ONE MORE TRY

A SECOND CHANCES COLLECTION

L.A. WITT

ONE MORE TRY: A SECOND CHANCES COLLECTION

Sometimes it's over... but it isn't really over.

Coworkers Marcus and Reuben broke up six years ago, but their feelings for each other have never faded. After a company Christmas party disaster makes things awkward, an out-of-town business trip together could douse this flame for good... or bring the smoldering spark back to life.

Childhood best friends Justin and Tyler lost contact for five years, but now Justin is helping Tyler pick up the pieces after his divorce. Justin has always been in love with his straight friend, and now he's wondering if he can really handle the man of his dreams living under his roof and out of his reach. Except maybe Tyler isn't as far out of reach as either man thinks.

Husbands Rhys and Derek are calling it quits, but they're not ready to tell their daughter until after her wedding. It doesn't matter how much they still love each other—trust is broken and there's no going back. Except could a road trip and a wedding be enough to bring their marriage back to life?

This collection contains three novels — Is It Over Yet?, The Torches We Carry, and It Was Always You, which are also available individually.

THE TORCHES WE CARRY

CHAPTER 1

REUBEN

"Could you swing by my office as soon as you have a minute?"

I squeezed my eyes shut and fought the urge to snap my desk phone in half. I didn't have a minute and wouldn't for a while, but when Dad summoned me to his office, it meant *now* so I forced the frustration out of my voice. "Yeah. I'll be right there."

He hung up without further comment. I sighed heavily and put the phone back on the cradle. With a knot in the pit of my stomach, I surveyed the paperwork spread out across my desk. I shot a plaintive look at my email browser, hoping the number next to New Messages hadn't increased in the fourteen seconds I'd been on the phone with my father. It had. Of course it had. By the time I came back from Dad's office, the pile would be higher and that number would be bigger. So much for not coming in this weekend.

And everyone wonders why I went gray so young.

Okay, so that was mostly genetics, but I suspected my dad had contributed more than just DNA to me being completely gray at thirty-five.

My phone started ringing because of course it did. According to the caller ID, it was Jan Harper, one of my engineers. I suspected it was about a set of schematics that we desperately needed to finalize by the end of the month, but I let her go to voicemail because the only thing more urgent than that project was whatever Dad wanted.

I got up and walked away from my desk, my phone still ringing behind me, and headed down the hall to Dad's office.

Maya, his secretary, smiled at me. "He's ready for you. Go on in."

I returned the smile. "Thanks." Then I continued past her, gave his door a cursory knock, and went inside.

"Have a seat." Dad's voice was terse as always, and he didn't look away from whatever he was typing.

I took my usual chair and waited while he finished his—I assumed—email.

When he'd finished a moment later, he faced me, folding his hands behind his keyboard. "Is there something I need to know about between you and Marcus?"

My heart stopped. "Uh..." Well, shit. This wasn't what I'd expected when I'd come in here. "Why... why do you ask?"

"Because you've seemed a little, I don't know, uncomfortable around each other lately."

If I hadn't been so startled by this line of conversation, I might have laughed. Uncomfortable around each other? A *little* uncomfortable? Right. That was a hilarious understatement. Or at least it would have been if I hadn't been filled with so much horror that my father had *noticed* the tension between me and the company's marketing manager. He was usually oblivious to things like that. Oblivious enough that my year-long relationship with Marcus had slipped completely under his radar. As had our breakup almost six years ago.

Then again, Marcus and I hadn't had to work together on a near-daily basis back then. And our split had been amicable, complete with a long conversation about making sure things didn't get weird at the office. These days, we were constantly in each other's space, and thanks to a certain incident at the company Christmas party two months ago, things were... well, weird didn't begin to describe it. We still couldn't even look at each other.

"Reuben?"

Shit, how long had I been sitting here like a dumbass, trying to come up with an answer? I cleared my throat. "Um. Sorry. Look, everything's fine. We've just both had a lot on our plates lately. Or at least I have."

Dad grimaced. "I suppose you have. How are things going with Michelle?"

Wincing, I avoided his gaze. "They're... moving along." Because goddamn, I needed to think about my divorce-in-progress on top of everything else right now. Fuck this. I had work to do. I pulled in a breath and looked at my father. "Is that what you brought me in here for? To ask about me and Marcus?"

My own phrasing almost gave me heart failure, as if Dad might read between the lines and realize there had ever been a "me and Marcus."

He obviously didn't, though. "That's not *all* I brought you in here for, no." His chair creaked as he settled back. "But I do need to make sure the two of you are getting along."

"We are. I promise." It was true enough. Wasn't like we were at each other's throats. Things were painfully awkward, but Marcus and I both took our jobs seriously, and we didn't let our bullshit interfere with our work. Much. We'd definitely need to sit down and clear the air about a few things, but Dad didn't need to know that. "It's all good. Seriously."

"Excellent." He nodded sharply. "Because I need you to go with him to next week's trade show in Boise."

I blinked, struggling to comprehend all the WTF in that sentence. A trade show. Me. On short notice. With Marcus. W. T. F. "I... really?"

Dad nodded. "You leave tomorrow."

"But... but I—"

"Listen, I know it's sudden," he said. "And I know you're busy. But—"

"He'll be there with John and Allen. What does he need me for?"

Dad sighed, shaking his head. "John's still sick. Doc says he can't travel for at least another week. And Allen..." Dad's lips tightened. "He just gave me his two weeks' notice."

Damn. The hits just kept on coming, didn't they?

"He's quitting?"

"Yep. Got poached by a competitor who shall not be named," Dad grumbled. "Which is why I can't go fill in at the trade show—Karen and I need to interview replacements for Allen."

I bit back a curse. Karen, the director who oversaw our field representatives, would have been my next suggestion to fill in. But with one field rep quitting, another out on medical leave, and both Dad and Karen occupied with scrambling to replace Allen, that didn't leave many options. I was pretty sure none of the other eight field reps could be pulled in for it either; their schedules were jam-packed as it was. We also had three in-house project managers who could theoretically fill in, but one was on maternity leave, one was in Germany to train our European reps, and the third was basically chained to his desk until the other two came back.

Which left me.

My mouth went dry. "I don't know if I can leave, though. I've got—"

"I don't have a choice, son," Dad insisted. "This is a huge trade show, and I *need* someone there who has a working knowledge of the products. Especially the new line of cutting torches."

I couldn't suppress the grimace. *No one* knew the new line of torches better than I did. I'd designed the goddamned things and built two of the early prototypes myself. "But if I'm there, I'm not here to keep the department moving so we can release the new products on time." I shook my head. "Dad, there's no way—"

"I need you on this, Reuben." There was a note of pleading in his voice that was so bizarrely out of character it rendered me speechless.

There really was no way out, was there? I was the only person who was both available—sort of—and knew the products. Marcus knew the products too, but only to a point. When potential customers had in-depth technical questions, they needed a field rep, a project manager, or an engineer. And since none of the engineers could be spared for something like this—and would probably resign in a heartbeat if someone said they were on trade show detail—that left me.

Deflating a bit, I said, "Okay. Just, um, email me the information about the show. I'll let my department know I'll be out of the office for a few days."

Dad blew out a relieved sigh. "Good. I'll have Maya forward you the itinerary."

"Great. Thanks."

Just please tell me Marcus and I won't be rooming together.

CHAPTER 2

MARCUS

"Make sure we've got two of the full-size banners," I told Aaron. "Just in case one gets torn or something again."

"Got it." The blond kid pulled two of the rolled banners down from a shelf and propped them next to the box they'd be packed into. "What about the smaller banners? Just in case you have less space than you think?"

I pursed my lips. We'd reserved an end cap booth, and this convention center had a ton of space, but the trade show itself sometimes had low-hanging banners of their own as well as displays that encroached on our space. And it wasn't like we had to pay shipping since we were taking everything in the company van. "Good thinking. Grab a couple of those too."

He nodded and did as he was told.

"Hey, Marcus?" Leanne poked her head into the storage room where we were staging everything. "Did you still need an HDMI cable?"

"Yes, please." I had two packed already, but I'd learned the hard way that there was no such thing as too many HDMI cables. In fact, that was the name of the game for pretty much anything when it came to conventions and trade shows—if you might need one, bring three.

I skimmed over the checklist in my hand. We'd packed the signs, pieces of our booth, literature, demo products, IT equipment, displays—

My phone chimed, snapping me out of my concentration. I swore as I tugged it off my belt. Always something.

Without even checking the caller ID, I tucked the phone against my shoulder. "Marketing, this is Marcus."

"Hey. It's Reuben."

My stomach flipped, and I froze. "Oh. Hey."

We were both silent for a couple of awkward seconds. Damn, when were we going to get over this? Guilt and shame twisted behind my ribs. For the millionth time, I vowed never to drink at a company Christmas party ever again.

"Listen." He cleared his throat. "Do you have a few minutes if I come by your office?"

I glanced around at the barely organized chaos of crap that needed to be packed into the van. A few minutes? No, definitely not. "I'm pretty slammed with getting everything ready for the trade show. Is it urgent?"

"Um." Reuben paused. "Yeah. It kind of is."

I closed my eyes and forced out a breath. So help me, if he'd chosen today—this minute—to settle things between us, I was going to lose my shit. I really did want to clear the air, and I knew all too well how hard it was for Reuben to initiate conversations like that, but not *now*, for God's sake. Especially since I'd have to do most of the emotional legwork, and even if I'd had the time, I just did *not* have that in me today. "All right. I have to keep it short, though."

"Yeah. No problem. I'll be down in ten."

After we'd hung up, I surveyed the mess Aaron and I were making of the storage room turned staging area. It always looked like this before we loaded the van, and it always made me twitchy because it seemed like a disaster area that would be impossible to clean up, never mind fit everything into the vehicle. It didn't matter that I knew we could do it—I'd be damn near breaking out in hives until I had visual confirmation that it had all fit this time and my storage room was back to some semblance of order.

But Reuben apparently had something to discuss that warranted us being in the same room together. He'd been avoiding me as much as I'd been avoiding him lately, so whatever it was, it must be important.

Fine. *Fine.*

"Hey, Aaron?"

"Yeah, boss?" He poked his head up from behind a stack of boxes marked CURTAINS.

"I need to step out for a few minutes. Can you take it from here until I get back?"

"No problem." He gestured at the clipboard in my hand. "Could you leave that here so I can double-check everything?"

I couldn't help but smile. Aaron was a boy after my own heart—worshipping lists and charts and checking them twice like he was goddamned Santa Claus. Why couldn't I find a whole army of employees like this?

I left the clipboard on top of a box of literature and headed back to my office. On the way, my heart was in overdrive. What was this about? What was so important that Reuben and I needed to meet one-on-one? Prior to the Christmas party, it hadn't been a big deal. In the eight weeks or so since, we'd gotten *really* good at having "meetings" via email. Sometimes face-to-face interaction was unavoidable, and we both frequently had to attend meetings with other departments—not to mention Bob, Reuben's father—but we body-swerved them as much as we could. Bob had even commented about how impressed he was that we'd streamlined a lot of interdepartmental communications to emails rather than time-consuming meetings. I was fine with him believing that.

So what the hell did Reuben and I need to talk about that couldn't be handled via email and needed to be handled right now?

Apparently I wasn't going to have to wait long to find out—when I reached my office, Reuben was coming down the hall from the other direction.

Our eyes met, and we both plastered on professional smiles, but said nothing. I keyed us into my office, and after a moment's hesitation, shut the door behind us.

"So." I sat at my desk and gestured for him to take a seat. "I have to keep this short, but I—"

"I don't think it'll take long." He sat down, and I didn't like how he was avoiding my eyes and wringing his hands. God, he needed to *Talk*, didn't he? Which he struggled hard with under the best of circumstances, so if he'd worked himself up to it now, it must have been eating him alive.

I rested my forearms on the desk. "What's up?"

Reuben swallowed hard. After a moment, he looked at me through his lashes. "I think we need to clear the air about—"

"For fuck's sake," I snapped. "Reuben, I'm leaving for Boise first thing tomorrow, and I don't have time to—"

"I'm going with you."

The words stopped my breath in my throat. My office was suddenly dead silent, and we stared at each other.

Reuben moistened his lips. Voice softer, he repeated, "I'm going with you. To Boise."

My jaw went slack. "You... come again?"

He sighed and leaned back in the chair as he once again avoided my gaze. "My dad just dropped it on me. John and Allen both had to bail, and I suggested everyone I could think of, but the punchline is I'm the only one who can go."

I watched him, waiting for the *real* punchline. I'd be pissed if he told me he was wasting my time with a joke, but I liked that idea a hell of a lot more than the prospect of him joining me for an eight-hour road trip, five-day trade show, and eight-hour return trip. Especially since the convention hotel was booked solid, and I'd already been less than thrilled about sharing a room with John (who snored) and Allen (who ground his teeth).

"Please tell me you're joking," I said.

Reuben pursed his lips. "Hey, I'm not thrilled about it either. But rather than waste your time going through all the possible alternatives that my dad has already shot down, I'm thinking maybe we should cut to the part where we figure out how to make this work."

That... that was definitely a Reuben answer. He'd always been the pragmatic one. Find a solution, and when the only available solution wasn't a palatable one, suck it up and make it work even if it meant ignoring the baggage that desperately needed unpacking.

I sat back and sighed. "Fuck."

"It's not a picnic for me either, you know," he growled.

Our eyes locked. There was a hint of hurt in his eyes, and I realized my reaction to this whole thing probably sounded a lot less like *I'm not looking forward to a week of awkwardness* and a whole lot more like *I don't want to be around* you. Which, to be fair, was true, but not because I disliked him. Quite the contrary. We just had a lot of history together, and I didn't think the jam-packed van was big enough to hold all our baggage.

"I'm sorry," I said. "So, what do we do?"

Reuben shrugged tightly. "Not really much we can do except—"

His work phone jingled on his belt.

He squeezed his eyes shut and swore, and now I could really see the frustration and worry radiating off him. He unclipped his phone. "Give me a sec." Before I could respond, he said, "Engineering, this is Reuben." Pause. The furrow between his brows deepened. Then he closed his eyes again. When he pinched the bridge of his nose, my heart sank. We weren't finishing this conversation, were we? And if we didn't do it now, we wouldn't have another opportunity before we left.

"All right," he said to the caller. "I'll be there as soon as I can."

Damn it.

Reuben lowered the phone, and as he clipped it back to his belt, he looked at me. "I have to go handle a crisis down in engineering." He rose. "I guess we'll have to deal with this…" His eyebrows pinched together.

"Well." I sighed. "We've got all day tomorrow."

We locked eyes.

All day tomorrow. In a car. Him and me. No escape.

Oh God. This was going to be one *long* trip.

CHAPTER 3

REUBEN

The universe was apparently conspiring to keep Marcus and me from snagging a few minutes to sort things out between us. He was up to his eyeballs in organizing supplies for the trip to Boise, and I was putting out fires left and right in my department. By the time I left the office that night, it was almost eight, and I still needed to pack and at least try to get some sleep before our early start in the morning. So much for suggesting we meet for a drink to talk things through.

Which I supposed wasn't entirely a bad thing. I was liable to drink too much just to numb all the guilt and the other unwelcome emotions that came to life whenever I looked at him. And drinking too much around Marcus was *never* a good idea. Lesson learned the hard way.

So I went home, I packed, and I tried to sleep, and when the Welding & Control Equipment van pulled into my driveway at four o'clock the next morning, I was an exhausted, queasy, nervous wreck. But hey, at least I could blame some of the fatigue on needing to be awake this stupidly early.

After we'd put my suitcase and garment bag in the back—there was just enough space—I climbed into the passenger seat, and we were off.

"You want to stop and get coffee?" Marcus's tone was flat but not unfriendly.

"Unless you want me dozing off on you before we even get across the bridge."

He laughed quietly. "Where do you want to go?"

Back to bed and not to this trade show. "There's a QFC a couple of blocks down. They've got a Starbucks inside."

Marcus grunted in acknowledgment, and minutes later, he'd parked in front of the supermarket. As I unbuckled my seat belt, I asked, "You want anything?"

He held up a 7-Eleven travel mug. "I'm good."

"'Kay. I'll be right back."

Just walking from the van to the store was almost enough to wake me up completely. It was cold as balls these days, even for February. Which got me thinking—had Marcus checked the forecast? We had to go over the mountains, through Eastern Washington, and into Idaho. There was probably snow on the ground right now, and there could still be more. Would we need chains? Did we *have* chains?

I barely noticed the warmth of the grocery store as I walked in through the automatic doors. My mind was going a million miles an hour, running through all the worst case weather scenarios and every possibility that Marcus might have overlooked. I was downright jittery when I stepped up to the counter to order my coffee. Thank God there was no line; probably because most people were sleeping soundly in their warm beds rather than being upright and "functional" at this hour. I ordered, paid, and waited, shifting my weight and gnawing my lip because I needed to get back out to the van and make sure we weren't going to wind up in a snowbank or something.

Coffee in hand, I hurried back to the van. I'd barely closed the door before I said, "Have you checked the weather for the pass and Idaho? And we have chains, right? Do—"

"Reuben." The firm sound of my name shut me up. Marcus

smiled across the console, the bright light from the grocery store casting harsh shadows across his face. He reached between his seat and the door and pulled out a clipboard. "I'm ten steps ahead of you."

One look at the clipboard, and all my panic was gone in an instant. Of course Marcus had thought of everything. He always did.

I swallowed, relaxing against the seat as I put my coffee into the cupholder. "And we've got chains?"

"Of course."

"Oh. Okay. Good." I felt like an idiot now. If there was anyone on this planet who could possibly be on top of things more than I was, he was sitting right beside me. That man took his organizing and scheduling as seriously as an air traffic controller.

Neither of us said anything as Marcus pulled out onto the road and wound his way to I-90. Seattle was mostly still asleep, so we flew out of the city and across Lake Washington. In no time, we were past Bellevue and Issaquah, and it wouldn't be long before we'd left North Bend in the dust too. At this rate, we'd be over Snoqualmie Pass before the sun came up.

"If you want me to drive," I said as I tucked my now-empty cup back into the holder, "just say so."

"I'm good for now. Thanks."

And... silence. Again. I thought about suggesting we put on the radio, but it would start getting staticky once we were up in the mountains. No point in turning it on now only to switch it off again later. Shame the maintenance department had never gotten around to upgrading the age-old AM/FM radio in this van to include XM or something that would still function even in the mountains.

I stared out the window, but of course it was still pitch black outside, so I couldn't see much. Well, aside from my own semi-transparent reflection. And Marcus's.

I caught myself staring at his reflection while he drove. He was barely visible—just a few features picked out by the faint blue glow of the gauges and what little light bounced back from his headlights on the blacktop. It was enough, though. I'd memorized his face years ago, so my mind filled in what the darkness covered up.

The longer the silence dragged on, the deeper it cut. Even after we'd broken up, even after he'd started seeing his now-ex-boyfriend and I'd married my soon-to-be-ex-wife, we'd always stayed friends. This awkwardness? This distance? It wasn't us. Never had been. Not until that damn Christmas party.

So what do we do now?

He'd always been better at talking about feelings and shit like that. I could follow suit once he guided me toward the right words, but I'd always had to let him take point on those conversations. I just wasn't wired for it. I sucked at it. So did my ex-wife, for that matter; the *irreconcilable differences* on my divorce papers may as well have said *we're terrible at communicating, especially him.* Hell, I couldn't count the number of times I'd gone to Marcus to ask how to approach my wife about something.

Now she's gone, you're all the way over there, and I don't have a clue how to fix this.

Oh yeah. I was in a perfect state of mind to be joined at the hip with him for the next several days. *Fuck.*

I-90 wound us through the Cascade foothills toward Snoqualmie Pass. As we inched up into the higher altitudes, we went from a sprinkle of white along the shoulder to deep, dirty snowbanks and repeated warnings about black ice. Marcus took the curves extra slowly, staying in control even when the van tried to fishtail a few times. Good thing he was driving—I was a perfectly competent driver in the snow, but I hadn't driven a heavily loaded van in these conditions before. Least of all in the dark.

Almost three hours after we'd left Seattle, we'd gone a total of about eighty-five miles. The sky was still dark, the silence still hanging between Marcus and me, when he pulled off the interstate in Cle Elum, a tiny town not far beyond the pass.

"I need to eat something," he declared as he slowed to a stop at a red light. "You want anything?"

I shrugged. "I could eat."

"Should we just grab fast food and get back on the road? Or do you want to sit down?"

The thought of us sitting down for a meal, especially without a buffer of potential clients who needed wooing, made me want to gag. I didn't want to say it, though. Things were awkward enough. "You're driving. Whatever works better for you."

He picked a sit-down place. Damn.

It was one of those all-night diners that catered to truckers. The menu could basically be summarized as *Reuben, if you order anything, your trainer will make you pay dearly,* but hopefully she'd give me a pass. After all, I was traveling on business, it was barely seven in the damned morning, and I was with my ex-boyfriend and our gigantic herd of living room elephants. The stress alone probably burned enough calories to justify biscuits and gravy or something.

I didn't get biscuits and gravy, though. I settled for a vegetarian omelet with cheese and an English muffin. And coffee, of course.

What came, however, was a vegetarian omelet hidden somewhere beneath a half-inch thick blanket of melted cheddar, a side of enough home fries to support Idaho's entire economy, and how the hell did I miss the part about a stack of pancakes the size of my head?

Forgive me, trainer, for I am about to sin.

Across the table, Marcus surveyed the similar mountains of food that had been spread out in front of him. "Are we... are we supposed to eat this all in one sitting?"

"I think so." I blinked a few times. "Pretty sure it's just one meal, too. Like, there's still lunch after this."

"Oh my God," he murmured. Then he chuckled. So did I. Our eyes met across the table and—

The laughter instantly dried up.

Right. It's you. And me. And things are awkward. Sorry.

We both dropped our gazes to the safety of our food and didn't speak as we started eating. I didn't rib him for slathering his omelet in A-1 Steak Sauce. He didn't tease me about putting the jam straight on my English muffin without butter. All the usual jokes—the ones we knew so well we could contain them in a couple of glances and smirks—were absent. Of course they were.

And suddenly I wasn't hungry at all.

Marcus put his fork down and cleared his throat. "We, um, never did finish our conversation yesterday."

My stomach lurched. Definitely not hungry anymore. I put my fork down too and nudged the barely-touched plate away. "No. We didn't."

We met each other's gazes over the table. I stared into his eyes. His warm brown eyes that were still so gorgeous even when he was this tired and worried.

Are we going to finish it now?

I swallowed, ignoring the ball of lead in my gut. If ever I'd needed him to take the lead and get a conversation rolling, it was now.

Marcus chewed the inside of his cheek. When he dropped his gaze, the disappointment almost broke me.

But then he said, "There's something I need to know."

I picked at my omelet to give my hand something to do. "Okay?"

He stared down at his food for a painfully long moment. Finally, he whispered, "Are you and Michelle divorcing because of what happened in December?"

Exhaling, I laid the fork down again and sat back against the hard bench. "It..." There was no simple answer to that, was there? "Kind of yes. Kind of no."

His forehead creased. "What does that mean?"

It was my turn to break eye contact. I stared at the food neither of us were touching, and tried to work out how to explain how things had gone down.

"For what it's worth," he said quietly, "I didn't want that to happen. I never wanted to cause any problems between—"

"I know." I met his eyes again. "I've never doubted that for a second."

He inclined his head, but didn't speak.

I took a deep breath. "Look, she and I were in a bad spot already. We'd been sort of skirting around the subject of separating for a while. Just... neither of us could figure out how to drop the hammer."

"So a drunken threesome with your ex-boyfriend was... what? A Hail Mary because neither of you could find another reason to call it quits?"

I didn't know what startled me more—the coldness of the accusation, or the undercurrent of hurt. "No. It wasn't that." I shook my head. "We were drunk. You were drunk." Sighing, I made a dismissive gesture. "Things got out of hand."

Marcus set his jaw, and the hair on my neck stood up. I knew that look. My answer may have been the raw, unvarnished truth, but it was the wrong answer somehow. His voice stayed flat and chilly. "So if it hadn't been me, it would've been someone else."

I blinked. "I... I don't know, honestly. We'd never talked about having a three-way with you or anyone else. Not seriously, anyway." When that didn't chisel away any of the hardness in his expression, I sighed. "We weren't out looking for the nearest warm body or anything. She knew I'm still attracted to you, and she thought you were hot, so when we all ended up in the same place at the same time, and everyone's inhibitions came down..." I half-shrugged. "It happened. I can't give you any rational reason for it. All I can tell you is we weren't using you to make or break our marriage."

"But it did break your marriage." It wasn't a question.

"It..." I sighed. "It made us realize a lot of things we'd been ignoring for a while."

"Such as?"

I held his gaze.

Such as how unsalvageable my marriage really was.

Such as how my feelings for you stacked up to my feelings for her.

Such as how much more it hurt to have lost you than it did to be losing her.

But I didn't know how to say any of that out loud. Not without making things even weirder between us. I couldn't risk pushing him further away than he already was, and anyway, I had no idea how to put any of this into words.

I broke the staring contest and glanced out the window. Daylight was just starting to warm the edges of the dark sky. "We should keep moving. You want me to drive for a while?"

CHAPTER 4

MARCUS

As soon as the question came out of Reuben's mouth, I deflated. I'd known him too long not to take it for exactly what it was—him shutting down. If I tried to push him now, he'd just keep putting up more walls until one of us snapped, and then we'd have a fight on our hands.

So much for making things less awkward.

I sighed and put my napkin on the table beside the food I'd barely eaten. "I can keep driving. Just let me get some coffee to take with me."

Reuben nodded, but didn't speak. Of course he didn't.

I supposed I couldn't be as pissed at him as I'd usually be when he did this. He and Michelle had only separated recently. Just days after the Christmas party, in fact. It was hard not to imagine that night's activities hadn't led to their split, but I couldn't blame him for not wanting to talk about it. Getting him to talk about things had always been like getting blood from a stone, but maybe it was just too soon for this. Maybe he needed to lick his wounds for a while first.

And maybe, just maybe, throwing us into a vehicle and forcing us to spend a week together in close confines isn't a good idea right now.

Not that either of us—or Reuben's father—had much choice. Plus we'd vowed long ago never to let our romantic history interfere with our jobs. No one at work knew we'd ever been a thing, and I intended to keep it that way. Which meant there had been no tactful way to tell Bob Kelly that we couldn't handle this trip together.

Keeping my frustration and resignation as far under the surface as I could, I flagged down the waitress for the check.

"Do you want a couple of boxes?" she chirped.

I looked at the food. I'd feel guilty asking her to throw all this away, so even though I didn't foresee any reheated eggs, potatoes, or pancakes in my future, I nodded. "That'd be great. Thanks."

Under normal circumstances, Reuben would have playfully rolled his eyes and given me a hard time for taking a doggy bag that I probably wouldn't eat. It used to annoy me when he did that. Now I wished he would.

After we'd paid the bill and collected our doggy bags, we went back out to the van. Before I'd even left the parking lot, Reuben was typing something on his phone. Probably a work email. I wasn't mad —my inbox was probably jammed already, and I'd be facedown in my phone once I wasn't behind the wheel anymore. That, and as long as he had something to do, it made the silence between us feel a bit less weird. A bit.

As I-90 whipped past us and Reuben took care of whatever crises were erupting in the engineering department, I had nothing to do but stare at the road and think about the night of the Christmas party.

We hadn't really been that drunk. All three of us had had a few— enough to make us all a little louder than normal, including Reuben, who was a notorious introvert—but no one had been incoherent or blackout drunk. Michelle had been buzzed enough to make a few playful comments about Reuben and me. Reuben had been buzzed enough to laugh about it instead of getting uncomfortable. And at the end of the night, I'd been buzzed enough to suggest we all pool our money for a single cab instead of calling one for them and one for me.

The three of us wedged into the backseat of a Crown Victoria had led to jokes about Michelle being between us (and we'd all been sober enough to remember that a joke about a "Reuben sandwich" would make him dry heave because he thought the actual food by that name was disgusting). Somewhere along the way, those stopped being jokes. And somewhere between the party and their house, we'd decided the cab didn't need to take me home after all.

Yeah, the alcohol had lowered our inhibitions, but I bristled at the idea that it had been a drunken threesome. That anyone in that room —in that bed—had been anything but into it. I never fucked people when they were drunk enough to do something stupid, and if I'd been that drunk myself, I'd have had my head hanging over the toilet long before we got anywhere.

No, we'd all been lucid.

Maybe if we hadn't been, things would have been different. Maybe I would've been too drunk to plant that long kiss on Reuben's mouth. Maybe he would've been too out of it to feel anything but turned on, and maybe he wouldn't have looked at me like that.

My throat ached at the memory of that look we'd exchanged when he'd broken the kiss. For a couple of heartbeats, I'd forgotten anyone else existed, even while I'd been buried inside Reuben's wife. A few seconds, that was all, but it had jarred me right to the core. Being naked and intimate with him after all that time had brought every feeling I'd ever had for him right to the surface, and it had all been seared at the edges by the knowledge that he was out of my reach. It had been exhilarating and excruciating, and I had never been so close and so far away from someone at the same time.

If we'd been drunk enough for that night to qualify as a drunken threesome, that moment never would have happened.

And Michelle never would have noticed.

But it had. And she had. She hadn't said a word, but... she'd noticed. We'd carried on, but no one's heart had been in it after that. I'd bowed out and gone home, and I'd spent the weekend sick to my stomach with guilt over what must have gone through her mind in that moment, not to mention berating myself for still carrying a torch for him after all that time. I'd promised myself I'd sit down with Reuben on Monday, and we'd talk things through, and we'd put all this to bed, and maybe I could find a way to apologize to Michelle without making everything worse.

But Reuben hadn't come to work on Monday morning and it hadn't taken long to figure out why. By lunchtime, the rumor had circulated all the way around the plant—Michelle was moving out of their house. By five o'clock, the rumor had been confirmed. Reuben and Michelle were divorcing.

Gripping the van's wheel as I stared hard at the interstate, I willed the sting in my eyes to go away on its own. I didn't dare wipe them. I didn't want Reuben to notice, especially because he wouldn't ask. He'd damn sure know what was on my mind, but he wouldn't ask, and we'd just continue in miserable silence because we both knew what he wouldn't say.

He and Michelle had invited me into their bed.

Within days, their marriage had been over.

Now things were unbearably weird between Reuben and me.

And I didn't know how—or if—we could come back from this.

Losing our appetites and only eating a few bites of our breakfast had one unfortunate side effect—within a couple of hours, we were both starving.

Of course, now we were out on one of those wide-open stretches of farmland and nothing. I didn't trust gas station food, and I doubted either of us wanted to stop long enough for a sit-down meal—especially since that would mean getting into Boise and out of this van even later—so that pretty much left drive-thru fast food.

I cleared my throat. "Do you still have any signal?"

He picked his phone up off his leg. "Three bars."

"You want to see if there's any place to eat coming up? Ideally with a drive-thru?"

He didn't answer, but when I glanced at him, he was tapping his phone. A second later, he said, "There's a Dairy Queen off the next exit, but it's about ten miles down the road from there."

"Works for me."

Silence followed us down the off-ramp, along a winding road through farm country, and into the parking lot of a mostly deserted Dairy Queen. The drive-thru was closed, most likely because of the huge snowdrifts and the broad, shiny patches of ice. So we went in, ordered, and came back out to the van with a couple of burgers and sodas. It bugged the shit out of me that he didn't make some joke about promising not to tell each other's trainers about the crap we were eating. We were both religious about our work-outs and diligent about our diets, and indulging in junk food wasn't nearly as fun without some conspiratorial chuckling and vows of silence.

We climbed into the van, and I started the engine while he unwrapped his burger, but I didn't pull out of the parking space yet. I also didn't take my sandwich out of the bag despite my grumbling stomach.

Ignoring my nerves, I said, "I think we should talk."

Reuben stopped chewing the bite he'd just taken, and his eyes darted toward me, wide with alarm. Yeah, that was one thing that would never change—Reuben *hated* uncomfortable conversations. Not that anyone liked them, but he stopped just shy of being allergic to them.

"Look." I twisted in my seat so I was facing him. "I don't like this any more than you do, but we're stuck together for the next few days. Starting tomorrow, we're actually going to have *work* together. Constantly."

He nodded, cutting his eyes away from me as he resumed chew-ing. After he'd swallowed, he said, "Yeah, I know."

"So we really should clear the air."

Reuben winced. He eyed his burger, and a pang of guilt smacked me in the stomach. He needed to eat—couldn't I wait to bring this up until after he'd sated his appetite? But he took another bite. Smaller this time, but encouraging.

Though my own appetite was iffy while we were discussing this, the throbbing in my temples was non-negotiable, so I took my burger out of the bag. As I unwrapped it, I said, "Are you mad about what happened the night of the party?"

Reuben stared out the windshield with unfocused eyes, chewing thoughtfully. Then he took a swig of soda, and when he spoke, he kept his attention on the wheat field. "Not at you, no."

More guilt. Damn it. "But it shouldn't have happened?"

He sighed, slowly shaking his head. "Probably not."

We ate in silence for a minute or so. I decided it was partly because we both seriously needed to eat, and partly to let the truth sink in—that the threesome we'd had with his ex-wife *had* been a mistake. I'd known it. He'd probably known it. Saying it out loud gave that truth some weight that hadn't been there, though, and getting it out in the open didn't make me feel any better.

Reuben wadded up his empty wrapper and dropped it in the bag. A moment later, I did the same, and got out to toss the bag into the snow-covered trash can.

As I pulled back out onto the road, I glanced at him. "Okay, so we agree it was a mistake."

He tensed.

"But it's not like we can go back and change it," I went on. "For what it's worth, I'm sorry if it caused any problems with you and Michelle. If I could undo that, I would."

Reuben nodded, jaw tight, but still didn't speak.

Drumming my thumbs on the wheel, I kept my attention on the two-lane road taking us back to the interstate. I started to speak, but so did he, and we both paused, exchanging glances.

I cleared my throat. "Go ahead."

He fidgeted in his seat, and finally said, "I really don't want things to be weird between us."

Relief rushed through me. "Neither do I."

"But... they *are* weird. They've been that way since the Christmas party. I..." He shifted around some more. "How do we fix that?"

I chewed the inside of my cheek. The on-ramp came into view, and I put us back on the freeway to continue toward Boise. "I don't know how to fix it, honestly. All I can think of is that we let things go as best we can, and try to be friends like we were before."

"Sounds like something that's easier said than done."

"It is," I admitted. "But it's worth it, right?"

Reuben tapped his nails on the console between us. "Yeah. Yeah, it is. And I guess it would be easier if we weren't stuck together like this."

"Maybe. Or maybe it's a good thing."

"How do you figure?"

"Well." I shrugged. "If your dad hadn't thrown us into this trip, how long do you think we would've gone before we talked about this?"

"Hmm. Yeah. Probably a while." He pulled his drink from the cupholder and took a deep swallow. "I don't think it's going to be fixed overnight, though."

"Doesn't have to be." I glanced at him again. "We're both professionals. We can handle the trade show like adults, and after we get back to Seattle, we'll work on the rest of it."

Reuben seemed to mull that over. "Okay. Okay, yeah. I can do that."

"Me too." I stole another look. "We've got this."

He brightened a little. "Yeah. We've got this."

CHAPTER 5

REUBEN

The rest of the drive to Boise was more comfortable. We still weren't back to being able to effortlessly shoot the breeze like we'd always been able to do, but it was an improvement. I'd take it.

Thanks to some shitty road conditions on the way through north-eastern Oregon and into Idaho—I fucking hated traveling in the winter—not to mention an eighteen-wheeler that had bitten the dust thanks to those shitty road conditions, it was almost six when we pulled into the hotel. The eight-hour drive had turned into fourteen hours, and we'd both been so tired we'd had to switch off almost every hour for the last third of that. And then there was the time change, so it was actually seven o'clock, and who knew one hour could make a man feel this jetlagged?

At least we didn't have to deal with parking. Marcus handed the keys off to the valet after we'd removed our suitcases, and we headed into the lobby.

"I am so glad we're not setting things up until tomorrow," Marcus muttered on the way through the revolving door. "I would seriously just burn the whole thing down."

I chuckled. "Now I know why Dad doesn't let you handle the cutting torch demos at these things."

He laughed, and I tried not to let it show how relieved I was to be able to make him laugh again. We weren't back on solid ground yet, but I finally had a tiny ray of hope that we could be.

There was a sizeable line of people waiting to check in, which wasn't surprising right before a big convention. There'd probably be twice as many showing up tomorrow—Marcus had explained that he and the field reps always came a day early so they'd have time to settle in, set up the booth, and go find an office supply store if they'd left something behind. As meticulous as he was about making lists and planning everything within an inch of its life, I couldn't imagine him forgetting anything.

As soon as we were in line, Marcus the Marketing Manager came to life. A pair of bald guys in suits struck up a conversation with him—they obviously recognized him—and like magic, all his fatigue and frustration vanished. The transformation was instantaneous and dramatic. One second he was barely holding himself up, his eyes heavy-lidded and his gait dragging like he wanted nothing more than to faceplant in bed. The next, he had on a broad smile and his eyes were bright as he chatted up the people around us. He was like a different person.

With a hand on my shoulder, he gently herded me closer. "Have you met Reuben Kelly? Bob Kelly's son? He's our head of engineering."

"We haven't met," one of the men said, extending a hand, "but we've talked on the phone. I'm Roger West from Rocky Mountain Analytics."

"Oh, right!" I smiled—not as easily as Marcus, but I managed—and shook his hand. "It's nice to finally put a face with the voice."

Others in line turned toward us, as if they were drawn in by Marcus's magnetic charisma, and I found myself being cheerfully introduced to a dozen people I'd spoken to or heard of, but had never met. Even as we all inched toward the registration desk, Marcus held court in the tightly wound cattle line, seeming to bring every tired person in the room to life with nothing more than a handshake and a smile. Jesus. I'd always known he was good at his job, but seeing him truly in his element was a sight to behold.

I couldn't say if the line moved quickly, or if time just seemed to go faster while Marcus charmed and schmoozed. Before I knew it, though, we were at the registration desk. After that, it was another fifteen minutes before we were on our way to the elevators, and a good five after that before we could finally get *into* one.

A couple of sales reps from our steel supplier were on the elevator with us. They got off on the fifth floor while we continued up to the tenth.

As soon as the doors slid shut behind them, sealing us in here alone, Marcus sagged back against the wall, closing his eyes and releasing a long breath. The transformation this time was even more dramatic than earlier, as if the spell had been broken and all the life had gone out of him at once. If things had been just slightly less awkward between us, I'd have put a hand on his shoulder to make sure he stayed upright.

"You okay?" I asked.

He nodded, eyes still closed. "I just don't have the energy to people today."

"Could've fooled me back there."

He looked at me, and a tired smile played at his full lips. "Can't let people see the man behind the curtain."

"Not even when you're off the clock?"

Marcus chuckled softly, like it took some actual work. He glanced up as the elevator stopped with a gentle lurch and a *ding*. "I'm never off the clock at these things. Trust me."

We filed off the elevator and headed down the hall to our room. As he tugged the keycard from its cardboard folder, my gut tightened. I'd been so mesmerized by his charisma downstairs, I hadn't even thought about the fact that we were sharing a room.

He touched the card to the sensor, and when the green light came on and the door clicked, my throat tightened.

Oblivious, Marcus pushed open the door.

I hesitated, but followed him.

"You have any preference about which bed?" He shuffled deeper into the room, dragging his suitcase like it weighed a hundred pounds.

"Uh. No." I shut the door behind us. "No preference."

"Good." He propped his suitcase next to the first bed, draped his garment bag over it, and then flopped unceremoniously onto the bed on his back. "Oh my God, I am so glad to be out of that van." The words came out as a groan.

I laughed. It was definitely a good thing we'd had a talk a few hours ago and made some headway toward clearing the air. Otherwise, I might've taken his comment personally. But things were a bit less awkward between us now, and the drive really had been draining.

I sank onto the other bed. "So, what's the plan for tonight?"

"No plan." Marcus rubbed his hands over his face before letting them fall to the bed at his sides. "Aside from room service, a shower, and sleep."

"Room service?"

"Fuck yeah."

"Accounting doesn't get their nose out of joint over that?"

He snorted. With a wicked smirk on his face, he turned to me. "Not anymore they don't."

I arched an eyebrow.

Chuckling, he looked up at the ceiling again. "They tried to tell us we couldn't do room service unless we wanted to pay for it ourselves. Then they realized that if I'm eating in the room, I'll just have a meal and maybe a glass of wine. If I'm down at the bar or the restaurant, and potential clients show up..." He shrugged, the smirk shifting to a poor attempt at innocence. "Well, I have to wine and dine them, right?"

I laughed. "You conned accounting into letting you expense room service. I'm impressed, Marcus. I really am."

"Just don't rat me out to your dad, all right?"

"Are you kidding?" I picked up the room service menu off the table between the beds. "Ordering in means I don't have to go out and deal with"—I wrinkled my nose—"people."

"Oh. Right. I forgot." He sat up with a theatrical groan and swung his legs over the side of the bed. "I'm traveling with an engineer."

I grunted as I flipped through the menu.

Marcus studied me, and when he spoke again, his tone was more serious. "Are you going to be okay for this? For the trade show, I mean?"

I looked at him through my lashes. "I told you. I can be professional, and we'll deal with our—"

"No, not because of that." He shook his head. "I know you. You're an introvert. This is going to be a lot of people in your face for hours on end." His forehead creased. "Are you sure you'll be all right?"

I gulped. All the way here, I'd been focused on whether I'd be able to cope with Marcus. I hadn't had time to think about everything else this show entailed. "I've, um... I've never been to one. So I don't know."

Palpable concern radiated off him. He leaned forward, elbows on his knees, and looked in my eyes. "It's going to be overwhelming, okay? You're pretty much installing a revolving door on your personal space. It's even overwhelming for me, especially after two or three days."

"Oh fuck. If it's a lot for you..."

"It is, but it's manageable." He shrugged. "Honestly, you won't have to deal with people as much as I will. You're there in case someone needs more technical specifics than I can give, and for demos. If it gets to be too much and you need a break for a while, just keep your phone with you and stay close by. I'll text you if I need you."

I held his gaze as some tension eased from my back and shoulders. "Really?"

"Of course." A small smile came to life. "Everyone here is used to dealing with engineers, and believe me, you won't be the only engineer hiding in his room or at the bar."

"Oh. That's... that's actually encouraging."

The smile broadened, lighting up his face as if I needed a reminder of what had drawn me to him in the very, very beginning. He was gorgeous anyway, and deploying that hypnotic smile was not playing fair. Especially not when he had five-o'clock shadow because damn, this man had always been hot with stubble.

I cleared my throat as I broke eye contact, shifting my focus back to the menu that had somehow not slipped out of my hands. "Thanks. I, um, might take you up on that." I chanced another look at him. Yep. Still smiling. Still hot. "So should we order some food?"

"Definitely." He pushed himself up and gingerly headed for his suitcase. "While you look at that, I'm going to change into something more comfortable." He paused, eyeing me uncertainly. "Should we, um, have some ground rules for things like changing clothes?"

Oh God. You. Naked. Or even without a shirt. Fuuuck.

"Um." I gulped. "We're both adults. I don't think we need to hide in the bathroom to change." *Though maybe that would keep me from losing my mind before this week is up.*

He watched me for a second, then dug through his suitcase, came up with a Seahawks T-shirt and a pair of gym shorts, and disappeared into the bathroom.

Well. In the full-length mirror, I watched the reflection of the door as he closed it behind him. *Guess that answers that.*

Maybe it was for the best, though. Neither of us was particularly shy, and we'd certainly seen each other naked before. But with the way things had been lately... yeah. A little discretion wasn't a bad idea.

With a sigh, I shifted my attention back to the menu and tried to find something appetizing.

———

Marcus was oddly quiet the next day. We'd agreed not to bother setting an alarm because it would be our last chance to sleep in until the trade show was over. That and we were in another time zone now, and even bumping the clocks an hour ahead was enough to throw both of us off.

So, between the time change and some decadent laziness, we didn't leave the room until almost eleven. The hotel lobby was buzzing with activity, and it was a good fifteen minutes before a valet was able to bring our van around. From there, we just had to drive across the street to the convention center's loading dock. We'd be able to walk back and forth from our room to the trade show after this, which would be so much fun in the bitter cold.

We unloaded the van and staged everything at our booth, along with the larger pieces that had been shipped ahead of us. We set up displays, hung banners, connected electronics, filled literature holders... and all the while, Marcus barely spoke.

It wasn't just that he was quiet or preoccupied. It was like he'd folded in on himself. Like he was barely aware of anyone or anything.

As I carefully arranged some literature according to a drawing he'd made—he really did think of everything—I watched him uneasily. What the hell was going on? I'd thought we'd made headway last night, breaking through all that bullshit that had been hanging between us for the better part of two months. We'd been able to make light, superficial conversation about the trade show, dinner, and what stupid TV show to watch until it was time to call it a night, and it had *almost* been easy. How the hell had we backslid so far already?

Except this was different. Or it sure seemed that way, since it wasn't just me he was apparently shutting out. Instead of joining me and several guys from one of our suppliers in the restaurant for lunch, he'd stayed at the booth under the pretense of needing to make sure the projector was working properly. When a convention center employee came to ask him about something, Marcus's answers were short, almost to the point of terse. When he had to talk to the facilities manager about a faulty electrical hookup, he spoke in a monotone, sounding either disinterested or irritated. He was still polite, of course, but he wasn't exactly warm.

Seriously—what the hell was going on?

As we headed up to the room after we'd finished setting up, I watched him out of the corner of my eye, wondering how in the world to figure out—and fix—whatever the problem was. I had never been good at approaching people about anything. Ever. If a conversation had even the minutest potential of being uncomfortable or awkward? I'd run for the hills.

But for the next few days, I would be as good as glued to Marcus's side. If he cold-shouldered me, we were going to wind up killing each other.

In our room, Marcus sank onto the edge of his bed, gaze fixed on his phone. I watched him, my stomach somersaulting at the mere thought of broaching the subject. Or even speaking to him at all since I had no idea where his mind was or if I'd done something wrong.

My eyes flicked toward my bed, which was all of two feet away from his. Our suitcases, which were parked side by side against the wall. Our garment bags, which hung next to each other in the open closet. Fuck. My ineptitude for uncomfortable conversations sucked, but so would spending most of a week in close confines with someone who was either ignoring me or—worse—quietly stewing over something we could fight about later.

Okay. Here goes.

Deep breath.

Fuck.

"Hey." I swallowed my nerves, and when he looked up at me, my heart beat even faster. "Is, um..." *Oh God. Fuck. How do I do this?*

His eyebrows rose, though his eyes still seemed oddly blank. "Hmm?"

I moistened my parched lips. "Is... everything okay? With us? I mean, I thought we ironed a few things out, but all day today..." That was the best I could do. Not even a full sentence, and I'd already run out of steam.

Marcus's shoulders dropped. So did his gaze. Then he put his phone aside and leaned forward, elbows on his knees. "I'm sorry." He exhaled and rubbed his neck with both hands. "I probably should have given you a heads up about this."

"About..." I blinked, then cautiously came closer and sat on the edge of the other bed. "About what?"

Eyes still down, Marcus kept kneading the back of his neck. "The other reps call it social hibernation. I didn't even realize I do it until one of them pointed it out, but I kind of, I don't know, close off for a day or so before a con starts." He sighed, then looked at me through his lashes. "Sort of priming myself for having to be 'on' for days on end."

"Oh." I wasn't sure how to respond to that. "I... never realized..."

He smiled a little, his expression closer to shy than I'd ever seen it. "Even extroverts wear out sometimes. I'll probably crash when it's over too, so if there isn't much conversation on the way home, don't take it personally."

"Okay. Good to know." I inclined my head. "So, you're okay, then? And we're..."

The smile grew. "Yeah. We're good."

I exhaled. "Thank God. I thought things might have gone back to being weird."

"No, no. I'm just having a little pre-con weirdness. It happens."

"You? Weirdness?" I put a hand to my chest. "I'm shocked."

He rolled his eyes and playfully swatted at my leg as he stood. "Asshole."

I just laughed and wondered if he knew how relieved I was that we were okay.

"Want to go find something to eat?" he asked.

"Or we could stay in and do room service again."

He turned to me. "You don't mind?"

"Not at all. Especially if you need to charge your batteries before you have to be Mr. Charisma tomorrow."

Marcus chuckled, though his shoulders were still visibly heavy with fatigue. "I wasn't all that impressed with their food, though."

"Want me to check GrubHub? There has to be someplace that delivers."

His lips quirked like he was considering the idea. Then, meeting my gaze with a hint of caution in his eyes, he said, "If we order pizza, do you promise not to tell my trainer?"

I couldn't help smiling. "You promise not to tell mine?"

The caution evaporated. "Deal."

We held each other's gazes for a few long seconds, my heart fluttering with giddy relief at the playful callback to our pre-awkwardness days.

Then I took my cell phone out of my pocket. "Extra cheese?"

His grin gave me goose bumps. "Fuck yeah, extra cheese."

CHAPTER 6

MARCUS

My alarm went off at six.

In the next bed, Reuben grumbled and buried his head under the pillow.

I would have loved to do the same, but I'd learned the hard way a few times how late I could be to a trade show if I started hitting the snooze button. So I was up, showered, and dressed in minutes even though I definitely didn't want to be.

There will be coffee. The words repeated in my brain like a mantra. *There will be coffee. All you have to do is get downstairs, and there will be coffee.*

In theory, I could have made some with the provided machine in our room, but I'd never been impressed with the taste of hotel coffee. That, and the smell would likely wake Reuben. Somehow, I doubted he'd magically transformed into a morning person in the last few years; even if it meant delaying my coffee, it was better to let sleeping engineers lie.

Once I had on my shoes, I tiptoed between the beds to get my phone, watch, and wallet, and before I turned to head out of the room, I froze.

A jolt of cold panic almost negated my need for caffeine. *Oh shit. Did I almost...?*

Yeah. I had. Because even though it had been more than half a decade since I'd woken up in the same room as Reuben, it was almost automatic to lean down, press a kiss to his prickly cheek, and murmur, *"I love you. I'll see you at work."*

I stood there, staring at him, slack-jawed and wide-eyed, my heart racing as it sank in just how close I'd come to going through those habitual motions. How easy it would have been. How awkward it would have made things.

I shook myself, double-checked I had my room key, and got the hell out of there.

In the elevator, I took a few deep breaths and forced Reuben as far into the back of my mind as I could. It was show time. The trade show didn't actually start for a couple more hours, but most of the attendees were staying in this hotel, which meant I had to have my game face on as soon as I stepped out into the lobby.

Or sooner, it turned out—when the elevator stopped on the sixth floor, three familiar faces stepped in. It took me a second to connect them, but I was already greeting them and shaking their hands before I remembered they were the president and two senior engineers from the company that manufactured springs for some of our product lines. I hadn't even had coffee yet, and it was already go time.

As it always did, the elbow-rubbing and ass-kissing continued through the coffee line, through breakfast at the hotel's restaurant—which was "meh"—and all the way across the street to the convention center. I was introduced to the vice president of a compressed gas supplier we'd been working with forever, got a business card from a start-up that had some promising ideas for expanding our online presence, and asked a field rep from our rival torch manufacturer to give my regards to his hospitalized coworker. In the convention hall, I paused to catch up with a couple of competitors' marketing directors —they were competition, but we considered each other colleagues and had always been friendly.

And *then* the convention started.

Trade shows like this naturally didn't attract much traffic from the general public. We'd sometimes get students coming through to do research for science projects or for business classes, but the vast majority of the crowd were people directly or peripherally involved in the compressed gas business. Regulator, distribution, and welding equipment manufacturers like ours. Gas distributors. New start-ups and crowd-funded innovators with fresh ideas for everything from product design to assembly line efficiency to marketing angles.

It was a big industry, though, and this was one of our biggest trade shows west of the Mississippi, so as soon as the doors opened at nine o'clock, the wide walkways between rows of booths were jammed with people. Voices echoed off the high ceiling. Demo machinery clanked, hissed, beeped, and whirred. A crackly loudspeaker occasionally broke up the noise with an announcement about a seminar, a featured demonstration, or a cell phone missing an owner.

Our booth was one of the endcaps, and we had no shortage of traffic. By ten o'clock, I was about to text Reuben and beg him to come down and help me out when—

Oh *hello.* There he was.

By all rights he should have blended in—another gray-haired white guy in a sea of the same—but nope. He stood out, at least to me.

Reuben usually wore a shirt and tie to the office, but it had been a long time since I'd seen him in a suit. Holy shit. Had he always been that hot in—oh, who was I kidding? Of course he had. Though he'd also gone a lot grayer since we'd dated—from salt and pepper to completely silver—and somehow that, coupled with the perfectly tailored dark suit, made him jaw-droppingly sexy.

"Marcus?"

I shook myself and turned back to Steve Horton and Greg Schaeffer, a couple of potential clients interested in one of our manifold systems. "Sorry. Sorry. Um." I cleared my throat. "Our senior engineer just got here, so let me grab him. He'll be able to tell you exactly what you need for your setup."

They both nodded, and I turned as Reuben stepped into the booth.

"Sorry I'm late." He was shrugging off his jacket. "Got hung up talking to someone from—"

"It's fine. It's fine." I gestured behind me. "Your timing is perfect, actually, because these two gentlemen are interested in one of the 7000 series manifolds."

He glanced past me, eyebrows up. "Oh. Okay. Um." He looked around. "I left a spiral notebook down here, didn't I?"

I picked it up off the table beside the projector. "Right here."

"Perfect." He flashed me a disarming smile, pulled a mechanical pencil from his shirt pocket, and went to where Steve and Greg were waiting.

I'd worried about how Reuben would handle a trade show like this. He was easily overwhelmed by people, especially people he didn't know, and a constant stream of strangers right in his face seemed like a recipe for disaster.

Clearly, I'd underestimated him.

When I glanced over from trying to charm some business out of another pair of attendees, Reuben seemed far more in his element than I'd expected. He'd rolled his sleeves to the elbows and tucked his tie into his shirt, and he was leaning over a table, sketching on that spiral notebook as Steve and Greg nodded along. He was animated and—hell, even a bit boisterous.

I smiled to myself. Apparently that was the secret to getting Reuben out of his shell. Put him in front of people who were interested in something he was excited about. The 7000 series manifolds had been one of his pet projects for the last couple of years, and he really did seem to get a thrill out of telling people how it worked.

The two guys seemed downright mesmerized by him. I couldn't say I blamed them. Hell, even our sales reps could learn a thing or two from him. They always sounded like they were excited to sell the client something. When Reuben told people about products, he sounded more like a kid who'd discovered a new game and couldn't wait to explain it to his friends.

Steve and Greg were at our booth for over an hour. A few other people had drifted away from the foot traffic and were listening, and by the time Reuben had finished, he had reps from three other companies waiting to ask him some questions as soon as he was done scheduling an on-site consultation for Steve and Greg.

"Nicely done," I said to him once there was a lull while people headed to a keynote speech. "Less than half a day on the floor, and I think you've made three major sales."

Reuben blushed, smiling shyly. He looked around, and now I could see him visibly running out of steam. As if he'd kept the energy going until the conversations were over, but now that there was a break, he was crashing.

"Hey." I touched his arm. "You all right?"

"Yeah. Just..." He exhaled, rolling his shoulders. "I think I could use some more coffee." When our eyes met, the subtext might as well have been written across his forehead—*I need to get away from the booth for a few minutes.*

"Why don't you go grab some, then?" I motioned at our surroundings. "It's probably going to be quiet until the keynote is over anyway, and after that is lunch."

Reuben released another breath. "And this show is how long?"

"Doesn't end until Sunday."

He groaned.

"You'll be fine. I promise." I paused. "Honestly, you're handling this better than I thought you would."

He eyed me like he wasn't sure how to take that.

"Come on. I know you. Crowds and people aren't your thing." I nodded toward the notebook he'd tucked under his arm. "But I guess all we have to do is give you a sketchpad and something interesting to talk about, and you're good."

Laughing, he shrugged. "I guess so, yeah." He scanned our surroundings. The throngs of people had noticeably thinned, but not everyone had gone to the keynote, so the place wasn't deserted. "Are you sure you can hold down the fort while I go get coffee?"

"Don't sweat it. In fact, would you mind grabbing something for me?" I pulled out my wallet. "I've got the corporate card, so—"

"I got it. Don't worry." He smiled. "I'll be back."

"You don't have to buy. We can expense this, you know."

Reuben winked. "I have a corporate card too, remember?"

"Oh. Right." Why were my cheeks burning? Clearing my throat, I pocketed my wallet. "Well then, I don't feel so bad."

We exchanged smiles, and as he left to find us coffee, I watched him disappear into the crowd.

Of course, it was just my luck that even though not everyone had gone to the keynote, most people had. The speaker was from one of the major laser cutting manufacturers, and a lot of people were interested in what she had to say, so for now there was a serious lull in traffic here in the exhibition hall. Which meant I had some downtime. Downtime with my thoughts. My thoughts about Reuben.

I hadn't expected him to be so comfortable in this environment. He wasn't a wimp by any means, or someone who was so painfully shy he couldn't hold his own. But one-on-one interactions with strangers intimidated the hell out of him. The spotlight scared him half to death. And yet, when he had something to talk about that excited him, he did all right. If I was honest, he'd impressed the hell out of me. Enough that I was sorely tempted to text his father and beg for Reuben to be sent to more of these events.

Except that would get weird. Reuben probably didn't have it in him to do this often, and anyway, he and I were still on shaky ground. Or at least uneven ground, which suddenly seemed tilted at a precarious angle as I fumbled with my feelings about how I wanted him here professionally, and how attractive he was, and how fucking delicate our sort-of truce was.

I blew out a breath and rubbed my eyes. Yeah, I was definitely still attracted to him. And I was professionally impressed by him. I wanted to protect him, escape him, fuck him, argue with him, and somehow I was supposed to keep all of that contained until we got back to Seattle.

Oh God. We're still stuck together for how *many more days?*

Trade shows always meant early mornings and late nights. By the time I made it back to the room the first day, it was nearly nine o'clock, my feet hurt, and my voice was scratchy. As much as I wanted to hit the hay, I needed to suck down some tea if I had any hope of being able to speak tomorrow.

Reuben had bowed out of going to dinner with me and some clients, which hadn't surprised me. He'd probably had all the people he could handle for one day and needed some downtime. That was fine with me. Wooing, wining, and dining clients was what *I* got paid for.

When I let myself into the room, he was still awake. Again, not a surprise. He'd always been a night owl. He sat cross-legged on his bed, a pillow between his back and the headboard, and his laptop propped on his thigh.

His eyes flicked up as I came in. "How was dinner?"

"Boring and overcooked." I pulled my conference badge's lanyard over my head and dropped it by the TV. "But I'm pretty sure I kissed enough ass to keep us in the good graces of everyone who matters."

Reuben laughed without a lot of feeling. "Better you than me."

I grunted as I thumbed through the box of tea provided by the hotel.

"Your voice going to hold out?" he asked. "You're sounding a bit hoarse."

"I'll be fine. Especially since this room has an actual teakettle." I pulled the device out from its hiding space behind the coffeemaker. "One that actually gets the water hot enough for tea."

He made a gagging noise. "Still don't know how you drink that shit."

"Well, drinking this shit will mean the difference between me still being able to speak and having to pawn off all the human interaction on you."

"Oh. In that case..." He made a *go on* gesture.

"That's what I thought."

I filled the teakettle and finally settled on peppermint tea. Tomorrow I'd see if the bar could provide me with some hot lemon water to drink while I was at the booth, but this would do for now.

While the water boiled, I stole a peek at Reuben. He'd shifted his attention back to the computer and was frowning at something on the screen. It wasn't a look of concentration, though. Maybe at first glance, but anyone who knew him—aka, me—could see the frustration and confusion in his eyes.

After I'd made my tea, I cautiously asked, "What's wrong?"

"Just some bullshit back at the plant." He drummed his nails on his laptop, then shook his head. "I don't know what anyone expects me to do about it, though."

I sat on the edge of my bed, carefully cradling the steaming mug between my hands. "Anything I can help with?"

"No. It's—" He paused. "Well, maybe."

I lifted my eyebrows.

Sighing, Reuben leaned against the pillow between his lower back and the headboard. "So, I keep butting heads with one of my leads, and I can't figure out why. Or how to fix it."

Well, that explained his frustration and confusion. I slipped the teabag out of the cup, and as I tossed it into the trash between the beds, said, "Tell me what's going on."

He eyed me uncertainly.

I waved a hand. "Nothing leaves this room. I'm not asking for gossip—just enough details that I can help."

Reuben chewed his lip. "Okay. So." He put the laptop aside on the comforter and rubbed his hand over his face. "I've got Stan Weitzel in charge of developing the new 9X series torches, right? He's overseeing the project, but like I always do, I'll sometimes send an email out to the entire team. Asking for status updates, giving them a heads up about a change to specs, that kind of thing."

I nodded, but didn't speak.

"And Stan..." Reuben glared at his screen and made a frustrated gesture. "Every single time, he emails me back—copying everyone—and questions everything. Even stupid shit like where we're going to put the part number label on the torch handle." He turned to me, brow pinched. "What am I supposed to do with that?"

"Well." I worked my jaw for a moment. "It sounds to me like you're both upset that the other is undermining you."

Reuben blinked.

"You put him in a position to be the lead," I went on. "Maybe he feels like you emailing his crew is making him look less like he's in charge, and that might make it harder for him to lead his people. And at the same time, he's undermining you by questioning your judgment at every turn." I whistled, shaking my head. "I guarantee all the people working for him are throwing up their hands and wondering when this dick-measuring contest will end so they can do their jobs."

His eyes flicked to the screen, and his lips parted. "Shit. I... never thought of that. I just thought I was being efficient, you know? Getting the information to everyone who needed it. But when you put it like that..."

I held back a smile. Sometimes it was actually kind of endearing to watch the pieces come together in his head. I had no idea why he short-circuited when it came to understanding and processing emotions, but once someone showed him how everything went together, he got it. He didn't fight it, and he didn't get annoyed if I was blunt about it. For as much as he second-guessed his ability to work with people, his sheer earnestness about *wanting* to understand them went a lot further than he imagined.

After a moment, Reuben laughed quietly. "That all makes sense. Honestly, this is why I hate that my dad put me in a supervisor position. I'm an engineer, not a manager."

"No, but you're not bad at what you do either."

"I'm good at managing projects, not people."

Okay, that was fair. Reuben was amazing at all the technical stuff that blew my mind, but he didn't read people well. Never had. He struggled to decipher and address his own feelings, never mind other people's. It wasn't that he was a cold, emotionless asshole or anything. In fact, he tried really hard to be mindful of how things affected other people, or how they responded to things. He knew when people were upset or unhappy—the struggle was with figuring out why. It was like somewhere between receiving the information and knowing what to do with it, something got lost in the translation.

"You know." I set my mug on the table between the beds. "If something like this comes up again, I'm always around the plant. You're welcome to bounce stuff off me and see if that helps."

Reuben's brows pulled together. "You wouldn't mind?"

"Of course not." I smiled. "I know you, and I know exactly why this kind of thing is hard for you. If I can help"—I shrugged—"let me know."

"That's..." He blinked. "That would be great. Thank you."

"Any time."

We held each other's gazes, and my heart did a little flutter. This was a small step, but it still seemed like one step closer to things being back to normal.

After the way things had been for the last several weeks? I'd take it.

CHAPTER 7

REUBEN

I had no idea how Marcus did this. For three solid days, he was Mr. Charisma at the trade show. Whether he was talking to a longtime supplier, a potential multimillion-dollar client, or a shy barista who mentioned in passing that she was just starting a marketing degree, he focused on people like no one else existed in the world.

His charm seemed effortless, but rooming with him gave me a new perspective on that. Every night, the instant we were in the elevator, the veil would drop and the exhaustion would show, and within fifteen minutes of getting back to our room, he'd have drunk some of that awful-smelling tea and be dead asleep. All the years I'd known him, I'd just thought being an extrovert was easy for him, but I'd never seen him in trade show mode. I'd never been around him when he'd had to be "on" for hours on end with person after person after person from the crack of dawn until nine or ten at night. Maybe it wasn't as easy as it looked after all. No wonder he'd had to go into that "social hibernation" the day before the trade show had started.

Which, I had to admit, made me feel a hell of a lot better about struggling so hard for even a fraction of his outgoingness. As we got ready to head to the bar after things had wrapped up on Friday night,

I still envied his ability to charm strangers and work crowds, but I had a much deeper respect for how taxing that ability really was. Even now, as he was fussing with his tie in the full-length mirror in our room, the cracks showed. His eyes were a little dimmer, his shoulders sagging slightly; I knew as soon as we left the room, he'd flip the switch and come back to life, but the fatigue was unmistakable now.

I pulled on my suit jacket. "You ready?"

"Just about." He adjusted his tie one last time, then looked himself up and down. When he faced me, all the tiredness was gone. It was almost like his reflection hadn't really been his; like the mirror had shown a different man entirely. One who was ready to collapse instead of the poised, energetic man smiling back at me right now.

So was he faking it? Or had I been seeing things?

Of course I knew he was human. I'd seen him clinging to his tea, heard how raw his voice could be at the end of a long day. Still, he seemed even more drained than he'd been letting on.

Oblivious to me, Marcus tugged at his sleeve. "You should think about coming to more of these things."

"Come again?"

Marcus met my eyes. "You haven't noticed people pretty much falling all over themselves to hear you talk about products?" He shifted his attention back to his cufflink. "If you can get away from the plant a few times a year, having you at more shows would be really good for the company."

"Oh. Um." I shook my head. "I don't know. I don't think this is really my scene."

His warm smile made my skin tingle. "You're better at it than you think."

"Doesn't mean I enjoy it."

Inclining his head, he asked, "Do you?"

"I..." I thought about it. "Well, it's not as bad as I thought it would be. It's just intimidating. Having all those people coming at me all day long. That, and I doubt Dad can let me out of the plant for more than a day or two at a stretch. Every time I so much as step out for lunch, the whole place seems to fall into chaos."

Marcus sniffed. "Maybe if your father would finally let you hire some more people into management positions." He gave his sleeve a sharp pull, as if it were the source of his irritation. "You're good at what you do, and it's stupid to distract you with everything else."

I wasn't sure what warmed me more—the hint of that protectiveness he'd always had for me, or the casual acknowledgment that I was good at my job. My own response made me feel kind of ridiculous, though. I knew I was good at what I did, and Marcus had a vested interest in the company being able to utilize me properly instead of wasting my time on something an actual manager would be better suited for. I was being stupid.

"Well, maybe I can reorganize the department when we get back." I rose from where I'd been sitting on the bed. "Should we head downstairs before the line at the bar gets too long?"

Marcus gave his reflection another critical down-up, then nodded. "Yep. Let's go." He picked up his room key, I took mine, and we headed out of the room.

As soon as we walked into the jam-packed bar, I knew I was in over my head. At the trade show, I'd held my own. Discussing products and troubleshooting was fine.

The bar, however, was a whole different world, and I was way out of my element. I couldn't even handle the bar scene when I was out with friends. What was I supposed to say? What was I supposed to do? How the fuck did anyone hear each other over the cacophony of voices roaring over the top of blasting music? How many times were you supposed to ask people to repeat themselves before you just nodded and pretended you'd actually heard them? How did people *do* this?

Unsurprisingly, Marcus navigated the whole scene like one of those Olympic athletes who does his figure-skating routine or handles a snowboard course and makes it look so fucking easy. He was the guy you watched on TV and thought, *well shit, that looks easy, I can totally do it*. And then when you made your first attempt at curling or skiing, you fell flat on your ass and broke something because, no, it really *wasn't* that easy.

Marcus knew exactly when and how to slide in or out of a conversation. He seemed to have this intuition about how close to stand to someone, or if they were okay with him touching their arm or shoulder. If he'd met someone before, he always remembered some detail about them, and if they'd never met, he always seemed to know just what questions to ask to get them to open up. No matter what they talked about—family, friends, shop talk, small talk—he listened like it was the most fascinating thing he'd ever heard. Sometimes I wondered if he'd actually caught everything they'd said—it was so loud, I sure couldn't—but if he was just nodding along, he was the most convincing bullshitter I'd ever seen.

I stuck close to him. He was the only person here I knew, and at least if he was the center of a conversation, that meant people were focused on him, not me. I was more than happy to hide in his shadow.

Especially because hanging back in his shadow meant getting a front row seat to him. I could see why people were so easily charmed by him. The smile alone had always made me weak in the knees. Back when we'd first been introduced—me an engineer trying to claw my way up through my dad's company, him a newly hired marketing genius—his smile had rendered me speechless. The way he'd looked right into my eyes had hypnotized me. To this day, he could still stop me dead in my tracks just by looking at me. Small wonder I hadn't said no back then when he'd boldly asked if I wanted to get drinks. Or that drinks had turned into closing down the bar before going back to his place for sex that woke up his neighbors. To this day, I still had no idea how he'd even known I was queer.

Tonight, as he'd done all week, he laid on that charm with everyone in the room. He said all the right things to get men and women alike falling all over themselves to talk to him.

It was interesting to sit back and observe him in his natural habitat. A lot of things about our clientele and our company's reputation were beginning to make sense. This was a male-dominated industry, and I'd heard stories for years about how hard it was for women to be respected and taken seriously. Watching Marcus at work, it was no mystery why the company had never had any trouble wooing women into becoming clients. While men from other companies flirted shamelessly, Marcus didn't. At all. He smiled and he schmoozed, but he never crossed the line into anything remotely suggestive. He kept a respectful distance instead of getting into their personal space, and he listened to them and asked questions and didn't treat them like they were stupid—a novel approach, from what I'd seen in this business.

Somehow, he managed to be as smooth as a salesman without being sleazy like a salesman selling used cars. It was charming and endearing, not to mention fascinating to watch.

Tonight, though, as I stayed with him while he floated from conversation to conversation, a few cracks started to show. One minute he was all smiles and handshakes. The next—when he'd pause for a drink, or excuse himself to the bar, or just didn't think anyone was looking—he seemed to struggle to hold himself upright. Then another person would walk up and start talking to him, and he'd instantly be back to Marketing Marcus as if he hadn't wavered at all.

It was hard to say if I was just more in tune to him than usual, so I was noticing things more, or if he really was letting the mask slip more and more as the night went on. Either way, it worried me. This was a long trade show, and it wasn't over yet. Everyone had their limits. Was Marcus getting close to his? And what happened if he hit that breaking point?

Maybe he needed the same thing I did right now—back up to the room and no more people. He probably needed some of that godawful tea, too.

I stepped closer so he could hear me over the noise. "Hey, if you want to call it a night, we can."

"What?" He smiled. "Aren't you having a good time?"

I shrugged. "I am, but you were looking pretty tired earlier. Are you sure you're doing all right?"

"I'm fine. What about you?"

"I'm fucking exhausted," I said with a tired laugh. "And I think you are too." I paused, hoping I wasn't stepping out of line, and spoke just loud enough to be heard. "Maybe turning in early would be a good idea. So you don't burn yourself out."

His smile faltered a little, and he searched my eyes, his own expression suddenly unreadable.

I tried not to squirm under the scrutiny. "What?"

"Nothing." He shook his head, dropping his gaze to the mostly empty glass in his hand. "But I think you're right. Maybe calling it a night is a good idea." He threw back the rest of his drink and gestured around the room. "Let me say goodnight to the important people, and we'll get out of here."

I fully expected those goodbyes to take three hours, but he was surprisingly quick about it. Within fifteen minutes, we were on our way out of the thick, deafening crowd.

As soon as we were clear of the core of the noise, the day's fatigue started pressing harder on my shoulders. It was like we'd broken a spell by getting away from the thrum of voices and energy, and now I was really feeling the last several hours.

Sleep. Oh sweet, sweet sleep. Come to Daddy.

Marcus seemed to be dragging a bit too, and neither of us spoke on the way to the elevator. He jabbed the button, and we both stared at the numbers above the door as the elevator took its sweet time coming down. Finally, it did, and we shuffled inside.

As the doors closed, he broke the silence. "You're right. I'm exhausted. If I never see another person, it'll be too soon." He paused, then turned to me. "With one notable exception."

Our eyes locked.

My stomach flipped.

"Yeah?" I managed.

"Mmhmm." He stepped closer, his presence pushing me flat against the wall. "And just my luck, we're sharing a room."

"Y-yeah. We are." I gulped. "So we—"

He kissed me, and my whole body sagged between him and the wall. Holy shit. One minute we were both collapsing under the weight of a long day. The next... this. Oh my God, *this*.

Marcus had never been a gentle kisser, and tonight, his kiss was almost violent. Crushing. Possessive. Demanding. I gripped the front of his shirt, moaning softly because it was the only way I could audibly beg for more. He pinned me harder to the wall. The bar bit into my lower back, and the wall wasn't exactly comfortable behind my head, but holy hell...

The elevator stopped. We didn't. Marcus's hand slid down between the wall and my ass, and I pressed my hard-on against his. Where all this energy had suddenly come from, I had no idea. I'd been dog-tired all day, but it was like Marcus's lips gave me a second wind. There was no way in hell I could deal with more people or handle another product demonstration. Fucking Marcus into the mattress? God, yes.

He broke the kiss and went for my neck, and I arched off the wall with a soft whimper. "God, Marcus..."

He groaned against my throat. "I'm so tired I can barely stand up," he said, his breath hot on my skin. "But I want you so bad right now."

If my brain had any objections, they were lost in the rush of arousal and the prickle of goose bumps as Marcus's talented lips explored beneath my jaw. I opened my mouth to suggest we get back to our room, but right then, the world shifted out from under me.

Marcus jerked back and looked over his shoulder. He cursed, and I realized it hadn't been my balance abandoning me—the elevator was moving again. Before he could redirect it back to our floor, though, it stopped. We pulled apart, muttering curses as we tried to mask our predicaments with our clothes. The doors opened, and damn them, a couple of guys I recognized from—well, some other company I didn't care about right then—joined us, offering polite smiles as I prayed to God they didn't look down and see our hard-ons.

They pressed the button for the lobby. Marcus and I exchanged glances.

Apparently we were on the same page—the one where there was no way in hell we were riding down to the lobby and back—because without another word, he caught the closing doors, and we stepped out of the elevator and we headed for the stairs.

CHAPTER 8

MARCUS

All I had to do was touch the keycard to the reader on the door, and we'd be home free. With Reuben's kiss still tingling on my lips, though, not to mention my hard-on straining the front of my pants, this stupid door might as well have had a twelve-digit cipher lock and a retina scanner.

By some miracle, I lined up the keycard with the reader, the light turned green, and the lock clicked. We moved into the room, and as soon as the door was shut, I had Reuben in my arms again. Kissing. Groping. Stumbling. I wasn't quite sure how, but despite being almost completely focused on exploring Reuben's mouth, I found enough coordination to toe off my shoes *and* not trip over his as he did the same.

I shrugged off my jacket. His had disappeared at some point too. Though we'd both been dragging when we'd left the bar, there was no sign of fatigue in either of us now, and no shyness in him. He pinned me to the wall and kissed me hard, grinding his erection against mine as I tugged the back of his shirt up. From the low growl to the roughness of his touch, he was in charge now, and I was putty in his hands.

Fuck, no one had ever kissed me like he did. He could be so shy and uncertain, but in the bedroom, he was self-assured and unapologetic. He touched me like he meant it. Kissed me like he knew damn well I wanted it that hard and hungry. Fucked me like he had every intention of breaking every piece of furniture in the room before he was done with me. There was nothing tentative about him, and nothing had ever aroused me like watching the switch flip between his shy self and *this*. Being on the receiving end of his needy, demanding desire was the single biggest aphrodisiac I'd ever encountered.

Small wonder I couldn't get through this week without putting my hands on him, and now that I had, there was no stopping either of us. We made out. We pulled at clothes. We ground together. If it weren't for the occasional gasp when he touched me just right, I probably would've forgotten to breathe at all.

Reuben pulled me away from the wall and across the remaining distance to the bed. He dragged me down, and as soon as we'd landed on the mattress, we were fumbling with each other's pants. Somehow, I got his zipper down, and we both inhaled sharply as I closed my fingers around his cock. A moment later, he made it past my clothes too, and then we were kissing hungrily and pumping each other's cocks.

He nudged me onto my back, and then moved like he was going to go down on me, but I stopped him.

"I've got a better idea," I murmured, and gave him a quick kiss before I shifted around so we both had easy access to each other's cocks. He turned on his side to mirror me, and I moaned as I took him into my mouth in the same moment he took me into his.

Yes. Oh God, yes. This was everything. This was the kind of sex I'd been missing for so long. Reuben moaned around my cock, stroked it, licked it—he sucked dick like he was single-mindedly driven to do anything and everything it took to send me into the stratosphere. It was almost impossible to concentrate while I was at his mercy like this, but I had that same determination to turn him inside out, and every time he took me higher, I poured that pleasure into returning the favor. He did the same, and we were locked in a delicious feedback loop of spine-tingling pleasure and the need for not just our own orgasms, but each other's.

I caught a glimpse of us in the mirror, and holy shit this was the most pornographic thing I'd ever seen. The two of us, sixty-nining across a still-made bed, both of us still dressed, ties loose and shirts half-unbuttoned, our pants undone just enough to get to each other's dicks.

The sight of us drove a groan out of me, which sent a shiver through him, and he gave my cock a mind-blowing lick before he deep-throated me. I did the same, and was rewarded with a low moan. Over and over, we drove each other on until I couldn't resist rocking my hips, pushing my cock into his mouth, and he moaned again. Some guys didn't like that, but Reuben? Oh, just the thought of all the times he'd *begged* me to fuck his mouth...

I forced myself deeper, and his cock got even harder and thicker between my lips. His balls pulled up. So did mine. We were both breathing fast, panting as we hauled each other toward the inevitable.

Reuben lost it first. He whimpered around me, and the first drop of salt on my tongue took me right over the edge with him. I grunted, fucking into his mouth as I stroked and licked him, and I came so hard that if my mouth hadn't been occupied with his cock and his cum, I'd have woken the entire hotel.

He exhaled. Then I did. We rolled onto our backs and stayed there for a moment, just catching our breath while the room spun. When I was sure I wouldn't pass out, I sat up. So did he. We came together in a salty kiss, and the scratch of his nails across my scalp made me moan against his lips. We both should have been collapsing under the weight of orgasms that powerful. We should have been falling asleep in a cloud of pure bliss. Any other night, a climax that strong would've knocked me out in no time.

Tonight? Not a goddamned chance.

Neither of us was twenty-five anymore—hell, I hadn't been for twenty damn years—but that didn't stop us. Maybe we weren't hard anymore, but I had no doubt we would be before long. In the mean-time, we had six years of lost time to make up for, and so we kissed and groped and pushed clothes off. I needed his naked body against mine right fucking now.

It didn't take long—minutes after we'd gotten each other off, our clothes were out of the way and we were on our sides, cocooned beneath the covers of my bed as we kissed like our lives depended on it. When we'd had that threesome back in December, there hadn't been a lot of opportunity for this. There'd been sex, of course, and it had been hot when it wasn't awkward, but it hadn't been the time or place for this unrestrained intimacy. Maybe this wasn't the time or place either, but I didn't question it and Reuben didn't hold back.

Even after all this time, I still had every inch of his body memorized. Oh, we'd both changed over time. He'd lost weight. I'd gained a little. We'd both gone grayer—him more than me. There was a scar on his arm that hadn't been there before, and I hadn't had the tattoo on my ribs back then. But the planes and angles were mostly the same now. He still loved my lips on his neck. I still couldn't get enough of his fingertips gliding up my back or digging into my ass cheeks. He still made that soft, breathy sound whenever I nibbled his earlobe, and I still shivered every time he carded his fingers through my hair. We picked up where we'd left off before we'd split up, and if not for the scars and ink and gray, it would've been like the last few years hadn't happened at all.

I had no idea how long we lay like that—kissing, sliding hands all over skin, holding our naked bodies as close together as we could get. For all I knew, we should've been getting up and going downstairs for the trade show. Or maybe it had only been a minute or two. Didn't know. Didn't care. There was literally nothing that could pry me out of Reuben's arms right then, and time wouldn't matter again until I'd had my fill of him.

Unsurprisingly, we both started getting hard again, and as soon as there were erections involved, the intensity ratcheted up. He didn't just run his fingers through my hair—he gripped it tight enough to sting. I didn't just kiss up and down his neck—I sank my teeth in. Before long, we were both out of breath just like we'd been in the moments after we'd sixty-nined into oblivion. Our bodies moved of their own volition and fell into sync, rubbing and rocking as if to tell us we needed to stop fooling around and fuck.

I nipped his collarbone, making him gasp and arch, and I growled in his ear, "Fuck me."

Reuben inhaled sharply, fingers twitching against my sides. "Did you bring any condoms with you?"

I stiffened. Then swore. "Did you?"

"No." Reuben exhaled, pressing his forehead into mine. "Damn it."

"Damn it is right." I pushed myself up. "The hotel has a shop downstairs. It might still be open." I paused. "Or..."

His eyebrows rose.

I swallowed. "I haven't been with anyone in months. Nobody except you and..."

Reuben licked his lips. "It's only been you and her for years."

Our eyes met.

He gulped. "What about lube?"

I thought fast, and glanced toward the bathroom. Hand lotion was usually a winner, and hotels always seemed to provide it. "Let me check for hand lotion."

"Oh, good idea. I hadn't thought of that."

I bit back a comment about how he probably didn't have a lot of impromptu sexual encounters that required improvisation. No need to tip my hand about how I'd spent the first couple of years after we'd broken up.

In the bathroom, there was the usual display of complimentary toiletries, and—yes. Hand lotion. I gave it a quick sniff to make sure it didn't have any strong scents that might burn—lesson learned the hard way in the past—and skimmed over the label. Nothing set off any alarm bells. Perfect.

When I came back, holding up the tube of lotion like a prize, Reuben grinned so wickedly I almost dropped the damn thing.

As soon as I was close enough, he took it from me. "Turn around," he ordered. "I want to do you from behind."

I bit my lip as I climbed onto the bed. He still knew how I liked it, didn't he?

Oh yeah, he did, and he also knew the easiest way to turn me into a trembling wreck—prep me for *ages*. He teased me with lotion-slicked fingertips. When he pressed them in, he took his sweet, sweet time sliding them in and out, fingering me like he absolutely could do this all fucking night. I gritted my teeth to keep my frustration under the surface; I knew all too well how long he could do this if he knew it was torturing me this much.

Come on, I wanted to beg. *Gimme your dick. C'mon.*

But I kept my mouth shut and let him finger-fuck me. It felt amazing, especially since I hadn't bottomed for anyone in a long time. It just wasn't his thick cock. And he did this slowly and gently— exactly the opposite of what he'd do once he was in.

Finally, he slid his fingers free and shifted behind me. The sound of him stroking lotion onto his cock made me claw at the sheets with anticipation. *Yes, yes, please, yes.*

He lined himself up, and with a low groan, pushed himself in. For a second, the whole world vanished except the head of his cock moving into me, and I whimpered as he withdrew and pushed in again.

Reuben leaned down, and he buried his face in my neck as he eased his dick into my ass. "God, Marcus..."

I just moaned, overwhelmed by the heat of his body and the stretch of being penetrated. The head of his cock slid past my prostate, and my elbows almost dropped out from under me. It had been long enough since my orgasm that I wasn't uncomfortably hypersensitive, but the sensations were still overwhelming and intoxi-cating. I rocked back, desperate for more, and he exhaled as he pushed in deeper.

"You still like it hard?" he purred.

"You know I do." I gripped the edge of the mattress as he sat up behind me. "You still like to give it—"

He answered with a thrust so violent I almost choked on my own breath, and he didn't stop. He gripped my hips painfully tight and slammed into me over and over and over, and thank God we'd both already come once tonight because I would have gone off way too soon like this. I wanted him to keep going until neither of us could walk.

"Oh, yeah," I moaned, almost sobbing with both pain and pleasure. "Yeah, baby..."

He slid a hand up to my shoulder. Then the other. I squeezed my eyes shut, my whole body humming with sensation as he used his newfound leverage to fuck me even harder. Everything around us disappeared. It was all sensation—pain, pleasure, tension, relief. I was delirious. Drunk. Desperate.

Then Reuben slowed down a little, panting hard as he kept up a slower but still frantic rhythm. The gentler pace let my vision come back into focus, along with my brain, and I was slightly more aware of everything. Of our surroundings. Of muscles trembling with exertion. Of hot hands sliding across my skin, which was wet because we were both sweaty now. He sounded even more out of breath than I was.

"Lemme get on top," I panted. "So you... so you can have a break."

Reuben slowed to a stop. "Mmm, I like the sound of that."

I grinned over my shoulder. "You've always liked letting me ride you."

He slammed in, driving a grunt out of me. "You know I do."

"Then get on your back where you belong."

He responded with another punishing thrust, then pulled out and rolled onto his back. I climbed on top, and in seconds, had his dick in me again, and despite the ache in my thighs, found a fast, hard rhythm I knew he'd like.

And... dear God. I'd thought our sixty-nining reflection was hot, but this? Reuben flat on his back, skin flushed and gleaming, sweat plastering the hair to his chest and darkening the edges of his gray to almost black again, features screwed up as he groaned helplessly under me... fuck, this was the sexiest man I'd ever seen.

He opened his eyes and met mine as he ran his hands up my chest. One hand slid around the back of my neck, and I instantly recognized the subtle pressure of his fingers: *come here.*

I leaned down, and he threw his arms around me as our lips met. As if this couldn't get any more perfect, now I was kissing him, holding him, and riding him—the perfect trifecta of letting myself be completely consumed by Reuben.

He held me tighter and thrust up into me, and as we always had, we found an effortless rhythm even in this slightly awkward position. He hit every nerve ending just right, and from the sounds he was making, I had the same effect on him. Just like when we'd blown each other earlier, I wanted nothing more than to drive him over that peak, and he fucked me from below like he had the same single-minded goal.

"You want me to come like this?" he asked shakily. "Or pull out?"

"Like this." I let my head fall forward beside his, squeezing my eyes shut as my own orgasm closed in fast. "God, yeah." My voice came out as a shaky near-sob as I said, "Come, baby."

And just like that, he did. His body arched under mine and his dick pulsed inside me, and every sharp gasp and curse cooled the side of my neck, and his fingers dug in painfully. He took a few more deep, needy thrusts, and then he dropped onto the mattress, panting and trembling—the most beautiful wreck I'd ever seen.

Without even giving himself a chance to recover, he reached between us, and I shuddered as he started pumping me. I was so close to the edge anyway, and his shaky, sweat-slicked strokes were more than I could take. In his hand, I wasn't a middle-aged guy who'd already come once tonight. I was a twenty-something with a hair trigger, and in seconds, he had me shooting cum across his stomach as I cried out and damn near *cried.*

I collapsed onto him, and he wrapped his arms around me again. For a while, we just lay there. I lifted my hips enough to let his cock slide out, but otherwise, we didn't move.

He ran his fingers through my hair. "Hope... hope you're not expecting a third round tonight."

I laughed and kissed the side of his neck before I pushed myself up to look in his eyes. "Yeah, not happening."

We both chuckled, and he slid his hand into my hair as we kissed again.

I had my eyes closed so I could kiss him, but I had a feeling I wouldn't have been able to keep them open anyway. The day was definitely catching up with me now. There might have been a time in my life when I could do a trade show and still fuck the nights away, but that time was over. Pure need had driven me through two orgasms, but that was all I'd had, and now I was fading fast.

"I've got about enough left for a shower," I slurred, "and then I'm gonna be out for the night."

"You and me both."

"Join me?"

"If I don't, I'll fall asleep before you're done."

On shaky limbs, we got up and made it into the bathroom to clean off all the sweat and cum. After we'd showered, we collapsed back into bed.

And my head had barely hit the pillow before I was out cold.

CHAPTER 9

REUBEN

Nothing in the world was better than waking up to the warmth of someone lying beside me, especially when I could still feel everything we'd done the night before.

And nothing was worse than the cold realization that the person next to me was my ex-boyfriend. And coworker. And the man I'd fucked in front of my wife the night before we'd separated for good.

Oh God.

Last night had been so hot. The sex had been amazing. He'd been unreal. Now Marcus looked sexy as hell in the faint light coming in from outside. He was sprawled beside me, sleeping peacefully with stubble darkening his jaw. It should've been perfect.

But what the fuck was I thinking?

That Marcus had kissed me, that was what. Once he'd locked lips with me, I'd been... well, not helpless. I'd been just as much a part of last night as he had. That kiss had just knocked down all my inhibitions and reminded me of everything I'd been missing, and rational thought had gone out the window. Yeah, I'd gone into it with both eyes open, and deep down I'd known I'd probably regret it in the morning, but in the moment it had seemed worth it. I'd missed

Marcus for years, and after the last several uncomfortable weeks, I'd *needed* everything that kiss in the elevator had offered.

So... now what? And hell, what time was it? Marcus's alarm hadn't even gone off yet. What the fuck was *I* doing awake?

Oh. Right. Getting knocked around by my conscience for stupidly fucking my coworker/ex-boyfriend. I hadn't had time to think last night. By the time the dust had settled and we'd calmed down, he'd been asleep and I hadn't been far behind him. So now, in the wee hours before we had to start another day of dealing with people, seemed like as good a time as any to agonize over it.

I knew why, against my better judgment, I'd ended up in bed with him last night. Being attracted to Marcus had always been a no-brainer. The man was hot, and he kept getting hotter as he got older, so no shit I was attracted to him. Especially when there was a break in the tension between us, I just couldn't resist going too far.

But acting on it hadn't been a good idea for a long, long time, and what the fuck had possessed me to think last night would be any better than December? There was too much baggage. Too much bull-shit. Too many things I couldn't say even when I wasn't drooling over his dick. Since we'd arrived in Boise, we'd come back to some semblance of friendship, but that still felt precarious. Like the concrete of the foundation hadn't set yet, and putting anything on top of it would bring the whole thing down.

I sighed heavily. Damn, I wanted last night to be right, but the queasy knot in my stomach said that wasn't likely. Everything felt all wrong and like we'd just done something we really, really shouldn't have even thought about. It was possible I was just overthinking it, but I suspected once Marcus was awake, I'd know without a doubt that we'd fucked up.

I didn't have to wait long to find out—Marcus's alarm made me jump, and with a grumble, he felt around blindly on the nightstand until he'd shut the thing off. For a moment, I thought he might've hit snooze and gone back to sleep even though he never did that, but then he felt around again and turned on the dim light between the beds. We both winced. After a moment, his eyes fluttered open. Slowly, they focused, and when they met mine, a sleepy smile formed on his lips.

It didn't last.

After a couple of beats, the smile faded, and I could practically feel the horror as all the pieces came together in his head. What we'd done. Every reason why we shouldn't have. How much more time we were stuck in close proximity. Okay, so I didn't know if that was specifically what he was thinking, but I doubted I was too far off the mark. I knew him and I knew what we'd done. I could put two and two together.

We fucked up, didn't we?

Without a word, Marcus sat up, and I couldn't help noticing he'd inched toward the edge of the bed. Even though I'd been expecting that much or worse, my heart sank. Son of a bitch. We were back to where we'd been before we'd left for the trade show.

Correction—we weren't back to where we'd been before the trade show. Things were *way* more uncomfortable now. We had way too much left unsettled for us to be hooking up. Though we'd kind of straightened things out—enough to make it through the week without incident—all the awkwardness from before came crashing back in with reinforcements.

Marcus reached for something on the floor. Then, as he stood, he pulled on his boxers. "I'm, uh, going to get ready to go downstairs." He glanced at me. "I'll meet you at the booth?"

"Yeah. Be down in a few."

We didn't look at each other while he quickly got ready for the trade show. Once he was shaved and dressed, he started to go, came back for his convention badge, and hurried out of the room.

Cursing softly, I lay back across the bed where I'd fucked him senseless last night. Well, shit. What now?

I hope you know how to come back from this, Marcus. Because I sure as shit don't.

Our booth seemed a hell of a lot smaller than it had yesterday. I seriously wondered a few times if the convention staff had come in during the night and squeezed all our displays and tables together. Had Marcus and I been bumping into and tripping over each other all week and I just hadn't noticed?

Not that it mattered. We couldn't get out of each other's way, and every time we stumbled or collided, the air between us turned even more awkward. Much more of this and people were going to start noticing.

I tried like hell to focus on what we'd come here to do. Marcus handled all the schmoozing, and all I needed to do was talk about the technical aspects of Welding & Control Equipment's product lines. I knew this stuff inside and out, so it should have been easy under even the most distracting conditions.

Should have been.

I'd never stumbled or fumbled my way through demos before. It was a good thing I wasn't actually firing up the torches and doing any cutting or welding. I was pretty sure that would be an unmitigated call-911 type disaster today. Just going through the motions, explaining all the features, harping on all the reasons our design was superior to other companies—it was like one of those dreams of being back in high school and having to give a presentation, but not being able to remember any of the material. I seriously wouldn't have been surprised to look down and realize I was in my underwear.

When there was a lull, Marcus turned to me and cleared his throat. "So, um, there's a demo going on for some new gas manifold designs. If you want to go check it out, I can hold down the fort."

"You trying to get rid of me?" The joke came out before I could think twice.

Our eyes locked, and the awkwardness ratcheted up so hard, I was amazed no one around us noticed.

Marcus broke the staring contest, his cheeks darkening.

I shifted my weight. "I think I'll just go get some coffee. Do you, um, want any?"

He shook his head without looking at me or making a sound.

"Okay. Well. I'll be back." I left, and I hated myself for feeling relieved to put some space between us. Last night I couldn't get close enough to him. Now this.

The line at the coffee shop was way too short, and in no time, I was on my way back to the booth.

Where did he say that manifold demo was? I had zero interest in the other company's demo, but it was an excuse to stay out of the booth for a while.

At that thought, my stomach got even heavier and sicker. Because nothing said *glad we fucked last night* like looking for the nearest available excuse to get away from each other.

Son of a bitch...

CHAPTER 10

MARCUS

If there was one thing I'd learned in years of going to trade shows, it was this—tearing down a booth was like putting up wallpaper. A royal pain in the ass. Way more headache than it was worth. A minimum two-person job that was guaranteed to throw gasoline on any conflict simmering between those two people.

Reuben and I didn't have the trade show itself to hold our focus anymore, so in came that crushing post-con fatigue, which was *really* good at shortening fuses and making small jobs into huge ones. I'd had more than a few quietly heated arguments with the other people who'd come to shows with me, usually over stupid shit that wouldn't have bothered any of us under normal circumstances.

Except I'd never had to do this with someone I'd slept with, never mind someone with whom I'd now shared *two* regrettable sexual encounters in fairly rapid succession. I couldn't even define everything I felt whenever I looked at him. There were so many emotions swirling together, they ceased to be their own feelings and turned into a single, combustible one—anger. Because anger hurt less than shame. Because lashing out was more palatable than breaking down.

Because wanting to read him the riot act was less painful, less exhausting, and less futile than telling him how I really felt.

In the interest of not damaging my professional reputation or losing my job, I kept that anger as far beneath the surface as I could. I didn't speak unless I absolutely had to. I didn't even look at him if I could help it.

"Do you need help with the demo cases?" Reuben's tone was flat, but somehow managed to mix in both boredom and uneasiness. The former was probably intended to hide the latter. *Please don't notice how wound up I am.*

You wouldn't be *this wound up and neither would I if we hadn't—*

I cleared my throat and spoke carefully. "It takes two people to lift it once everything is in it. If you can pack everything, I'll help put it in the van."

Reuben didn't respond. He put the empty case on the cart the venue had provided, and started dismantling the demo equipment.

Normally, I'd be hovering like a hawk or handling the demo stuff myself, but Reuben was already on top of it. Hovering would piss him off on the best of days.

Besides, I reminded myself, he'd played a role in designing most of that equipment. He knew how to handle it without damaging anything.

So I shut off my inner control freak and focused on my own task —rolling the banner so it wouldn't get wrinkled and would fit into its container.

Okay. We'd interacted without blowing up at each other. We could do this. Maybe. Hopefully. No, we could, damn it.

We did have a couple of things working in our favor and keeping us from an explosive confrontation. First, Reuben's allergy to drawing attention to himself unless he absolutely had to. Second, both of us having *years* of practice at (mostly) keeping our personal issues out of sight at work, even when it sucked.

So, aside from a few loaded glances and terse comments through gritted teeth, we made it through tearing down the booth without anything actually happening. Which was good—neither of us needed our boss catching wind of us losing our shit at each other in front of half the industry. If someone had cared to look, they probably would have noticed the tension between us. God knew it felt about as subtle as a pissed-off bull about to be turned loose at a rodeo, but I supposed it was more obvious to me or Reuben than everyone else. They were all busy with their own booths, so I doubted we registered on anyone's radar. I hoped, anyway.

That tension wasn't going to contain itself forever, though. We still had one night together in the hotel room followed by tomorrow's painfully long drive back to Seattle. Throughout the entire process of breaking down our displays and packing our van, I dreaded the moment we were alone together. By mid-afternoon, I wasn't even sure we'd make it back to the room. On our eightieth or two-thousandth or whatever trip to the van, we suddenly found ourselves alone in the parking garage. When we locked eyes over the bin of demo equipment we had to lift together, I could almost feel the confrontation exploding between us.

But then the elevator had opened and a couple of people from a company I didn't immediately recognize trooped in with some plastic crates, and the moment passed. It wasn't like the tension had vanished. More like someone had been holding a cutting torch dangerously close to a stick of dynamite, but then moved it away from the fuse. The dynamite was still there, and the torch was still lit, but for the time being, they were far enough apart to let us breathe.

In silence, we loaded the case into the van, closed and locked the doors, and wheeled the cart back into the convention hall.

And all the while, I tried and failed to ignore the ticking time-bomb between us.

———

We could only put off the inevitable for so long, and I saw it coming from a mile away. All the way back to the hotel, up the elevator, and down the hall, I could feel it brewing in the tightness in my chest, and I could see it in the twitch of his jaw muscles. If there was such a thing as an emotional relief valve, we'd crossed the threshold of anything it could contain. It didn't even need a spark to blow at this point.

It didn't need one, but it got one, and that spark came in the form of me nudging the door closed *slightly* harder than I needed to. I hadn't intended to. I wasn't slamming it or anything. Any other time, we both might've jumped at the unexpected bang, and that would have been the end of it.

Not this time.

The door hit home like a gunshot going off, and we both damn near jumped out of our skin, and I could almost literally feel the relief valve give.

Reuben spun around, lips pulled back across his teeth and eyes narrow as he jabbed a finger at me. "What the fuck were you thinking last night?"

I straightened, showing my palms. "Me? It took two, you know."

He scowled. "Yeah, but it only took one to make the first move."

"You weren't exactly protesting in the elevator," I snapped. "And I definitely didn't hear any protests once you had my dick down your throat."

"Of course you didn't," he shot back. "You knew you wouldn't because you know I've never been able to say no to you."

The words were like a slap across the face. We stared at each other in stunned silence.

"Do..." I swallowed. "Do you think that's why I kissed you? Because I knew you wouldn't say no?"

He tightened his jaw and folded his arms. "Would you have done it if you thought I'd shoot you down?"

"That's not the same as going for it because I was taking advantage of you or something." I showed my palms. "Look, I don't know why I made a move. It just felt right, and I—"

"Yeah, I'm sure it did."

I glared at him, not sure if I was more pissed or hurt by the accusations. "I can't believe you think I was just making a pass at you because... because..." I threw up a hand. "Seriously, Reuben? Is that seriously what you think?"

"Well, I can't imagine it was because you thought it would make the rest of the trade show bearable, so you tell me."

I gaped, unable to process all this. He'd lashed out in the past, and God knew in the heat of the moment we'd both said things we didn't mean, but I couldn't get my head around what he was saying. Did he really think...? Did he actually believe...?

Fuck. I couldn't do this. Not now. I was too raw and too tired to stand here and listen to him tell me he thought last night was... like *that*. Maybe it had been a mistake, but I'd wanted him, and not because I knew he'd say yes. Hell, I'd been scared shitless he'd shove me away and tell me off. I didn't have it in me to absorb all this. Not tonight.

"You know what?" I put up my hands again. "I'm done. I'm exhausted, and we're going to be stuck in the van all day tomorrow, so if it's all right with you, I'm going out for a while."

"Be my guest." He took off his shoes and nudged them up against his suitcase. "I'll be here."

Not like I cared. As long as he was somewhere other than where I was, that was fine by me.

So I double-checked I had my wallet and room key, and without another word, got the fuck out of there.

CHAPTER 11

REUBEN

The constant avalanche of emails—most of them urgent—were turning out to be more blessing than curse. If nothing else, they gave me something to do to pass the time while Marcus was gone.

I was pretty sure he'd gone to the hotel bar. The trade show was over, so a lot of the attendees were heading down for an informal get-together. From what I'd heard, that pretty much meant everyone was getting hammered and being loud for a night before they had to trudge back to work. That was where, legend had it, the biggest trade show mistakes happened. The ill-judged, alcohol-fueled hookups. The drunken leaks of trade secrets. The shit-faced shit-talking that could sever professional relationships and create hostile work environments.

Not my scene.

And anyway, I didn't really care where he'd gone—I was just glad he wasn't here. The awkwardness was tenfold what it had been on the way to Boise, and the less time we had to spend together, the better. Maybe once we got back to Seattle and our normal lives, we could think about clearing the air between us again, but right now I didn't want to talk. I didn't see myself sleeping any time soon, I had no desire to go party with anyone, and as long as he didn't come back up to the room, I could seethe in peace.

I'd be dead on my feet in the morning, but whatever. Marcus could drive. He was the morning person, so he was better suited for the job anyway.

Well, assuming he got some sleep first. And he had been gone a long time, hadn't he?

I checked the time. Almost eleven thirty.

I gnawed the inside of my cheek. It wasn't at all like Marcus to go out and party, particularly into the night like this. He was a morning person. Late nights had never been his thing, especially not if he had to be up early.

Okay, Marcus could function on less sleep than most people, but he still needed some sleep, especially if he was going to navigate a fully loaded van down treacherous roads in shitty weather. Plus we had to leave early because the weather was supposed to get ugly tomorrow. We couldn't afford to leave later than six or seven, and I *knew* Marcus. That man ran on too little sleep like a car ran after someone had poured sugar in the gas tank.

I groaned, picked up my phone, and sent him a text.

Where are you? We need to get some sleep.

No response. He saw the message, but... no response.

Fuck. I tossed my phone onto the bed beside me. Even if he didn't need to sleep, I sure did, and that wasn't going to happen if I was lying there wondering when he'd come back. Or if he came in and turned on all the lights or something.

Damn it, I should have booked a separate room. Then we could avoid each other in peace.

But I had an expensive divorce looming, so I wasn't exactly flush with cash. Marcus might have been able to convince the company to let him expense room service, but there were limits. I really didn't want to explain to my dad or the accounting department why two people couldn't share a room big enough to comfortably accommodate four, and I doubted Marcus did either. I was pretty sure the hotel was sold out anyway, so the only other option would be finding some other place to stay. Which suddenly didn't seem like such a bad idea. If my dad roped me into another trade show, that was exactly what I would do.

For this show, however, Marcus and I were rooming together, and even though I didn't want to be anywhere near him, it bothered me that he wasn't back yet. Especially when I went to text him again and realized it was almost midnight.

No sign of Marcus. He'd read my texts, so unless he'd been kidnapped or something, he was still alive and looking at his phone. He just wasn't replying and didn't seem to be in any hurry to come back up to the room.

Well, there wasn't much I could do, short of going down to the bar and dragging him back to the room. So, I took a quick shower, brushed my teeth, and got ready for bed. As I settled in for the night, the clock between our beds said 12:13.

It took me a long, long time to finally drift off to sleep.

And my last thought before exhaustion finally took over was that Marcus still hadn't come back.

CHAPTER 12

MARCUS

As the bartender poured me another neat whiskey, I checked my phone. It was after midnight.

Gnawing my lip, I glanced at the drink. I was seriously buzzed, and it was getting really late. The bartender was already making the drink, though, and there was a chance Reuben was still awake. He'd texted me half an hour ago, after all. Staying down here for as long as it took me to finish this one wouldn't make much of a difference, would it? Except maybe giving Reuben a little more time to fall asleep so we didn't have to face each other?

I took the glass, paid, and leaned against the bar, looking out at the familiar faces who were all well on their way to getting drunk. It had been a long time since I'd joined them; for the last few years, I'd carefully avoided staying late at the bar on the last night of a trade show. This was when people let their hair down, got shit-faced, and did things the rest of us would be gossiping about for years to come. I'd been the subject of that gossip a few times, and had learned early on it was better to just make an appearance, say goodbye to a few people, and then bow out under the pretense of needing to leave early the next morning.

It wasn't even a pretense this time. There was a blizzard moving into the region in the next twenty-four hours. Reuben and I needed to get on the road early and be well on our way home before the storm showed up mid-afternoon. As long as we made it into Washington by around two or three, and assuming the storm didn't suddenly change its strength or trajectory, we'd be well in the clear. I wanted to be back in Washington by noon just to be safe.

Staring into my drink, I debated leaving it on the bar untouched. I was still coherent and steady on my feet. By the time I made it to the bottom of this glass, though, I would be well on my way to joining my colleagues for a night of public unprofessional behavior.

But at least I'd be numb. I'd be away from Reuben, and I'd have some more time to think about anything other than how much longer and more awkward our drive home would be now that we'd...

I winced.

Damn. I obviously wasn't drunk enough because I was still lucid enough to cringe at what we'd done.

Fuck it.

I took a deep swallow. Another.

Then I downed the rest, flagged down the bartender, and ordered a double.

I was halfway through that one when a chirpy squeal broke through the noise of the crowd: "Marcus!"

I turned to see Sheila Brown from... fuck, whatever company she was from. With a forced smile, I let her hug me—one of those drunk hugs that was more like a controlled fall in hopes I would hold her upright. As I righted her again, I said, "How are you doing?"

"I'm..." She held up her mostly empty beer bottle. "Well, I think you know." She nudged me and slurred, "What're you still doing here? You're never at this party."

Because I'm not usually rooming with someone I can't look in the eye.

I sipped my drink and smiled again. "I've been missing out, haven't I?"

"You have." She looped her arm in mine. "Come on. My field reps don't believe me when I say you can dance."

I balked, digging my heels in. "Oh, no. Not—"

"Come on!" She tugged my arm. "Just a song or two!"

"I know, hon, but I need to..." What? Go back to the room and feel like shit? Try to sleep even though there was no way in hell I would with Reuben in the next bed?

Well, damn. I could either toss and turn, or I could stay down here and dance for a while. I wasn't going to sleep either way, and at least this would be fun.

So I shrugged, threw back the rest of my drink, and let her lead me out onto the dance floor.

CHAPTER 13

REUBEN

At 5:00 the next morning, my alarm jolted me out of a restless sleep.

At 5:01, anger jarred me fully awake.

Marcus was sprawled across his bed, snoring the way he only did when he'd been drinking. He was still dressed—hell, he still had his shoes on—and the alarm didn't seem to have even registered. When had he come in? Apparently during one of those brief intervals when I'd actually been asleep.

I got up and shut off the alarm. He still hadn't moved, so I leaned over to nudge him. The smell of booze wafted off him so strongly it made my eyes water. I swore under my breath and shook his shoulder. "Marcus. Hey. Marcus?"

He groaned, but his eyes stayed shut.

"Marcus. Get up. We have to get going." I shook him harder. "Goddammit, Marcus!"

This time, he grunted, and then his eyelids fluttered for a second before they opened completely. He winced, squeezing them shut again, but not before I saw how bloodshot they were.

"Okay, okay," he muttered. "I'm up."

"Bullshit."

He shot me a glare, then sat up with a groan and rubbed his face. "Just let me—" He paused, and his eyes lost focus as his balance seemed to waver.

I studied him, forcing my irritation beneath the surface. "What?"

"Just—" His teeth snapped shut. Some color slipped out of his face. Then he bolted for the bathroom and treated me—and probably our neighbors on all sides—to the sounds of him retching for a solid minute. On any other day, I might've been smug because he richly deserved to be as miserable as he sounded, but not today. It wasn't funny that he was way too hungover to drive. Hell, he might've still been drunk.

I rubbed my gritty eyes with the heels of my hands. Fuck my life. I was driving, wasn't I? Even though I was the night owl and had gotten almost no sleep, I was driving. The only alternative was to stay another night in Boise and hope for the best tomorrow, and... no. *Fuck* no. I didn't care how much caffeine it took—we were going back to Seattle *today.*

Marcus emerged from the bathroom looking green and wobbly.

I gritted my teeth. "You all right?"

"I think so," he croaked. "Let's get going. We need to..." His eyes unfocused again.

"Get out of Idaho before that blizzard shows up?"

He snapped his fingers. "Yes. That. Let's go."

I rolled my eyes, and said nothing. I just started getting dressed. I didn't bother shaving, but at least brushed my teeth and splashed some cold water on my face. Marcus was, unsurprisingly, slower about getting ready to roll, but he got his shit together. Neither of us said a word as we headed out of the room.

In the elevator, he leaned hard against the wall, squeezing his eyes shut and swallowing like he was struggling not to puke again.

I could relate. It was hard to believe we'd had a ridiculously hot make-out session in here the night before last. Now, just being this close to him made me want to hurl too, and not because of the alcohol fumes still radiating off him.

When we got to the lobby, I gave him the van keys and sent him down to the garage to wait for me by the van. No sense letting anyone see him here in the checkout line while he was such a mess. I doubted he'd know how to check out at this point anyway.

Checking out was uneventful and easy, and I grabbed a cup of coffee at the espresso stand before I headed down to the garage. As I walked up to the van, Marcus eyed my cup, and he actually managed to look even greener.

I couldn't resist, and raised the cup. "Coffee?"

Marcus winced and shook his head wordlessly. From the way he was clenching his jaw, I didn't have to ask why he didn't want anything. I couldn't imagine he had much left to throw up, but he could still surprise me, so I didn't push the issue.

And he was completely miserable. I *almost* felt bad for him because he had to feel like shit right then. But I really didn't. Not after he'd chosen to stay out that late and drink that much when he knew we had to be up this early.

Serves you right, asshole.

We hadn't even made it to the freeway before Marcus had dozed off in the passenger seat. I kind of wanted him to stay awake and keep reminding me why I was pissed at him. Being angry kept me awake. The combination of the van's heater, the quiet between us, and the monotony of the pre-dawn road threatened to lull me to sleep. Would it be wrong to wake him up and pick a fight with him just to keep myself awake?

Maybe, maybe not, but I let him sleep. Truth was, I was too tired for that. At this rate, if we started fighting, I was liable to break down in tears. There was just so much, and I couldn't even put it all in order, and the one person I could usually ask to help sort things out was on the other side of this giant trash fire.

Later. After we'd both had a chance to catch our breath. After some coffee. Maybe after we'd both gotten some sleep, too, because I was running on fumes. Driving was way more difficult than it should have been. My eyelids were heavy. So heavy. Each time I blinked, it was harder to open my eyes again. Damn. Next exit with anything that sold coffee—Starbucks, 7-Eleven, some shady dude in a rusty food truck—we were stopping. Clearly I hadn't had enough caffeine.

I gripped the wheel and forced my gritty eyes to stay open, if only so I could watch for someone selling blessed coffee.

After a mile or two, they started getting heavy again.

They slid shut.

I let them stay there.

Just for a second.

Just a second of rest.

Just—

A loud rumble jolted me awake, and I swerved back into the lane. Thank God for those strips on the shoulder to wake up truckers. Turned out they worked for van drivers too.

Beside me, Marcus jerked a bit. "What was that?"

"Nothing." My face burned. I was awake now. "Just trying not to hit a deer."

On any normal day, he would've called me out on the bullshit, but he probably didn't even know it *was* bullshit. Today, he didn't question me, and a second later, he was snoring again.

Irritation kept me going for a little while. Only a little while, though. There was still no place to buy coffee yet, though one sign promised something in a few miles. My eyelids... fuck.

They slid down again.

Okay, a second wouldn't—

A horn blared.

My eyes flew open. I swerved to avoid the pickup truck in the next lane, and the ass end of the van found some ice. We fishtailed. Then spun.

For a few seconds, my vision was reduced to flashes of white, gray, and black.

Before the van jolted to a violent stop.

And everything was still.

CHAPTER 14

MARCUS

Weightlessness and a surge of panic had knocked me awake, and I'd had seconds to try to make sense of things before the van slammed against something solid, and stopped.

For a couple of heartbeats, Reuben and I sat in stunned silence. The van was at an odd angle, the windshield half-covered in snow, and everything was still except the idling engine. Outside, I could hear cars going by. There were voices and footsteps too, so maybe someone had stopped.

Slowly, hands still gripping the wheel, Reuben turned to me and shakily asked, "You okay?"

"Yeah." My head was throbbing even harder now, but he didn't need to know that. As I tugged at the shoulder strap of my seatbelt, which had tightened enough to be painful, I swallowed to make sure I didn't puke. Then I croaked, "You?"

"Yeah." He faced the front again, staring slack-jawed at the snow-dusted windshield. "Yeah, I think... I think I'm good."

"You sure?"

He paused like he really needed to give it some thought, but then nodded. Hand unsteady, he shifted the van into park even though it didn't feel like it was going anywhere, shut off the engine, and opened his door. The door scraped on something. Frozen ground, maybe. Pavement. Hard to tell.

Jittery with adrenaline, I got out and stepped carefully on the icy ground. I had visions of the van being completely destroyed, but it turned out the scene wasn't as bad as I'd anticipated. The van was partly in the ditch, nose buried in a snowbank, which had thrown a bunch of powder onto the windshield. As far as I could tell, we probably just needed a tow truck to pull us free, and with any luck the wheel and axle were still intact.

But what about everything inside?

My guts knotted, which wasn't a good feeling when I wasn't sure I was done hurling, thanks to my hangover. I hurried around to the back of the van, opened the doors, and checked inside. Fortunately, not much had moved. Everything had been packed in here so tight, there hadn't been a lot of room for anything to slide or fall, so nothing seemed out of place. When we made it back to Seattle, I'd have to check some of the demo equipment and make sure it had all stayed intact. I wasn't too worried, though—it was all heavy-duty industrial-grade machinery anyway, and we'd packed it like Grandma's best bone china.

Relieved, I swung the doors shut. Crisis averted. Well, *one* crisis averted. With my stomach still knotted, I went around to the front again. Reuben was scowling at his phone.

"Any signal?" I asked.

He nodded without looking up. "Just trying to find a tow company that will come out here."

I grunted in acknowledgement and glanced at the freeway. We hadn't slid far, but we were a good fifteen feet from the flow of traffic. Safe enough, I decided, though I'd keep an eye on the road in case someone started to spin out. Though with as fast as everyone was driving...

I looked around. "Maybe we should wait inside the van. Just in case someone else slides."

Reuben's jaw worked as he cut his eyes toward the interstate. After a few seconds, he nodded. "Yeah. Good idea."

We climbed back into the cab. It was still sitting lopsided, so the seats were at an awkward angle, but at least it was warm in here and we were safer than if we stayed outside.

I stayed quiet while Reuben made some calls. It took a while—not surprising, given the road conditions—but he finally found someone who could be here before the Second Coming.

"Probably a couple of hours." He tossed his phone onto the dash and rubbed his eyes. "We're going to be here a while."

"So much for getting home before the storm," I muttered.

Reuben said nothing.

I kneaded my throbbing temples. "What the hell happened, anyway?"

Reuben clenched his jaw, avoiding my gaze.

"Reuben? What—"

"I nodded off, okay?" he snapped. He turned to me, eyes full of fury. "Guess I should've let you drive."

I blinked.

"We had to hit the road early," he went on. "You knew that. But you were still out drinking until—"

"Yeah, because I couldn't stand to come back to the room."

He stopped. So did I. We stared at each other, eyes wide.

Finally, he shook his head, muttered something I didn't understand and got out of the van again. When he slammed the door behind him, the sound hit my aching head like a two-by-four. I winced and tried not to puke.

Outside, an eighteen-wheeler shot past us, the wind off the truck rattling the van. Damn it, as much as I needed a few minutes away from Reuben, it was not safe out there. Not while the roads were this slick.

I swore and got out. "Reuben, come on. Get back in the van."

Standing in the track the van had carved into the snow on its way to the ditch, he turned and glared at me. "I think I'd rather stay out here."

It took all the restraint I had not to roll my eyes, and I schooled my expression as I joined him so I wasn't standing to mid-shin in snow. "It's dangerous out here, and it's cold. Just..." I motioned toward the van. "Come on."

"No thanks." He fixed that glare on me. "I can't believe you're going to try to pin this on me."

"I wasn't driving."

"No, but you would've been if you hadn't stayed out drinking last night." He narrowed his eyes. "Oh wait, that's my fault too."

We locked eyes. Tiny snowflakes drifted down, probably freezing solid in the icy air between us.

With a sigh, I broke the staring contest. I watched the sparse traffic whipping past us, ostensibly to be alert in case someone lost control. A line of eighteen-wheelers barreled toward us, staying well between the lines but still worth keeping an eye on. The first passed in a roar of diesel engine and tires, the next four trucks right on its tail, and the noise gave me a chance to gather my thoughts. As the last truck faded into the distance, leaving nothing but a few cars and pickups to fill the silence, I turned to Reuben. "Look, I'm sorry. Things have been really uncomfortable ever since we fooled around, and I..." I exhaled a cloud into the cold air, sending snowflakes scattering. "I needed some downtime, and I got carried away."

He laughed bitterly. "Is that what you call it?"

I glared at him for a second before turning my attention back to the interstate. "I fucked up, all right?"

"Which part?" he asked through his teeth. "Last night? Or the night you spent with me?"

I closed my eyes and sighed. Truth was, the answer was both. I really, really didn't want to call the other night a mistake, but I'd known from the moment we'd made eye contact the next morning that it had been. There'd been too much left unresolved for us to be jumping into bed together, and now things were even weirder than before. And yes, last night had been a mistake too. I'd known better than to party that hard when I knew I was driving out the next morning even if there *wasn't* a blizzard to contend with. Somehow being stranded on the side of the road with a possibly busted van seemed like the logical outcome after I'd been such an idiot recently. It was the closest we could get to a literal train wreck, so why the fuck not?

Facing Reuben again, I kept my voice and expression as neutral as possible. "Let's just worry about staying warm and not getting run over." I nodded toward the passing cars. "Once we figure out what's going on with the van and when we have a shot at hitting the road, then we can deal with everything else."

His eyes were colder than the bitter wind whipping at our clothes. "We've got nothing but time right now. Why wait?"

I swallowed. *Because I'm afraid we'll make things worse and it already hurts like hell?*

Before I could respond, though, he gave another bitter laugh and headed for the van, and as he did, he threw over his shoulder, "Fine. We'll wait until you're done being hung over."

I watched him go, unable to speak. My stomach was sick, the back of my throat sour, and I honestly couldn't say how much of it was from last night versus feeling like an utter asshole.

Reuben was right. This was my fault. We both knew he didn't function early in the morning, and he'd been depending on me to be able to drive us out of Boise in time to beat the snowstorm. And the other night, I'd made the first move. It didn't matter why. It didn't matter that I was used to carrying everyone and everything at trade shows, and I'd been overwhelmed by someone actually caring about how I was holding up. It didn't matter that I'd apparently been subconsciously looking for a reason to get close to Reuben again. It didn't matter that all those feelings I still had for him needed to stay buried. I'd let them come out anyway, opening a Pandora's box I didn't think I could ever close again.

I exhaled through my nose, keeping my jaw clenched so I didn't hurl again. God, this was all such a mess. The van was in better shape than Reuben and me. Even if it turned out the axle was toast and the oil pan was punctured.

So who the hell do I call to tow this *wreck out of a ditch?*

CHAPTER 15

REUBEN

It was a long, silent wait for the tow truck. Almost three hours, and neither of us said a word the entire time. When our cell phone batteries died, we resorted to flipping through literature we'd picked up from other companies at the trade show.

Mercifully, though, the tow truck eventually showed up.

He took us to a town I'd never heard of and dropped the van at a garage with three bays and about a dozen cars waiting. Shit. Once the van was in the hands of a mechanic, we took our luggage and walked across the street to a single-story motel with a buzzing *Vacancy* sign in the window.

"Just one room?" the lady at the front desk asked.

Without even looking at me, Marcus said, "Two, please."

I wasn't offended. Relieved, actually. We needed some space right now.

But the lady frowned and shook her head. "I've only got one left. Queen bed, double occupancy."

Marcus and I looked at each other, my own horror etched across his face. Clearing his throat, he faced her again. "Are there any other places in town?"

Another head shake. "Sorry, hon. People are getting waylaid left and right because of this storm. Only reason I've got a room is someone left fifteen minutes before you came in."

Behind us, an engine grumbled and tires spun on the snow. I glanced back to see a car pulling into the motel's lot.

"If you don't want this one," she said, "they probably will. It's up to—"

"We'll take it." Marcus pushed his corporate card toward her. To me, he added, "We can make do."

I nodded silently.

Minutes later, we were in the room, and I wanted to be ill. I had held out hope there might be a couch or something. No such luck. There was a queen bed—and they were using "queen" generously— under a pastel pink comforter, a couple of chairs by a tiny coffee table, and a dresser with an old CRT television on it. That was it.

Without looking at each other, Marcus and I settled in. We plugged in our dead phones, took our shaving kits into the bathroom, found places to put our suitcases so we didn't trip over them, and draped our jackets over the top.

Before long, though, there was nothing left to do, and the cold, empty space between us was getting louder by the second.

Trust Marcus to finally break the silence. "Listen, we should talk."

I winced. *Yeah, we probably should, but you're gonna have to start because hell if I know how we go back from this.* "We should."

He sat on the bed while I stood in the bathroom doorway, shoulder pressed against the frame and arms folded loosely across my chest. Without looking at me, he took a deep breath. "I really am sorry about last night. I should have come and talked to you. I was just... overwhelmed, I guess."

I was about to respond, but he picked just that moment to lift his gaze, and when our eyes locked, words failed me. I could have lived with him being angry or even contrite, but that hurt in his eyes cut me right to the core.

"Look," he said, voice shaking worse than it had the night I'd broken things off six years ago. "I can't change what happened the other night or last night. I can't change what happened in December. But I don't want things to be like this between us." He swallowed. "I still want us to be friends, and even if we can't be, we still have to work together."

I forced back my own emotions. "I know. And I... I want that too. But how do we do this?"

Marcus pressed his lips together. Shifting his gaze away, he shook his head. "I have no idea."

I stared at him. Fuck. If he didn't know, then... shit. Marcus had always been the one who could parse feelings and put names on things that were just nebulous and abstract to me. I'd looked to him when we'd dated and when we'd been friends. Let him put all the pieces out on the table and label them neatly so I could make sense of them. Maybe it hadn't been fair to him—and he'd said more than once it wasn't—but I'd never known what else to do. It wasn't that I wanted him doing all the work. I straight up *couldn't* do it. He could read feelings like psychics read palms and tea leaves and stars and whatever, and more than that, he could figure out what to do once things had names.

So if he didn't know what to do now...

"Do you really think we screwed up?" I whispered. "The other night?"

Marcus's jaw worked. He took a breath like he was about to speak. Hesitated. Started again. Hesitated again. Finally, he exhaled hard and faced me again. "Nothing has ever felt as right as being in bed with you."

My heart stopped as suddenly as my breath did.

But he wasn't done. Voice still shaky and raw, he said, "In the moment, it's always right. And before December, it had never fucked anything up, you know? Now suddenly—" His voice cracked. He paused to clear his throat, and it sounded like one hell of a struggle when he finished: "Suddenly I've slept with you once and possibly killed your marriage. Slept with you again and fucked up our friendship." He met my eyes with tears in his. "I don't want anything I've ever done with you to be a mistake, but I don't know what else to call it now."

"I don't either." The heavy silence was worse than the conversation, so I pressed on. "What do we do now?"

Marcus's shoulders sagged and he shook his head. "I don't know." He pulled in a ragged breath and let it out slowly. "Maybe we just need some time. To... I don't know. Let things settle down."

The lump in my throat was impossible to ignore now. "How do we know when it's been long enough? Or that things have settled down?"

Please, please have an answer because I have no idea what we're doing.

But he shook his head again, and repeated in a barely audible whisper, "I don't know. I... I don't fucking know." He paused. Then he cleared his throat and got up, and as he reached for his jacket, said, "I'm going to walk down to the mechanic's and see if there's an ETA on the van."

I bit back a comment about how our room had a phone, we had cell phones, and he didn't actually need to walk through the bitter cold. Figuring out my own emotions and putting them into words wasn't a strong point of mine, but I *could* read when Marcus needed to be alone. When he needed to be away from me.

Neither of us said a word as he collected his phone and charger, and a moment later, the door shut behind him. I sank onto the edge of the bed and rubbed the back of my neck, wondering when those muscles had gotten so stiff. I didn't think it was from the crash earlier. I'd had whiplash before. This felt more like the kind of tension I got after a long meeting with my dad or a fight with my ex-wife.

Things were bad with Marcus, and as per usual, I had no idea what to do. In fact, it was worse than usual. What the hell kind of territory were we in that even Marcus couldn't read the tea leaves and line everything up so it made sense?

I needed some advice. Desperately. Maybe then I could pick up where Marcus hadn't been able to continue, and we could fix this. Or... something.

My phone had finally charged enough to be useful, though I kept it plugged in after I'd turned it on, and I pulled up my ex-wife's contact. I hesitated, wondering if this was against some protocol I didn't know about. Eh, fuck it. Who else was I going to talk to about this?

So, I sent the call.

"Oh hey," she said. "What's up?"

I swallowed. "Well, I'm stranded in the middle of Eastern Washington for the night."

"What? Are you okay? Do you need a ride or—"

"No, no." I pinched the bridge of my nose and sighed. "I just need to talk."

"Oh." Beat. "What about?"

"About us. And what happened."

Silence. "All right."

I swallowed hard. "There's something I need to know. And I'm... I don't even know how to ask."

"Okay." Her voice was soft and patient, just like it always had been when we weren't fighting. "Well, tell me what it's about, and we'll go from there."

I almost smiled. When it came to things like this, she knew me as well as Marcus did. The smile didn't come, though. I chewed my lip, staring blankly at the wall as I struggled to find the words. Finally, I closed my eyes and took a deep breath. "Do you think we could have fixed our marriage if we hadn't had that threesome with Marcus?" I winced. It was a relief to get the words out, but I felt like an idiot too. I wasn't even sure why.

Michelle didn't answer immediately. She stayed silent, though I could hear her breathing, so I knew the call hadn't dropped. I didn't press; just getting the question out had taken everything I had, and I couldn't have prodded her if my life had depended on it. Plus, she struggled almost as much as I did with this kind of thing, so I wouldn't begrudge her if she needed a moment to process things.

Finally, she spoke. "No. I don't think we would have made it. In fact, to tell you the truth, I knew before the Christmas party that we wouldn't. I wasn't ready to go through the motions yet, but... I knew."

I swallowed. "You did?"

"Didn't you?"

Gnawing my lip, I watched myself playing with the edge of the pastel comforter. "I guess I did. Hadn't really admitted it, though. I just keep wondering if things might have been different if we hadn't hooked up with Marcus that night."

"I don't really think so." She spoke so softly I barely heard her. "If anything, we would've dragged it out a little longer. Which I don't think is a good thing."

"No, probably not. I guess I've just felt so guilty ever since that night. We weren't in a good place, and we definitely shouldn't have been fooling around with someone else. Especially not my ex."

"Maybe not." She sounded resigned, but not bitter or angry. "We also shouldn't have been pretending things would work out when we knew damn well they wouldn't. So it wasn't like that threesome was the only mistake we made. Or even the biggest."

Something about hearing her admit that the threesome *had* been a mistake hit me in the chest. I hated that sex with the two most amazing lovers I'd ever had was a mistake. I knew it, and I accepted it, but I hated it, and knowing all three of us had been hurt by it was awful.

"And I guess..." Michelle was quiet for a moment, then sighed. "Part of me had always kind of fantasized about seeing you two together."

My teeth snapped shut. "What?"

She laughed shyly. "Come on. You're hot. He's hot. Knowing you guys had been together and that you were still into each other..." I swore I could see her half-shrugging on the other end as she added a soft, "It was kind of a hot mental image, you know?"

I had no idea how to respond to that. It had never been a secret between us that I was still attracted to Marcus any more than it had been a secret that she was still attracted to her ex-girlfriend. We'd always been open about it. We'd gotten a lot of things wrong in our relationship, but not that part.

"So when things got flirty at the Christmas party," she went on, "I guess I thought, well, why not? I wasn't going to have you for much longer, and maybe..." She sighed heavily. "It sounded good in my head that night. And it was fun, right up until I saw how you two were looking at each other."

I sat up. "What do you mean?"

"What? You didn't notice?"

"Um..."

"Jesus, Reuben. How do you not notice a man looking at you like that?"

My heart jumped into my throat. "Like... like what?"

Michelle exhaled. "Like there isn't anything in the world he wouldn't do for you, including letting you go. Even if it kills him."

Tears suddenly pricked at my eyes. I couldn't breathe. I'd already had my heart in my throat, and now there was an intense ache that I couldn't quite push back.

"And the worst part," she went on as if I wasn't ready to break, "was realizing you were looking at him the same way." Her voice sounded especially brittle as she added, "I don't even think either of you knew I was there right then."

She might as well have been in the motel room and slugged me in the gut. Eyes squeezed shut, I whispered, "I am so sorry, Michelle."

"I know. Listen, the threesome didn't end our marriage, Reuben. It just made me realize I was only torturing myself by pretending we weren't already over."

I rubbed at my stinging eyes. Who knew a simple statement could bring so much relief and guilt at the same time? "God, I'm sorry, Michelle. About everything."

"I know. And I don't blame you. Just so you know."

I moistened my lips. "What do you mean?"

"I mean, we both stopped trying a long time ago. Even if we hadn't admitted it out loud, let's face it—we gave up on our marriage long before we ever hooked up with Marcus. I'd..." She paused for a deep breath. "I won't lie—I was checking out coworkers and thinking about other people for the last year."

A few months ago, that revelation would've pissed me off and hurt me, even though the truth was I'd done the same. But tonight it was oddly reassuring. As if we'd both been on the same page about *not* being on the same page, and that even if we could've handled the end of our marriage better, it *had* been inevitable and it *was* for the best.

"I'm so sorry, Michelle," I said again.

"Me too."

"And thanks. This really helps."

"Any time. I know we're over, but I really hope we can still be friends."

I did manage to smile at that. "I hope so too."

We ended the call a moment later, and I stared at the dormant phone for a long time.

I would never have cheated on Michelle with Marcus or anyone else, but she was right that we'd both started checking out of our marriage. I just happened to work with a man I still had feelings for after all this time, and once I'd stopped focusing all my energy on trying to save my marriage, those feelings had made themselves known.

A threesome should have been—and could have been—a lot of fun. If Michelle and I had been in a better place. If Marcus and I hadn't been exes.

And, I thought with a sinking feeling, if I hadn't still been in love with Marcus.

Maybe that was why things with him were so hard right now.

Because no matter how much I wanted to hate him sometimes, I was *still* in love with him.

CHAPTER 16

MARCUS

Hands tucked into my pockets and face nestled into my zipped-up jacket, I shivered against the cold as I left the garage. I'd been here for over an hour waiting for the mechanic to give me some kind of ETA on the van. He'd finally assured me that the part he needed was on its way over from another town, and we'd be on the road in the morning.

So I left, but I didn't go back to the room. I'd have to eventually. After all, this was one of those little towns that rolled up its sidewalks at night even when the weather wasn't shit, so it was either stay outside, or go to the motel.

But I still had a few hours of daylight left, and I wasn't in any hurry to spend them cooped up with a man who struggled to even look at me. Not until I knew what to say to make things better.

There was a diner next to the motel, so I went over there to kill some time. As luck would have it, there was an outlet at my table. Thank God, since my phone was so dead I couldn't even switch it on. I plugged it in, then started perusing the menu. Typical diner fare. Nothing sounded good, but I ordered an apple pie and a cup of coffee to justify occupying a table.

When it came, I picked at my food. What little I'd eaten was really good, but I felt like shit. Some lingering hangover, yes, but also... Reuben. Just when I'd thought things couldn't get any more fraught between us, they had, and now we were stuck in a room together for one more night. That was to say nothing of tomorrow's drive. I doubted that would be pleasant. Sharing a bed with him, though? I winced. Glancing at my phone, I wondered if I'd find anyone in this area on Grindr. I could muster up the energy for sex as long as it meant staying in a different bed than the one Reuben would be sleeping in, right?

Yeah, probably not. Just walking back to the motel was going to take what little I had left.

As I nibbled another bite of my apple pie, I couldn't help letting my mind go back to the days when things had been easy with Reuben. Back when we'd both thrilled in the excitement of a clandestine office relationship, sneaking around and stealing kisses in the supply closet or the men's room or wherever we could have a few seconds of privacy.

Like he occasionally did, Reuben slipped into my office and shut the door behind him. "You busy?"

I looked up from my computer screen, chest fluttering at the sight of him and that wicked grin. "I'm always busy, but never too busy for you."

"Good." He came around the side of my desk. "Everybody thinks I'm back in the plant working on a prototype." He turned my chair toward him and put his hands on the armrests. "Nobody will miss me for a few minutes."

I hooked my fingers in his belt loops and drew him closer. "You assume a few minutes is enough time?"

"Enough time for me to tease you and get you all worked up for tonight, yeah."

"Mmm, you're a bastard." I lifted my chin and he kissed me. "Shame I won't have you all weekend."

"You won't?"

"Trade show in Atlanta. Remember?"

His smile fell. "Oh yeah. Damn."

"And we can't even stay up late my last night in town." I wrinkled my nose. "I have to leave for the airport at four in the morning."

"Four? Ugh. That's early even for you."

"I know, right?"

"Well." He kissed me softly. "We'll just call it an early night before that, and I'll make sure you sleep like the dead."

I shivered, my chair squeaking as if to make sure Reuben noticed. Trailing my hands up his arms, I said, "You always do."

"Damn right. And when you get home…" He nipped at my lower lip. "I'll be waiting with a bottle of wine."

"And a bottle of lube?"

Reuben grinned. "Costco-sized."

After a few more kisses and some more flirting, he left my office so nobody would get suspicious. Of course that left me with a hard-on and a big grin on my face, but I didn't complain. His drive-by visits were always exactly what I needed to carry me through the rest of the day. Nothing made work-related stress seem less relevant than knowing Reuben wanted to get frisky that evening.

I sighed into the stillness of my office. Oh, it was going to be a good night.

In the present, I swiped at my eyes. My feelings for him ran so much deeper than I'd realized, and for some damn reason, it had taken battering ourselves emotionally for the last few weeks—and especially the last few days—for me to realize just how much I wanted him and how far out of my reach he really was. I loved Reuben so much it hurt, and I had a feeling it would still hurt to some extent even if we hadn't fucked up in December. If things were good between us right now, and we were giving it another go as boyfriends, I could totally see myself looking at him and getting that ache in my chest because I just loved him *that* much.

Having that same ache while we couldn't stand to be in the same room was fucking torture.

After a few hours and some various à la carte items I ate despite not wanting, I couldn't justify hanging out at the diner any longer. I left the waitress a generous tip for putting up with me for so long, then headed out into the bitter cold. In the time I'd been sitting there feeling sorry for myself, the snow had stopped falling, but the temperature hadn't.

I hurried across to the motel and up to our room, but despite the cold, I stood outside the door for a moment, trying to steel myself and collect myself and talk myself into walking inside. It wasn't like I could stay out here forever, and at least the room had heat.

I took a deep breath, keyed myself in, and stepped inside, pausing to stomp the excess snow off my shoes.

Reuben was sitting cross-legged on the bed with his laptop. His expression offered nothing. "Any word on the van?"

I nodded as I deadbolted the door. "Yeah. It'll be ready tomorrow."

"Oh thank God. How did he pull that off? I thought he needed parts or something."

I shifted my weight. "He does, but they're on their way. The ones he couldn't get his hands on were to repair the cosmetic damage and the bumper. So by tomorrow he'll have everything he needs to make the van drivable. It just won't be *pretty* until we take it to a body shop."

"As long as it'll get us home." Reuben tapped his nails on the edge of the laptop. "Did he say what time he thinks it'll be done?"

"Early afternoon, probably."

The subtle drop in Reuben's shoulders was hard to miss. Then again, he'd probably caught the resignation in my tone.

We're stuck together for a while.

Reuben sighed as he closed his laptop. "It's been a long day. Let's just get some sleep, and tomorrow we'll deal with getting home."

"Good idea." I surveyed the room. "So, how do we do this? We've got one bed."

His lips quirked. He stared at the pastel comforter like it might volunteer a solution, but the bedding didn't have any ideas either.

"There's an extra blanket in the closet," I said. "Whoever sleeps on the bed can use that, and whoever takes the floor can use the comforter. The room's warm enough for—"

"This is stupid." His shoulders sagged and he shook his head. "Your back will never forgive you for sleeping on the floor."

"And your neck will never let you forget it if you do. Especially after this morning."

"Exactly."

I raised my eyebrows. "So...?"

Reuben sighed. "Look, we're stuck for the night. There's only one bed." He set his jaw and met my gaze. "We can either share the bed, or one of us can take the floor, and whoever gets the short straw is going to be miserable tomorrow." With a heavy, resigned gesture, he motioned toward the bed. "Let's just share it."

Don't sound so thrilled about getting into bed with me.

Okay, that thought wasn't fair. We weren't jumping between the sheets to have sex. We were just trying to make the most of a situation neither of us liked, and no, he probably wasn't any more thrilled about sharing a bed than I was.

But sleeping on the same surface as him did sound better than making do on the floor.

So we went through the motions of getting ready for bed without saying a word or looking at each other. That had kind of been our M.O. for the whole week, but there was an undercurrent of uneasiness that hadn't been there before. We weren't hostile now, but we were a long way from okay.

Stripped down to our boxers, we slid into opposite sides of the bed. It was probably a decent-sized bed for most couples, but for two guys who absolutely didn't want to touch each other, it was *tiny*.

Is this how straight guys feel when they have to share a bed?

The thought might've made me laugh any other night.

Tonight? Not so much.

Closing my eyes, I tried not to sigh with audible frustration. I'd known this was going to be a long trip, but tonight was going to be a *long* night.

With a gun to my head, I couldn't have said if Reuben had fallen asleep. His breathing was always slow and steady in bed whether he was wide awake or out cold.

I hoped he was asleep. It wouldn't do us any good if neither of us could function tomorrow. Me? Sleeping? Nope. I rolled over. Then again. This bed was probably comfortable as hell, but I was too tense to enjoy it. Things were too screwed up between me and Reuben. I'd been losing sleep since December anyway, and after this week, that was only going to get worse. I didn't see any way around it. Not now that my own emotions had bubbled to the surface, keeping me from denying how much I still loved him after all this time.

Guilt was tearing me apart over what we'd done to his marriage and how much we'd fucked up our friendship. I didn't know how to fix us, and I didn't know how to coexist at work like this.

My chest tightened.

At work.

Oh God.

I loved my job, and I was happy at Welding & Control Equipment, but maybe it was time to move on. There were other companies within the industry who'd tried to poach me over the years. I'd made enough of a name for myself that finding a job wouldn't be too hard, even in this economy. I might have to leave Seattle, and I might burn a few bridges within the industry—Bob Kelly did not take kindly to his people leaving for competitors—but in the end, that might be worth it.

For about two seconds, I entertained the idea of being honest with Bob and explaining I had to leave the company because I had feelings for his son that were compromising my ability to do my job.

But no. Everyone knew I was queer, but Reuben wasn't out, and there was no way in hell I would out him. As it was, him being in the closet had been part of what had driven us apart six years ago. The secrecy had been thrilling at first, but it had quickly become a source of stress for both of us. That, and he hadn't been able to cope with his fear of coming out to his father and potentially torpedoing our jobs. Or more to the point, torpedoing *my* job, since he'd been convinced Bob would can me over him out of nepotism. We both knew now that our boss was way more cutthroat than that, and he'd either fire both of us or whoever the company could more easily live without. And if I was honest, I didn't know which of us would draw the short straw in that situation—Reuben was a critical member of the engineering team, and I didn't shy away from acknowledging that I was equally critical to the marketing department.

It didn't really matter now anyway. We weren't together anymore. We couldn't *be* together.

As for work, well, I'd deal with that when I got there. Right now... sleep. I needed to fucking *sleep*, even if that seemed impossible with Reuben lying this close to me and this far away at the same time.

I closed my eyes and exhaled into the silence of the room. Tomorrow, we'd get back to Seattle. The day after that, we'd be back at work.

And when I got home that night, I'd start polishing up my résumé.

CHAPTER 17

REUBEN

Surprise, surprise—I couldn't sleep for shit. I'd dozed off for a while, but now it was damn near three in the morning and I'd been wide awake for hours.

It didn't help that Marcus kept moving. This wasn't one of those fancy mattresses with the commercials where the lady jumped on one side and the wineglass on the other didn't spill. Every move he made registered like I was a seismograph specifically calibrated to pick up every twitch and tremor.

I wanted to be frustrated with him, but I couldn't be. We were stuck in this situation together, and he was probably as stressed about it as I was. He'd managed to go to sleep and stay that way, so he had one up on me, but I doubted he was all that relaxed. Though Marcus had always been a restless sleeper, he was practically vibrating now. Not just shifting, tossing, and turning, but thrumming with tension.

Guilt burned in my chest. He wouldn't be tense or stressed if I weren't in this bed with him. Maybe I should have taken the floor after all. Or... something.

Like maybe not having sex with him, not letting things get weird with him, and not losing so much sleep you crashed the van and got stuck with him?

The thought made me wince. Hadn't there been a time when sex had been easy for us? Okay, so the sex had definitely been easy. It was the aftermath that was the problem.

A million miles away on the other side of the bed, Marcus sighed heavily in his sleep and rolled over. His foot kept moving, rubbing against the sheet with a quiet whisper, the motion carrying to all four corners of the stupid mattress. He mumbled something into his pillow. Rolled over again. Sighed. He still sounded like he was asleep, but I still doubted it was restful.

I didn't want it to, but a memory surfaced. One from when we'd been dating, and we'd spent more nights together than not. His place, my place, sex, no sex—the vast majority of nights found us sleeping side by side. And when he was stressed out—some bullshit at work, another argument with his mom—he'd move around constantly... until I curled up against him.

My throat ached. What I wouldn't have given to be able to do that for him now. Just slide up next to him, wrap my arms around him, and silently soothe him enough that he could get some sleep.

So... what's stopping you?

The thought made me jump. What was stopping me? Oh, I didn't know. Maybe the fact that I was the reason he was so restless?

I turned my head and watched him in the darkness as he fidgeted again.

Any reason I couldn't be the cause and the cure? It could make things worse between us, but they were already shitty. If there was some chance I could make them better, even if it was just for the night...

Didn't really have much to lose at this point, did I?

I casually turned over, closing some of the space between us. Paused. Waited. My heart was pounding, but I reminded myself it wasn't likely he'd actually hear it or—once we were touching—feel it.

For all he'd know, I'd moved in my sleep. Unconsciously. Accidentally.

Hoping like hell I wasn't about to ignite a battle or some fresh awkwardness, I inched closer. Then closer still.

We finally made contact when my shoulder landed gently against his back and my hip nudged his ass. He didn't recoil. He didn't tense or anything. In fact, he seemed to settle a bit.

I considered staying just like this instead of pushing my luck, but now that I could really feel his body heat, it was impossible to resist moving in closer.

Cautiously, I slid toward him. When he didn't resist, I rolled onto my side, molded myself to him, and draped an arm over him.

Marcus made a soft noise. A wordless murmur. Then his hand moved, fumbled a little beneath the covers, and found mine. For a split second, I had visions of him shoving my arm—and me—off him.

But then he closed his fingers around my hand and brought it up to his chest, tucking my arm under his elbow in the process. His breathing slowed again, and in no time, he was well and truly asleep.

I closed my eyes and inhaled deeply through my nose, indulging in a taste of that familiar scent. Though I was pressed up against him, I wasn't worried about an ill-timed hard-on making things weird; I was still way too wound up and exhausted to get turned on. I wasn't too far gone to let this wave of relief wash over me, though, and I just held him close and savored his familiar shape against me. This was one of the things I'd missed the most after we'd split up—falling asleep to the warmth of our bodies pressed together.

I wished it was this easy in the daylight. As soon as the sun came up, everything between us would be a minefield again, but in the darkness, all the mines weren't just hidden. They were gone. Like this, it was easy to say everything because I didn't have to say anything. All I had to do was touch him and hold him the way I had years ago, and we'd both be calm enough to sleep. Why wasn't there a way to do this when the lights were on?

Please don't push me away, Marcus.

Please don't hate me for doing this.

I squeezed my eyes shut, willing my emotions to settle so I didn't wind up literally crying on his shoulder. That wouldn't help anything. He'd wake up. He'd want to talk. And right now I was saying everything I could work up the courage to say.

Don't ask me for more—this is all I have.

I don't know how else to tell you I love you.

I sighed, and he stirred a little before settling again. I had to fight hard against the urge to press a kiss to his neck or his shoulder. Nothing to get him spun up or frisky—just a soft, affectionate touch because goddammit, I wanted to. But that might wake him up, and then this would be over. I wasn't ready for it to be over yet.

Tomorrow, we'd be back to fucked-up, and God knew if or how we'd ever get past that, but for now—for just a little while—I had him in my arms.

And for as long as I could, I was going to enjoy this.

CHAPTER 18

MARCUS

My eyes fluttered open to thin, gray daylight coming in through the gauzy curtains. I remembered I was in this godawful motel in the middle of nowhere, but it took my tired senses a moment to catch up with all the details.

Especially the part where someone was cuddled up against me. The warm, strong arm slung over my midsection. The bare foot woven between my lower legs. The tingling in my fingers because my arm was wrapped around broad shoulders and I'd lost circulation in my arm because someone's head was resting on my chest.

Someone being... Reuben.

My breath hitched. I tilted my head as much as I could without disturbing him, and... yeah, there was no doubt about it. Unless I'd hooked up with another gray-haired guy with shoulders that sexy.

Except I was pretty sure we *hadn't* hooked up. In fact, I knew we hadn't. I'd have remembered. Sex with Reuben was anything but forgettable, and waking up this morning, I'd have noticed all the aches and twinges before I'd even noticed him lying against me.

So no, we hadn't done anything.

Then how the fuck...

I opened and closed my hand to get some blood moving. Before I realized what I was doing, I let my tingling fingers brush his arm. Down. Then up. Then down again. Slow, lazy arcs like I'd sometimes done in the past when he'd been asleep on my shoulder.

Lying like this, I could almost convince myself everything was back to the way it was six years ago. Like if I squinted at an old car, I could see it in all its perfect, shiny glory without the rust, dents, bald tires, and dead battery.

I sighed, still caressing his arm. I'd hate myself later for it, but I made no move to disentangle myself from him. Aside from that morning in Boise, it had been far too long since I'd woken up with someone, and much longer since I'd woken up with him.

Do you have any idea how much I miss you?

That had been killing me anyway, but now this, the way we were lying together? God, it reminded me so much of the handful of times we'd fought when we were dating. We'd argue, and somehow we'd wind up in the same bed even though we didn't live together. It was like no matter how pissed off we were, neither of us could justify sleeping apart. We wouldn't necessarily have sex, but we'd at least land on the same surface, and that had always given me hope that we could work things out.

And somehow, in the middle of the night, we'd drift back together and wake up like this. Sometimes his head was on my shoulder. Sometimes mine was on his. Or one of us would be spooning the other, or... something. But we'd fall asleep miles apart and wake up in the middle of the bed, and over coffee, I could usually find the words to ease whatever had pushed us away in the first place.

Pressing my lips together, I fought back tears because it felt so good to be holding him like this, and it was also excruciating to realize I couldn't find those magic words this time.

Oh, there were words. There were three in particular I wanted to say to him.

But I couldn't. Not now.

Sure, I could tell him. I could sit him down, look him in the eye, and pour my heart out until there was no doubt left in his mind that I missed him, I wanted him, and I loved him.

But not while the ink was still wet on his divorce. He couldn't possibly be ready for anything with anyone, never mind with an ex-boyfriend who'd played a part in the closing act of his marriage.

All I could do now was unfuck what we'd done to our friendship, and try to keep things on an even keel until he'd moved on from his marriage. Then... well, it was up to him if we had a shot at getting it right this time.

It was too soon after his divorce, and things were too raw between us, and...

I closed my eyes and exhaled. There was never going to be a right time, was there?

Beside me, he stirred. Then, slowly, he pushed himself up on his elbow and turned his head toward me, features puffy with sleepiness. "Hey."

"Hey." I wanted so desperately to smooth his sleep-tousled hair, but I wasn't sure if I should.

His hand went to his lip, and his eyes filled with horror. "Oh God. I drooled on you."

I glanced down and wiped the hint of wetness off my chest. "It's okay. Isn't like it's the first time."

The horror held for a second, but then he laughed. "Eh, you've done the same to me a few times."

"Exactly."

We met each other's eyes, and the amusement faded. Yeah, we'd done things like that in the past. Back when we'd slept together all the time. When we'd been together. A long, long time ago before things got weird.

Reuben scooted over a little, putting some more distance between us, which the room's cool air rushed to fill in. Goose bumps prickled all the skin he'd been pressed up against a minute ago.

Damn it. Come back.

He swung his legs over the side of the bed and sat up. "So, um."

He cleared his throat, staring down at his wringing hands. "I guess... while we wait for the van..."

"We might as well go find something to eat."

"Yeah. Good idea. Any, um, ideas?"

"There's a diner next door. I ate there yesterday and it wasn't half bad."

"Okay." He nodded. "Just, um, let me grab a shower."

"Okay."

Reuben stood, but he only made it a couple of steps toward the bathroom before he stopped. He stood there for a moment, rocking on his feet, and finally turned back to me. "Look, I know we've got a lot to sort out, but... that thing I said about the other night? About you only coming on to me because I was a sure thing?" Cheeks coloring, he broke eye contact. "I'm sorry. That was a cheap shot."

I swallowed. "I kind of figured you didn't actually mean it."

"No, I didn't, but I said it." He met my gaze again. "I'm sorry."

"Apology accepted."

A faint smile flickered across his lips. One tugged at mine too.

Then he disappeared into the bathroom, and the moment was gone. As soon as the bathroom door was shut behind him, I released a breath and covered my face with both hands. I was relieved he'd apologized for that much, but I had no illusions that we were back on solid ground. The air between us hadn't been this uncomfortable the night we'd broken up, for fuck's sake. That hadn't been a fun evening, and leaving had hurt like hell, but somehow that was more appealing than this. Maybe because there'd been some finality that night. Today, everything was up in the air, and even letting it all crash and burn at our feet sounded better than continuing like this. Even after waking up in each other's arms and that apology, it was all so daunting. In fact, that tiny bit of progress we'd just made seemed to make things worse, as if it pointed out how far we still had to go. How much distance we still had to cross.

And how impossible that seemed.

CHAPTER 19

REUBEN

So much for the van being fixed.

"Still waiting on some parts," the mechanic said with a shrug. "I've got a buddy running them up from out of town. The roads were too bad for him to get here yesterday, but he should be here in another hour. Two if the roads are bad."

"How long do you think it'll take after that?" Marcus's voice was still calm and collected, but he was tense all over. "We need to get on the road so we can clear the pass before dark."

The mechanic shrugged again. "Probably won't be ready until this evening, I'm afraid."

My heart sank. Tomorrow? Fuck, no.

Beside me, Marcus exhaled, a cloud of breath forming between the three of us as we stood in the freezing cold garage. "Just... send me a text as soon as you have an ETA."

"Will do."

The mechanic walked away, and Marcus turned to me. "So, what do we do now?"

"Well, first things first," I said, "we should try to snag our room again. If we're stuck here for another night, let's grab it before someone else does."

"Good idea."

We hurried back across the street, and fortunately our room hadn't been snatched up in the twenty minutes since we'd checked out. With our key in hand, we dragged our luggage back to the familiar room and parked our suitcases beside the familiar bed with its pink comforter still rumpled from last night.

There was one thing working to our advantage—being at the trade show all week meant we both had a crapload of work to catch up on when we got back to the office. With no transportation and an entire day to kill in a tiny no-name town, there wasn't much to do except hunker down, fire up our laptops, and make some headway on all that crap.

I sat against the headboard. Marcus took one of the chairs. For hours on end, the only sounds were our fingers on keyboards and the odd diesel engine roaring by on the interstate.

More times than I could count, I stole a glance at him. Sometimes I got an ache in my chest because I hated how uncomfortable things were between us. A few times I wanted to put my laptop aside and suggest we talk about this, but that thought terrified me because I was afraid of what either of us might say. Other times, I wanted to grab the alarm clock, hurl it at his head, and tear into him for... hell, I didn't know what. It wasn't fair anyway. Things were awkward, and it was no more his fault than it was mine. This tension between us wasn't as hostile as it had been before, but it was still uncomfortable. It was fucking *painful*. And I had no idea what to do about it. I was pretty sure that wasn't just my emotional short-circuiting; Marcus wasn't one to just wallow silently if he thought he could fix the situation.

Marcus left around one to get some lunch. After he came back, I went out. Dinner was the same deal. I was simultaneously bothered and relieved that we'd both assumed without saying a word that we were eating alone today. After a week of being too close for comfort,

I was pretty sure we'd both needed the breathing room. I knew I did.

Eventually, we both started rubbing our eyes more than looking at our screens. I gave up first and put my computer aside. A few minutes later, he did the same.

The silence continued as we went in for our respective showers, brushed our teeth, and got ready to call it a night.

Which brought us to...

Aw, Christ.

Marcus sat on his side. I stood by mine. Over the mattress, we exchanged uneasy looks. This bed wasn't nearly big enough for us to sleep in. Not when we were like this. Last night, sure. When we'd cuddled up in the middle of the mattress, it had been fine, but—

Maybe that was the key. Maybe instead of staying as far apart as a "queen" bed would allow, we should just leave all the bullshit outside and come together in the middle again. It wouldn't solve everything. It didn't have to. But it had to be better than this.

Before I could stop myself, I said, "We could always fuck."

He eyed me, eyebrows climbing his forehead.

"I'm serious." My face burned, but I kept going. "Shit's already awkward between us. But we're good at sex, and at least we'll get off. Then maybe we can go to sleep."

We'll both sleep better, and maybe we can say some of the things we don't know the words to say.

"You don't think it would make things weird?" he asked so softly I barely heard him.

"I can't imagine it'll make them weirder than they already are."

Please don't push me away.

Swallowing hard, he searched my eyes.

Experimentally, I pulled the covers back and sat on my side of the bed, still holding his gaze as I closed some of the space between us. He tensed, but didn't move away.

With my heart in my throat, I reached for his arm. "We both need to sleep." *And I need you.*

He held my gaze, still tense and still not coming closer. I took it as him trying to formulate a rejection that would get the point across without making this any less bearable than it already was. Message received.

I started to withdraw my hand, but he caught my wrist.

We both froze.

And then, without making a sound, Marcus crossed the chasm between us, draped his arm over me, and kissed me. Relief hit me even before arousal did. I shifted so we were facing each other fully, wrapped my arms around him, and opened to his gentle but insistent tongue. We were already down to our boxers, so as we sank together on the bed, warm skin touched warm skin all over. After a solid week of feeling like shit, not to mention a miserable day of being next to each other in uncomfortable silence, I felt so good I wanted to cry. And I wanted to make *him* feel so good *he* cried.

My mind kept trying to take me back to everything we were screwing to avoid, but I fought it hard. I tried to think of how much I wanted him right now. I tried to think of all the times we'd been in bed in the past, but only two times kept coming back to me—Boise and December. Hot, impulsive sex that had been amazing in the moment, but disasters in the aftermath. No matter how hard I tried to focus on the sounds he made and how my whole body reacted to his touch, my brain fixated on Marcus not being able to look at me. On me not being able to hear his voice or see him or even let him cross my mind without a wave of guilt crashing over me.

I held him tighter and kissed him harder. Still, guilt kept trying to elbow arousal out of the way, and despite my best efforts, it was winning. I wanted him, and I wanted things to be okay between us, but now I wasn't so sure I wanted to go through with this. I wasn't so sure I could.

Then Marcus sighed, and not in a good way.

He broke the kiss.

I pulled back.

We locked eyes, but only for a second.

"Maybe we should just try to sleep." Marcus's words didn't hit me nearly as hard as the resignation in his voice.

"Yeah. Maybe we should."

And just like we had done almost everything today, we didn't say a word. We separated. He killed the light. And we lay there, both stone-still and breathing slowly. Was his heart thumping as hard as mine was? Did he feel sick like I did?

I didn't know. All I knew was that the bed seemed tinier than it had last night, but the space between us seemed like miles.

And I didn't know how to cross that space tonight.

"Goddammit." Marcus hung up his phone and exhaled, pinching the bridge of his nose.

My stomach turned to lead. "Please tell me it'll be done today."

"Today, yeah." He huffed out another breath. "This morning, no."

"Fuck," I muttered.

"I know, right?"

"Want to hang out at that diner until the van's ready? If we stay here, we'll get billed for another night."

"Probably not a bad idea," he grumbled, and went into the bathroom. A second later, stuff started rattling and crinkling; he was probably repacking his shaving kit.

I slid my laptop into its case and started putting my stuff back together too. Then, in awkward silence—man, that was becoming a thing with us—we gathered our luggage and left the motel room. While we waited behind an elderly couple to check out, we avoided each other's gazes, and a sick feeling soured my stomach. The words *"last night was a bad idea, wasn't it?"* hung on the tip of my tongue, but there was no point in saying them out loud. He knew. I knew. We knew.

After we'd checked out, we walked over to the diner and

hunkered down at a booth near the back, our suitcases tucked behind the bench so they were out of the way.

We probably spent longer than we needed to perusing the menu. It was generic diner food. Nothing unusual. As queasy as I was, it was mostly a matter of finding something that didn't make me want to retch. And then reading over the menu one more time just to put off having to face Marcus without an easy distraction.

After we'd ordered, we still didn't talk. At least we had cell signal so we could focus on our phones and ignore each other. Maybe that wasn't the healthiest thing for us to be doing right now, but it was damn sure the easiest, and I was too tired for anything else.

That wasn't to say I completely ignored him, though. The only time I could really draw an easy breath was when he stepped out for a minute to use the restroom. Otherwise, I was on pins and needles, my body painfully tense all over from nerves.

The silence between us was... weird. The air between us was taut, but it wasn't hostile anymore. And I kind of wished it was. Anger and resentment were less painful and draining than the dogpile of guilt, regret, and an almost irresistible need to reach across the space and touch him. It was the only way I could think to reach out to him because I flat out fucking didn't know what to say.

Figure it out, idiot. Before you lose him completely.

Fresh guilt jabbed at me. I knew I'd always relied too heavily on him—and later, Michelle—to help me walk through what all these feelings meant and how to convey them to someone else. I needed to be able to work that shit out myself before I could approach a partner and start fixing whatever was wrong. I needed to, but hell if I knew how.

Though it occurred to me that maybe this time it wasn't that I didn't know what I was feeling—it was that I was afraid to put a name on it. There was some truth hiding under all those jumbled emotions, and the thought of seeing it and not being able to ignore it scared me.

Maybe last night hadn't been a mistake. Maybe the mistake was all the stuff we still needed to say.

I surreptitiously watched Marcus. He looked exhausted. His skin was a shade or two paler than usual, and the dark circles under his eyes made it even worse. He was usually so quick to smile, but now his lips were a thin, straight line.

And he wasn't talking. All throughout our relationship and friendship, he'd been the one to speak up and define everything so we could work it all out.

But what if he didn't have the words this time? What if this time, Marcus needed *me* to find the words?

Just the thought sent panic skittering through me. I didn't even know where to start. I was terrified that if I tried to tell him all the things on my mind, I'd screw up somehow and make things worse. That I'd explain my feelings wrong, or just freeze up and not be able to speak at all.

But, I thought as I watched him across the table, was that worse than leaving everything unsaid?

Right then, Marcus's phone vibrated, buzzing loudly on the table and startling me so hard I almost knocked my drink over. He checked the screen, and the relief washing over him was palpable. "Oh, thank God. The van will be done in another half hour."

I exhaled. "Awesome."

He gestured for the waitress to bring us the check. While we waited for that, he turned to me. "Well, we have a choice. We can try the roads this afternoon and hope the pass is clear. Or we can stay in town for one more night and leave in the morning."

We locked eyes across the table.

Then, at the same time: "Let's get moving."

CHAPTER 20

MARCUS

Not a moment too soon, the van was ready.

We paid with the company credit card, and then Reuben and I checked the back to make sure nothing had gone missing—we didn't distrust the mechanic per se, but there was no harm in being vigilant. Once we were sure everything was where it belonged, we tucked our luggage in, and Reuben climbed into the driver's seat.

I said nothing as I buckled my seat belt. He didn't say a word as he started the van. The silence followed us onto I-90, and I stared out the window at the snow-covered farms flying past. I hated that we couldn't talk to each other, but I was kind of relieved by it too. I didn't think I could handle a conversation now. Small talk would be too awkward. Anything more than that would be too painful, either because the subject itself would be salt in too many wounds or because we'd be pointedly avoiding the shit we desperately needed to talk about. And all that assumed I could even speak without my voice breaking, and I didn't have a lot of confidence in that department.

The sex we'd tried to have last night made me want to cry now. The Reuben I was used to in the bedroom had been MIA, replaced by someone who second-guessed his every move before we'd both finally given up. Lying beside him last night and riding shotgun beside him now, I didn't think I'd ever been so certain that what we'd had in the past was dead, and that our friendship was quickly following suit.

Yeah, it was definitely time to look for another job. I couldn't come to work every day and see him. Not when I still felt this strongly for him and neither of us could look each other in the eye.

First things first—get home and decompress.

Then work on the résumé.

Then start applying for—

Abruptly, the van started slowing down. Then his signal came on, and he nosed off onto the shoulder.

Panic skittered up my spine. "What's wrong? Why are we stopping?" A zillion worst-case scenarios crashed through my brain. Had a warning light come on? Was the van still fucked up? "Reuben, is—"

He put up his hand. "I need to do this now before I lose my nerve."

My teeth snapped shut.

Do what?

Lose your nerve?

Oh God, what's happening?

My heart pounded and my meager breakfast threatened to reappear, so I focused on clenching my jaw and swallowing hard enough to keep from getting sick.

Reuben put the van in Park, but didn't face me. He stared straight ahead, still gripping the wheel for dear life even though the van was idling on the shoulder. I wanted to ask what was going on, but something told me to stay quiet so I didn't break his concentration.

Finally, he took a deep breath. "When you asked if the threesome killed my marriage," he began tentatively, "I couldn't give you a straight answer. And it's because I didn't know how to tell you the truth."

My tongue tried to stick to the roof of my mouth, but I managed, "So what is the truth?"

Reuben swallowed hard, still staring out the windshield. "I knew going into that night that Michelle and I were in a bad place. I thought we had a shot at making it, but she'd pretty much written us off, so really, it was a matter of time. So we were... well, we shouldn't have been thinking about a threesome, that's for damn sure." He wiped a hand over his face and exhaled. "But that night... I don't know. I guess the idea of a threesome got us both turned on, and even though I knew it was a bad idea, I couldn't say no. I..." Another hard swallow, and this time he turned to me, eyes full of too many emotions to parse. "I just couldn't say no to the way I felt that night. Someone was actually excited about sex with me, even if you and she were both just excited about having a threesome."

I bit my tongue to keep from telling him it hadn't been the threesome that had drawn me into their bedroom that night. As much as I wanted to say it, I didn't dare interrupt him while the words were finally coming.

"The next day," he went on unsteadily, "we both knew it was over. I think we both knew it anyway, and had for a long time, but that was the end of it."

I winced.

"I'm not blaming you for the end of my marriage," he continued. "You didn't do anything wrong. We did. And I'm sorry we pulled you into the middle of it."

"You didn't," I said. "We were all in on it that night. I just... didn't realize..."

"I know. You couldn't have known. The thing is, that night sped up the inevitable with me and Michelle. And that's probably a really good thing. If we'd dragged it out much longer, I don't think we would have broken up *nearly* as amicably. But what I'm trying to say..." He took a deep breath, staring out at the lazily falling snow and passing cars. "The threesome forced me and Michelle to acknowledge some things we'd been trying like hell to ignore. And I think getting thrown together on this trip forced you and me to deal with how weird things have been... and also a lot of things we've been ignoring for a long time. Or at least things I've been ignoring."

"Such as?"

"Things like..." He shifted uncomfortably. Then he closed his eyes for a moment, lips tight and brow furrowed like he was concentrating hard. Finally, he looked at me again. "My marriage had probably been dead for a solid year. Michelle and I didn't want to admit it, but there it is. That night, though, I realized that after all this time, I'm still carrying a torch for *you*."

My heart stopped. "What?"

"I realized after that night that I still want you. And that I..." His lips tightened again, frustration radiating off him as if the words were there but just out of his reach. Finally he pushed out a breath, and his voice shook badly as he went on. "You know me, Marcus. You know how much I suck at saying all this shit. So if it's not coming out right, I..." He threw up a hand. "I don't know." He met my eyes, and in a shaky whisper, he added, "I just know that I love you."

I couldn't breathe. I stared at him in disbelief. Had he... was this... he loved me? Okay, deep down I'd always believed he did, but the fact that he'd tapped into God knew what and managed to say the words out loud... ironically, it left me speechless.

He shifted a little, eyes flicking away for a second before he continued. "I'm not going to tell you I'm over my divorce or that I will be any time soon. But I can deal with that and still know how I feel about you." He pressed his lips together, then wiped a hand over his face before he stared out the windshield again. "Maybe I'm not ready for something. I don't know. But to be honest, nothing has felt right in my life since we broke up."

I blinked. "That... that was six years ago."

"I know," he whispered. "And to this day, I couldn't tell you why I ever thought it was a good idea."

"You couldn't deal with the secrecy at work." It came out flat, edged with a hint of the accusation I couldn't quite hold back.

Reuben winced. Then he sighed. "I was a fucking coward." He turned to me, eyes shining with tears and wide with regret and hurt. "I was afraid to come out to my dad, and I was afraid if he found out about us, you'd lose your job. But there is nothing in this world I've ever regretted more than walking away from you."

Disbelief kept me mute for long seconds. I'd known about his fear of coming out, and I'd known about that certainty that one or both of us would lose our jobs, but I'd convinced myself our breakup had been easy for him. Or at least, not this hard.

I steeled myself. "There's something I need to know."

Reuben watched me expectantly, eyebrows up.

I searched for the right words, and finally settled on the direct approach: "Did you love Michelle?"

No surprise registered on his face. It was as if he'd been ready for it.

His eyes lost focus. "Yeah. I did. And I do." He paused, regained focus, and looked at me. "And yeah, I meant my vows to her. I... the thing is, I thought I'd blown my chance with you. I'd broken up with you, you'd moved on to someone else, and I made myself move on too." He swallowed, and his voice wavered, "I *thought* I moved on."

"And you think you and Michelle still would have split up?" I asked because I was a fucking masochist. "If we hadn't... in December..."

Reuben nodded without hesitation. "Yeah. I mean, I was still in love with you, and I still had a shitload of regrets, but that doesn't mean I didn't pour myself into my marriage. I wanted it to work, and I tried to make it work. But we..." He shook his head. "Michelle and I had problems that would've killed our marriage even if you'd never existed at all." He let his head fall back against the seat, and suddenly looked ten times more exhausted than he'd been this entire week. "So that's... that's everything I needed to say."

I silently drank in the sight of him for a long moment. It would've taken a lot out of me to spill my guts like that too, but knowing what I did about Reuben... Christ, no wonder he'd had to pull off on the side of I-90. He must've been working up the nerve, and as soon as he'd had it, didn't dare wait another minute or else he might never find the courage again. And then he'd said all of that. This was probably more than he'd ever opened up in a single conversation—hell, in a single *week*—in his life.

He turned toward me, brow pinched, tired eyes studying me from across the console.

My heart sped up. He'd just bared his soul, probably scared himself half to death, and he was still waiting for me to respond, wasn't he?

I moistened my lips, then cleared my throat and hoped that was enough to keep the words steady. "Maybe now's a good time to mention that in six years, I've never stopped loving you."

His breath hitched. "Really?"

"Yeah." I reached across the console, and as soon as I found his hand, we both closed our fingers and held on tight. His palm was as damp as it was hot; he really was a nervous wreck. Sitting up, I beckoned to him with my free hand. "Come here."

He leaned closer, and we met over the console, but not in a kiss—we wrapped our arms around each other, buried our faces in each other's necks, and just held on for... God, I had no idea how long.

When I was sure I could trust my voice to hold, I whispered, "I love you, Reuben."

"I love you too."

I drew back and looked in his eyes. There'd been something on the tip of my tongue, but as soon as I met his gaze, words didn't seem important anymore. So instead, I cupped the back of his head and kissed him, and the instant our lips met, it was like the whole world had righted itself. Everything that had been off-kilter for the last several years was back where it needed to be. I could breathe—*really* breathe—and when I did, I caught his familiar scent, and everything from relief to arousal to tears wanted to overwhelm me at the same time.

This wasn't the kind of kiss we'd shared when we were trying to wind each other up. It was just his lips against mine, both of us sliding trembling fingers through each other's hair. There'd be time for tongues and gasps later, and I didn't imagine the sun would go down before we were naked in bed, but right now it was just this quiet, earth-shaking return to something I hadn't fully understood how much I'd been missing.

He touched his forehead to mine. Neither of us said a word, but I supposed nothing needed to be said right then. Which was good because I couldn't think of anything except *you're here*.

The crunch of tires on gravel cut through the noise of the interstate. Reuben twisted a little to glance in the side mirror, then jerked back and muttered, "Shit!" Confusion had me paralyzed until he added, "Cop."

I dropped back into the passenger seat, and a second later, a state trooper appeared at my window. She hadn't seen anything, had she? As I rolled down the window, I glanced in the rearview and was relieved to confirm what I already knew—that everything packed into the van completely obscured the rear window.

The chilly wind from outside blew in, snapping at my face, and the cop asked, "Everything all right, gentlemen?"

"Yes, ma'am," Reuben said. "Just stopped to find an address." He tapped the GPS.

Wow. He'd certainly thought faster than I had, and bullshitting was my *job*.

"All right, well." The trooper gestured up ahead. "There's a ramp about half a mile up. Gas stations and plenty of safer places to pull over." She motioned toward the traffic speeding past us. "Isn't safe out here, so move along."

"Right." Reuben cleared his throat. "Sorry."

The cop gave us a nod, then headed back to her patrol car.

Neither of us moved or even breathed until she'd pulled back onto the interstate and was disappearing into the distance. As the dirty Crown Vic faded, we both exhaled.

Then we looked at each other, and after a beat of silence, burst out laughing.

Wiping his eyes, he said, "It figures the one time I manage to say what's on my mind, the cops get involved."

I snorted. So did he. We both doubled over laughing again.

As I pulled myself together, I said, "We should probably get going before another cop stops."

"Good idea." But he didn't put the van in gear yet. Instead, he slid his hand over my thigh and smiled, relief written all over his face. I wasn't sure how much of it was because we'd straightened things out between us and how much was because the cop had bought his bullshit, but I'd take that gentle smile however I could get it.

"We should get back on the road," I said again.

"Yeah." He gave my leg a little squeeze. "The sooner we get over the pass, the sooner we get back to your place."

"Are you suggesting what I think you're suggesting?"

The smile grew. Then he winked.

My pulse went wild.

"Good..." I swallowed. "Good idea. Let's go."

Reuben leaned across the console for one more quick kiss, then returned to his seat and carefully merged back onto I-90.

And I prayed like hell that nothing slowed us down.

CHAPTER 21

REUBEN

The hour and a half between when we'd pulled over and when I drove up Marcus's driveway felt like days. Finally, though, we were here, and I actually breathed a sigh of relief as I put the van in Park.

Neither of us said a word—though this silence was nothing like the many we'd shared over the last week—and we didn't make any move to get his luggage out of the back. We just got out and went inside.

As soon as we were clear of the door, he shut it behind us and turned the deadbolt. Then he faced me, and for a moment, we just stood there in the entryway, gazing into each other's eyes as if we needed to savor how relaxed the air was between us now. There'd been so much wrong and now there was so much right, and I didn't even know if I could handle it.

"Come here," he whispered, and drew me in for a kiss, and... yes. God, yes. I wrapped my arms around him and lost myself in him.

I'd half-expected us to start ripping clothes off and throwing each other around, but we didn't. We let this long, languid kiss go on, holding each other close as we lazily explored each other's mouths. Clothes stayed put, and so did our feet, and right there in the entryway, I held on to Marcus and let his kiss assure me that I hadn't said the wrong thing out on the road. That somehow, I'd found the words and put them together and laid myself bare and he'd understood it all. Understood and reciprocated.

"I love you, Reuben," his words echoed inside my mind.

When we came up for air, he touched his forehead to mine, and we just panted for a moment, holding each other close and letting our breath mingle between our mouths.

"We're going to end up fucking right here," he breathed.

"Your bed's not that far away. Maybe we should go there."

Marcus laughed softly, and kissed me. Then, without a word, he took my hand and led me upstairs. We sank onto his bed, still dressed, and kissed just like we had in the entryway. Gently. Tenderly. There was heat between us, and hunger, but mostly there was relief. Like the world had been on its ass for so long I couldn't remember what it felt like on its axis, and now we had to get used to things being right again. Fine by me—I could do this as long as either of us needed.

Even as the clothes started coming off and the touches became more frantic, we were subdued compared to what I was used to with him. Usually, he brought out the side of me that loved rough sex. Tonight, I wasn't sure I could handle that. Even the softest touch of his lips or his fingers almost broke me. There was so much relief and pent-up need and so many years of distance to cross, and somehow it didn't feel right to have the frantic, bruising sex we'd nearly always had.

This was everything I'd hoped for in the hotel room last night and then some, and it was perfect. Unrestrained kissing. Unhesitant touching. We held each other tight and just felt each other all over as if neither of us could believe this was real. I sure couldn't.

"Want you to do something." His voice sounded strained and shaky, like he was struggling to form words.

"Yeah?" I kissed my way down his neck. "Tell me."

"I want—oh God..." He squirmed under me, dragging his nails up my back as I continued exploring his neck.

I grinned against the hot skin of his throat. "Talk to me. What do you want me to do?"

"Fuck—" He lifted his hips a little, pressing our hard dicks together and making me gasp, and whispered, "Fuck me like you did back then."

It was my turn to forget how to speak. Just the thought of burying myself in him and riding him hard was... oh Christ, how were we not doing that already?

I lifted myself up on my arms and gazed down at his flushed face. "You have lube?"

Marcus nodded. I moved out of the way, and he leaned toward the nightstand. He started to come back with a bottle of lube and a strip of condoms, but hesitated. "Guess we don't need to bother with these." He tossed the rubbers back in the drawer, then handed me the lube.

I took the bottle, but instead of opening it, slung an arm around his waist and kissed him. He didn't protest. For a long moment, we knelt in the middle of the bed, kissing lazily, and I probably could have done that all night long if he hadn't murmured against my lips, "I want you. Now."

With a soft groan, I broke away and nodded toward the pillows. "Turn around."

He did, and I quickly slicked up my fingers and my cock. As fun as it was to drag this part out just to tease him, I needed him too much right now, so once I was sure he was relaxed enough to take me, I slid my fingers free and guided myself in.

"Oh God, Reuben," he whimpered, arching under me. "Oh God, yeah..."

God yeah was right. Marcus was the only man I'd ever been inside bareback, and sliding into him made my eyes water with emotions I didn't need to label. Somehow, despite everything, we'd made it back to this, and feeling him around my cock with nothing between us just made it all that much more real.

How did I breathe without you for six years?

It didn't matter. I was breathing now, and every breath tasted like his familiar scent, and I couldn't get into him fast enough. I still took my time, of course—I didn't want to hurt him—but Jesus, I needed to be as deep as he could take me.

Before long, I was moving easily inside him, taking smooth strokes all the way in and out while he rocked back against me.

"Harder, baby," he whispered. "C'mon. Please."

"Mmm." I kissed his shoulder. "Harder? How much harder?"

He rocked his hips like he wanted to egg me on. "You know how I like it."

I shivered. Because yes, I did know. Because I'd been with this man before, and it was the best sex I'd ever had, and oh, yeah, I knew how he liked it.

I nipped the side of his neck. "Go all the way down. On your stomach."

Marcus groaned softly, shuddering beneath me, and did as he was told. I followed, and once he was on the mattress, I slid my hands under his chest and hooked them over his shoulders for leverage.

And then I gave it to him hard. Exactly as hard as I knew he loved it.

"Yeah!" he cried. "Fuck. Oh my God. *Yeah!*"

I gritted my teeth and kept riding him, and every thrust knocked a moan out of him, and every sound he made drove me higher, until I was long past thinking I'd come and starting to wonder if I might just explode instead.

"Fuck..." Marcus tensed under me, and arched, and his ass clenched hard around my cock as he came. "Oh God, Reuben..." He sounded close to tears, and I loved it, and I pounded him until I unloaded inside him with a groan that didn't even sound like me.

And then... we were both still. Panting, trembling, but otherwise still.

Even after I'd pulled out, I didn't pull away. I kissed the side of his neck, savoring the warmth of his skin, and murmured, "I missed this."

"Me too." He turned his head toward me. "I missed *you*."

I smiled and brushed another kiss across his lips. "Want to grab a shower?"

His playful grin almost turned me on all over again. "Like I'd say no to a shower with you."

We did manage to actually shower, though there was plenty of playful kissing and touching too. If we'd been a little less exhausted, we probably would've wound up fucking again, or at least jerking each other off. That would've been fun, but I wasn't going to complain about what we ended up doing instead—cuddling up under the covers and just holding each other.

"I really have missed you." He smoothed my damp hair. "I swear nothing's been right since we broke up."

"Tell me about it. It's so good to be back to this."

He smiled, but it faltered. "So, do we tell people at work? Or keep this under the radar?"

I considered it for a moment, and shrugged. "I don't feel the need to hide it, but I don't really want to put up a neon sign either."

"Fair enough. What about your dad, though? If we start seeing each other, he's going to know you're queer."

I laughed softly. "He, uh, already knows."

Marcus made a sound like he was almost choking. "Come again?"

Absently running a hand up the middle of his chest, I said, "First Christmas I was married to Michelle, he made a comment about how he'd always expected me to be gay. So I looked at him and said he was half right."

"Whoa. How did that go over?"

"Eh." I shrugged. "Kind of anticlimactic compared to how it had always played out in my head. I'd always expected it to be a huge blowup or something, but then I was suddenly explaining bisexuality to my family over Christmas dinner, and it was just... a non-issue."

"Maybe because you were married?" Marcus suggested cautiously. "So they thought it was a non-issue?"

"Maybe." I smiled. "But at least if I bring a man home, they can't say I didn't tell them."

He smoothed my hair. "Good point. And we know we can do this. We made it work while we were dating and after we broke up. We know damn well we can handle our jobs and this at the same time."

"True." I released a long breath. "Fair warning—it's gonna take me some time to get through everything with my divorce. That doesn't mean I don't want to do this. Just... be patient with me."

"Patient." He kissed me softly. "I've waited six years just to be able to touch you again. I've got all kinds of patience, baby."

I smiled back and caressed his cheek, but the smile didn't last as his words sank in. "You didn't wait all this time for me, did you?"

He shrugged. "I didn't think I'd ever have you back, if that's what you're wondering, but I mean it when I say nothing has felt quite right since we split." Covering my hand with his, he pressed a kiss to my palm. "And now it does."

A million emotions crowded in, everything from being moved by his confession to feeling guilty as hell for leaving back then, and I did the only thing I could think to do—I wrapped my arms around him and pulled him close. How had I ever wanted to be *away* from him? Thank fucking God I'd broken past that mental block that kept me from talking about things as easily as he could.

This time.

"You know today might be a fluke, right?" I avoided his eyes as my face burned. "I'm never going to be that guy who can..."

"Reuben." He tipped up my chin, and the warmth of his smile made my toes curl. "I've known that about you since we met, and I fell in love with you knowing damn well it was probably who you'd always be. That hasn't changed."

A lump rose in my throat. "It's got to be frustrating, though."

He half shrugged, the smile staying firmly in place. "If the last six years have taught me anything, it's that helping you figure out what you're feeling isn't nearly as frustrating as not having you at all. Trust me—I can work with it."

I laughed, more out of relief than anything, and leaned in for a kiss. When I broke away, I whispered, "I love you."

"I love you too." Then he pulled me back in and let me rest my head on his chest, and we just lay there for a while. We'd probably wind up fooling around again before too long, but for right now, this was perfect.

I still couldn't believe we were even here. I hadn't thought it was possible. I hadn't even realized I'd wanted it to be.

But it was. After a long time and a rough road, Marcus and I had found our way back to each other. I had no illusions that the future would be smooth and uneventful, or that every moment together would be the same bliss as this one right now, but this was right. This was where I'd needed to be for all this time, and it was where I wanted to be until the end of time.

And lying here in Marcus's arms, with *I love you* still tingling on my lips, I had no doubt we'd make it.

EPILOGUE

Marcus

Two Years Later

The bleating alarm jarred me awake. Fuck. Was it six o'clock already? In *any* time zone, never mind the one I was in?

I reached for my phone, then remembered the nightstand was on the other side of the hard hotel bed. Carefully, I leaned across Reuben, felt around for my phone, and shut off the alarm.

"Mmf." He grumbled, burrowing into the pillow.

I chuckled and kissed the back of his shoulder. As stealthily as I could, and with only the bathroom light on so I wouldn't wake him up, I got dressed. I grabbed my trade show badge and held it up in the light to make sure I hadn't picked up his by mistake. Then I put it over my neck, and collected my wallet, phone, and room key.

Before I left, I paused by the bed and leaned down to kiss

Reuben's scruffy cheek. "I love you. I'll see you downstairs."

"Mmf."

I laughed, gave his shoulder a little squeeze, and headed out, making sure I turned off the bathroom light. In the elevator, I took a few deep breaths and rolled my shoulders. Okay. Time to be *on*. I'd get some coffee, get to the booth, and the day would start.

Downstairs in the exhibition hall, Karen, the field representative director, joined me a few minutes later, steaming cup of coffee in her hand. "Morning, sunshine."

"Morning."

She looked around. "Where's Reuben?"

"Still asleep." I sipped my coffee. "He'll be down around nine, remember?"

She frowned, but didn't press. As much as she liked having him come to trade shows with us now, she was still less than impressed with the arrangement I had with Reuben. Probably because she'd never tried to make Reuben function like a normal human being before the sun came up.

Not long after our trip to Boise, Reuben had agreed to start coming to trade shows on two conditions, and one of those conditions was that he didn't have to get up at the crack of dawn like I did. I'd never argued; the man simply did not function before at least eight, so I'd readily agreed.

The other stipulation was that we had one night to ourselves at each show. It could be after the con was over. It could be before it started (though that wasn't likely since I needed my social hibernation before things kicked off). Most of the time, it was somewhere in the middle.

As it happened, tonight was date night, and I had no problem with Reuben stealing another hour or two this morning if it meant he was not only functional today but raring to go tonight.

In the meantime, Karen and I had work to do, and we'd just finished refilling literature holders and straightening displays before the exhibition hall doors opened.

"And we're off," she muttered into her coffee cup.

Indeed we were. The minute the doors opened, the room was flooded with people. Karen and I were ready with our game faces, and in moments, were deep in conversation with potential clients. As soon as those potential clients moved on, others moved in.

I was in mid-conversation with a brass supplier when my neck prickled, and I turned just in time to see Reuben strolling through the crowd in that charcoal gray suit I loved so much. He had coffee in his hand and flashed me a quick smile, one that made my whole body tingle, and joined us in the booth.

I only missed a beat in my conversation, fortunately, and recovered enough to continue with the supplier. When I'd finished talking to her and she'd left me with some flyers, I had a momentary lull, which I used to zero in on Reuben.

He was, unsurprisingly, having an animated conversation with Karen and a couple of guys about our newest laser cutting apparatus.

I smiled as I watched him. It still amazed me how much he'd become a fixture at these events. Especially now that he had another manager handling most of the crises in the engineering department, Reuben had started coming to more and more trade shows with me. They still overwhelmed him sometimes, but as long as he could decompress and I didn't drag him to the bar in the evenings, he did all right. In fact, he'd really found his groove with this, and occasionally even joined me at early-for-him hours if it was just the two of us or someone else had had a late night.

Reuben was finding his groove with a lot of things, actually. Not long after we'd gotten back together, he had surprised the hell out of me one day by declaring that he was going to start seeing a therapist.

"*It's not fair for you to do all the work,*" he'd told me. "*I need to learn how to sort out my own feelings and all that shit, so I'm going to go to someone who gets paid to help me do that.*"

And wow, what a difference. He still struggled sometimes, and if we had a fight, it wasn't unusual for him to get on the horn with his therapist before we sat down to work things out. In the beginning, she'd have us both come in so she could mediate. As time went on and he'd gotten a better handle on things, it hadn't been so bad. He was actually getting pretty good at it, and sometimes blew me away by how self-aware he'd become. Plus, she'd helped him sort out some lingering feelings about his divorce. They'd even had a few appointments with his ex-wife, which had helped Reuben and Michelle put everything to bed and move forward as friends. Michelle and I were still overcoming some awkwardness, but we were getting there.

At work, most people knew we were a couple, but we weren't out to anyone outside the company. People had probably caught on, and rumors were probably circulating, but it wasn't openly talked about. That was fine with me. I didn't feel the need to broadcast it, particularly when we had some outspoken homophobes floating around in our industry, and at the same time, was relieved I didn't have to try to keep it a secret. If people found out, they found out. Our coworkers mostly knew, Reuben's family knew, and while Bob had been iffy about us dating at work, he'd ultimately decided it was better than us struggling to be in the same room.

"Mr. Peterson?" A voice jarred me out of my thoughts, and I turned to see Jim Grainger and Connie Yates from Sparks Magazine —one of the industry's biggest trade magazines—approaching.

"Jim! Connie!" I shook hands with each of them in turn. "Great to see you both. How are the families?"

"They're well, thank you." Connie smiled brightly. I'd always liked her. "We wanted to talk to you about that article about your company's new line. Do you have time for a chat this week?"

"Of course," I said. "I've been looking forward to talking to both of you since you emailed. We're very excited about this."

"As are we," Jim said. "In fact, why don't you join us for dinner tonight? We can talk more details then."

Oh, it was tempting because this article would be huge, but I restrained myself and apologetically shook my head. "I'm so sorry. As much as I'd love to, I've already got a commitment this evening."

They both looked a little disappointed. Still, Jim clapped my shoulder and smiled. "Well, the week is still young. We'll figure something out."

"Sounds good. You know where to find me."

We shook hands again, and he left.

As they walked away, I glanced at Reuben. He'd taken off his jacket and rolled up his sleeves like he often did, and he was excitedly gesturing and talking to three people who looked absolutely riveted.

The article in Sparks would be huge for the company, and a dinner meeting with Jim and Connie was incredibly difficult to nail down, but... no. There would be time. We'd figure something out.

Tonight, though, I was having dinner with Reuben and no one else.

———

Dinner was oddly quiet.

We were both tired from the trade show, both of our throats a little raw from constantly talking, but I didn't get the impression the silence had come from protecting our voices. Reuben had struggled to make or keep eye contact a few times, and seemed... elsewhere. Not hostile, but not there either.

Rather than bring it up in a public place, I'd decided to wait until we were back in the privacy of our room. I tried, anyway. As we rode the elevator up to our floor, I couldn't take it anymore and touched the small of his back. "Hey. You okay? You were kind of quiet during dinner."

"Yeah. Yeah. I'm sorry. I was..." He swallowed. "Preoccupied, I guess."

"With?"

Reuben pressed his lips together. His gaze was intently fixed on the numbers above the door.

Okay. I'd wait until we got to our room.

A moment later, we did, and I shut the door, the quiet click making him jump. His back was to me, and though he shrugged out of his jacket, he didn't otherwise move or make a sound.

Cautiously, I stepped closer. "Hey." I wrapped my arms around him and kissed the base of his neck. "Talk to me."

Reuben exhaled, leaning back against me. After a moment, he turned around in my embrace, met my eyes for a second, then dropped his gaze. I thought he might clam up on me, but then he set his shoulders back and took a deep breath as he reclaimed eye contact. "I was quiet during dinner because I was nervous. Because I *am* nervous."

"About?"

He brought his hand up between us. "About whether or not you'll take this."

The soft lights caught the band he was holding between his thumb and forefinger. It wasn't gold or even silver. In fact, I couldn't identify the dark, somewhat matte metal. It was smooth with a few telltale imperfections that made my heart go wild—it was handmade. Reuben was... he was offering me a ring. One he'd made. Because... oh my God.

I looked in his eyes. "Reuben..."

"I'm not good at big public gestures," he whispered. "I'm not even doing so great at a small private one. But I..." Swallowing hard, he pressed the ring into my palm and closed my fingers around it. "I love you, Marcus. And I want to be your husband if you'll have me."

I stared at him as I ran my thumb along the edge of the band, disbelief keeping me from speaking until I saw the worry beginning to crease his brow. Was he really that afraid I'd say no? Yes, of course he was. Because that was how he worked, and he'd probably spent weeks if not months psyching himself up to do this.

I smiled and reached into my pocket. As I held up a band not unlike the one he was holding—though it was gold and one I'd bought —I said, "This answer your question?"

It was his turn for awestruck silence. He stared at the ring just like I'd stared at the other one. When he met my eyes, he broke into a relieved smile, and I didn't think he'd ever looked sweeter than he did right then.

And then we both laughed. I wrapped my arms around him, and he leaned into my hug as we chuckled.

"This so doesn't surprise me," he said. "Both of us on the same page without even realizing it."

"Story of our lives." I kissed his cheek. "I've had this for a couple of weeks—I just couldn't figure out when to ask. I didn't think you wanted some big public spectacle, and I guess I got tongue-tied every time I tried to work up the nerve when we were alone."

Reuben pulled back and smiled. "You know me too well." He looked down at the ring in his hand, and blushed again. "I honestly thought I could pull off something in public. Just... seemed like..."

"That's not you, though."

"Maybe not." He looked at me through his lashes. "But you deserve it, you know?"

My heart somersaulted. "What?"

"I'm *proud* of being with you," he said. "I want people to know we're together, and I want the whole world to know that I want to marry you." He swallowed hard and finally met my gaze for real. "We broke up before because I couldn't handle the secrecy. Now, it's not just that I don't want to keep it a secret, I want everyone to know. Being with you, now I get why people do proposals in the middle of basketball or football games with thousands of people watching."

"Reuben." I touched his cheek. "I don't need that kind of gesture from you. Just... I mean, the fact that you *made* that ring—" I raised my eyebrows to ask, *right?* He nodded, and I went on, "That means more to me than any public proposal."

"Really?"

"Of course. And I know you. You're not someone who wants the spotlight on you, least of all when you're as nervous as you obviously were." I took his hands between mine and kissed the backs of his fingers. "I don't need a big public spectacle. All I want is you."

Reuben studied me uncertainly. "What about a wedding?"

"I don't care." I shook my head. "We can do something quiet in your dad's living room, or we can rent out the goddamned Space Needle and have fireworks. As long as we're married at the end of it, I just don't care about the details."

"Good," he said with an obviously relieved laugh. "Because I have no idea what I want either. Something quiet sounds good, though."

"Then that's what we'll do."

We exchanged smiles, then looked down at the rings we were both still holding.

"Whatever we do," he whispered, "we should do it sooner than later."

"Agreed. I think we've waited long enough."

Reuben nodded. Then we traded rings and slid them on. The band I'd bought for him was slightly loose, but fit for the most part. The one he'd made for me? Fit perfectly. Somehow I wasn't surprised.

We stared down at our rings for a moment before meeting each other's gazes again. Wrapping his arms around my neck, Reuben looked in my eyes, and I loved how relaxed and happy he was right then.

"We'll figure it out," he said softly. "How about we just spend tonight enjoying being engaged, and worry about all the details later?"

"Sounds perfect." I grinned, cradled his face, and kissed him.

Yeah, the details could wait. Just enjoying each other and being engaged sounded like the best possible way to spend the rest of the evening.

And that was exactly how we spent it.

THE END

IT WAS ALWAYS YOU

CHAPTER 1

TYLER

Glad you made it. See you at baggage claim. :)

I smiled at Justin's text, relieved it hadn't been along the lines of *sorry, couldn't make it* or something. He wasn't flaky like that, and it would have been seriously out of character for him to bail on me, but with the way my life had been going for the last couple of months, I was taking nothing for granted—not even my best friend coming to the airport to pick me up. Or letting me live with him until I got my shit together, even after he hadn't seen me in five years.

Guilt jabbed me in the gut. I'd all but ghosted Justin five years ago, and still he was picking me up and taking me in.

Man, I'm gonna owe you so big, I thought as I reread his text. As if I didn't already. At the very least, he was probably going to want an explanation for me disappearing on him. And I supposed I owed him that much, even if the thought of that conversation made me want to retch.

One thing at a time. Get off the plane. Go meet up with him. Settle in. And then... then talk. Eventually. Fuck my life.

The plane lurched to a stop at the gate, and as soon as the seatbelt light went off, people jumped out of their seats and started popping open overhead bins. Clear back here in row thirty-nine, it seemed pretty pointless, but that didn't stop anyone.

I was shoehorned in by the window, so I didn't bother getting up. Wasn't like I could stand anyway—coach was clearly not designed for anyone over about five feet tall, and if I stood now, I'd be hunched over to keep from clocking my head on the bin. My whole body ached from sitting for the past few hours, and that ache seemed to intensify as the forward rows started clearing out and people filed off the plane. Just a few more minutes, and I could stand and stretch.

At least the flight was over. I'd made it. All I had to do now was get up, collect my crap, get to baggage claim, collect the *rest* of my crap, and meet up with Justin. After that...

I sighed, deflating a bit and leaning against the rigid seatback. I was here. I was in Seattle. So... now what?

As I took off my seatbelt, I glanced at my left hand, momentarily puzzled when my ring didn't click against the buckle. Oh. Right. I wasn't wearing it anymore. Hadn't worn it in weeks now, but I still wasn't used to that thick gold band being gone. It seemed like such a small thing to even notice, given how chaotic my life had been lately, but under this much stress, every little thing registered. My lack of a ring was just one more on the heaping pile of shit to obsess over. And it was less stressful than worrying about if the new job would work out, how I'd manage to get a car and a new place, if I could still find my way around the Seattle area, if Justin was angry at me over disappearing, if—

God. Tyler. Get a grip. One thing at a time.

Shaking myself, I tamped down the fresh anxiety prickling along my spine. I had time to figure things out. Today's priority had been to get to Seattle and settle into my temporary home. I was halfway there. Everything else could sit tight until tomorrow.

My seatmates moved out of the row, and I pried myself up as well. After another couple of minutes, it was our turn to make our way up the aisle. I tried not to glare at the first class seats. The upgrades had been relatively cheap. A hundred bucks or so, if I remembered right. Tempting, especially for all that extra legroom, but I couldn't justify it. Not with a divorce-in-progress, rapidly depleting savings, and that minor detail about being between jobs. Okay, I had another job lined up—I started a week from tomorrow—but until my paychecks actually started rolling in, I was going to continue budgeting and spending as if I were unemployed.

So no first class upgrade. Even if that meant folding all six-two of me into a seat designed for a hobbit.

After a bit more shuffling, I was off the plane. I strode through SeaTac International, thrilled to be up and moving. The aches and knots loosened with every step, and my heart fluttered with... shit, was that excitement? Yeah, it was. My life had been utter chaos for the last few months, and things I enjoyed had only served to remind me how crappy I felt, and thus made me feel worse.

But suddenly the prospect of seeing Justin—my best friend since elementary school—had me walking a little faster. And smiling. And nervous. And, yeah, *excited.*

We'd been joined at the hip until we'd graduated high school. College had taken us to other states. His career had brought him back to Seattle while my marriage had kept me in Chicago. Whenever I'd come to visit, we'd always made a point of meeting up, and we rarely went more than a few months without seeing each other.

And then I'd stopped going to see him. Stopped talking to him on the phone. Our only connection had been on Facebook, and I'd nearly unfriended him so many times, I was queasy with shame just from thinking about it. When all was said and done, we'd gone five years without seeing each other in person. Without really staying in contact at all besides that passive presence in each other's newsfeeds. If not for social media, God knew if I'd have ever been able to find him again.

One thing was for sure—he wouldn't have reached out and offered to help me.

I don't deserve you, Justin.

The final stretch to baggage claim was an escalator, and at the top, people were gathered around, watching for whoever they were meeting, and—

There.

Holy shit. There he was.

Smiling down at me, arms folded on the chest-high railing overlooking the escalator, was Justin. His brown eyes sparkled like they always had, and the scruffy beard—little more than some heavy and carefully groomed five o'clock shadow—had been in some of his recent Facebook photos, but it looked even better in person. Or maybe I was just *that* thrilled and relieved to see him.

How did I go five years without you?

Well, no time like the present to start making up for it.

He grinned as the escalator brought me closer. "Hey sweetie!"

"Hey you." I smiled back, heart thumping and my throat suddenly tight. As soon as I was clear of the top of the escalator and out of everyone else's way, Justin threw his arms around me and hugged me tight. I dropped my bag, closed my eyes, and held him. He'd always given the best hugs. He was a touch shorter and narrower than me, and somehow we'd always fit together perfectly. After all this time, and after all the hell I'd been through recently, his enthusiastic embrace was exactly what I needed. He held me so tight I could barely breathe, and I just didn't care.

"Oh my God, I missed you," I said.

"I missed you too," he said into my shoulder. Without letting go, he added, "How are you doing? How was your flight?"

I groaned. "Don't ask about the flight."

Justin pulled back and frowned up at me. "That bad?"

"That bad. But it's over now. I'm ready to get out of here."

The smile came back to life, and he gestured past me. "Let's see where your bags will come out, then."

Fortunately, it was only a couple of carousels down, and by the time we joined the thickening crowd, the bags were starting to appear. Sometimes it wasn't so bad, being one of the last to deplane. At least I wouldn't have to wait long for my damn suitcases.

In theory, anyway. The first showed up almost immediately. The second wasn't far behind. The third, however, took its sweet time, and as bag after bag that wasn't mine appeared, I prayed like hell it hadn't been lost. With my luck lately, I wouldn't have been surprised. I just wasn't sure if I could deal with yet another hiccup while I tried to start my new life.

I glanced at the two suitcases standing beside Justin. "Those will fit in your car, right? I didn't even think to ask if—"

"Relax." He winked. "Honey, I've *always* got room for your junk in my trunk."

A lady next to him scowled, and I chuckled, rolling my eyes before turning my attention back to the carousel. It felt good to be the target of his crude banter again.

The third suitcase finally showed up, and Justin and I lugged them out to the parking garage. I was still a little dubious about fitting all of this into a single car, but the trunk and backseat of Justin's Prius turned out to be remarkably spacious.

"See?" He slammed the trunk lid. "Got it all in and didn't even need lube."

I laughed. Justin's sense of humor obviously hadn't changed, and that little touch of normalcy—that piece of the past that had remained constant the whole time we'd known each other—eased my anxiety. Some part of me had wondered if we'd still be able to get along. We'd spent twenty years in different worlds, and hadn't crossed paths in five—what if we'd both changed too much? What if living together proved that we'd drifted too far apart and were too different and things went to shit like they had with my now-ex-wife?

I already lost her. What if I lose you again?

That fear had been careening around in my head ever since he'd reached out on Facebook and offered to let me stay with him. But now, as we climbed into his car and started out of the labyrinthine parking garage, Justin's playful comments and easy smile settled my nerves more than he probably realized.

"So." He kept his eyes on the road as he drove down the dizzying, tightly-coiled ramp from the parking garage. "Do you want to grab something to eat? Do you need anything?" He glanced at me. "I went grocery shopping this morning and made sure everything's well-stocked but I don't really know what you eat these days." The near-frantic concern in his tone warmed me all over. That had always been him—the mother hen who made sure everyone around him was taken care of.

"I'm good. I'm just glad to be off the plane."

"I believe it. Flying is such a nightmare these days."

I just grunted in agreement. While he drove, I surreptitiously watched him, trying to be absolutely sure he was there and not a hallucination. Oh, he was there. He had a few more lines than he'd had in our younger days, and he wasn't as tanned as he'd been the last time I'd seen him. Still had the high cheekbones. Still had the sharp jawline. I couldn't see his eyes now because he had on sunglasses, but I'd seen them in the airport, and they were definitely etched into my mind. Still as amazing as they'd ever been.

Remind me not to go another five years without looking at you.

We finally made it to the end of the ramp, and I handed Justin a twenty so he could pay for parking at the booth on the way out. Once that was squared away, he got us on the freeway... which was basically a parking lot.

"What the hell?" I said. "Isn't it a little early for rush hour?"

Justin barked a laugh and patted my leg. "Oh sweetheart. You really have been gone a while, haven't you?"

"Huh?"

"Rush hour has always started this early."

"Seriously? It's—" I paused as my jetlagged brain finally caught up. "Oh right. Two-thirty means Boeing just let out."

"Exactly." He settled back against the seat, one hand resting on top of the wheel. "So it's going to be a while. If you want to stop for food or something, just holler. There's plenty of off ramps between here and home."

"It's fine. Honestly, I'm okay."

Justin glanced at me again, brow pinched with skepticism and concern. "Are you, though?"

You mean aside from guilt eating me alive over deserting you?

I swallowed. "I am. Just a bit jetlagged and stiff from that stupid seat. But I'm good. I promise."

"How about in general?"

I stared at the line of bumpers and rear windows extending into the distance, not sure how to answer the question. Things were improving, or at least calming down. I was adapting as much as anyone could under the circumstances. Nothing in my life felt remotely stable, and just thinking about that brought all the anxiety to the surface so violently I had to fight back an unexpected wave of panic. Everything in my world had been in constant motion lately, and I was suddenly desperate to be still. Not on a plane. Not in a car. Just... not moving. Not needing to move. The last several weeks had been go, go, go, and I... fuck, I was exhausted. None of this was over, and there were wheels turning that wouldn't stop any time soon, but was it too much to ask for an hour to catch my breath?

"You know," I said quickly. "I *could* stand to eat something after all." I gestured at the upcoming ramp for Southcenter Mall. "Why don't we swing in there and I'll buy us lunch?"

Justin didn't push the issue.

He just turned on his blinker and started crawling toward the ramp.

CHAPTER 2

JUSTIN

I'd been worried sick about Tyler, and now that he was here, that worry didn't back down at all. Oh, I still had some questions, and I still ground my teeth whenever I tried to figure out why he'd vanished on me, and I'd still cursed his name a few times in recent years, but all of that could wait. Sitting opposite him at some hipster bar and grill across the street from the mall, I ignored my menu and stared at him, more worried than angry.

He'd always been a gym rat, and it still showed in his physique. Though fatigue pushed down on his shoulders, it couldn't hide the broadness or the way his muscles stretched his snug black T-shirt. His dark hair was longer than it had been when I'd seen him last, and I liked it on him. The heavy five o'clock shadow probably would have been a nice touch too, but his face was so pale and the circles under his eyes were so dark, it just made him seem tired.

He looked amazing and he looked terrible. Like time had been kind to him—he was even hotter than he'd been in high school—but life had been a dick, and now this incredibly sexy man seemed like he'd had the shit kicked out of him. He was simultaneously pinging all those brain cells that had been fantasizing about him since we were teenagers, and tripping my drive to take care of him until his life was right again. I barely had room for that simmering resentment, though it would probably elbow its way in at some point.

Of course I'd expected him to look like shit. After everything he'd been through lately, a physical toll was inevitable. I doubted I'd be in any better shape if both my job and my spouse had booted me to the curb in the space of a month. Who was I kidding? If I'd been through half that shit, I'd have been curled in a fetal position and begging for wine, ice cream, and death, and not necessarily in that order.

So yeah, it wasn't surprising to see him like this, but it was hard to take in. Tyler had always been so optimistic and happy. A human ray of sunshine who had somehow been the perfect friend for a prickly ball of cynicism like me.

That light had dimmed, though, and I hoped it was just the exhaustion that had dulled the shine in his eyes and made his sweet smile into something rare and halfhearted. Maybe a few decent nights of sleep, not to mention starting his new job and getting his feet under him, would bring him back to life. Maybe he needed to get laid.

Say the word, sweetheart, and I will have ladies lined up outside your bedroom door.

Oblivious to me, Tyler closed his menu and laid it beside the placemat. He absently sipped his ice water and stared at the center of the table with unfocused eyes. Neither of us said a word until the waiter came to take our order.

I hadn't even scanned the menu, but I'd been here before, so I just ordered something generic—a BLT with truffle fries—and another water. Once Tyler and I were alone again, I folded my hands on the table and broke the silence.

"Hey."

He lifted his gaze, and for the first time, I could *really* see the fatigue in his blue eyes. Not just that, but the... emptiness, for lack of a better word. Like all the life and spark had been sucked right out of him.

I swallowed. "Tell me honestly, hon—are you okay?"

Tyler sighed, breaking eye contact again, and ran a hand through his hair as he sat back against the faux leather bench. "I'd love to tell you I am, but..." He shook his head. "I'm not. I'm really not."

I sat up and folded my arms on the edge of the table. "Talk to me."

"What is there to say?" His voice sounded as brittle as he looked. "My wife's gone. My job's gone." He laughed humorlessly. "I'm one lost dog away from starring in a bad country song."

"Sounds like a pretty rough patch."

"Just a bit."

Chewing my lip, I studied him for a moment. "What happened, anyway?" We'd talked a fair amount lately on the phone and on Facebook, but the majority of that had been to work out logistics of him moving in with me. He'd been understandably focused on putting out fires, so we hadn't discussed much else.

Tyler wrapped his hands around his water glass and stared into it. "Basically, the company I was working for merged with another one, and that one is pretty much in bed with one of the big home lenders in Illinois." He sighed. "They promised they wouldn't lay off any of the appraisers, but before the ink had even dried on the merger..."

I'd meant his ex, but okay. "Was there something shady going on? Or just merger bullshit?"

"They tried to tell us it was a cost-cutting measure or whatever." Tyler rolled his eyes. "But there were some rumors. In fact, there was a lawsuit against the bank claiming their appraisers under-appraised or over-appraised houses depending on which outcome was better for them."

I cocked my head. "I thought appraisals were done independently."

"On paper, they are. But anyone can be bribed. So the appraisers who were willing to massage the numbers stayed onboard, and the rest of us were shown the door." He brought his drink to his lips and added a bitter, "Allegedly."

"Jesus. You guys should fucking sue."

Tyler scowled, shaking his head. "The legal fees would kill us, even if we went in on it together. That, and we have no proof, and if any of us ever want to work as appraisers again, we're better off not having our names attached to a wrongful termination suit."

"Oh. Yeah." I grimaced. "Fair point."

"And anyway, I found a job out here, so I'll be fine. I really didn't want to work for the new parent company, and I was ready to get out of Chicago." He met my eyes again, his expression sad and tired. A little smile formed, which didn't help. "It was time to come home."

I chewed the inside of my cheek. What I really wanted to ask about was his divorce, but I supposed I didn't need to. They'd been doomed from the start as far as I was concerned, and the only questions were why it had taken so long and what had been the last straw.

Which wasn't fair. Or objective. Not that I was remotely capable of *being* fair or objective when it came to Tyler and his relationships. After all, I'd been in love with him since our sophomore year and he was (rudely) *straight*. I'd made peace with that. I couldn't have him as a partner, but I was grateful to have him as a friend and I'd always genuinely wished him the best when it came to women.

So it killed me, and had for fourteen years, that he'd married Gina. Standing beside him at his wedding, smiling through the worst heartbreak I'd ever felt, I'd had to fight back the urge to grab him by the shoulders, shake him a few times, and steer him toward the row of five bridesmaids. I didn't know any of them, but at least one of them had to be better for him than Gina.

It wasn't fair. I would have literally moved mountains for this man, and he'd wound up married to *her*. I wasn't bitter that he was straight—I was bitter that out of millions of wonderful women on this earth, easily a hundred of whom I would have personally set him up with, he'd had to marry *that* one. It wasn't fucking fair to love someone this much and have no choice but to sit back and watch them fall for people who didn't deserve them. Like *Gina*.

And I hated that he was hurting over her. He deserved to be

happy, and hopefully he would be, but right now, he wasn't. Even having him back in my life wasn't a big enough silver lining if it meant he was this miserable.

Tyler exhaled, absently swirling his glass so the ice clinked against the sides. "By the way, I know I've said this a hundred times already, but thank you. For putting me up and everything. The prospect of getting back on my feet is a lot less daunting now."

I smiled. "You're welcome. You know I've always got your back."

I'd do anything for you.

A lump rose in my throat. I really would have done anything for him, especially if it meant getting him out of this awful funk. Staring across the table at him now after he'd inexplicably pulled away from me half a decade ago, though, I realized just how true those words were. The worst part was that despite everything, all those feelings I'd had back then were as strong, if not stronger, today. Just like when we were teenagers, I would have sold my soul for him to even *look* at me as something more than a friend. But if that wasn't possible—or even in some parallel universe where it *was* possible—I could think of literally nothing I wouldn't do for this man.

Shifting in my seat, I forced back my emotions and gazed into his eyes. "So, you're planning on staying in Seattle now?"

"As long as the new job holds out." He smiled a bit more genuinely. "I'm kind of looking forward to it, actually. The divorce and all that shit has been rough, but it's good to be home, you know?"

I smiled back. "Well, circumstances notwithstanding, it's good to have you home."

Even if having a front row seat to you finding someone new is going to be torture.

CHAPTER 3

TYLER

Traffic was still a nightmare when we left the restaurant. In fact, there was a wreck on I-405, which brought everything to a standstill. Justin took some back roads, though, and we spent well over an hour driving through areas that I'd either never seen before or had changed so dramatically I didn't recognize them.

Eventually, we made it into some familiar territory. Redmond had changed a lot since I'd lived in the area, but it was still Redmond, and I knew a few streets and buildings. Enough to figure out where I was, at least.

Justin lived a few miles outside of Redmond, but not quite to Fall City. There were a lot of farms out here, plus some scattered clusters of condos and apartments, all with eye-watering price tags. I'd checked out some apartments in this area, and the rent was staggering.

So I was more than a little surprised when Justin pulled into the driveway of a modest blue split-level on what must have been at least an acre of fenced-in land. My appraiser brain whirred into action, and... holy shit. How much was Justin *making* these days?

I craned my neck, peering at the place through the windshield. "This is yours?"

"Yep." Justin killed the engine. "Has been for the last two years."

I shot him an incredulous look. "*How?* Are you selling cocaine or something?"

Justin laughed, patting my thigh. "No, I'm not selling cocaine." He motioned toward the house. "It was a foreclosure. I got lucky—even foreclosures have been going for a lot, but this one needed so much work, nobody wanted to pay for it."

"Oh." Well, okay, that made sense.

"Come on in." He opened the car door. "We'll put your stuff in the guest room, and I'll show you around."

We unloaded everything and took it inside. Once we'd walked in, it made a bit more sense that he'd been able to afford the place. It certainly had potential to be really nice, but it was very much a work-in-progress. The front door was on the landing between the first and second floors, and what I could see of the first floor hallway was bare plywood, like the carpet had recently been ripped out. A ladder peeked out from behind the wall, and there were paint buckets and tools stacked neatly beside it.

As we lugged my suitcases up to the second floor, more signs of construction were visible, especially in the living room. Sheets of plastic covered a section of wall where the sheetrock had been removed, exposing studs and pink insulation. The brick mantel had been partially torn out, as had half the carpet. The kitchen was partially gutted, with a gaping hole where I assumed a dishwasher was meant to be.

"You've been busy," I said.

"Yeah." He chuckled self-consciously. "It's a lot better than it was, believe me."

"I do. This part looks great." I nodded toward the side of the kitchen that appeared to be finished. "Did you do all of it?"

Justin nodded. "I lived downstairs in the rec room for the first six months because this floor was such a wreck. But now the kitchen is usable and the master and guest bedrooms are done. The master bathroom is done too. Still working on the other upstairs bathroom." He paused. "I mean, it's usable, but you might have to use mine for a little while until I unfuck the shower in yours."

I shrugged. "That's fine by me. In fact, now that you mention it, do you mind if I grab a shower now? I still feel gross from being on the plane."

"Sure. I'll show you where everything is."

He took me down the hall to the guest room, which was directly across the hall from his bedroom. It was fairly sparse with a queen sized bed, a dresser, and a pair of nightstands. The off-white walls were bare aside from a framed print of a sailboat against a vivid sunset. It was impersonal, but cozy—not unlike the hotel room I'd been staying in recently.

As he parked one of my suitcases beside the bed, Justin gestured at the wall between the dresser and nightstand. "There's a power outlet here, and I can get you a power strip if you need to plug in a computer or something. Wi-Fi network is *I'm Not Paying For You To Surf Porn*, and the password is *fuck you Jim*, all one word, all lowercase."

I snorted. "Am I sensing some animosity with your neighbors?"

Justin tsked and rolled his eyes. "Cheap motherfucker likes to steal my bandwidth. I thought I'd fixed it when I changed the password, but then it started getting slow again." He turned to me, lips quirked. "Would you believe that when my ex moved out, he gave that jackass my Wi-Fi password just for spite?"

"What? That's fucking *low*."

"I know, right? I just figured it out like a month ago. Hence the new and mildly passive aggressive network name."

"Mildly, eh?"

"Well, by my standards." Justin batted his eyelashes, and I laughed. Which felt pretty damn good, and probably shouldn't have surprised me. I should've known that even when my life was at its absolute shittiest, Justin could make me laugh. No wonder the last five years had seemed so dark.

He cleared his throat. "Okay, so, the bathroom is across the hall, one door to your left. My bedroom is straight across, and the master bathroom is... well, let me show you." He gestured for me to follow him.

His bedroom wasn't nearly as sparse as the guest room. There were framed photos on the wall—mostly family who I hadn't seen in years—and he had some odds and ends on his dresser and hanging by the mirror. Mardi Gras beads. Some lanyards with what appeared to be passes for conventions or concerts. A pink and white lei hanging from the same thumbtack as a postcard with white sand and palm trees on it. I'd seen some photos on his Facebook from the trips he'd taken, and for some reason I decided it was incredibly endearing to see the sentimental side of him that kept his favorite memories where he could see them.

The California king bed was covered in a bright blue comforter and some matching throw pillows, plus a very large long-haired cat—mostly silver-gray with black head and legs—curled in the middle. The cat lifted its head and looked at me coolly with icy blue eyes.

"That's Azrael." Justin pointed at the cat. "She's kind of a bitch, but if you let her warm up to you on her terms, she's super sweet when she wants to be."

"Good to know."

"And don't be surprised if she shows up on your bed. She loves the guest room, and she's a total cuddlebug once she decides you're worthy."

I glanced at the cat, who was peering at me with pure disdain. Somehow I doubted she'd be cuddling with me any time soon, but okay.

"This is the bathroom." He motioned toward the door beside his closet. "Towels are in the linen closet in the hallway. Also the hot water doesn't last very long." He huffed. "I'm working on getting the hot water heater replaced because the new one is shitty as hell, but the company's acting like the warranty is—" He waved a hand and shook his head. "Anyway. If it starts getting cool, get out because it's about to turn ice fucking cold."

"Duly noted," I said. "I take pretty short showers anyway. Kind of comes with the territory when you—" I caught myself before I let the comment come to life. I really, really didn't want to discuss the things my ex-wife and I had fought about. Especially the stupid petty shit. Clearing my throat, I shifted my weight. "My last place was the same way."

He studied me like he was curious what I'd left out, but if he was, he let it go. "Okay, so." He looked around as if to make sure he hadn't forgotten anything. "I'll leave you to it."

"Great. Thanks."

We exchanged smiles, and my heart fluttered. He'd always had the most gorgeous smile. That, and even though my whole world was on its ass, I actually got to see my best friend now. Every day.

Why did I ever let her keep us apart?

I swallowed the lump that had suddenly materialized in my throat, and with it my guilty conscience. With a smile that was more forced than it had been a second ago, I said, "Right. So, I'll get a shower, and then I'll buy you dinner tonight. I owe you."

"Don't worry about it. I know cash is probably tight, and I have plenty of food here, so—"

"Then at least let me cook something." I put a hand on his shoulder. "You're bailing me out big time. Just let me do something for you."

Justin studied me, features taut for a moment, and finally shrugged, his shoulder lifting slightly under my palm. "If you want to, I'm not going to say no." Now his smile had changed too—turning a little nostalgic and maybe kind of sad as he looked in my eyes. "You always were a great cook."

We held each other's gazes a second longer before I took my hand off his shoulder and he left so I could take a shower.

I cleaned myself up as quickly as I could, taking to heart his comment about the water heater crapping out quickly. The water was still hot when I was finished, so I indulged in a minute or so of just enjoying the warmth rushing over me. I'd been staying in a hotel for the last two weeks, and the shower hadn't had much pressure, so I couldn't help savoring the luxurious feeling of water beating on my stiff neck and shoulders.

The water did quickly start cooling, though, so I got out. I dried off in the bathroom, wrapped the towel around my waist, and headed back to my room. On the way across Justin's bedroom, I glanced at the souvenirs he'd tacked on his wall or arranged on his dresser, and one caught my eye: A little plastic Space Needle keychain dangling from the pushpin that also held a faded and slightly wrinkled ticket that read *Senior Party – Class of 1998.*

My breath hitched. I vividly remembered that night, and for reasons I couldn't quite define, it warmed my heart to see that our graduation party had made the cut for his wall of apparently cherished memories. And that it was still there after two decades.

That night seemed so long ago. Like something that had happened in another lifetime. At the same time, though, the memories were as clear as if it had been last night. How we'd all been ecstatic over graduating, a little sad over not seeing each other every day anymore, and equal parts terrified and excited about the future.

They'd had karaoke, and while I usually loathed karaoke, several of our friends had wanted to do it, so I'd tagged along.

When it came time to pick songs, Justin had picked *My Heart Will Go On.* We'd all laughed since he'd obviously chosen it ironically, sort of like when our buddy Aiden had done *Like a Virgin* or when my girlfriend at the time, Madison, had badly sung some Pink Floyd song I couldn't recall.

Justin had stepped onto the stage, the music had started, and he'd...

God. He'd nailed it. Like, made the whole room go silent, gave everyone goose bumps, hit all the notes flawlessly, *nailed it.* In his own voice, too. Not some attempt to make himself actually sound like

Céline Dion. It was the first and only time that song had ever come close to bringing me to tears, and to this day, I couldn't hear it without getting those goose bumps all over again.

Or think about it, apparently, because I was getting them right now.

With a shiver, I pulled my gaze away from the tiny piece of senior party memorabilia and continued across the hall to my room. As I got dressed, I couldn't get the memories out of my head, especially Justin singing. That was the thing I remembered most clearly about that night. Watching him up there onstage, singing his heart out until that last, long note had been drowned out by applause and cheers, and being utterly mesmerized by him.

We'd all been convinced after that that he would wind up with a recording contract and an armload of Grammy awards. When *American Idol* had been a thing, I'd always watched the audition episodes under the pretense of enjoying a little schadenfreude, but truthfully, I'd been hoping for a glimpse of Justin singing for the judges. So it was kind of weird, now, him being settled into a modest house with a normal job, a regular car, and a judgmental cat. He was obviously doing well, and he seemed to be happy, but he wasn't a rock star.

Then again, I guess most of us weren't. We'd all had big dreams, and now he had some corporate job, I appraised houses for mortgage lenders, and we commiserated with our old classmates on Facebook about student loans. Everyone had more or less average lives aside from Vince Graham (he'd been picked up by the NFL) and Jade DeYoung (I had no idea what she did, only that it involved globe-trotting). And maybe that was okay. We didn't all have to be rock stars.

Hell, at this point I'd have been perfectly happy with a dull, average existence. It would be a lot less chaotic than things had been for me recently. After all of that, boring sounded just fine by me, and I was looking forward to getting back to it.

I wondered about Justin, though. Was he happy? Did he like his job and his life?

And I realized, then, how little I knew about him anymore. *Was* he happy? *Did* he like his job and his life?

I didn't know. This man was my best friend, and I'd stupidly cut him out of my life until recently, and now I just... didn't know who he was anymore.

Well. No time like the present to fix that problem.

CHAPTER 4

JUSTIN

As much as I didn't want Tyler to feel like he was obligated to do anything, I really couldn't say no when he offered to cook. From the time we were teenagers, he'd always been amazing in the kitchen. We'd all encouraged him to go to culinary school, but his mom had insisted he needed a more useful degree. As if being a chef wasn't a respectable job where he could make a solid income, but hey, what did we know?

Anyway, he obviously hadn't lost his touch, and my unfamiliar, half-demolished kitchen didn't slow him down. Once he knew where everything was, he was good to go, only occasionally pausing to ask me where a particular utensil or something was stored.

I stayed out of the way, leaning on the other side of the kitchen island with a cup of coffee while my kitchen filled with the smells of garlic, sizzling ground beef, and some kind of savory sauce. I took in a deep breath through my nose. "My God. I don't think my house has smelled this good since I moved in."

Tyler chuckled. He was facing me, chopping some celery on the cutting board. "Don't tell me you've been living on boxed crap and takeout?"

"What?" I put a hand to my chest, feigning offense. "I'll have you know I do cook once in a while."

His eyebrow arched.

I huffed. "I said once in a while."

Tyler laughed. "You're obviously not just living on crap, though." His eyes flicked toward me, almost giving me a down-up despite the counter blocking everything below my ribs. "I mean, you're still in really good shape."

My cheeks warmed, and I smiled. "Oh. Thank you. That's, uh, probably got a bit more to do with religious gym attendance than eating right." In a stage whisper, I added, "Don't tell my trainer."

Chuckling, he pushed aside the pieces of one celery stalk, then started on the next one. "I need to get back on that myself."

"What?" It was my turn to give him a down-up, something I usually couldn't do this openly with my straight friends, but Tyler had always been an exception in that department. "You don't look like you've been slacking."

His good humor faded. "I... well, I was going to the gym, and I was eating decently, but the last couple of months..." He sighed. Then he put a hand on his flat stomach. "This is probably more from not eating enough than anything."

I straightened, concern making my own stomach flip. "You haven't been starving yourself, have you?"

"No, no." Tyler shook his head, and he focused intently on chopping the last stalk of celery. "It's just, between the divorce and losing my job, I haven't had much of an appetite for a while. It's been kind of depressing, you know?"

I slouched a little. "Yeah, I guess it would be. But you're doing better now?"

He met my gaze for a second, and let a tiny smile come to life. "Better, yeah." Without elaborating further, he finished with the celery, scooped it all up, and put it into the pot with the sauce. He stirred it a couple of times, then put the lid on to let it simmer while he came back to the cutting board and started dicing some tomatoes.

Silently, I watched him, wondering how much to press about his state of mind. I wasn't at all surprised that he'd been depressed, even to the point of not eating, but how deep did that depression run? How bad had the last few months really been?

I was still formulating a tactful way of asking when he spoke up.

"You know, it's crazy. I feel like I know nothing about you anymore." His voice was tinged with sadness, and maybe some regret. "Are you... I don't know. How *are* you doing? In general?"

A pang of way too many emotions hit me in the gut. Resentment was in the lead, and I had to fight to keep the accusations out of my tone as I countered with, "Why don't we know much about each other anymore?"

His eyes flicked toward me. "You didn't answer my question."

"No, but mine feels a little more pressing." I leaned over my arms on the island. "We were tight for years, even after we ended up in different states. And then we just... weren't." I cocked my head. "What happened?"

Tyler's hands stopped. He stared down at the tomatoes he'd been dicing, and sighed. Then, pushing his shoulders back, he looked at me across the island. "It isn't like we can change the past, but maybe we can do better in the future." He smiled again, though it didn't reach his eyes. "Living in the same state will help, right?"

"True," I whispered. *Don't change the subject. I deserve an answer, damn it.* "I guess living in the same *house* will too."

Tyler nodded. As he resumed chopping, he said, "Hopefully that part won't last too long." Beat. "I mean, I don't want to impose on you forever, you know?"

"Of course. I gotcha." So why did the thought of him moving out depress me? He probably wasn't leaving the area. We'd be able to see each other. I didn't need to keep him under my roof to keep in my life. Right?

Ah. That was it. He'd been gone so long, I was afraid of losing him all over again. The last time we'd seen each other five years ago, we'd hugged goodbye as always, and I'd walked away without worrying for a second that it was the last time. He'd come back to town. I'd get to see him. There'd been no way in hell that moment would be the last one we'd have until *today*.

I watched him silently. He was at the stove, dealing with the meat and sauce, oblivious to me staring at him. Oblivious to the question that had been burning in my chest ever since we'd started talking again recently, and it was still burning there even after he'd tried to avoid it. I hadn't planned to throw it at him quite so soon. Let him get here. Let him settle in and get over the jetlag.

But damn it, now that we were in the same room, I couldn't hold it back anymore. Truth be told, it had been eating at me for the last couple of years. That had only gotten more intense recently, and now it was unbearable. *You were my best friend. Why did you leave?* So, carefully schooling my tone, I said, "I'm curious about something."

"Okay?" He glanced over his shoulder, but didn't turn around. Fine—I understood needing to keep an eye on things so they didn't burn.

Thumbing the handle on my coffee cup, I took a deep breath. "I really do want to know—why haven't I seen you in five years?"

Tyler's whole body stilled. For a long moment, the kitchen was completely silent except for the faint sizzle of the meat in the skillet.

"One day everything was fine," I said, fighting a losing battle to keep my emotions out of my voice. "Then you left after a visit, and after that, every time I said I'd be coming through Chicago or something..." I was afraid to continue because the hurt and anger would take over.

Again, he was silent. I waited, giving him a moment to gather his thoughts.

Finally, he turned a couple of dials—probably lowering the heat under the various pots and pans—and came back to the island. He wasn't looking at me as he pressed his palms on the counter and leaned over them. "Listen." He sounded even more tired than he'd been earlier. "I... I should've had more of a spine when it came to my friendship with you."

I blinked, not sure what he meant.

He swallowed. "I had a lot of 'pick your battles' moments with Gina. Especially after the first year or two."

Fury piled on top of the hurt. "Are you... are you saying she wouldn't *let* you see me?"

Tyler pursed his lips, still avoiding my gaze. "I'm saying that every time I wanted to come to Seattle, or whenever I mentioned you might come visit us, it turned into a fight. A bad one."

"What?" I could barely breathe all of a sudden. "Why? I didn't think she... well, okay, I know she didn't like me, but..."

He finally met my eyes. "I'm not proud of it, okay? I let her dictate a lot of things in my life, and if there's one I regret more than all the others, it's letting her interfere with our friendship. I was just... I was so exhausted from fighting, and any time there was something I could do to give us one less reason to fight..." He dropped his gaze again, and released a long breath. "For what it's worth—and I know it doesn't change a thing—I've missed you like crazy." With a bitter laugh, he shook his head and stood pushed himself upright. "That should've been a clue, you know? How much it hurt being away from you, and how much I resented her for keeping us apart like that."

I struggled to absorb everything he'd said. "Why, though?"

He met my eyes. "Why did I let her dictate who I spent time with? Or why did she have it out for you?"

"Both, now that you mention it."

Tyler blew out another breath. He turned away to deal with the food on the stove, though I had a feeling it was partly to give himself an excuse to break eye contact. "If you ask my therapist, he'll tell you the part about me letting Gina run my life was because I married a woman just like my mother. It's what I was used to, so it's what I was drawn to."

I frowned, but didn't speak. I'd never been a big fan of Tyler's mom. My own mom had insisted that Mrs. Schaeffer's overbearing ways just came with the territory of raising four boys alone. As I'd gotten older, I'd wondered if those overbearing ways had played a part in her husband vanishing off the face of the earth when Tyler was three. Tyler's older brothers had all gotten the fuck out of Seattle as soon as they'd graduated, and so had he.

Which was also why I'd never bought that he'd stopped coming to Seattle because she'd moved to California. Two of his brothers had moved back here. His friends and the extended family he got along with all lived here. And it wasn't like he spent much time in California, at least not according to his social media posts.

Deep down, I'd always suspected it was a different woman in his life who'd kept him from coming home. A woman who Tyler's therapist—and his best friend—thought bore a striking resemblance to his mom. Sometimes it sucked being right.

I cleared my throat. "So why did she have it out for me?"

Tyler's shoulders sagged. He wasn't doing anything with the food now, but he still didn't turn around. When he finally broke the silence, it was with the last answer I could have possibly anticipated:

"Because she thought I was going to leave her for you."

CHAPTER 5

TYLER

I couldn't face him. Now that the words were out, I wanted to throw up, and I wasn't even sure why. Gina and I had fought more times than I could count over her obsessive fear that it was only a matter of time before I packed up and left her for Justin.

"I've seen the way he looks at you, Tyler! That man is in love with you."

"So what if he is? I'm straight."

"You sure about that? Because I've seen how you look at him."

Movement behind me made the hair on my neck stand up. Justin was coming around the kitchen island, bare feet landing softly on the linoleum. He stopped behind me, maybe an arm's length away, and I couldn't breathe as I waited for him to speak.

"Tyler."

I winced. Then, slowly, I turned to face him. I had no idea what expression to expect, but what I saw hit me in the chest—a mix of hurt and concern in his wide eyes and creased forehead. Like everything I'd told him had cut him to the bone, but he was still worried about me, which did nothing to soothe my conscience.

Can't you just be mad for once? Please?

Justin swallowed, and his voice was so soft it was barely audible. "Did you ever think I would try to break up your marriage?"

I stared at the floor between us, and slowly shook my head. "No. Never. Not even when..." I winced again.

His hand materialized on my arm, the gentle touch almost moving me to tears. "You know whenever I asked if you were happy, or if things were—"

"I know," I whispered.

"It wasn't something selfish. I really want you to be happy." He squeezed my arm. "I would never have tried to take you away from her even if you *were* into guys. I just wanted you to be okay."

Nodding, I exhaled. "I tried to explain that to her, but she was... I mean, hell. She was convinced I was sleeping with everyone who moved. Male or female. Especially since I had to go to people's houses to do my job."

Justin made an aggravated sound, and I didn't even have to see him to know he was rolling those beautiful eyes. "Insecure much?"

"You think?" I held back the part where Justin was the one and only person she'd ever forbidden me from seeing at all. She'd been convinced I was fucking anyone and everyone, but she was utterly certain that whatever was happening between me and Justin ran deeper than sex. Why that was more of a threat, I had no idea, only that she didn't try to stop me from seeing any of the other people I was allegedly fucking. She'd guilt the shit out of me over them, and call me or show up at my office at random times to try to bust me, but she'd put her foot down with Justin. She'd scream at me and browbeat me over everyone else, but she'd cry over him, and what the fuck could I do? The only thing more exhausting than fighting was groveling.

I glanced at everything on the stove to make sure it was all cooking properly. Then I turned to him again. "You want to know what's really fucked up?"

His lips twisted. "This is not a very enjoyable line of 'but wait, there's more'."

"You're telling me."

He tilted his head, expression softening. "So, what's really fucked up?"

I moistened my lips. "We're divorcing because Gina's leaving me for her boss."

"You're shitting me."

"Nope. I caught her cheating with him about a year ago, and then—"

"Wait, wait, wait." Justin shook his head. Leaning against the island, he stared at me incredulously. "You busted her cheating a *year* ago? But you didn't leave her?" Before I could answer, the surprise in his expression melted into something more like sympathy. He sighed, still holding my gaze. "She apologized and promised never to do it again, right?"

"Apologized isn't really the word I'd use."

His eyebrow rose and his lips pursed to one side, and I almost had to laugh with the sheer relief of seeing his classic *"I'm about to say something bitchy"* expression.

Do you have any idea how much I've missed you?

"So what word would you use?" he asked in a flat tone.

"Well, my therapist went with deflection. After I caught her, she just kept going back to how I kept lying and obviously fucking around, so she'd had to go find someone else too."

Justin covered his face with his hands and almost muffled a few choice names for my ex-wife. When he lowered them again, he looked in my eyes. "She really had you beaten down, didn't she?"

"Just a bit." I rubbed my eyes. "I can't decide if it was all a smoke-screen. Like, if she was so paranoid about me cheating, then she must hate cheaters, and so I'd never suspect a thing." I dropped my hand. "Or if she genuinely thought I was cheating, and that me cheating on her was this horrific sin even while she was doing the same damn thing."

Justin winced. "She really is like your mom, isn't she?"

I nodded. I'd been around that block with my therapist enough times, I didn't even bother getting defensive about it anymore. "I should've left a long time ago, but it's over now. All I can do is move on." I paused for a deep breath. "And apologize to you for not sticking to my guns."

"Don't." He shook his head. "You're back in my life now, and that's all I really care about." His words made my guilt burn even hotter.

I gave you up to keep the peace with her?

Before I could think of something to say, Justin stepped closer and hugged me. I stiffened for a split second, startled by the gesture, but then I wrapped my arms around him even tighter than I had at the airport. Squeezing my eyes shut, I just held him for a moment. Some of my other friends had always been weirded out that I was so close to a gay dude, especially one as touchy-feely as Justin, but I'd never cared. Justin had been my best friend since long before he'd come out, and nothing had changed since then. He'd always been more physical with me than he was with other straight guys because he had no reason to believe I'd get upset or defensive.

And right now, standing in his kitchen with confessions and apologies hanging in the air, I had never been more grateful for his touchy-feeliness. I'd never told anyone, but I'd always loved how it felt when he hugged me like this. And for that matter, I hadn't even realized until this second how much I needed his effortless physical affection or how starved I'd been for *anyone's* touch.

"*Don't try to tell me that man doesn't love you,*" my ex-wife's tear-filled voice echoed in my head.

I held him a little tighter. I was pretty sure he did love me. Not in the way she'd been convinced he had. Not like he was going to try to seduce me away from my marriage. Not like he'd ignore my hetero-sexuality and move in for the kill.

No, he loved me exactly the way I'd desperately needed someone to love me for a long, long time—unconditionally and without asking for anything in return. Which, hell—maybe Gina had needed to worry about Justin luring me away from her. Not because I'd

suddenly turn gay and decide I was into him, but because my friendship with him was a hell of a lot better than my relationship with her
had ever aspired to be. If he was this amazing as a friend, he must
have been one hell of a partner, and I caught myself hoping that
somewhere out there was a man who would someday make Justin as
happy as he deserved to be.

Wherever you are, I hope you find him soon.

—————

"Oh my *God*, that was amazing." Justin put his fork down on his
empty plate. "I'm going to have to step up my sessions at the gym now
that you live here."

I laughed, laying down my own utensils. "So you wouldn't protest
if I made this again?"

"Honey, I'd protest if you *didn't*."

"Good to know. I'll keep it on the list." It had been ages since I'd
made stuffed bell peppers. The recipe was one I'd modified over the
years, and I'd added a sauce that was more or less like a red sauce for
enchiladas. They were definitely different, and they got mixed
reviews, but Justin the picky eater had gone back for seconds, so I
figured his compliments were more than lip service.

I started to stand so I could take the dishes, but he motioned for
me to stay put.

"I got it." He collected our plates and utensils. "You cooked—like
hell are you cleaning too." I started to protest, but he wagged a finger
at me. "*Sit*."

"Okay, okay." I put up my hands. "Can I at least join you in the
kitchen?"

"Fine. But no cleaning."

"Oh, twist my arm." I picked up my wineglass and followed him
into the kitchen. Fortunately, there wasn't too much left for him to
do. Even when I had a dishwasher, I was in the habit of cleaning
while I cooked. I hated washing dishes, and doing one or two at a

time was a lot less daunting than facing down a whole sink full of the damn things.

While he scrubbed our plates, he said, "You know, I could go for something sweet."

"Hmm, me too, now that you mention it."

"When I'm done here, you want to go get ice cream?" He grinned sheepishly. "My trainer's already going to kick my ass, so I might as well get some ice cream out of it."

I laughed. "I won't tell if you don't. But yeah, that sounds really good."

"Great. Just give me a couple of minutes, and we can head up to Cold Stone."

"Oh man. I haven't been there in ages."

He glanced up from rinsing off the plate. "Chicago doesn't have Cold Stone?"

"Oh, they're out there. I just never went for some reason." The mood between us had lightened over dinner, and I didn't feel like mentioning that I'd lived with someone who would give me hell if I ate anything that might make me gain weight. Or that the whopping fifteen pounds I'd gained in the last two years had been part of why she'd had to resort to sex with her slimmer and more attractive boss. Kind of ironic that I'd lost a significant portion of that weight in recent weeks. Being dumped for another man really didn't do much for a guy's appetite.

"Hey." Justin's voice nudged me out of my thoughts. "You spaced out on me." He put the plate into the drying rack and reached for the other one. "You okay?"

"I'm good. Sorry." I laughed as heat rushed into my cheeks. "Just, uh, trying to think of all the other places I haven't eaten at in a long time. Is that Greek place we used to go to still open?"

"The one on Capitol Hill?"

"Yeah, the one with that lemon and rice soup you and Chloe were hooked on?"

"I wish," he muttered as he scrubbed the plate. "They shut down a couple of years ago. There's some new Greek places around downtown and one or two here on the Eastside, but none of them are as good as that place."

"Damn."

"I know, right? Still plenty of good food around here, though. Lot of new restaurants that I will absolutely drag you to."

I smiled. "Since when have you ever had to drag me someplace when there's good food?"

"Fair point." He returned the smile, a mix of warmth and playfulness in his eyes. "But you've been gone a long time, so I've got a lot of places to show my favorite food snob. So if I *do* have to drag your ass to every amazing restaurant in the area?" He pushed his shoulders back and sighed dramatically. "Then it's what I'll do. For the greater good."

I snorted. "For the greater good, right."

Chuckling, he winked and continued with the dishes.

As we continued shooting the shit, I wondered if he knew how much good it did me just to know he was planning on reintroducing me to Seattle's food scene. To know that in his mind, it was a foregone conclusion that we'd pick up where we'd left off years ago and go back to being inseparable.

And I hoped that was exactly what happened.

CHAPTER 6

JUSTIN

For once, finding a parking space at Redmond Town Center wasn't too difficult. There were two large restaurants beside the biggest parking lot, and on the other side, the open air mall and the movie theater. On a Friday or Saturday, it would be absolutely teeming with people.

It was Tuesday, though, so the crowd was pretty light. There wasn't even much of a line at Cold Stone, and before long, we were seated at one of the tables outside by the fountain. I dug into my cake batter ice cream with chocolate chips, and Tyler—upon taking his first bite of double fudge with caramel sauce—made a sound that was almost orgasmic.

"Good, isn't it?" I grinned and hoped he didn't notice me trying not to squirm. It was not fair for my incredibly hot and very straight friend to make any sounds in my presence that could be in any way interpreted as sexual. Even if it was directed at his ice cream. Not. *Fair.*

Presumably unaware of my thoughts and goose bumps, Tyler nodded. "I can't believe how long it's been since I've eaten here." He chuckled as he scooped some more ice cream out of the waffle bowl. "Thank you. For 'dragging' me to this place."

"Any time." I paused to spoon out some more of my own. "So, what's your plan? Now that you're here?"

Tyler took a bite, and after he'd swallowed it, he shrugged. "Step one, get a car and get started at the new gig." He rolled his eyes. "Getting a car should be fun with my job situation, but..." He gestured dismissively. "I'll figure it out. Car, job, place to live..."

"Would it help if I co-signed for the car?"

Tyler jumped like I'd kicked him under the table. "What?"

I shrugged. "If it helps, I'm happy to do it."

He stared at me, lips parted. "You'd... really do that?"

"Tyler." I laughed dryly. "Stop acting so surprised when I try to help you. You're my friend and you're in a shitty situation." I shrugged again as I scooped out another bite of ice cream. "I'd do it for any of my friends."

"Even after—?"

"Yes. Even after the last five years."

"Oh." He relaxed a little. "I... wow, I really appreciate it. Hopefully I can do it on my own, but yeah, I..." His cheeks colored. "I might take you up on that."

"Just let me know."

We ate in silence for a few minutes. After I'd finished, I pushed the empty cup aside and sat back with my soda. "So, what about everything else?"

"Everything else?" He cocked his head. "Like what?"

"You tell me. You're pretty much starting over. New job. Sort-of-new city."

"Oh right." He sighed, staring down at his remaining ice cream as if he wasn't so sure he could finish it. "I guess I haven't thought very far ahead. Getting to Seattle, starting the new job, and getting a car were about it." He paused, snapped off a piece of the waffle bowl, and nibbled on it. "I'm... sort of thinking about downloading Tinder or something."

Good thing I wasn't taking a drink just then. And I had no idea why it surprised me so much. Or did it? Shit, maybe I was just caught off guard by the idea of a newly-liberated Tyler putting himself back out there.

Oh, you lucky ladies...

I took a sip, then cleared my throat for good measure. "Oh yeah? Thinking about actually dating, or just hookups?"

Tyler blushed. "I don't know. I've been with Gina for fourteen years, and now I'm out on my own, so I guess I... well, I wouldn't say I want to play the field. I just want to get myself out there and see what happens."

"Good. Good." I smiled across the tiny table. "I mean, there's no reason to rush into another relationship, but getting out there again seems healthier than moping over Gina."

"That's what I'm thinking." He watched himself break off another piece of the waffle bowl. "It'd be nice to get laid, too."

Lord help me, if I thought this man possessed one single bisexual molecule, I'd have offered to assist him with that. But he was straight, and I'd never allowed myself to so much as joke with him about us sleeping together. I made the odd crude joke about fitting his junk in my trunk or whatever, but there was a line I carefully toed between saying something clearly meant to be raunchy and ridiculous, and making a comment he might interpret as an actual suggestion. I'd flirted playfully with straight guys who I knew wouldn't get pissed about it, but never with Tyler because I was terrified he might see through to my pathetic gooey pining-for-him center, and then things might get weird.

I swallowed, my mouth suddenly dry.

Before I could speak, Tyler laughed self-consciously. "I'm sorry. That might've been a bit TMI."

"What?" I waved a hand. "You want to get laid. That's not TMI. Hell, *I* want to get laid."

Tyler met my gaze. "You mean you're not... uh..."

"Not a shameless slut who uses Grindr as my personal dick buffet?"

"Uh..." He blushed again, darker this time.

"Relax." I laughed. "To be honest, I've just been so busy the last few months, I haven't met many guys at all since my ex left."

"How long has that been? I didn't even realize you'd broken up with anyone until you mentioned him earlier."

I tried not to flinch at the reminder of how separate our lives had been and for how long. "We broke up in November."

"Oh. I'm, uh, sorry to hear it."

"Eh." I made another dismissive gesture. "I was with him for a year that I'm never getting back, and I'm glad the fucker's gone. I wish he'd come and get the rest of his crap from my house, but otherwise, I'd just as soon never see him again. And since he left, I just... haven't done much dating or hooking up." I laughed bitterly. "Guess I got so used to having someone in my bed every night, I got out of practice with putting in the effort to meet anyone."

"I get that," he grumbled. "I don't even know where to start. I met Gina the same way I met every girl I've ever dated—in class."

"You could always sign up for a class, then."

"Maybe. But do people even meet that way anymore? Seems like it's all apps and websites and shit."

"Pretty much. I've met some guys in clubs, but the online stuff is so much more efficient." I paused. "I don't know how it is for you straight weirdos though."

Tyler laughed, sending my pulse skyward. I'd forgotten how much his smile could light up a room. The fact that we were talking about going out and getting laid didn't do much to keep my vitals from responding to his beautiful laugh.

"It's too bad there aren't clubs we can both go to," he said.

I furrowed my brow. "What do you mean?"

"I mean, like..." He crunched thoughtfully on a piece of waffle bowl. "Like obviously we can go into the same places, but they're different scenes, you know?"

"Pfft. You make it sound like dudes never blow dudes in dive bar restrooms."

His eyes widened. "They do?"

"Sure." I smirked. "We walk among you, sweetheart, and sometimes we even get laid right under your nose."

"Oh. I did not... I did not know that." He broke eye contact, but only for a second. "So that means we *could* go together?"

Into the men's room of—

I blinked. "Would you *want* to?"

"Why not?" He looked at me through his lashes, oblivious to how adorable he was when he was this shy. "I'm not gonna lie—going out alone is kind of intimidating. It's been so long since I've even set foot in a club, and I..." He lowered his gaze.

I wasn't sure what to say. I'd never been a wingman for a straight guy, and I'd never had a wingman at all, so I had no idea how effective either of us would be at getting laid if we went somewhere together. Still, I was quickly warming up to the idea of going out clubbing with him. It was time with my friend after way too many years apart. I'd get to see him happy and relaxed. I'd get to see him dance, and good God, this man could dance. Just because there wasn't a snowball's chance in hell of him ever dancing with me didn't mean I couldn't enjoy the show.

"That sounds like fun," I said.

His eyebrows jumped. "Really?"

"Sure. You let me know when you want to go, and you're on."

"Awesome." His face lit up again. "I can't wait."

You and me both.

When I walked into the dealership, I immediately zeroed in on Tyler and the salesman sitting at a desk by the windows. As I came closer, Tyler gestured at me. The salesman nodded, but deflated a little. I swore I could see *oh fuck, another Millennial* written all over his face.

Suppressing a smirk, I continued in their direction.

I'm not as young as I look, darlin', but thanks for the compliment.

When I reached the desk, the salesman rose. "Hi, I'm Chris." Smiling tightly, extended his hand. "You must be Justin."

I shook his hand. "That's what my office door says, yes."

He blinked.

Now it was Tyler obviously trying to hold back a smirk. Schooling his expression, he said, "Sorry for the short notice."

"Don't worry about it. I work right up the street, so I took an early lunch. Easy peasy."

"Well, this shouldn't take long." Chris cleared his throat and took his seat again as he gestured for me to take the empty seat beside Tyler. "Just have some forms for you to fill in." Beat. "And of course we'll have to do a credit check." He eyed me expectantly, as if he was certain I'd balk.

I took a pen out of my shirt pocket and clicked it. "Bring it on."

More confusion and uncertainty played in Chris's expression, but he slid a clipboard with some papers across the desk. "Can I get either of you some coffee?"

"Oh, I could go for some." I smiled sweetly at him as I crossed my legs and balanced the clipboard on my thigh. "Just a little bit of sugar, but otherwise black."

He blinked. I wondered what he'd expected. After a couple of awkward seconds, he got up and left.

As soon as the salesman was out of earshot, Tyler muffled a snort.

I glanced at him, the innocent face still plastered on. "What?"

Tyler rolled his eyes. "Some things never change, do they?"

"Like what?" I gestured after Chris with my pen. "I never used to put sugar in my coffee at all."

Chuckling, he gave my leg a playful kick. "Not that. I'm saying you're still the same guy who used to gloat when he got carded for R-rated movies."

I half-shrugged as I started filling out the form. "You would've gloated too if your fake ID was as good as mine." I wagged my pen in his direction. "In fact, I seem to recall you gloating over the fact that nobody ever carded you for shit."

He smirked, and damn if it wasn't that same smug expression he'd always gotten when the box office handed him a ticket without a second glance when we knew damn well they'd want fourteen pieces of ID and notarized permission from my parents for good measure despite him being four months younger than me.

"Guess that baby face of yours is still a double-edged sword?"

"Uh-huh." I rolled my eyes and started writing again. "You know I still get carded for drinks sometimes?"

"I don't doubt it." He spoke without missing a beat, and when I met his gaze, there wasn't even a hint of self-consciousness in his expression. If there had been, I might have cautiously asked just how much he'd been looking at me since he'd moved in. But it was like he didn't even realize it was unusual for a straight dude to notice so much about another guy, and I was afraid me pointing it out would *make* him self-conscious. It might mortify him.

It might make him stop looking at me like that.

I cleared my throat and once again focused on the paperwork. "Give it time," I said. "Sooner or later, my age is going to catch up with me. I'll wake up one morning looking forty-seven."

He laughed. "Yeah. Probably the day you turn eighty." Something about his tone made my spine tingle. Something... wistful? Shit, was I imagining that?

But I didn't let myself steal a glance at his expression to see if his eyes betrayed anything. Truth was, this had always been Tyler's way. It was one of the reasons having a crush on him had always been so excruciating—because every now and then he'd make some comment, or he'd touch me, or we'd make eye contact, and I'd seriously wonder if maybe he wasn't so straight after all. I'd tortured myself with that when we were teenagers. I wasn't going to start that shit again now.

I'm just not used to it anymore. That's all.

Which explains why I can't remember how to spell my last name, what my address is, or where the fuck I work...

I shook myself and managed to start coughing up all the information the dealership needed to let me co-sign on Tyler's car.

Chris returned a moment later with the coffee I *so* didn't need. I thanked him before taking a polite sip and restraining a decidedly less polite gag. What part of *just a little bit of sugar* did he not understand? I swore this man had just rendered the sugarcane extinct in the process of making my coffee. Blech.

But I not only had a baby face, I had a damn good *poker* face, and I was pretty sure I made it to the end of both the forms and coffee without tipping my hand. Chris didn't seem to notice how nauseated I was by his weapons-grade sweetening job, and Tyler didn't seem to notice the wheels spinning in my head. Mission accomplished.

"Okay." I handed the clipboard back to Chris and pocketed my pen. "That should be everything."

Chris took the paperwork and skimmed over it. Then he cleared his throat and shot us both a smarmy salesman smile. "Everything looks good." He got up and gestured at the opposite end of the dealership. "I'll have the financing department do their thing, and *if* it comes back approved"—he grimaced like he wasn't optimistic—"we'll go from there."

With a wink, I said, "Do your worst, sweetheart."

His features tightened slightly at the endearment. I smiled to drive it home, and he cleared his throat as he hurried out with the paperwork.

Beside me, Tyler was almost vibrating with amusement.

I kept my poker face firmly in place. "What?"

Tyler patted my thigh as if that was a totally normal thing for a straight man to do, scrambling my thoughts with a gentle touch. "You know what you did."

I'm pretty sure you don't know what you did, though.

My mouth had suddenly gone dry, and I had to fight to speak, never mind keep my tone casual. "What? He implied my pristine credit wouldn't be approved, and he made my coffee so sweet I'm going to have to swing into the dentist on my way home." I hoped my exaggeratedly indignant huff masked how much my head was spinning. "He deserved it."

"Fair enough." And now he was watching me. No, studying me. Focused on me with an intensity I didn't remember from our younger years. Okay, so it had been hard to focus that hard when we'd been stoned off our asses, but we hadn't *always* been stoned, so was this something new? Or was my memory fading?

I fought a losing battle against the urge to fidget. "What?"

He tilted his head and narrowed his eyes just slightly. "You okay?" He tensed a bit. "You... don't mind this do you? Me calling you down here to co-sign and—"

"Oh my God, no!" A laugh burst out of me. "Are you kidding? Honey, you know me."

"Yeah, I do, but..." He trailed off, but didn't look away. Fuck. His eyes. So focused.

I finally let myself fidget. Goddamn. I was suddenly nervous enough that my internal censor was liable to go completely MIA, and I had to almost literally bite my tongue to keep from suggesting he use a body part *other* than his eyes to drill into me.

That thought made my breath hitch, and there was no hiding it. What the hell was wrong with me?

Apparently I wasn't the only one wondering that—Tyler's gaze intensified even more. "What's wrong?"

Well you see it all started with this hot straight man who doesn't even know *he's eye-fucking me and—*

I coughed again and managed to laugh. "Sorry. I'm sorry." I shook my head. "I guess part of me is still just getting used to having you back." As soon as the words were out, I wanted to curl up and die. Really? *Really?* That was the best I could come up with? I should've just made the "*drill me with your dick instead of your eyes*" comment and been done with it.

But Tyler... smiled. He blushed, too. Dropping his gaze, he said, "Yeah, same here."

I blinked. "Really?"

"Well, yeah." He hesitated, and then with some work, faced me again. "I practically ghosted you without explanation, and then when my life fell apart, you opened your door to me and..." He gestured at our surroundings. "You don't think it's been a little mind-blowing for me?"

I swallowed. "You didn't... you didn't ghost me. We've still been in touch this whole time." As much as seeing each other on social media and posting *Happy Birthday!* once a year on each other's Face-book walls counted as staying in touch, anyway.

Tyler broke eye contact and stared at something on Chris's desk. "I stopped coming to see you. We practically stopped talking." In a low, bitter tone, he muttered, "Would've been more than that if my ex had had her way."

Instantly, my hackles went up. I knew about Gina's nonsense, but it still made my teeth grind. "Ty. Look at me."

He did, eyebrows drawn together and forehead creased.

"Stop beating yourself up, okay?" I said. "And yeah, I know it's surreal to be back in each other's lives, but tell me you know me better than that. Like you don't actually think I'd leave you up Shit Creek."

"I do know you better than that." His shoulders sank, and the dealership chair creaked under him as he squirmed. "I just thought I blew it, you know? I wouldn't have held it against you if you hadn't reached out." He paused, and his voice was a little thick as he added, "I'm just really grateful you did."

I held his gaze and smiled. He smiled back. Then I ran my thumb alongside his hand and—

Wait.

I dropped my gaze to where my hand rested on top of his on his leg. When the fuck had I taken his hand?

My head snapped up, and I almost jerked my hand away, but Tyler was still smiling at me, and *he* wasn't pulling *his* hand away.

Of course he wasn't. Casual contact like this had been easy for us back in the day. Apparently it was still easy now—I just needed to get used to it again.

The sharp snap of dress shoes on linoleum broke the spell, and we both turned—and I casually withdrew my hand—as Chris strode toward us. From the way his eyes flicked toward our laps, he'd noticed, but he didn't say anything about it. Instead, he held up another form. "You're approved!"

Tyler exhaled. "Oh thank God."

"Honey." I elbowed him and said in a stage whisper, "I told you not to call me that in public."

He laughed, and there was some kind of comeback, but I didn't catch it because I was way too hypnotized by his broad smile after that fraught moment we'd just shared.

You have no idea how beautiful you are.

Chris flopped down in his chair, dramatically breaking me out of my trance because fuck him. "And you got a *much* lower interest rate than finance or I expected."

I glared at him, as much for pulling my attention from Tyler's laughter as the implication that my credit deserved anything but the best interest rate available. "You sound surprised."

"Well, I..." He met my eyes, and when he blushed, he wasn't nearly as adorable as Tyler. Coughing into his fist, he started shuffling papers around. "Most people end up a little higher than that, so it's... it was... Anyway. We just need to finalize a few things, and you'll be on your way."

Good. Fewer opportunities for you to put your foot in your damn mouth.

I glanced at Tyler, and my heart sank a little. He was serious again. Sobered, focused, and not touching me. Or letting me touch him.

How do I make that happen again?

I banished that thought, though. I knew from experience I was only torturing myself if I read too much into our casual, platonic touches. Or the way he looked at me. Or those offhand comments that made me wonder just how often—and how intently—he looked at me. Or if I encouraged those moments and touches and comments to happen more often.

But damn if torturing myself like that wasn't tempting as hell right about now.

CHAPTER 7

TYLER

I was seventeen the day I bought my first car. I'd spent the last year constantly begging my mom to let me take her car so I could go out with friends or drive myself to school instead of taking the bus. Suddenly, I'd been the proud owner of the clunkiest, ugliest piece-of-shit Nissan monstrosity that had over a hundred thousand miles, a few million dents, and made suspicious noises, and I'd been *free*. Any time I'd wanted to—assuming I could put a couple gallons of gas in the tank—I could go anywhere. It was easily one of the best days of my youth.

And somehow, that had nothing on today. Standing there in the parking lot of a car dealership with the keys to a well-used Toyota Camry in my hand, I found myself getting weirdly emotional. Why was this so damn overwhelming?

Beside me, Justin softly asked, "You okay?"

"Yeah. Just, uh..." I coughed, then turned to him and smiled. "A lot more liberating than I expected."

Justin smiled and put a hand on my shoulder. "Of course it is. You can get around now. And you're a step closer to getting your life back together."

I blinked. How the fuck could he read my mind better than I could?

Because he's always been able to do that.

Facing the car again, I nodded. "That's about the size of it, yeah. Maybe there's hope for me yet, right?"

"Of course there is." He gave my shoulder a squeeze before withdrawing his hand, leaving a cool spot behind. "I never had any doubt."

"That makes one of us." *Put your hand back.*

"Come on, hon. You've been dealt some shitty cards recently, but none of it's the end of the world. You've got a job. You've got a car." He paused, and there was a wicked smirk in his voice as he said, "All we need to do now is get you laid."

I groaned. "Yeah, we'll see about that."

Justin cocked his head. "You don't sound very optimistic."

"Yeah, well." I shrugged, spinning my new key ring on my finger. "I've been out of the game for a while, you know?"

"Eh." He looked me up and down, not even trying to be subtle. When he met my eyes again, he winked and patted my arm. "I don't think you'll have any trouble, hon."

I felt myself blushing, and laughed. "So I've got the Justin Tucker Seal of Approval. Hear that, ladies?"

He snorted. "Okay, seriously. As long as you don't do something dumb like sending dick pics before the third date, you'll be fine."

"Wait, so it's okay to send dick pics after the third date?"

"Don't know." Justin shrugged. "I just figure if you play your cards right, she won't need to see pictures of it by the third date, if you know what I mean."

I chuckled. "And here I didn't think you were the type to wait until the third date to get into bed."

"I'm not," he said with mock indignance. "I'm talking about you, not me, darling. If I haven't gone hands-on with his junk by the end of the first night, he's not getting my number."

Someone coughed, and we both turned to see a middle-aged

couple and a balding salesman, all three of whom were staring at us with a mix of bemusement and horror.

Clearing our throats, we turned away again, and both struggled to contain our laughter.

"Okay, okay." He glanced at his phone. "I really need to get my happy ass back to work."

"Right. I don't want you getting back late." I paused. "Thanks again. You're a lifesaver as always."

Justin smiled, all traces of his mischievousness replaced by warm sincerity. "You're welcome, sweetheart." He pulled me into a hug. "Enjoy the new ride."

I held on for a second. When had I started actually liking being hugged?

Oh. Right. When it was Justin. *No one* disliked a Justin hug, and I'd missed this almost as much as I'd missed him.

As he let me go, he said, "See you tonight?"

"Yeah. See you tonight."

"So." Justin smiled as I came up the stairs to the kitchen a few days later. "How was your first day?"

I blew out a breath and loosened my tie. "Good. It was good. Boss seems pretty chill, and the rest of the staff is nice so far."

His smile broadened. "Excellent. Seems like it'll work out, then?"

"Well, it's a little early to tell, but so far so good. No complaints."

"Awesome. You hungry?"

"Oh my God, yeah." I took off my jacket and draped it over a chair. "You?"

"Starving, but I don't feel like cooking or going out. It's not too far below your refined palate, I was thinking maybe we could order a pizza and park in front of a movie."

Pizza. A movie. Being lazy. Oh fuck yeah.

"That actually sounds really good." I paused. "You mind if I change clothes first?"

"Of course not." He shooed me out of the kitchen with a wave of his hand. "I'll go ahead and order. You still do pepperoni and pineapple?"

That gave me pause. "You still remember what I put on my pizza?"

Justin snorted. "Honey, a man doesn't forget when his friend insists on eating something that gross. Don't flatter yourself—I'm just traumatized."

"Traumatized by pizza toppings. Okay, Justin." I laughed as I headed down the hall, and threw over my shoulder, "We won't talk about what you put on your burgers."

"Shut up."

Still chuckling, I went into my bedroom and shut the door. For a moment, I just stood there, letting the day's fatigue wash over me. It had been a long day, even if it had been relatively easy. I was still learning my way around the office, and they hadn't sent me out on any appraisal calls yet. That would start next week. Still, I was drained from meeting an entire building full of new people, being briefed on protocols, and trying to ignore that ever-present certainty I was going to screw up and get fired. I'd had that at every job since my first under-the-table part-time job in a shipping department when I was fifteen. I'd thought it would go away, but apparently not.

Then again, I *had* been fired fairly recently, so it was probably a reasonable thing to be worried about.

I rubbed my eyes with the heels of my hands and took a few slow breaths. Everything would be fine. I still had to learn the ins and outs of this particular company, but I knew appraisals. I knew my job. As long as I did it properly—which I always did—I'd be fine. Well, as long as my company didn't get involved in shady shit with a housing lender or throw me under the bus for doing my job...

I shuddered. No point in thinking about that. I had a job. I had no reason to believe this one would take a nosedive like the last one. And for God's sake, I was home for the evening. It was time to relax. Pizza and a movie with my best friend were waiting at the other end of the hall, so why was I standing here in my work clothes, wallowing in worries about things I couldn't control?

With that, I pushed myself off the door and started unbuttoning my shirt while I toed off my dress shoes. I changed into a pair of sweats and a faded Seattle Mariners sweatshirt, and that alone was enough to kill some of the day's tension. Work was a distant memory. I had nothing to do tonight except be comfortable and chill.

Feeling a hell of a lot better than I had when I'd gotten home, I headed out to the living room to join Justin for a night of sloth and gluttony.

I opened my eyes, and panic knifed through the heavy fatigue. Where the hell was I? What time was it? Had I overslept? Oh God was I late for my *second* day at the new job?

It only took a second to orient myself, though. The room was dark besides the Netflix menu screen glowing on the TV and gently illuminating the pizza boxes still spread out on the coffee table.

Justin's downstairs rec room. On the sofa.

And Justin was...

I turned my head.

He'd fallen asleep too—leaning against me. His head rested on my chest and at some point, I'd wrapped my arm around his shoulders and he'd draped his across my stomach. We weren't on opposite ends of the couch anymore, either. Somehow, we'd wound up in the middle.

For a moment, I just stared at him and tried to make sense of how we'd gotten here. Should this have been weird, having another dude sleeping against me like this? Maybe. Probably? Hell, I didn't know. All I knew was that I liked how he felt against me. Which must have meant I was more desperate than I'd realized for some human contact. Justin had always been on the touchy-feely side, but we'd never... *cuddled.*

Some of the guys I used to work with—not exactly people I'd call friends—would have been on the other side of the room by now, probably losing their ever-loving minds. Then again, they never would have allowed themselves to be on the same piece of furniture as an openly gay man.

I'd never had an issue with Justin being gay, and it didn't even seem all that relevant. This wasn't anything sexual. And the more I sat here enjoying the warmth of another human being for the first time in ages, the more I liked it. Like... a lot. In fact, I must have been seriously starved for human contact because having someone pressed up next to me—having a *man* pressed up next to me—was making me hard. I tried not to fidget as my erection made sitting like this uncomfortable. There was no way to adjust myself without disturbing him, and I decided I could deal with the discomfort more.

After a moment, though, Justin twitched a little. Then he stiffened. Slowly, he lifted his head, and when our eyes met, he jerked back. "Oh shit!" He scrambled away, putting up his hands. "I'm sorry. I am so... oh my God, Tyler, I—"

"Hey. Easy." I patted the air, almost breathless from the sudden coolness where his body had pressed against mine. "It's okay."

He looked in my eyes, his filled with palpable panic. The light was too dim to tell for sure, but I would have bet money he'd lost a few shades of color. "I..."

"Relax. I'm serious—it's okay."

He held my gaze, still rigid with panic.

"I mean it. I..." I could feel myself blushing, especially as I tried to surreptitiously shift to accommodate this hard-on. "Kind of liked it, actually."

That brought his freak-out down a few notches. "Really?"

"Yeah." I half-shrugged. "It's, um, kind of nice to be touched, I guess." *Really nice. Please come back.*

Some more tension melted out of his posture, and the embarrassment and panic in his expression shifted to concern. "How long has it been?"

"Too long." Two words, and my shoulders suddenly felt heavy. That conversation had way too much potential to get depressing as hell. "Anyway, just... don't worry about..." I gestured at him, then myself. "It's not a big deal."

He studied me uncertainly. "Are you sure? A lot of straight guys... they don't..."

"They're assholes, okay? They're not me." *And they have no idea what they're missing.*

He held my gaze again, and after a second, a playful glint appeared in his eyes. "Are you trying to tell me you're not an asshole?"

"Why? You trying to say I am?"

He pressed his lips together, but a smirk still came to life.

I laughed and elbowed him. "Jackass."

He chuckled too, and paused to stretch. "Well, I should probably call it a night. I've got a stupid meeting first thing in the morning." He stuck out his tongue and wrinkled his nose. "Boss might get pissy if I fall asleep in the middle of it."

"Bosses are such dicks like that."

"I know, right?" With a groan, he stood. "What about you?"

I checked the time on my phone. "Yeah, I should get some sleep too." I stood, and for a second, we held each other's gazes. It was almost like we needed to say something more about how we'd found ourselves a minute ago. I didn't know what to say, though, and he didn't offer anything, so in silence, we headed upstairs and down the hall to our respective bedrooms.

He paused in his bedroom doorway. "Good night, Tyler."

"Good night."

We exchanged tired smiles. Then his door closed behind him. I closed mine behind me.

As I flicked on the light, Azrael lifted her head and glared at me, one eye still closed and the other full of contempt.

"Sorry." I scratched behind her ears, which earned me a swat and an even more offended look. "Hey! That's my bed, you know."

The other eye opened. *Bitch, this is my dad's bed and we both know it. Fuck off.*

I laughed, and opened the door a crack in case she wanted to leave. Hopefully that would please Her Highness.

As I started getting undressed, I chuckled. Trust Justin to have a cat with as much attitude as him, if less filtered. Somehow I didn't foresee Azrael sneaking up to cuddle against me during the night.

I stopped, belt partially unbuckled, and stared at one of the two doors separating us from each other. I'd never imagined Justin cuddling up with me like that either. Or me moving toward him for the same. Who had initiated it, anyway? Had either of us been awake for it, and my brain was just too fuzzy to recall the details?

Mind still whirring, I continued getting undressed. Justin had always been extra careful with his straight friends. Whether he knew how we felt about gay dudes or not, he wasn't naïve. A guy could insist till he was blue in the face that he was fine with his friends being gay, but a split second of unintentional contact would bring out his true colors in a big hurry. So I didn't see Justin throwing caution to the wind with a straight guy. Not even me.

And now that I thought about it, as much as I was itching for someone—or even for Justin's crabby-ass cat—to curl up with me tonight, it was entirely possible I'd been the one to make the first move. Consciously or unconsciously, I might have been the one to reach out to him.

I swallowed hard as I tossed my clothes in the hamper. Apparently I was hungrier for human contact than I'd realized. Maybe Justin was right and I really did need to go out and get laid.

Except tonight hadn't been about sex. God knew what had happened and how we'd ended up arranging ourselves the way we had, but it hadn't been sexual at all. Okay, so my body might have thought otherwise, but that probably had more than anything to do with the fact that I hadn't touched anyone—sexually or otherwise—in ages.

Whatever it was, now I was seriously craving affection. I wasn't sure how to suggest deliberately doing what we'd accidentally done tonight, so cuddling on the couch with Justin was probably out of the question. Putting myself out there in the dating pool, though? I could do that. Maybe. Or a hookup? Casual sex with a stranger didn't sound appealing, but it did sound better than sleeping alone.

And yet, somehow not nearly as appealing as waking up with Justin leaning against me.

What the fuck was I supposed to make of that?

CHAPTER 8

JUSTIN

For the first time since he'd moved in, I dreaded seeing Tyler in the morning. He'd been cool with things last night, but how would he feel now that he'd had a chance to sleep on it?

I could always leave early for work. Get there in time to catch up on emails before the meeting. Then I—

Quiet footsteps came down the hall. Shit. So much for ducking out like the coward I absolutely was this morning.

Azrael trotted in a few steps ahead of Tyler, and bumped against my leg hard enough to almost buckle my knee.

"Hey." I wagged a finger at her. "You make Daddy spill his coffee, we're going to fight."

She sat down and glared up at me, long black tail twitching behind her on the linoleum.

I put my coffee cup aside, crouched, and scooped her up. "Listen here, Little Miss Attitude Problem."

Tyler took a mug down from the cupboard. "She's a cranky little shit, isn't she?"

"Who, Azrael?" I hugged her tighter, and she planted her paws against my chest, shoving back and staring at me in abject horror. "What makes you say that?"

"Besides the fact that I think she's trying to kill you with her mind?"

"Yeah, well..." I balanced her on my hip like a toddler and, with my free hand, pulled the can of treats down from above the fridge. As soon as it rattled, Azrael perked up. Instead of trying to push me away, she started kneading on my shoulder and purring.

Tyler laughed. "Ah, so bribing her is the secret."

"Uh, yeah?" I popped the lid with my thumb. "You want the love of a little black heart like hers, you *buy* that shit."

"Like cat, like owner?"

"Hey!" I scoffed as I dug a few treats out. "I resemble that remark."

"Uh-huh. That's what I thought."

I gave Azrael a couple of treats, kissed the top of her head just to see that look like I'd offended all her ancestors, and then set her down. She huffed audibly before strutting out of the kitchen, probably to the laundry room for her breakfast.

"She really knows how to keep you in line, doesn't she?" Tyler said into his coffee cup.

"Yeah, she does." My humor quickly faded. Without my cat to hold the spotlight, last night was front and center in my mind. My skin prickled and my stomach twisted; when had being in such close proximity to Tyler ever made me this twitchy?

Okay, this wasn't going to work. If I left for the office now, I'd be worried all day and wouldn't be able to concentrate or even sit still until tonight. Might as well do it now and be done with it.

"So, um." I pressed my palms onto the counter. "Just to clear the air—we're cool after last night, right?"

Tyler blinked in surprise. "Of course we are."

I raised an eyebrow.

He raised one too. "What?"

Drumming my fingers, I shifted my weight. "I don't have too many straight friends who'd be okay with me going full spider monkey on them while they were asleep on my couch."

"To be fair, unless you physically dragged me to the middle of the couch, I did my part."

I straightened. "Physically... what?"

Tyler smiled sleepily. "When I first sat down, I was at the opposite end from you. When we woke up, we were both in the middle."

The memory of waking up in his arms played through my mind, and I realized he was right. In fact, I distinctly remembered coming back from the kitchen with drink refills and sitting closer to the middle. Then later, after he'd gotten up to use the bathroom, he'd come back and taken the cushion beside me instead of the one on the end. Not quite touching me, but not exactly avoiding me either. I wasn't sure he'd even realized what he was doing. I was always hyperaware of my proximity to someone straight, so I'd been absolutely zeroed in on how close we were.

Until I'd fallen asleep, anyway.

I swallowed. "So, you know I wasn't trying to cop a feel or something."

"Of course I know that. And to be honest..." He gnawed his lower lip and stared at the linoleum between us. "I didn't mind it. At all. I meant what I said about liking it."

"You did?"

"Yeah." He took a breath and met my gaze again. "I'm serious about how long it's been since anyone's touched me. It was... I guess it was just nice to know someone wanted to."

My jaw fell open. "What?"

Tyler sighed, leaning hard against the counter and half-shrugging. "It's only been a few weeks since Gina and I signed the papers, but believe me when I say our marriage has been over for a *long* time."

I wet my suddenly dry lips, but had no idea what to say.

"I mean, we still fucked sometimes, but even that was more..." His eyes lost focus. "I guess it was more like scratching an itch. Or something to do besides fight. But all the affectionate stuff? A kiss goodnight or cuddling after sex?" Gaze still distant, he shook his head. "All that dried up so long ago, I couldn't even tell you how long it's been."

"Jesus, Tyler," I whispered.

"It is what it is." His shoulder lifted in another half-shrug, though this one seemed to take some work. "And it was on both of us. We both stopped putting in the effort, and..." He rolled his hand as if to say *do the math.*

"Still. I can't imagine living with someone and never—" My teeth snapped shut when he met my eyes. I quickly added, "Living with a partner, I mean."

He smiled. "I know what you meant. And it sucked, believe me. That's something I don't ever want to have again when I do find someone else." He turned serious, and looked right in my eyes. "So yeah, last night wasn't something I expected, but I'm really glad it happened."

My heart wanted to literally break at the twin realization of how touch-starved he was and that my touch was just a stopgap until the right woman came along. Maybe that second part made me selfish, but emotions were what they were, and being in love with a man like Tyler could really fucking hurt sometimes.

I cleared my throat and managed an uncomfortable laugh. "And here I thought it would make things weird between us."

Tyler smiled, stepping a little closer and putting a hand on my arm. "Come on. You know me better than that."

Pretending not to notice all the sparks that gentle touch sent all the way down to my toes, I said, "Yeah, I do. And if something happens again, I promise I won't post on Facebook about our manly cuddle nights."

He laughed, and I couldn't help laughing too. My heart still ached for him and for that stupid torch I was still carrying, but it was hard not to smile when he did. Especially when he stepped even closer, wrapped his arms around me, and hugged me tight.

"Thanks for everything," he whispered.

"Any time, hon." I shut my eyes and held on for a moment. At the end of the day, last night had been good for him, and it had been good for me too. A bit like torture, but still. That—and this—was as close as I'd ever get to him, so I wasn't going to complain.

At least he wasn't out of my life anymore.

"Hey, did you get an email from Annika Davies?"

I looked up from grating cheese for a salad. "Annika Davies? As in, Annika Davies from high school?"

"Yeah." Tyler glanced over from the stove, where he was sautéing some chicken. "I got an email from her this afternoon. I guess she's coordinating our class reunion."

"Our class—" I did a double take. "Lord, please tell me it is *not* time for our twenty-year already. We just graduated, like, last week."

"Afraid so." He nudged the sizzling chicken around the pan. "Looks like they're renting out a hotel ballroom."

I snorted as I took out my phone. "Classy. Well, let's see if I made the list." I opened my email browser, and sure enough, Annika had sent me an email too.

It's that time already!!!! I could practically hear her chirping through the Comic Sans and exclamation points. *It's been 20 years, and we want you to come join us for a night of nostalgia and catching up with friends!!!*

"Catching up with friends, huh?" I quirked my lips. "Because we're such good friends that we stayed in touch for the last twenty years."

"Like we did?"

I lifted my gaze, not quite sure how to respond to that.

Tyler sighed, and continued chasing pieces of chicken around the frying pan. "I mean, sometimes people lose touch, you know? And we graduated before social media was a thing, so losing touch was easy." He paused, shoulders dipping slightly. "Imagine how hard it would have been for us to stay in contact at all if it hadn't been for Facebook."

"Good point. But I actually wanted to stay in touch with you. There weren't a lot of people in high school who needed to stick around, you know?"

"Fair enough."

I watched him for a moment. "You planning on going?"

Tyler shrugged. He took the frying pan off the heat and started guiding the pieces of chicken onto a plate. "I think I will. I can't think of anyone I want to reconnect with in the long term, but there are a few people I wouldn't mind catching up with for an evening."

"Hmm. Yeah, I can see that. And I can think of a few people it would be nice to see for a few minutes."

He glanced at me. "So you'll go?"

"Maybe." Beat. "Probably. But you're driving so I can drink."

Tyler laughed. "Deal."

We continued making dinner, which consisted of me throwing together a salad and opening a bottle of wine while he did everything else. He made chicken with some sort of sauce that smelled amazing, a side dish that was like turkey stuffing but somehow different, and fresh green beans cooked so they still crunched instead of going limp. And he made it all from scratch, too, and cleaned the kitchen as he went so it was spotless by the time we sat down to eat. Fucking showoff.

While we ate, we mused a bit more about the people we might see at our reunion, and the more I thought about it, the more I warmed up to the idea of going. Especially if I had Tyler with me. My high school years had been rough at times—being an out gay kid in the late nineties was not for the faint of heart—but there'd been good times too. There'd been classmates who were friendly even if we'd never become friends. Like the girl who'd sat next to me in history our senior year. I'd have to go dig up a yearbook to remember her name, but we'd always gotten along. We'd run in different circles and had different interests, but for fifty-five minutes every day, we were buddies. I hoped she came to the reunion.

Halfway through dinner, my phone buzzed. "Oh God," I muttered, putting my fork down. "If this is work, I will blow my fucking stack."

"No rest for the weary, eh?"

"Not at that place, no." I checked the screen. And instantly, my mood soured. Fuck. This? Now? *Really?*

"Work?" Tyler asked.

"Nope." I sighed. "My fucking *ex.*"

Tyler straightened, alarm widening his eyes. "What about him?"

"He's finally coming by to pick up some of his crap." I slammed the phone facedown on the table. "About damn time, but ugh, I do not want to see him."

"When is he coming by?"

"Tomorrow night." I picked at my chicken, furious that my ex-boyfriend's mere existence was screwing with my ability to enjoy this amazing food. "He'll be by around six." I paused, then peeked at Tyler. "I'm sorry. I'd tell him to come back when you're not here, but he's threatened me with a lawyer if I—"

"Like hell he's coming when I'm not here," Tyler growled with startling fury. "If he's enough of an asshole to be threatening you, and to make you that pissed off just by texting you, I think it's better if I'm here."

Ah, I'd forgotten about his snarly protective side. "Eh, he's harmless." I speared a piece of chicken. "Just loud and obnoxious."

Tyler frowned.

"I mean it. He's an asshole, but I'm not scared of him or anything."

"Still." He picked up his wineglass. "I think I'd rather be here just in case he decides to get cute."

The familiar protectiveness sent warmth rushing through me. "You sure?"

He met my eyes, and his expression was a mixture of sweet and fierce. Oh, it had been a long time since I'd seen Mama Bear Tyler. The last time had probably been senior year when I'd been trying really, really, *really* hard not to turn into a sobbing mess over that asshole Chad Wickham dumping me on Valentine's Day.

"I *will break him in half,*" Tyler had seethed. "*Where is that fucker?*"

Tonight, his voice was much calmer if still *faintly* menacing as he said, "I'll be here."

Fridays were supposed to be relaxing. The weekend was here, for God's sake!

But no, I had to spend the whole day with indigestion over the thought of facing my ex. By the time I got home, my hands were achy from gripping the wheel and trying to calm my nerves.

"Hey." Tyler watched me from the kitchen doorway as I shakily filled a glass of water. "You all right?"

"I will be once he's been here and gone." I took a deep swallow, wishing someone had magically replaced the water in the pipes with gin or something. No such luck.

"Listen," he said, his voice gentle. "I have no idea how this is gonna go down because I don't know much about this guy. But you're obviously nervous."

I set the glass on the counter, the double clink giving away the unsteadiness of my hand. "I told you—he's not dangerous. I just... don't like being around him anymore."

"I know." Tyler came closer and put a hand on my shoulder. "And I promise, I'll stay back, but if you want me to step in or if you want me to call the cops, just say so. I won't do anything unless you ask me to, but I'll help any way I can if you do."

I smiled for the first time in hours. "You're the best, you know that?"

He smiled too, giving my shoulder a squeeze. "I just want to make sure you're okay."

I think I will be as long as you're here.

But I just said, "Thanks."

"Any time."

The sound of a car pulling up nauseated me. I closed my eyes and steeled myself. "Well, here we go." I started for the door, but Tyler stopped me with a hand on my elbow.

"I'm serious," he said softly. "Say the word, and I'll step in."

I nodded and repeated, "Thanks."

He let me go, and I went downstairs and out onto the porch as David was getting out of his car.

"Hey," David said with a huge smile. "It's good to—" He froze, eyes flicking past me, and the smarmy smile vanished. I didn't have to glance back to see if Tyler had joined me on the porch, but I did, and damn—if looks could kill, Tyler would've dropped David where he stood.

"Easy," I whispered.

Tyler put up his hands and said nothing.

"Can we just do this?" David slammed his car door, all traces of his over-the-top cheerfulness gone in an instant. "Where's all my shit?"

Without speaking, I came down the steps and entered the code for the garage door. Everyone exchanged icy glares while the door took its sweet time opening, and once it was high enough for me to duck under and go inside, I did. "It's all right here." I gestured at the stack of plastic totes. "Right where you left it."

He stomped up and grabbed the handles on one, but didn't pick it up. "You got a new man already?"

I set my jaw. "Already, hell. And not that it's any of your business, but he's just a friend."

David glared at Tyler, who was off to the side just outside the open door. My ex gave a grunt of annoyance, then picked up the tote and started toward his car again.

As he passed Tyler, he said, "You got a problem?"

"Nothing that won't be solved by you getting the fuck out of here," Tyler said coolly.

They exchanged a long, venomous glare before David continued toward his car.

Tyler turned to me, and a faint smile played at his lips. He shrugged apologetically as if to say *What? He started it.*

Rolling my eyes, I pressed my lips together to stifle a laugh. Tyler had promised to keep his mouth shut, but David had initiated the conversation and, well, I didn't disagree with anything Tyler had said.

It was kind of surprising how quickly the two of them had started hating each other. Well, not David. He didn't like *any* man speaking to me. But prior to about two minutes ago, Tyler hadn't even *met* David. My entire relationship with the dickwad had come and gone in the five years since Tyler. I didn't think I'd said much about him, but maybe I had. Or maybe he'd just caught on to me being twitchy as fuck after David had texted me. I didn't do subtle very well when it came to assholes like him.

And as it turned out, for as much as I'd worked myself into a frenzy over David coming by, the encounter wasn't so bad. Aside from some nasty looks and muttered comments, nothing really happened. He collected all his shit, put it in his car, and left.

And... that was it.

He was gone.

Completely exorcised from my house, out of my life, and *gone.*

"Well that was anticlimactic." Standing there in the empty driveway, I raked my hand through my hair. "Now I feel kind of stupid for making such a big deal out of this."

"No, don't." Tyler stood beside me, leaning against the garage as his hackles went down. "You should see me whenever I have to deal with Gina. I get it."

I searched his eyes as if I actually thought I'd find anything but total sincerity. Of course I didn't. Tyler wasn't like that. "Still." I sagged against my car. "The way I spun myself up, you'd think he was going to come over here and..." I didn't finish the thought. My stomach was still too queasy for that. "I need a fucking drink."

"If you want to go out for a few drinks, I'll drive."

I turned to Tyler. "Hmm?"

"I've got a car now. Why don't I drive, and you can cut loose for an evening?"

God, he was sweet. "I would so take you up on that except I was thinking of going downtown to meet up with some friends at Celebz. It's, um—"

"A gay bar?"

I nodded.

Tyler shrugged. "I don't mind a place like that." He put up a hand. "But I mean, if you've got plans with friends, I totally understand if—"

"It's not that," I said quickly. "I'd... I mean, I'd really love to bring you along." *I don't want to be away from you. Ever.* "And introduce you to everyone. Just... it's a queer bar and all my friends are queer. That might not be your scene." *Please come anyway.*

He laughed dryly. "You make it sound like I even know what my scene *is* these days."

Presumably not a gay bar, sweetheart.

On the other hand, the place where I usually met my friends was more like a karaoke bar that happened to be frequented by queer people. It wasn't a meat market like Wilde's up the street—just a place for people to chill with a few drinks, some awful singing, and their friends without getting the stinkeye from the straight folks. I could think of a lot of people who wouldn't be able to handle a place like that—God forbid they be confronted with queer people in the wild—but Tyler? Yeah, he'd probably do all right.

"If you really think you'll be comfortable," I said, "you're more than welcome to join us."

He searched my eyes. "What about you? Do you mind me tagging along?"

I smiled as if I hadn't been mentally begging him to be glued to my side for the night. "Not at all. In fact, let's get an Uber so you can have a couple of beers too. I think you deserve it after putting up with my ex."

"He wasn't so bad." Tyler paused. "Not for me, anyway."

"Still." I gestured at the house. "Let's go get dressed and I'll get an Uber on the way."

"You're sure you're comfortable with this, right?" I asked Tyler as the Uber stopped in front of Celebz.

"Of course." He shrugged. "Why wouldn't I be?"

"Because... I mean, this is..."

"Justin. Come on." He rolled his eyes as he opened the car door. "Are you really asking me if I'm comfortable going into a gay bar?"

"Well..." I chewed my lip. "Kinda, yeah."

He shot me a look. Then we got out of the car, and after I'd tipped the driver on the Uber app, Tyler added, "If I wasn't comfortable, we wouldn't be here."

I held his gaze.

Tyler smiled. "Chill. You know me."

"Yeah, I do. But have you ever *been* to a place like this?"

"You mean besides the time we drove up to Canada so you could drink on your nineteenth birthday, and we went to a drag show? A drag show that, if memory serves, was at a gay bar?"

I pursed my lips. "Okay. Fair point." And now I kind of felt stupid for bringing it up. I hadn't known a lot of straight guys who'd voluntarily join me at a place like this, but Tyler had a point. We'd gone to that club in Vancouver, laughed ourselves senseless during the hysterically funny drag show, and then basically made friends with everyone in a twenty-foot radius. I couldn't imagine Tyler suddenly deciding he wasn't into that.

So, I led him inside and searched the room for my friends. They weren't hard to find—my group nearly always claimed the same booth. It was far enough from the speakers to allow conversation, close enough to the bar we didn't have to walk thirty miles for a drink, with a perfect view of the dancefloor if anyone was on the prowl or just wanted to enjoy the scenery, and with an equally awesome view of the stage for karaoke nights like tonight. Someone always showed up early to commandeer it, and it was rare for us to wind up at another booth. Or "in the slums" as Charley always said.

The music was loud enough that we had to raise our voices a little, but this wasn't one of those places where you had to shout or resort to texting just to have a conversation. Perfect place to hang out as far as I was concerned, and exactly where I needed to be. I'd barely stepped in through the front door before the tension from my encounter with David started melting away.

My friends waved from across the room, and I nodded in acknowledgment. The group was comprised of some friends I'd met in chat rooms about ten years ago, and the various other people we'd all brought in over time. Some had introduced their friends and partners to the group. Occasionally we picked up a stray wallflower looking lonely at a club, or befriended someone who was getting creeped on. People came and went, and when we met up, there was usually about a dozen of us, give or take one or two.

After Tyler and I had snagged a couple of drinks, we joined the group, and I introduced Tyler around. There were enough people here tonight that we'd overflowed from the booth, so some were clustered around tables, some were near the bar, and the rest were at our usual booth and the one next to it. I wandered from group to group, and Tyler stuck close, sitting or standing beside me pretty much constantly. That had nothing to do with being a straight man among queers, though, and everything to do with Tyler. Once he'd warmed up to people, he was outgoing and confident—the kind of guy who could make friends with anyone—but sometimes he had a shy streak, especially if he was the new guy in a group of people who knew each other. In a situation like that, he'd stick with anyone he did know until he was comfortable mingling on his own.

In fact, within an hour, we'd drifted away from each other. He was lost in conversation with Van, who was raving about her girlfriend's band and trying to get him to come to their next show. I ended up back at the booth having a heated debate with Les and Jackson about where we thought the writers were taking a particular show we were all hooked on. Then Jackson's partner showed up, and they disappeared to the bar for another round while Les and I continued talking about work and random shit like that. After our conversation had wound to an end, he left to chase down Zach, who'd just arrived with his other boyfriend.

Tyler appeared beside me and held up his empty glass. "I'm going to get a refill. You want one?"

"Thanks, sweetheart." I reached for my wallet. "How much do—?"

"I got this one." He waved me away. "You bought the last round."

I shrugged. "Fair enough."

He turned to head to the bar, and just for the hell of it, I watched him go. Mm-*mm*, the things I would do that man if I ever had half a chance. I didn't bother tamping down the thought. I was pretty much used to my brain tormenting me like that when Tyler was in the room. Especially when he'd worn jeans that held onto that perfect ass like—

I jumped as Sidney sidled up next to me and nodded toward Tyler. "You didn't tell me you had a new man."

"I don't."

They arched an eyebrow. "Could've fooled me."

I scowled. "I wish, believe me. He's my roommate."

"But..." They glanced at him, then back at me, the beads on their braids rattling with the sharp motions. "How...?"

"That man"—I pointed emphatically at Tyler—"is straight."

Sidney snorted and shook their head. "Bullshit."

"Trust me. I'd have snagged him twenty-five years ago if he had a single queer bone in his body, but..." I sighed. "Nope."

My friend watched Tyler for a long moment. Then they shook their head again, beads clattering even more emphatically this time. "I don't buy it, hon."

I shot them a look. I really wasn't in the mood to get my hopes up about the man I couldn't have, especially a couple of hours after he'd been poised and ready to play knight in shining armor if my ex had gotten out of line.

Sidney smirked. "Okay. Let's say hypothetically that you're right, completely ignoring the fact that he is a straight cisdude who's completely comfortable in a queer club full of queer people with his queer roommate."

I glared at them, and wanted to protest that we'd had other straight guys tag along with our group before. But I didn't because... well, because guys like that were pretty fucking rare. And usually came with us because they were attached to one of the girls in the group. And they usually clung to those girls for dear life as if all the scary queer people might pounce on them the instant they weren't making blatantly heterosexual contact with women. And they were usually guarded as hell if a remotely flamboyant man so much as peeked in their direction because apparently being this fabulous was contagious.

Tyler wasn't like that at all. He chatted with anyone. If someone was particularly handsy and casually touched him, he didn't recoil. When someone approached him for a dance, he bowed out politely and didn't act like the proposition had offended him. None of that surprised me because I'd always known Tyler was different from the majority of straight men I knew, but bringing him here made those differences stand out.

I cleared my throat and shifted in my seat. "Okay, ignoring all of that... go on?"

Sidney glanced at Tyler, then back at me, and as they met my eyes, they wagged a finger in Tyler's direction. "If he's so straight," they said in a conspiratorial whisper, "then why have I seen those pretty blue eyes following at least three male asses across the room?"

I fixed my gaze on Tyler, who was talking animatedly with a guy in a purple Mohawk while he waited for our drinks.

And I had no idea how to answer Sidney's question.

CHAPTER 9

TYLER

The club was great, and within about ten minutes, I'd decided I loved Justin's friends. It usually took me a while to warm up to new people —I'd always been that way—but this group was fun and relaxed. It was impossible not to get into the groove of bantering and chatting. A couple of drinks had me feeling damn good too; I was really glad Justin had suggested taking an Uber instead of one of us driving.

As I sat at the booth next to Justin while Zach told us a wild—and probably somewhat exaggerated—story about a road rage incident from earlier in the week, my phone vibrated in my pocket. Who the fuck was calling me this late on a Saturday night? I took it out, read the screen, and groaned. "Aw, fuck my life." Apparently Justin wasn't the only one whose ex could drop the buzzkill hammer at the most inconvenient times.

"What's wrong?" Justin slung an arm around me, leaning in so close his warm cheek brushed mine, and peered at my phone. I could tell the instant he recognized my ex-wife's photo by the way he tensed all over, as if his irritation with her had effortlessly eliminated all the alcohol in his system. "What the hell does she want?"

"No idea, but I better take this." I gestured at the door. "I'll be back in a minute."

Justin frowned. I suspected it would've been a barely noticeable shift in his expression had he been sober, but alcohol did tend to make him a bit less subtle. "Dude, don't let her kill your buzz."

"I won't." I flashed what I hoped was a reassuring smile. "She probably just needs to touch base about the divorce."

Justin didn't look convinced. The frown deepened. One eyebrow arched.

"Relax," I said. "If I'm not back in fifteen minutes, come and drag me back in."

His lips quirked. "Ten. Because they'll be calling me up to do karaoke soon, and you'd better be here."

"Deal." I touched my forehead in a mock salute, then made my way through the crowd and out into the parking lot. Of course by then her call had ended, but I speed-dialed her back. "Hey," I said when she picked up. "Sorry about that. What's up?"

"Driving?" she asked as if she cared.

"No, I'm..." *Out with people you wouldn't like. Out and about, wondering if it's too early to get drunk, laid, or both. Out with the man you think I'm in love with.* I cleared my throat. "What do you need?"

"I..." She sighed.

My gut knotted. "You, um... is this about the divorce?"

"Yeah. It is." Another heavy sigh, and I squeezed my eyes shut. Oh God. I knew that tone. Three words and an exhale, and I could pretty much read her mind from here—Gina had always been the type to wear regret on her sleeve. So, I was preemptively cringing when she said, "I think I fucked up, Ty."

You think *you fucked up?*

"Uh. What do you mean?"

"I mean..." She was quiet for a long time. I swore I could feel her shoulders slumping and her gaze dropping. "The divorce isn't final. We could always put things on hold and—"

"Put them on hold?" I blinked a few times as I tried to make sense of what she was suggesting. "Like... get back together?"

"Or at least give it a try."

I barely kept a laugh from escaping. That would only piss her off and make this conversation ten times worse. "No."

"No? You're not even going to consider it?"

"Um. No. Why are you considering it?"

She sighed. "I've just been doing a lot of thinking, and I mean, we invested fourteen years in each other. Is that really something we should throw away without at least trying to fix it?"

I stared at the pavement, dumbstruck for a moment that she had the brass balls to suggest we could fix what had gone wrong in our marriage. What in the world would have brought—

Oh.

Oh.

"He left, didn't he?"

The harsh breath said it all.

I pursed my lips and rolled my eyes, but when I spoke, I kept my voice calm. "Gina, I'm sorry you're going through a tough time, but we're over. I mean, I've moved to Seattle. I have a new job. I'm starting a new life here. And, Jesus. You—" I paused, nerves almost getting the best of me. "You cheated on me."

Holy shit. Did I actually say that out loud?

"For God's sake," she snapped. "Don't act like you never—"

"I never cheated." The words came out thick with emotion. "Never, Gina."

She huffed. "Tyler, I don't want to argue about this. We both made mistakes, and we—"

"And *you.* Cheated. On *me.* And then tried to blame me." I could hear her getting ready to speak again, and put up my hand as if she could see it as I continued talking. "I'm sorry you're having a hard time, but we're done. I have to go."

I have to go.

My own words resonated through my head, as if the gravity of the sentence had been lost on me until I'd actually said it out loud.

I have to go.

Yeah, I did have to go. Not just disconnect this call, but *go.* Move on. Leave Gina, our marriage, and our life in Chicago behind. Because even if things were uncertain right now, they were better than what I'd left behind.

Then Gina released a long breath. "You're with him, aren't you?"

I almost dropped my phone. "Come again?"

"You went back to him, didn't you?"

"Back to—" My gaze landed on the club I'd walked out of, and the pieces came together. "Justin."

She sniffed with disdain. "Yeah. *Him.*"

I rolled my eyes. "You know, I doubt it matters at this point, but I never did anything with him before you or while we were married, and I'm not doing anything with him now." *Except cuddling up on the couch, something we stopped doing years ago.* That thought started to choke me up, and I had no idea why. I just knew I suddenly wanted to be back on that couch, or at the very least, back in that booth. "And while we're on the subject, if there's one thing I can't forgive you for, it's for pushing me and him apart for all these years. Letting you do that was the biggest mistake I ever made."

Another sniff, this time with extra sarcasm. "But you never touched him. Okay, Ty."

I didn't say a word.

I just ended the call.

For a moment, I stood there staring at my phone, my hand shaking and my knees starting to join in. The screen was black now. Gina's name, number, and picture had vanished, but it was like I could still see them. Like an obnoxious after-image that came from stupidly staring into the sun.

I'd told her off. I'd hung up.

Swallowing hard, I let my gaze drift back to the club.

I called her out for pushing me away from Justin.

A flurry of emotions tried to take hold. I'd never been any better at standing up to Gina than I'd been at standing up to my mom. I'd defend myself, but calling her out on her bullshit? Ending the call before she was good and ready to end it for me? That was new.

I have to go.

The phone buzzed to life and the screen lit up.

Gina calling.

Without a second thought, I tapped *ignore*, and then I turned off my phone. She'd leave a message, no doubt, and there'd probably be an email too, but... no. I was here to have a good time and to help Justin unwind after his ex's visit, not to listen to Gina try to blame me for our divorce in the same breath she asked me to take her back. Whatever fucks I'd had to give about exes, I'd already used tonight while waiting for that dickbag ex-boyfriend of Justin's to leave. I didn't have any left for my ex-wife.

I took a deep breath, stuffed the phone into my pocket, and headed back inside to where there was beer, music, people, and Justin.

I'd barely made it back to the booth before Justin appeared beside me. "Hey, hon. Everything okay?"

I nodded. "Yeah. Yeah. It's..." I forced a smile. "Just bullshit with the ex. You know how it goes."

"Ugh. Yeah." He rolled his eyes. "I so do." He looked at me, brow pinched, but before he could speak, the deejay's voice boomed through the club.

"And our next singer is Justin. Come on up, Justin!"

"Oh!" Justin thrust his drink into my hand. "Hold this."

I barely had my fingers around the half-empty glass before he was on his feet and sprinting across the dancefloor to the stage. I laughed. No one was as enthusiastic about karaoke as he was, and even with my jittery fucked-up mood, it was impossible not to smile.

He took his place onstage and nodded at the deejay. He hadn't even started yet, but people were already falling quiet and turning toward the stage. I wasn't surprised; if he was a regular here, I couldn't imagine people were unaware of his karaoke prowess.

As the intro started playing, I was admittedly a little disappointed that it wasn't *My Heart Will Go On* this time. In fact, it took a few notes for me to recognize *Amazed*. I chuckled to myself; Jesus, how many girls had I slow-danced with to that song in high school? In fact, I was pretty sure this was the song that had led to me and Amy Nguyen making out in the back of the gym at Homecoming when she was a senior and I was a sophomore, and I—

Onstage, Justin started singing.

And my mind went blank.

And my ex-wife's call faded into the past.

And I... just... stared.

His voice had always been beautiful, but time had given him more control. More resonance. Even after a couple of drinks, he hit all the notes just right, and I would have bet my entire year's salary that there wasn't a single person in this room without goose bumps. No one was making a sound. I didn't think they were even moving.

Or maybe they were. I didn't know, and I didn't care. A marching band could have gone by right then, and I wouldn't have seen or heard a thing except the man singing onstage.

Justin's friend Sidney nudged my shoulder. "Talented, isn't he?"

Mute, I nodded.

"It's good to see him getting up there and singing again," Sidney said.

I glanced at them. "What do you mean?"

Sidney shrugged. "He just hasn't done it in a while. Guess he decided to pick it back up."

I looked at Justin again, and smiled to myself. "Good. He's too talented not to."

Sidney said nothing. We watched and listened, and Justin had the entire room on their feet as he finished the song. I didn't even hear the last couple of lines over the roar of applause.

Justin handed the microphone back to the deejay, hopped down from the stage, and headed toward us. He was waylaid every few steps by people who I assumed were telling him how awesome his performance was. Still, it didn't take him long to get back to the booth and drop onto the bench beside me.

He was—unsurprisingly—out of breath, and leaned against me as he quickly downed the last of his drink in three deep swallows.

"That was awesome!" Van sat on the bench across from us, followed by Sidney and someone I hadn't met. "Not that any of us are surprised, right?"

Justin blushed, still shamelessly leaning on me. I didn't mind in the least.

"She's right," Sidney said. "It's a crying shame you aren't off making millions of dollars with that voice."

Justin snorted, though even in this light, he was clearly blushing. "Pfft. You all just want me to get a recording contract and a big mansion so you can come leech off me."

"Yeah?" Sidney shrugged. "And?"

"I don't do freeloaders, darlin'."

I cleared my throat.

He laughed, swatting my hand. "You're not freeloading."

"I'm, uh, not exactly paying for—"

"You cook for me." He made a gesture like he was banging a gavel on the table. "Case closed."

"He cooks?" Sidney's ears perked up.

"Oh my *God!*" Justin put a hand to his heart and sat straighter, taking my breath with him as he broke contact. "I'm telling you, I am going to gain a hundred pounds with him in the house."

A few other heads turned, and people leaned in. I recoiled a little, not sure I liked suddenly being the center of attention, but Justin effortlessly held the spotlight.

"The first night he stayed at my house," he went on as if he were telling some wild story. "He made these stuffed peppers. I don't know what was different about them, but oh my God. *Oh. My God.* You *guys.*" He flattened both hands on the table. "I never thought I'd describe a dish like that as orgasmic, but—"

I almost spat out my beer, which had everyone cracking up. Justin flashed me a wicked grin. I tried to glare at him, but the grin turned into an innocent puppy-dog look, and I burst out laughing.

He went on with his stories about my cooking, regaling them with everything I'd made recently and peppering the tales with some of the disasters of my early years. I was amazed he even remembered the time I'd accidentally put too much brown sugar in a meatloaf (which turned out to taste amazing) or the infamous blueberry pie incident of 1997 when I'd somehow put way too much lemon juice in the filling (which turned out to taste *not* amazing). I found myself listening as raptly as everyone else, laughing at my own fuck-ups and getting more than a little nostalgic over the memories he was awakening.

There were few days I thought back on as fondly as the surprise eighteenth birthday party we'd thrown senior year for his boyfriend. The memory was kind of bittersweet because the guy had turned out to be a jackass, but that day had been a good one, and apparently Justin had never forgotten the honey barbecue wings I'd made. Before that there was the time in ninth grade when we'd been studying Russian history, and our teacher had offered us extra credit if we brought in a Russian dish. To this day I had no idea if I'd screwed up the recipe or the cooking time, but that rum cake had left us all a bit woozy. And it had turned out the recipe had actually come from New Orleans or something, so I hadn't gotten the extra credit after all. On top of that, we'd had P.E. right after history, and I'd almost thrown up on Justin during our extra miserable mile-and-a-half run.

"I still think that was from your sad excuse for a stroganoff," I said.

"Bitch." Justin elbowed me. "Your cake wouldn't have passed a field sobriety test. Don't tell me my stroganoff made you weave and stumble."

"I think he needs to make that cake for all of us," Sidney said, nodding sagely. "So we can decide if it was as boozy as Justin's making it out to be."

Van grinned. "Oh, I agree. How about it, boys?"

Justin turned to me, eyebrows up. *Well?*

I shrugged. "Sure. Why not? I'm pretty sure I can dig up the recipe online."

To my surprise the group broke into applause. My cheeks burned, and Justin nudged me with his shoulder. Loud enough for everyone to hear, he said, "I think you just won over all their drunk-ass hearts."

"Oh shut up." Van threw a peanut at his head. "You were practically drooling when you told us about it, so don't act like you won't be sampling the cake batter and stealing the biggest pieces."

"Hey!" Justin pouted.

"She's got a point." I batted my eyes innocently. "How many times have I had to threaten you with kitchen implements because you kept stealing batter or whatever?"

"What?" He scoffed, shaking his head. "That's a lie."

I arched an eyebrow.

With a huff, he leaned back against the bench. "Fine. But it's not my fault it takes so long for some of that stuff to cook, and I just want a *taste*."

I rolled my eyes and elbowed him. He elbowed me back.

"Bastard," he muttered.

"Asshole."

We glanced at each other, laughed, and went for our drinks.

Across the table, Van and Sidney exchanged looks I couldn't quite read—eyebrows up, lips quirked—but neither said a word. I didn't ask, and neither did Justin. Besides, he was already launching into the tall tale of me nearly burning my grandmother's kitchen down on Thanksgiving when I was fifteen. I didn't stop him. The story wasn't nearly as entertaining if you knew the fire was contained to a frying pan and the only casualty was one of Grandma's hideously ugly oven mitts. And anyway, she'd wanted new oven mitts for Christmas, so it all worked out.

After a few more stories, the group broke apart as people went to sign up for more karaoke, get drinks, or hit the restroom. Justin and I stayed in the booth, and I was grateful to have a lull for a minute or two.

I turned to him. "I can't decide if you just made me out to be the next Gordon Ramsay, or completely incompetent in the kitchen."

He side-eyed me. "Please. I guarantee I had everyone's mouths watering. Now that I've sold them all on your cooking, we probably have to have a house party. No pressure or anything."

"Yeah?" I brought my beer to my lips. "That before or after you finish building the place?"

"Hmm." He scowled. "Okay, we'll have a party outside on the deck."

"I think they call that a barbecue." I sniffed with as much snobbishness as I could muster. "And I don't *barbecue*. I *cook*."

"Uh-huh." Justin rolled his eyes as he took a drink. Then he turned to me. His expression was completely serious, and he lowered his voice so only I could hear it even though the music provided a fair amount of privacy already. "Are you having a good time?"

"Yeah, I am. In fact, this is probably the most fun I've had in a long time. Even with my ex-wife calling to bend my ear in the middle of it." I absently played with the label on my beer bottle as I glanced at him. "So, thank you."

"Thanks for coming." He put his arm around my shoulders, and I leaned against him—*ah, so nice*—as he added, "Next time we go out, either block her number or shut your phone off. She almost killed my buzz."

I laughed, enjoying this closeness a lot more than I probably should have. "Got it."

And... next time we go out? There would *be* a next time?

I didn't push the issue about when next time would be, though.

I just smiled.

Because I couldn't wait.

CHAPTER 10

JUSTIN

My temples were throbbing when I woke the next morning, but the hangover wasn't too bad. I'd had worse. A little coffee and some water, and I'd be golden.

Moving carefully—something I'd learned the hard way during my college partying days—I sat up. Beside me, Azrael paused in the middle of licking her paw, shot me a look that was somehow a combination of disgusted and disinterested, and went back to bathing.

"Don't judge me, wench," I grumbled, and tousled her fluff. She side-eyed me, but that was about it.

Gingerly, I got out of bed and headed to the bathroom for a shower. Then I dressed and started my zombie shuffle toward the kitchen in search of coffee.

Tyler was already there, leaning against the counter with his phone in one hand and a mug in the other. He lifted his gaze from his screen and smiled. "Morning."

Despite my faint headache, it was impossible not to return that sweet smile. "Morning. Please tell me there's still coffee."

"Nope." He sipped his. "Just made enough for me."

I channeled my inner Azrael and glared at him.

He laughed and stepped aside, revealing a mostly full coffeepot. "I'm kidding."

"You're a bastard."

"Eh. You knew what this was."

I grunted in agreement and started making my coffee. Once I'd had a few life-giving swallows, I turned to him. "So did you have fun last night?"

That smile again. God.

"Yeah, I did." He put his cup down and pocketed his phone. "I like your friends a lot."

"They liked you too. Don't be surprised if you have a dozen friend requests on Facebook before the weekend is over."

He chuckled. "Already had five this morning."

"See?" I sipped my coffee again. "We meet up at that place a lot, so any time you want to join us, you're welcome to it. Even if I'm not there."

Tyler shifted his weight a little. "Well, maybe not by myself yet. They're... it's kind of your group, you know?"

"Oh honey. I'm pretty sure half of them forgot you were there with me."

"Well, aside from when you were telling them all about my cooking, right?"

"Okay, there's that." *Plus Sidney being convinced you were there with* me*. I shrugged. "But seriously—you don't need me to be there."

"Good to know. But... we'll see." He paused for a sip of coffee. "And by the way, you do know most people suck at karaoke, right? It's, like, a tradition?"

I sniffed indignantly. "Maybe *they* do, but if I'm going to sing in front of people, I'm going to sound good."

"Of course you are. I wouldn't expect any less."

"I should hope not."

"And you did sound really good," he said softly. "It's been a long time since I've heard you sing."

I swallowed. *It's been a long time since there's been someone worth singing to.* "Thanks."

Now that we had coffee in our systems, we went about making ourselves some breakfast. Tyler scrambled some eggs, and we lounged on the couch with our plates because we were too lazy to sit at the table.

As we settled in with our food, I realized Tyler had gone quiet for a while. He sometimes did when he cooked, but not when it was something as basic as scrambled eggs. Now that we were eating, he was still quiet.

No, not just quiet—distant. Gaze fixed on something else. Eyebrows pulled together. Chewing slowly and thoughtfully.

I watched him for a moment, and he didn't even seem to notice. "Hey."

He shook himself and turned to me. "Hmm?"

"You were spacing out."

"Oh. Sorry."

"It's okay, but..." I cocked my head. "You've got something on your mind, don't you?"

Tyler smiled sheepishly. "Am I that transparent?"

"To someone who's known you as long as I have, yes." I gave him a gentle nudge. "What's up, hon?"

The sheepish smile faded, and Tyler lowered his gaze. "So, you know when Gina called last night?"

Instantly, my teeth were on edge. "Yeah?"

He sighed. "It was to tell me her new man dumped her, and oh by the way she wants me to take her back."

"She *what?*"

"I know, right?" Tyler rolled his eyes. "She cheated, and now that her new guy is gone, she's—"

"She's got the brass balls to think you might let her come crawling back to her sorry ass?" My voice went shrill as I said it, and I didn't care. "What the *fuck?* You're not taking her up on it, are you?"

"Of course not!" Chuckling, he patted the air and shook his head. "Don't worry about it."

"Good. Because I just... I mean... the fucking nerve!" I threw up my hand, almost letting go of my fork. "Does she really think she can walk all over you like that, and accuse you of cheating, and cheat on her, and—"

"Justin. Justin." Tyler put his hand on my shoulder. "Take it easy, okay? I'm not going back to her."

I studied him, and after a moment, started to calm down a little. "Promise?"

"Promise. It's been hard, but it's over. I swear."

"Good." I looked in his eyes. How in the world was this man single and lonely? There was no justice in the universe if he didn't have legions of women pounding down his bedroom door. I tapped the center of his chest. "You know what? It's time to take you out and get you laid."

Tyler threw his head back and laughed. "What?"

"You heard me."

"Yeah, I did. But..." He sobered. "Are you serious?"

"As a heart attack."

"Weren't we kind of doing that at the club last night?"

"Uh, no." I shook my head. "Darlin', we were just out having a good time, and anyway, that was pretty much a gay bar. You haven't *seen* me trying to get you laid."

His eyes were instantly huge. "Well shit. Now I'm kind of intrigued."

I quirked my lips. "Kind of?"

He gulped. "Okay, really intrigued. What exactly does this entail?"

Basically taking you out into a public place and letting every straight or bi woman with standards do the rest.

"Well for starters, we need to find something for you to wear."

Tyler inclined his head. "Is this going to be one of those movie montage things where you sit outside of a dressing room, and I come out and model a bunch of different ridiculous outfits while you shoot me judgmental looks?"

"Right up until you step out in the perfect pussy magnet ensemble and I give you a thumbs up or something?"

"Exactly."

"Well, as fun as that would be..." I shook my head. "It won't be me playing dress-up with you."

"It won't?"

"Nope. I wish I could tell you I'd be your magic fashion guru, but what I'm actually going to do is turn one of my girls loose on you."

"One of..." He blinked. "Your girls?"

"Mmhmm." I picked up my wallet and keys. "Come on. You're driving."

As it turned out, it might as well have been one of those movie montages he'd asked about. The only difference was I wasn't the one giving the judgmental looks and sending him back in to change.

I did chill in a chair and watch everything, but it was my friend Kelsey doing the "nope," "not happening," "oh Lord," and "what was I thinking?" Tyler was a good sport about it. Occasionally he'd mutter under his breath or ask if she was absolutely sure this shirt or those pants or that pair of shoes didn't make the cut, but otherwise, he'd dutifully go back in and change out of whatever she'd rejected.

For me, it was hilarious, mostly because I was watching instead of doing the rapid fire rejection fashion show this time. I'd been there, done that. Most of my friends assumed that my penchant for sucking dick made me a fashion savant, but the truth was, the only reason I'd gotten away with appearing halfway fashionable in high school was because I'd grown up during the grunge era, something Seattle had embraced like nobody's business. When we'd first met ten years ago, Kelsey had joked about me being her gay personal shopper, and I'd dared her to let me pick out clothes for her. Five minutes into that hilarious shopping trip, she'd cried uncle and declared herself *my* personal shopper. Which was awesome because she had a sixth sense or something about what would make a man spectacularly fuckable.

And when Tyler stepped out of the dressing room for the hundredth time, my breath caught.

It wasn't anything extravagant—just near-black jeans paired with combat style boots and a green button-up shirt. On one guy, it might've looked stupid. On another, just average.

On him? Fuck. The green was the perfect shade to make his hair seem just slightly lighter and his eyes a lot bluer. The jeans weren't stupidly tight, but sat just right on his hips and ass. The boots had a slight lift in the heel, which worked magic on that gorgeous ass, and— son of a bitch. Kelsey really was a magician with this shit, even when it was nothing more than picking the right color shirt and style of shoes, but I hadn't thought it was possible to make Tyler any more fuckable than he already was.

"So?" He gestured self-consciously at the ensemble. "How does this look?"

Like I want to rip it off your person and—

"Oh, I think we have a winner." Kelsey studied him intently, then turned to me. "What do you think, hon? Would you tap that?"

I gulped. *I'd have tapped that in any of those atrocious outfits you made him try on, but—* "I think it looks great."

Tyler smiled shyly at me. "Really?"

"Mmhmm."

Kelsey waggled a finger at him. "Maybe another pair of those jeans and the same shirt in blue." She inspected him from head to toe, nodded, and wandered off to find what she needed.

He watched her go, his expression full of bemusement. Then his eyes flicked toward me. "This is really entertaining for you, isn't it?"

I shrugged, pushing myself up from my chair. "Eh, she's put me through it more than once, so I feel your pain. But she's good at what she does." I raked my eyes over him. "You wouldn't think something this simple would make such a difference, but it really does."

"Seriously?" He smoothed his hands down the front of his shirt. "I mean, it's just jeans and—"

"Trust me. It looks great. And if that woman approves, then—"

"So I've been downgraded to *that woman?*" Kelsey strode out from between two rows of clothing, a couple of shirts and jeans draped over her arm.

I showed my palms and smiled brightly. "You know I mean it with nothing but love and—"

"Oh shut up." She snorted and set the clothes down beside her purse and jacket. "I'm immune to your bullshit, my dear."

"Damn it," I grumbled.

Tyler made a half-assed effort to smother a laugh. When I shot him a pointed look, he stopped bothering to make any effort at all. "Sorry, man." He clapped my shoulder. "It's always hilarious when someone puts you in your place."

I rolled my eyes and muttered, "Whore."

He chuckled, then went back into the dressing room. When he came back out, he was in his normal clothes, and it seriously wasn't fair how much he rocked casual jeans and a faded T-shirt. I mean, really.

Kelsey beamed as she collected everything. "Okay, let's go ring you up."

Tyler hesitated. "Hang on. I should probably make sure I can afford all this."

"Don't." I touched his shoulder. "It's my treat, okay?"

"Justin." He shook his head. "I can't keep spending your money."

"Honey, I sicced the Fashion Police on you. The least I can do is buy what she picked out."

His brow creased.

Before he could protest, I squeezed his arm. "It's fine. Promise."

"So..." Kelsey eyed us. "Are we doing this, or...?"

"Yes, we are." I turned to him. "You can buy the first round when we go out, okay?"

He didn't seem convinced, but he shrugged, and we headed up to the register.

After I'd paid for the clothes, I took him and Kelsey to lunch. Then she had to get back to the bar where she worked, so we hugged goodbye and parted ways.

As we walked to the mall's parking garage, Tyler said, "Remember this morning when you thought I was spacing out during breakfast?"

I glanced at him. "Yeah?"

He nudged my elbow with his. "You've been doing the same thing for the last hour. What's up?"

I blinked a few times. Was I? I backtracked the last hour or so, and hell, I had been kind of off in my own little world, hadn't I? While Kelsey and Tyler had chatted over paninis like they'd known each other forever, I'd sat back and watched, not unlike what I'd done while he'd tried on clothes. I'd been there, but... not.

Taking a breath, I slid my hands into my pockets. "Okay. Well. I was thinking a lot, I guess." I moistened my lips, slowed to a stop, and turned to him. "There's something I need to ask because that conversation we had this morning is bugging me."

Tyler lifted his eyebrows. "Which conversation?"

"The one when you were spacing out. About your ex. And that phone call." Squaring my shoulders, I held his gaze. "You really aren't going back to her, are you?"

He laughed. "No. My God, no. I'm..." His humor faded and he lowered his gaze. As his posture sagged a little, he said, "I can't go back. I just can't."

"But would you want to?"

"No." Something in his voice sounded a lot like uncertainty, and that did not sit well with me.

I inclined my head. "Are you sure you don't want to?"

"Yes, I'm sure."

"Okay, but just on the off chance that a demon possesses you or you become a pod person, I think we should get something completely clear."

He smirked. "Uh, okay?"

"If you—or the demon controlling you—*do* decide to go back to her, do you want me to support your decision? Or should I chase your ass down, block you from checking in at the airport, and forcibly restrain you until you see reason again?"

God. I loved the way this man laughed. Especially when there was a hint of shyness in his eyes.

Shaking his head, he said, "I don't think you have to worry about that." He met my gaze, his expression completely serious. "Listen, I loved her, and in a way, I still do. But we're done. There's no going back. I can't be with someone I can't trust. And even if I could trust her again, we've..." He paused, eyes unfocusing as if he were trying to figure out how to put his thoughts into words. Finally, he sighed. "When you're with someone for a long time, things get kind of boring. You fall in love, you want to be with this person, and then you just kind of... get comfortable with each other. It's normal, you know? But with Gina, it's like we've reached a point where I can't even *remember* that giddy, falling-in-love feeling."

I cocked my head. "So, you don't know why you were with her at all?"

"Not... not really. We've just gone so far down the rabbit hole of resenting each other that it's hard to remember ever feeling any other way." He patted my arm. "Look, it's kind of terrifying to start my life over right now, but I'm not going back. We're done. I promise."

I held his gaze for a moment, searching for any reason to be skeptical. When I couldn't find one, I nodded. "Okay. I just don't want to see you get hurt again, you know?"

"I know. And I really appreciate it. It's, um..." He lowered his gaze, and his voice was soft as he added, "It's nice to have someone give a shit about me and how I feel."

He might as well have punched me in the gut. Jesus fuck.

"I do. You know I do." I paused, worried the moment might be getting too heavy, and quickly added, "Which is why next Friday night, I'm taking out and getting you laid."

He gulped. "You weren't kidding about that, were you?"

"Definitely not." I grinned. "I'm taking you out, and we're going to have a few drinks, and you're going to be mobbed by the ladyfolk until you can't get it up anymore."

He laughed, his cheeks turning an adorable shade of deep red. "Uh..."

"Relax, hon." I gave him a gentle nudge. "You'll do fine."

"I guess we'll see. But, um, thanks for helping me out. Getting back out on the singles scene after all this time is intimidating as hell."

"Any time."

We exchanged smiles, and I hoped he couldn't see me dying inside.

Oh yeah. Friday night, he'd dress up in everything Kelsey had put together for him, and I'd take him out. I'd turn him loose in one of those clubs where everyone was looking to get laid, and he'd have women lining up in no time. Probably some men, too. At least one.

I tamped down the selfish feelings that made me want to bail. There was no point in jealously pining after him instead of helping him find someone he was actually interested in. Tyler deserved to be happy, and I would do everything in my power to make sure he was happy.

Even if it killed me.

CHAPTER 11

TYLER

The taxi let us off in front of the club, but Justin led me across the street.

"Nobody really shows up until after ten," he explained on the way into the bar. "It's just loud and boring when it's empty, so we can grab a couple of drinks and relax a bit here before we go over there."

"Sounds good to me. I could stand to pre-game a bit."

He eyed me. "You're not planning on getting hammered, are you?"

"No! Of course not." I sheepishly met his eyes as I held open the bar's door. "Just something for my nerves. That's all."

"Nerves?" He smiled sweetly. "Honey, you're going to have women knocking each other over to get to you. You've got nothing to be nervous about." He gave my arm a pat, then swept past me into the bar.

I chuckled, but didn't argue as I followed him inside. I'd done all right in clubs when I was in college, but I wasn't twenty-two anymore. We'd see how things went tonight. At least I had Kelsey's fashion wisdom to keep me from looking like a trash fire, so as long as I didn't do or say something stupid, maybe I'd be okay.

Justin led me across the lounge. This place wasn't a dive bar per se. A little too clean and modern for that, and without the smell of fry grease permeating everything. There were some games on television, but none of my teams were playing, so I didn't pay any attention to them.

There were a few pool tables, too. One was occupied. The others were empty.

As we sat down in a booth, I gestured at the pool tables. "Hey, you remember that pool hall that was open in Redmond back when we were in junior high?"

Justin smiled. "Joey's? God, how could I forget that place? Shame they closed it or I'd probably still go there."

"Yeah?"

"Sure, why not?" He shrugged, the smile turning a little bit shy. "It wasn't exactly a place to go pick up guys, but there were worse ways to kill an afternoon than shooting pool and bankrupting myself feeding the jukebox."

I laughed. "Man, those were the days. I don't think I've ever found anyone who made better fries than they did."

"Oh, no kidding. Shit, maybe it is good they shut down, or I'd have gorged myself to death on those damn crinkle fries."

"You and me both."

He chuckled. He started to bring his drink to his lips, but paused and looked at me with a nostalgic smile. "Remember the time we almost got thrown out for putting *Danger Zone* on repeat on the jukebox?"

I threw my head back and laughed. "When the owner threatened to ban us for life if we played that song one more time?"

"He had no sense of humor, I'm telling you."

"Cranky old bastard."

We both laughed, and I let some more of those memories rush through my brain. More and more lately, I'd been realizing that all the best memories of my formative years had one thing in common— Justin. And not just the best ones, but all the important ones. He'd been there for the good times and the horrible times. For the hormone-saturated crushes on girls who were way out of my league and the breakups that had seemed like the end of the world. The fact that he'd been absent from my life for five years seemed like even more of a travesty than it had before tonight.

But that's over, so I'm going to enjoy being here with him in the present.

"Hey, so." I cleared my throat. "You want to shoot some pool while we're here?"

"Fuck yeah!" His face lit up. "Eight ball?"

"Unless you want to grab some random stranger and play Cutthroat."

Justin wrinkled his nose. "Nah. It's more fun to kick your ass on my own."

I laughed. Oh, didn't that bring back memories? He and I had always been competitive as hell no matter what we were playing— pool, video games, and even badminton during P.E. Our shit talking had been legendary at that pool hall, especially with our friends egging us on. It had always been good-natured, too. Competitive without being mean, but *definitely* snarky.

"You guys sound like an old married couple," a friend had laughed during a game of pool eons ago.

We took the table at the far end of the row, and Justin went up to the bar to get everything we needed. After we'd selected and chalked our cues, it was game on. I broke, sank a striped ball, and thought I was doing pretty damn good until Justin started dropping solids left and right. That game didn't last long. The second, I did a little better, but once he was on a roll, there was no stopping him.

As he got down to his last ball, the cue ball was tucked in a hard-to-reach position behind the twelve and eight. A lot of opportunity to scratch or accidentally sink the eight.

Justin leaned back over the table, reaching behind himself to line up the shot. Somehow he'd always managed to make even the most acrobatic shots without being clumsy or awkward. When the rest of us had to sprawl across the table with all the grace of three-day-old roadkill, he could always angle himself to both make the shot and look good doing it. Like he could line up a seemingly impossible shot, and not only sink it but showcase his ass in the process.

And of course, being the bastard he was, he made the shot this time. And looked good doing it, showcased ass and all.

"Oh." He put a hand to his mouth and stared at the table, feigning shock. "Am I... am I down to the eight ball? Again?"

I rolled my eyes. "Smug motherfucker."

He sank the eight ball with an emphatic *thunk*, and did a little victory dance because he was an asshole like that. Grinning, he said, "You want to do three out of five? Or is two out of three enough?"

I sighed, rolling my eyes again. "Apparently I need to practice a bit if I'm going to play against you."

He toasted me with his beer bottle, winked, and took a swallow.

"What about cricket?" I asked. "You still halfway decent at darts?"

"Halfway decent?" Justin scoffed. "I'll have you know I still kick ass at darts, thank you very much."

"Oh yeah?" I grinned. "Prove it."

Justin smirked at me. "All right. You're on." He jutted his chin at the bar. "Go get us some darts."

"What? I have to pay for them?"

"Bitch, I'm getting you laid tonight." He shooed me toward the bar. "Go."

"Fair enough." And he had bought me these clothes, so I supposed it was only fair.

I went up to the bar. I gave the bartender ten bucks plus my driver's license as collateral, and he handed me a case of six darts—three red, three blue.

"All right, smartass." I set the darts down on a table by the dartboards. "Let's see what you've got."

Justin picked up the blue darts. "Bring it."

"You got lucky." Justin clicked his tongue as he plucked the darts from the board.

"Please. Beating you that many times by that many points wasn't luck. That was years of practice and—"

"And dumb fucking luck."

"Aw, come on." I beamed. "Don't hate me because I'm better at darts than you."

He huffed, but there was a playful sparkle in his eye as he put the darts on the table between our beer bottles. "Another round?"

"Of darts or beer?"

"Yes."

I considered it, then shrugged. "Sure, why not? I think it's your turn to buy anyway."

He sighed dramatically as if buying a round was the biggest imposition in the world.

"Go on, drama queen," I said with mock exasperation. "You can handle it."

"Fine." He gathered our empty bottles, winked, and headed for the bar.

I chuckled, and as he walked away, I glanced at my phone.

12:35.

I did a double take. What the...

That couldn't be right.

I looked around and found an old neon Rainier Beer clock above the bar, and the hands confirmed it—12:35. Holy shit.

I followed Justin to the bar. "Hey, did you notice what time it is?"

"What time—" He took out his phone, and when the screen lit up, his eyes widened. "Oh my God. Time got away from us, didn't it?"

"Yeah, I guess it did."

"Well, do you still want to go over there?" He gestured in the club's general direction. "It's open for another hour and a half."

"Honestly?" I shook my head. "I think I'm ready to call it a night."

"Getting too old for—"

"You're four months older than me, jackass." I picked up my beer. "Why don't we finish these, maybe play another game, and then get out of here?"

"Sounds good." He took a deep swallow from his own bottle. "Let's roll."

On the way out twenty minutes later, I glanced at the club across the street. There was a line outside, and the music thumped so hard I could feel it in my teeth.

That was where we were supposed to be tonight, but we hadn't made it. Justin hadn't had a chance to work his magic at getting me laid. I wasn't disappointed, though. I'd enjoyed our evening together. I'd gone out intending to at least try to hook up with a woman I hadn't yet met. Instead, I'd spent an evening relaxing over some beers, darts, and pool with a friend who'd been out of my life for way too long. A friend who I'd stupidly *cut* out of my life, and who by the grace of God, was somehow back in it.

Before I could think twice, I said, "Justin?"

He turned to me. "Hmm?"

"I, um..." I swallowed. "I wanted to apologize again. For ghosting you. The last five years were—"

"Ty. Sweetie." He faced me fully and touched my arm. "You're back now. That's all I care about."

"But I fucked up. Cutting you out of my life was easily the biggest mistake I ever made. I just need you to know I'm sorry."

He smiled, looking right in my eyes. "I know. And I appreciate it. I'm just really glad you're back now."

"Yeah. Me too." *I don't think you'll ever understand how grateful I am.*

"Anyway, next time we go out? We'll definitely get to the club." Justin nodded toward the club, then flashed me a devilish grin and winked in the low light. "I will get you laid. That is a promise."

"Deal. Oh hey, there's our Uber."

We got in, and just before the driver turned the corner at the end of the block, I glanced back at the club once more time.

No, I hadn't gone anywhere near that place tonight. I hadn't danced. Hadn't checked anyone out. I hadn't made eye contact with a woman, never mind made a connection.

But as I continued down the road with Justin, I definitely wouldn't say the night had been wasted.

CHAPTER 12

JUSTIN

The following Saturday, we actually made it to the club. It helped that we left a bit later this time, so we weren't getting there so early that we needed to kill time across the street.

I parked around the block, and after waiting in line for half an hour, we finally went inside and headed for the bar. While we waited for our first round, I gave the club a sweeping glance. This wasn't usually my scene. I liked the places that were more upfront about being queer-friendly. They were safer, for one thing. It was a lot easier for guys like me to start up conversations and flirt with someone when we weren't scared shitless they might be a homophobe.

But this club did attract the queer crowd too, and anyway tonight wasn't about me—it was about Tyler. I was *going* to get this man laid and help him move on from his shitty marriage.

First things first, we got a couple of drinks and found a table. Tyler took a pull from his beer as he gazed around, and I wondered if anyone else noticed his deer-in-the-headlights look, or if it was only obvious to someone who knew how much places like this intimidated him.

I touched his arm. "Hey. Relax."

"Easy for you to say," he muttered into his beer bottle. "Is it just me, or is everyone here half our age?"

I scanned the room. "They're not *all* college kids."

"And it doesn't make you feel old to think about college kids being half our age?"

Scowling, I huffed. "It didn't before tonight, asshole."

He chuckled, which seemed to ease some of the tension in his features. "Okay, but seriously—is anyone here over twenty-five?"

"Usually, yeah." I scanned the room again, and okay, the crowd was a bit younger than I remembered it being. How long had it been since I'd come here? Still, there were a few scattered faces with that hint of world-weariness that came with being over thirty. "We're not the only escapees from the old folks' home." I tilted my glass toward a group in the corner. "If anyone at that table is under twenty-nine, I'm the Pope."

Tyler snorted, then burst out laughing.

"What? Do you really doubt my ability to tell people's ages at ten paces?"

"No." He tried and failed to smother his laughter. "Just the thought of you as the Pope..." Shaking his head, he snickered some more.

I huffed with mock offense. "Bitch, I'd make a fucking badass Pope."

Tyler shot me one of those incredulous looks I hadn't realized I'd missed. "I don't know, man. I can't imagine anyone letting you wear white to anything."

A laugh burst out of me. "Just what are you implying, Mr. Schaeffer?"

"Nothing." He shrugged, bringing his beer to his lips again. "Nothing at all." Just before he took a sip, he coughed "*slut*."

"Oh, I am not." I smacked his arm, and grinned triumphantly when the bastard choked on his drink.

"Okay. Fine." He sputtered. "But you're not exactly a saint, either."

"And you are?"

"Hardly. I'm not the one claiming I could be the Pope, though."

I rolled my eyes and laughed. I couldn't begin to tell him how much I'd missed the random bullshit our conversations had a habit of devolving into. Nobody in the world had ever appreciated my nonsense as much as Tyler, and no one else had ever brought the same kind of nonsense to the table.

God, I missed you.

And I was here to play wingman so he could get laid, which meant I definitely needed another drink. Like... now.

I plucked the drink menu off the stand at the edge of the table. Though I was driving tonight, it was still early. I gave myself a two-drink limit when I was DD, and I'd just finished number one. In search of drink number two, I perused the laminated pages of colorful cocktails that, at those prices, had better come with long, enthusiastic blowjobs from the bartender of my choice. Most of these places had overpriced cocktails with way more fruit juice than booze, but once in a while there was a diamond in the rough. Something with a little sweet and a little buzz, and maybe not requiring a credit check to prove I could fucking afford it. Fifteen dollars for a shot of Comfort and some sloe gin mixed with—

"Whoa." Tyler's low, awestruck voice pulled my attention from the drink menu.

"Hmm?" I realized he was focused on something, and followed the trajectory of his gaze. Despite the crowd, it wasn't hard to zero in on her. She was probably a few years younger than us, and she was about five foot eight of Tyler's type. Dark hair tumbling over her shoulders. A tattoo around her wrist and a beer bottle in her hand. Carrying herself like she owned the place and dressed to show off every curve of her body without trying to hide or apologize for anything someone might consider an imperfection. If she had a sense of humor, she'd have Tyler wrapped around her finger.

Right then, she looked his way. Her eyes slid up and down him, and she winked, and dear God, I *felt* him react. I didn't hear it, but I had no doubt his breath had hitched and his heart had gone wild. He might've even been getting hard, but I wasn't about to torture myself by stealing a glance at a tent he was pitching in his pants for someone other than me.

"Why don't you go talk to her?" I nudged his arm. "What do you have to lose?"

"Uh..." He swallowed so hard I swore I could hear it over the music.

"Worst case scenario, she says no."

"Yeah. That's... kind of the scenario I don't—"

"Go on. Ask if you can buy her a drink." I paused. "If she says no, I'll do your laundry and all the dishes. For a *month*."

He turned to me, one eyebrow flicked up. "A month?"

"Yes."

His lips quirked.

"Oh my God, just *go*." I gave him a shove. "Or so help me, I'll go ask her for you like we're in seventh grade."

"You wouldn't."

I lifted my chin and narrowed my eyes. "Complete with a hand-written note asking her to check yes or—"

"No!" Tyler laughed, putting up a hand. "Jesus Christ, no."

"Then are you—?"

"I'm going, I'm going." He put his empty drink down and took a step back. "Just... I'm going."

I shot him a pointed look. *You better be.*

He laughed again, rolling his eyes, and turned to approach the brunette. His nerves were visible from here—*I'm nervous* might as well have been scrawled in red neon across his tight shoulders and tense features.

When she turned to him again, she smiled. So did he, though he was still obviously terrified. I held my breath just like I had when he'd asked whatshername to homecoming in tenth grade. She'd said no, and he'd been crushed, and I hoped that if this woman turned him down, she was at least kinder about it than that girl in high school had been.

Say no if you have to, but don't tell him he's batting out of his league.

A smile lit up her face. She nodded, and even though his back was to me, I could feel the smile on his face too. She said something to the friends she'd been standing with, and then broke away to head to the bar with Tyler. As they did, he cut his eyes toward me, and that shy *holy shit she said yes* look on his face melted my heart.

"That your boyfriend or something?" A male voice startled me, and I turned to see an *incredibly* attractive Hispanic man approaching with a smile on his full lips.

"My boy—" I glanced over my shoulder, and zeroed right in on Tyler, who was ordering a drink at the bar. Oh, I wish. Laughing, I faced this hot man again and shook my head. "No, no. He's my roommate." I raked my eyes over him. "I'm here alone."

"Oh yeah?" He stood straighter, grinning at me. The rising confidence was almost palpable. In seconds, we'd completed that little dance gay men did in predominantly straight clubs—feeling each other out to make sure we were both gay, being cautiously forward without tipping our hands and accidentally hitting on a straight man. Not too many people mistook me for a straight dude, though, so he'd probably already decided I was gay before he'd engaged me. Now that he had, and I'd silently confirmed that oh, yes, I was definitely a man who loved men, it was game on.

"I'm Hector," he said.

"Justin."

His grin broadened. "So, Justin." He narrowed some of the space between us. "Any chance I can buy you a drink?"

I licked my lips. "I'm driving tonight, but I won't say no to a Coke." I gave him a quick once over, perusing the tight body he had on display in snug jeans and a painted-on black shirt. When I met his gaze again, I winked. *I can think of a lot I won't say no to if you offer, sweetheart.*

He returned the wink and snaked an arm around my shoulders. I let myself be led toward the bar, and as we made our way through the crowd, I scanned the room to make sure Tyler was doing all right.

When I found him, I almost tripped.

Oh. Yeah. I think he's doing just *fine.*

They were huddled beside a table near the edge of the room, and they were standing so close. He had his hand on her arm, and she was doing that smiling-eye-contact-hair-tucking thing that basically screamed *I am so into you.* He was gazing at her like he'd forgotten anyone else in the world even existed, and his smile... oh God. Oh my *God.*

Satan, my soul for a man to look at me like that just once.

I tore my gaze away and turned to at Hector. Right. Trying to connect with him— not obsessing over *him.*

At the bar, Hector bought me a Coke. I couldn't hear what he'd ordered for himself, but it was strong if the smell was any indication. Then we found a little pocket of space where we could talk over our drinks.

Here we go. Commence small talk and flirting in between stealthily checking for passable breath and hygiene. Yay.

I didn't mind this part of the game. I just found it kind of tedious sometimes. Hookup apps were much more my speed because the profile covered a lot of these bases in a much more straightforward manner, and by the time we actually started interacting with the over-the-top politeness of two strangers, I'd be ten steps ahead of where I was with Hector.

That, and I wasn't usually scrutinizing Grindr profiles while Tyler put his hand up a woman's skirt twenty feet away.

I squirmed on my barstool, hoping Hector took it as a response to his knee brushing mine.

Tyler was way too distracting while I tried to connect with Hector. Every time I glanced in his direction, a million emotions threatened to kill any shot I had at pulling off sex this evening. Jealousy made my teeth grind. Envy made my throat ache. There wasn't a man in this room I wanted more than I wanted him, and even if it made me a selfish bastard, I hated watching him charming her like that.

I would never have interrupted them or tried to cockblock him. I *wanted* him to make a connection with her, whether they fucked each other senseless for a night or fell head over heels in love with each other. I *wanted* her to either give him the night of his life, or end up being the partner I would have sold my soul to be for him.

I don't care if it's just for tonight or the rest of his life—make him as happy as I wish I could.

I took a swig of Coke to push back the sudden lump in my throat. Christ, why was I so emotional over him tonight? This was what I wanted for him. To meet someone. To have a good time. I'd long ago made peace with the reality that I was not and would never be someone who piqued Tyler's interest. So why did I suddenly feel like teenage me? The kid who'd been overdosing on hormones just like everyone else in my peer group, and who'd wound up crying in a bathroom at a dance because he'd been slow-dancing with Carrie Sable and it had seemed like the end of the world to accept that my best friend would always be out of my reach.

For fuck's sake. I rolled my eyes at my own thought, took another drink, and ordered myself to get the fuck over that stupidity this instant. I had the full and undivided attention of an extraordinarily hot man, and I needed to give him the same before he lost interest and found someone else.

So I twisted in my seat and faced Hector completely. The motion slid my knees between his thighs, which brought a grin out of him. I returned it, pretending I was way more into this than I was. Just to make sure, I slid my hand up his leg.

Having my back to Tyler wasn't working. Neither was having my hands on Hector. It was like I could feel Tyler even when I couldn't see him, and I gritted my teeth like I was fighting back the urge to spin around and demand, *"What do you want?"* Because that would make me look seriously sane.

I usually wasn't in a big hurry to drag a guy out of a club and into bed. And truthfully, the getting into bed part wasn't as appealing as it could have been. I just needed to get out of here. How the fuck was I supposed to concentrate on dancing and seduction with Tyler so close by?

No way around it—I just needed to not have Tyler in the same room. I needed to *not* be able to see him, with or without a woman on his arm.

So I turned to Hector. "Hey. You want to get out of here?"

He grinned like he'd just won the lottery. "You don't want to stay and dance?"

"Meh." I shrugged. "They're not really playing anything I can dance to."

"Works for me." The grin got even bigger. "Your place or mine?"

"Mine works. Just, um, let me tell my friend we're getting out of here." I winked as I slid my hand up the middle of his chest. "Stay right here."

He licked his lips and squeezed my ass. "I'm not going anywhere without you."

I grinned, and I winked again, and I felt like absolute shit because he probably thought I was as into this as he was. And maybe once we were alone, I would be.

To my surprise, Tyler was alone.

"Where'd that lady go?" I asked. "Seemed like you guys were clicking."

"Oh, we are." He gestured over his shoulder toward the bar. "She's getting us a couple of drinks."

I followed his gesture, and sure enough, she was leaning over the bar, talking to the cute bartender. I tsked, shaking my head. "Making your woman buy the booze?"

"Hey." He kicked my shin playfully. "I bought the last one. She offered to buy this round."

"Uh-huh."

He rolled his eyes. "What about you? Looked like you were having a good time with that guy."

"Oh, I was. In fact, that's why I came over here—is it okay if he and I take off?"

"Is it okay?" He laughed. "I'm not your adult, Justin."

"No, but I am your designated driver."

His lips pursed. Then he shrugged. "I'll get an Uber. Don't worry about it." With a grin that seemed just a touch halfhearted, he added, "Get out of here. Go get some ass."

I snorted. "Such a gentleman."

"Never claimed to be. If I was, I wouldn't hang out with you."

I *almost* flinched. *You* didn't *hang out with me for five damn years.*

But that wasn't what he'd meant, I knew it wasn't what he'd meant, and there was no point in dragging ourselves through that emotional minefield all over again. We'd already talked things over, and we were cool.

So I laughed as if the offhand comment hadn't struck a raw nerve. "Birds of a feather, I guess."

"Exactly." He chuckled too, with a tiny bit more feeling. Shooing me away, he said, "Go get laid. I'll see you tomorrow."

We exchanged grins

"See you tomorrow, sweetie. Good luck with her."

"Thanks."

One last glance, and then I turned to go join Hector.

Hector was pulling on his coat. "Ready?"

"When you are." I smiled, but... kind of wasn't feeling it all of a sudden. Not that I had been earlier, but now? Ugh.

I quickly brushed that off, though. I hadn't spent much time on the club scene recently, and I wasn't used to being out this late anymore. I was just tired. That was all.

As Hector and I headed for the door, I glanced over my shoulder to steal one last glimpse of Tyler. He was looking right at me, and he smiled before turning toward the bar. Probably searching the crowd for the woman who was getting them both drinks. The woman he'd no doubt be in bed with before the end of the night.

Good. I faced forward again, walking beside Hector. He put a hand on my lower back, and we flashed grins at each other, and... my stomach felt heavy. The thought of going home and going through the motions made me tired.

Which was stupid. It was ridiculous. This was why Tyler and I had come to this place. I was getting laid. Tyler was getting laid. Mission accomplished. Sex acquired. Orgasms imminent.

So why did I feel like the whole night had been a bust?

CHAPTER 13

TYLER

I watched them leave, and I had no idea why my heart was sinking or why I couldn't pull my gaze away from that hand resting comfortably on the small of Justin's back.

Or why I jumped when they disappeared out the door, and were gone.

The bouncers let in another pair—a couple of college-aged women—as if to emphasize that the packed club's population had momentarily dipped by two.

Well, shit. Apparently I was on my own for the evening.

"*Finally.*" Colleen reappeared beside me, triumphantly holding up two bottles of beer.

I laughed as I took one. "Thanks. Slow service?"

She groaned, rolling her eyes before she took a deep pull from her own beer. "Can't really blame them." She absently brushed her long hair back over her shoulder. "I don't know how they hear a thing over the music and everybody yelling at them."

I nodded, then sipped my own. I felt a little guilty about thinking I was alone for the rest of the night. Justin was gone, but Colleen wasn't. It wasn't like I needed him to hold my hand and guide me from here; once conversation had gotten moving between Colleen and me, I was good to go on my own. And hell, Justin had been halfway across the room for a while now, getting flirty with the man who'd had his hand on Justin's back when they'd left.

I worked my jaw, wondering why my teeth had started aching. Had I... had I been *clenching* them?

"Tyler?" Colleen's voice startled me, and when I turned to her, she cocked her head, silently asking why I'd spaced out.

"Sorry." I swallowed some more beer, then smiled. "I, uh." Fuck, I had no idea what she'd been saying, and I felt like a dick for tuning her out, even for a second.

She laughed, though. "I was just asking if you wanted to go dance." She tilted her beer bottle toward the dance floor. "There's actually some room now that that bachelorette party cleared out."

Sure enough, there weren't quite so many bodies crushed together anymore. And maybe that was what I needed. I wanted to say I was getting a little tired—more like lethargic—but then realized I was probably tired and lethargic because I'd been still too long. Get out there and move, and my energy would come back. After so many years, the thought of cutting loose and dancing for once in my life sounded damn good.

So I smiled. "After you."

We quickly finished our beers, and then I followed her out onto the floor. Within a few beats, we'd been swallowed up by the crowd. Her ass pressed against me, and I held on to her hips, ostensibly to keep us from being separated by the undulating mob.

It was impossible not to be aroused when I was this close to an incredibly hot woman, and there was no way she didn't feel my hard-on just like I couldn't miss how she squirmed every time I exhaled against her neck. Much more of this, and we'd wind up fucking in the restroom or making out in the backseat of a cab on our way to some-place with a bed. I could picture us pressed up against a wall, or giving a bed frame a run for its money, or not even making it past her living room and winding up on the couch instead, or—

Why did the thought of all that make me so tired? It wasn't the beer. I hadn't had nearly enough to make me feel like this. For whatever reason, the thought of leaving with Colleen and having some long overdue sex just made me... meh.

Even this close to her, rock hard with our bodies grinding suggestively in the middle of the thick crowd, my heart wasn't in it. I tried to tell myself I'd just gone through that last beer a little too fast and the alcohol was making me sluggish, but I didn't believe my own bullshit. Fact was, the bottom had fallen out of my enthusiasm, and I wasn't sure there was enough beer in this place to bring my spirits back up. It was like being at a party after the *life* of the party had left. That point in the evening when fatigue sets in and people start checking their phones and realizing how late it is, and everything starts quickly winding down as people meander toward the door.

Except no one was leaving. The dancefloor was still packed. The crowd at the bar was still two or three people deep. The music was still loud and the bouncers were still letting people in because it was still pretty early.

No, it was just me. From the moment Justin had left, I'd been halfhearted at best about all of this. Which was stupid. I hadn't come here to hang out with Justin. Sure, he'd kind of come along as my wingman, but this wasn't a guys' night out. I'd come to this bar tonight to get out of my funk and try to break my post-divorce dry spell. I was supposed to be stepping out into the singles scene and figuring out how much things had changed in the decade and a half since I'd taken myself off the market.

Maybe I just wasn't ready. A night out with my friend? Can do.

Getting back in the saddle this soon after my divorce? Yeah, maybe not.

Okay—definitely not.

And now that I'd accepted that, what little enthusiasm I had left drained away.

I tapped Colleen's shoulder, and when she twisted around to look at my face, I gestured toward the side of the room. She nodded, and we made our way through the thick crowd and off the dancefloor. When we stopped, she was close to me. Really close. Just to hear me, or...?

Well, whatever. I was going to disappoint her either way.

"Listen, um..." I swallowed, and it was a struggle to speak over the loud music. "It's been a long week. I think I'm just gonna call it a night."

The letdown in her eyes was unmistakable. Her shoulders sagged, and she put a fraction of an inch more space between us as she said, "Oh."

"I'm sorry. I... I really did have a good time, and..." And was there anything I could say that didn't sound like some cheesy rehearsed copout of a line?

"Any chance we could meet up again another time?" Her eyebrows lifted. "Maybe for a drink?"

"Sure. Yeah. We can definitely do that." I took out my phone. "Can I get your number?"

"Of course."

I unlocked the phone and handed it over. She entered her number, then gave me back my cell. With a smile that should have had me rethinking my escape, she said, "Text me sometime."

I smiled back, not sure if I was lying when I said, "I will."

Colleen kissed my cheek, and a moment later, she was disappearing into the crowd. I stared down at her name and number on my phone. Was I an idiot? She'd been everything I'd come here to find. Maybe just a hookup for the night, or maybe some potential for an actual connection, but whatever the case, there was chemistry. Everything from conversation to dancing had come easy. If I had a brain in my head, I'd hurry after her, tell her I'd changed my mind, and suggest we get out of here.

But instead, I closed my contacts and opened the Uber app.

"Aw, shit," I muttered as I started up the driveway. Up ahead, in front of the garage and beside my car was Justin's Prius. Which meant he was here.

Oh what a shock—he's at his own house.

Why I'd convinced myself he'd go to the other guy's house, I had no idea, but it didn't matter—they'd come here.

Of course my Uber was already driving off, so there was no jumping back in and having her take me someplace else. And I was too tired to go anywhere else anyway, so... not much to do but suck it up, go inside, and hope he and the other guy were done for the night.

As quietly as I could, I keyed myself in, shut the door, and headed to my room. I was halfway down the upstairs hallway before I knew Justin was here and he wasn't alone. It was impossible to miss the tell-tale sounds of two people getting intimate—the mattress creaking softly. Quiet murmuring. A muffled laugh.

I stopped a few feet shy of my door and glared at his. The rec room downstairs was mostly intact, right? After all he'd lived down there the first few months he'd had the house. I could go crash on that couch.

Except I'd have to make sure I was back in my own bedroom before Justin woke up in the morning, or things would get spectacularly awkward.

"Oh, hey, don't mind me. I slept downstairs so I didn't have to listen to you guys."

No, that wouldn't fly. Plus the rec room was directly under his bedroom. Nope. So instead, I continued down the hall to slip into my bedroom. I started to carefully close the door when something shoved it open again and brushed past my leg.

I rolled my eyes and whispered, "Hello, Azrael." The rustle and thump behind me told me she'd hopped up on my bed. Great. Now I couldn't shut the door all the way, which meant no escape from the Justin Getting Laid Theater production across the hall.

I could kick her out, but... eh. She'd already been booted out of her usual bed, and she liked it in here anyway. I let her stay.

After I'd stripped down to my boxers, I got into bed, carefully situating myself so I didn't disturb Azrael, who had flopped down near the footboard.

Now that I wasn't moving around anymore, the house was quiet.

Or, well—this room was quiet. The one across the hall?

Justin laughed, but the sound was abruptly aborted by a gasp. I could see him in my mind's eye, laughing before he was suddenly caught off guard by a touch. Maybe a kiss. A caress. A bite?

I shut my eyes tight, trying to will away the images, but another laugh carried across the hall. This one slightly quieter. Kind of muffled. Almost conspiratorial. They were probably looking in each other's eyes, murmuring playfully while they got each other spun up, and *why was that thought driving me up the wall?*

I'd heard friends and roommates having sex before, and it had been funny or maybe a little awkward sometimes. They hadn't all been straight, either. So why was it fucking with me so much to hear Justin in bed with another man?

And why...

Why the fuck...

Why the fuck was it making me *hard*?

Someone moaned in the other room. It was a sound that was both distinctly masculine and unmistakably made of arousal. I had no idea which of them it was, only that the sound sent a shiver through me. I was really horny tonight, wasn't I? Damn it, I should have stuck with Colleen. She would have been a lot more fun than using my hand while I listened to Justin and the other guy turning each other on.

Not... not that I was planning on jacking off to this.

Except I really was hard. And I'd been out looking for a hookup tonight, so I'd been horny all evening. I wasn't getting turned on by the sounds of two men having sex—I was turned on because damn it *I* wanted to be having sex.

To hell with it. I pushed my boxers down far enough to free my dick, and closed my fingers around it. I was so damn turned on, that first stroke was all it took to make me gasp.

And right then, across the hall, someone cried out, "Oh fuck!"

I bit my lip and pumped myself slowly. I felt like such a creeper, jerking off to my best friend getting laid, but damn, I was too turned on to ignore this stupid hard-on. I definitely should have stuck with Colleen. If I was this horny, then it would've been a hell of a lot more fun to do something about it with someone else, especially if I could be driving her wild too, just like Justin was apparently doing to—

God, what is wrong *with me?*

Another moan gave me goose bumps. Every time someone in the other room made a sound, my mind was instantly flooded with images of the two of them. I had no idea what they were doing, but in my head I could clearly see Justin's face, flushed and sweaty and contorted with pleasure and...

That's not supposed to turn me on.

I licked my lips and kept right on stroking myself. I could think about everything that was wrong with this later, but I was too fired up to analyze anything. I just chalked it up to being desperate to get laid, and let the mental images match the soundtrack coming from across the hall.

"Oh my God..." Not Justin's voice. "Do that again. That thing with your tongue. Just—yeah! *Yeah! Oh God!"*

My toes curled and my back arched off the bed. I could suddenly see Justin eagerly blowing the other guy—no, blowing *me*—and I'd obviously gone too long without getting laid because that was seriously, *seriously* hot, and I jerked myself faster as the moans across the hall intensified. Fuck, what would he look like with a cock in his mouth? My cock? And if he let his eyes flick up while he was deep-throating, and—

Then came a helpless cry, the unmistakable sound of release, and it took every bit of self-control I possessed to keep from crying out with the force of my own orgasm. Lips pressed together, eyes squeezed shut, I stroked until it was too intense, and then loosened my grip and relaxed back on the mattress. My head spun, especially as I tried to catch my breath without making a sound, and I needed a minute before I could summon the coordination to reach for a tissue.

At the end of the bed, there was some movement, followed by the heavy flop of Azrael lying down against my foot with an audible huff of disdain.

Then the whole room was quiet again. The whole house was quiet. I thought I heard some heavy breathing and subtle movement next door, but my heart was beating so hard, it drowned everything else out.

Whoa. That was...

I swept my tongue across my lips. I had no idea how to feel having just jerked off to two men getting laid. Or that one of those men was my best friend.

And I *definitely* didn't know how to feel about the fact that I'd never come that hard in my life.

CHAPTER 14

JUSTIN

What was I thinking?

I'd had that morning-after thought a few times in the past, especially back when I used to drink too much. Even sober, it wasn't unheard of for me to wake up, turn to the naked guy sleeping next to me, and wonder what the fuck had possessed me to think hooking up with him had been a good idea.

It was different this time. I didn't bother analyzing why. I didn't have to.

Suppressing a frustrated sigh, I got up. I took a quick shower, keeping it extra short in case he wanted to take one too. I really did need to do something about that stupid water heater. In fact, I'd had every intention of replacing it weeks ago, but I'd been a little... distracted recently.

I sighed as I rinsed some shampoo out of my hair. This thing with Tyler was getting out of control. Especially since there *wasn't* a thing between us. Just my decades-old pining that had been in high gear ever since I'd picked him up at SeaTac, and it wasn't going to stop until I made a conscious effort to stop it.

Last night was a good step, I told myself as I got out of the shower.

I hooked up with someone for the first time since Tyler got here. That's something, right?

Sure, if I ignored the fact that I'd grabbed onto the first available distraction so I wouldn't have to watch Tyler getting cozy with that brunette. So I didn't have to think, from moment to moment, about what the two of them were getting up to. Having Hector's dick down my throat had kept me from thinking of Tyler's fingers running through her hair. Making out with Hector had meant not torturing myself with Tyler's lips skating up the side of her neck. Begging Hector not to stop had shut off the flood of images of Tyler arching under her and swearing as he got closer.

Damn it. Maybe we should go one more time just to give my brain a break.

When I came out of the bathroom, though, Hector was sitting on the edge of the bed. He'd already put on his jeans, and he had his shirt in one hand and his phone in the other.

"Morning," I said.

"Morning." He looked up at me, smiled, then quickly finished something on his phone before he rose. "Just nailing down an Uber."

"Oh. Already?"

"Yeah. I mean, last night was awesome." He kissed my cheek. "But I really have to get going. You don't mind me bailing, do you?"

Saves me the trouble of kicking you out.

I regretted my unspoken thought. I wouldn't have kicked him out. I wouldn't have been rude or treated him like shit—I'd vowed never to do that a long time ago, especially after a couple of my hookups had all but relegated me to the same level as the wadded up tissues from the night before.

"No, of course not." I smiled. "Do you want some coffee before you go?"

He checked his phone, then shrugged. "I've got fifteen minutes before the driver gets here. I could go for some coffee."

"Great. Come on."

I should have been disappointed that he was making such a quick escape. I should have wanted him to stay so we could maybe fool around one more time. After all, he was perfectly attractive, and he'd been into me. Unselfish, enthusiastic, and hung like he hadn't pissed off a deity in a past life.

But my heart hadn't been in it. Oh, I'd gone through the motions, and I'd made sure he'd got off a couple of times, but all the while, I'd wanted to be anywhere but here. Or at least here but alone.

All because I couldn't get my stupid mind off my stupid roommate.

I sighed as Hector and I left my bedroom and headed for the kitchen to get some coffee. It was pathetic, being this hung up on a man who I knew was straight. A man who was most likely in that woman's bed. Probably getting another round in before he kissed her goodbye. They'd probably rocked each other's worlds last night, and maybe they were drinking coffee while they flirted some more and debated going one more time and—

I skidded to a halt so suddenly, Hector almost crashed into me. "Tyler. Hey. I... didn't think you'd be..."

Behind me, Hector tensed. "Uh..."

"Oh. Um." I cleared my throat and turned around. "This is Tyler. My roommate. Tyler, this is Hector."

They exchanged awkwardly murmured hellos from across the kitchen island, where Tyler was sitting with a cup of coffee in his hands.

"I..." I coughed again. "Didn't realize you came home last night."

He shrugged weakly. "Surprise?"

Alarm bells went off in my head. Had something gone wrong? Should I have stuck around?

Suddenly Hector's Uber couldn't get here fast enough. Again, I felt like a dick for thinking like that, but he had one foot out the door already and I wanted the other one to follow so I could find out what was going on in Tyler's head.

Not a moment too soon, Hector and I were at my front door,

exchanging one of those chaste kisses that meant we still wanted a kiss but didn't want to inflict morning breath on each other.

"I'll text you," he said.

"Sounds good."

We smiled at each other, and I was pretty sure I wasn't going to see him again. That was fine—this was all we'd signed up for.

As soon as he was in the car, I went back inside and jogged up the stairs to the kitchen. Tyler was at the counter, low-slung jeans snug on his hips and thin T-shirt showing off the body I couldn't touch. I gave myself a nanosecond to ogle him before I cleared my throat and casually pulled another mug from the cupboard.

"So when did you get home?" I asked. "I didn't even hear you come in."

"Last night." He stirred some sugar into his coffee. "I, uh... bailed."

I stared at him. "You didn't go home with her?"

He shook his head. "No. I..."

He didn't finish the thought, and I didn't press because all I could think was if he'd come home early, he'd probably heard a lot. Hell, he'd probably heard everything. I'd never been quiet in bed, and I'd been louder than usual last night in a desperate bid to sound more into it than I actually was. I hadn't realized... *fuck*.

I met his eyes. Some blush crept into his cheeks. Warmth rushed into mine.

We quickly broke eye contact, and he moved away from the coffeepot, letting me fill my cup while he took his seat again. I glanced at him. He was distant and tense, and I had no idea how to read him right then. Once I'd finished making my coffee, I faced him and cautiously said, "I really thought you two were into each other."

"Yeah. Me too." He laughed humorlessly, probably going for self-deprecating and landing closer to mortified. "Guess I just suck at closing the deal."

I didn't laugh. Cradling my cup in both hands, I watched him over the counter. I had no idea what to say.

Tyler stared into his coffee cup for a moment, then sighed. "I thought we'd end up... I mean, I really wanted to ... I don't know." He exhaled hard, shoulders sagging. "Maybe I'm just not ready for this after all."

"You don't think so?"

He half-shrugged. "If last night was any indication, I need some more time before I put myself out there. I mean, I was doing fine with her, and we were having a good time, but then it was like my heart suddenly wasn't in it. She was turning me on like crazy, but I..." He lifted his gaze, his eyes so full of emotion they almost shoved me back a step. "I couldn't do it."

"Then don't push yourself, sweetheart," I said. "There's no rush, you know? You just got out of a long marriage, and you're still getting your whole life back together." I cringed. "Maybe I pushed you too hard to—"

"No, you didn't." He shook his head. "I wanted that. The push was exactly what I needed to put myself out there, and I wanted to meet someone... right up until I didn't."

I frowned, wishing like hell I could read his mind and understand what had changed. What in the world had flipped that switch? I settled on quietly murmuring, "I'm sorry it didn't go down the way you'd hoped."

"Eh." He cracked a faint smile and looked at me through his lashes. "How did your night go?"

"Um." I cleared my throat, my face on fire now. *As if you don't know how my night went.* Except... he really didn't. Oh, he knew about the loud sex. He probably knew Hector and I had both gotten off more than once.

But he didn't know the rest, and I didn't know why the rest bothered me so much. It wasn't like Tyler was homophobic; he lived with a gay man, after all, and that meant overhearing two men in bed was always a possibility. And he didn't seem disgusted or upset about it.

So why was *I* disgusted with myself and upset about the whole thing? Or... hell, what *did* I feel about it all? Because there were a lot of feelings coursing through me right then, and I couldn't put a name on a single one of them.

"Justin?" He appeared beside me, startling me. I'd been so caught up in my own thoughts, I hadn't noticed him getting up and coming around the island. "You okay?"

"Yeah. Yeah, I'm..." I took a sip of coffee to buy myself some time, but it still wasn't enough to come up with a decent explanation. Instead, I settled on, "Just feel kind of bad for subjecting a roommate to..."

"It's okay." There was a smile in his voice, and when I chanced a look at his face, the smile was on his lips too. "You didn't know I was there, and I'm glad you were having a good time."

Oh honey. If you only knew.

"Well." I forced a smile. "If you're not ready, we can bail on the whole club scene for a while."

Tyler nodded. "Probably not a bad idea. Guess I need to spend a little more time getting back on my feet than I thought."

"It's okay. Everyone bounces back from things like that in their own time." I couldn't resist, and gave his arm a gentle squeeze. "You'll get there when you get there."

"Hopefully sooner than later." He paused. "Anyway. I need to get down to the storage place today and get things arranged so my stuff can be delivered. I should probably make myself halfway presentable."

"Do you need help with things at the storage place?"

"Nah." He shot me a lopsided little grin. "I'll drag you there when it's time for the heavy lifting."

"Bring it, darlin'." I flexed my bicep. "I've been training for this."

He laughed with some actual feeling, rolled his eyes, and went to put his coffee cup in the sink. "There enough hot water for me to get a shower?"

"Should be."

"Okay. Well. I'll see you later today?"

"Yeah." I brought my own coffee up for a sip. "See you."

One last quick smile, and he left the kitchen. As he walked away, I lowered my cup without bothering to take that sip. My throat tightened, and what little coffee I'd swallowed threatened to come back up.

I'd always known I had it bad for Tyler.

But somehow knowing the man I loved had overheard me having sex with someone I'd only been with because he'd pulled my focus away from Tyler—that left me with a sick knot burning in my gut. I still didn't know how what to call any of these feelings, but I didn't like them at all.

Question is—what do I do about them?

CHAPTER 15

TYLER

No matter how much I tried to avoid them, phone calls with my ex-wife were inevitable. Once the divorce was final, we could both move on and never have to talk to each other again, but in the meantime, a certain amount of communication had to happen. In theory, we could have had our lawyers play go-between for a lot of it, but that got really, really expensive, so when she called me at work one Thursday afternoon, I bit the bullet and answered.

"Hey. What's up?"

"Hey." She paused as if she wanted me to say something, but then she took a deep breath. "I just wanted to let you know we're probably getting an offer on the house soon."

"Oh. Good." That was a hell of a relief—we wouldn't make much money off it, particularly after we'd split it, but even a little windfall would be seriously helpful. "Do I need to sign anything?"

"Not yet. The buyer was going to back to talk to her agent, so we'll probably see an offer tomorrow. She sounds pretty eager to close it as quickly as possible, though, which is why I wanted to give you the heads up."

"Sounds great. I'll keep an eye on my inbox."

"Okay."

Silence set in again. My stomach was in knots—its default state whenever she called—and I suspected I'd be tense and distracted for the rest of the day. Always happened after we'd talked, even if it was a peaceful conversation about something benign.

Always happened... except one time.

Minutes after our last conversation, I'd been back in the club watching Justin sing, mesmerized by him the same way I'd been at prom. Then he'd regaled his friends with stories of my cooking, and we'd found ourselves casually cuddled up in the booth almost like we had on his couch that one night. Any other night, I'd have been grinding my teeth and tearing my hair out over talking to her, but that night, her call had stopped mattering because... Justin had happened

Gina exhaled on the other end. "All right, I need to go. That's all I—"

"Wait." I glanced at my office door. It was shut, and half the staff in this part of the building were in a meeting. There probably wasn't anyone around to overhear, and these walls were pretty thick. "Before you go..."

On the other end, she sighed. "Yeah?"

"Can I ask about something?"

"Okay? I guess?"

I swallowed, eyeing the closed door again. "Why were you so convinced I was going to leave you for Justin?"

There was a subtle catch of breath, so that probably wasn't the question she'd been anticipating. "What?"

I closed my eyes and rubbed my forehead. "I mean, you thought I was screwing some of my coworkers, including some of the guys. You thought I was going to leave you for Justin. Was... was there something that made you think I was into men?"

My ex-wife was quiet for a long moment. I was about to tell her she didn't have to answer when she finally spoke.

"Sometimes there was just this vibe, I guess. When you were talking to a guy, or even looking at one." She paused. "You don't look at men the way other straight guys do. You never have. And I guess that made me wonder." Another pause. "Why?"

"I don't know. I'm... I was just curious."

"And as for Justin..." She didn't sound defensive and hostile like she usually did when we discussed Justin. Resigned if anything. Maybe sad. "Whenever you've been around him, you're practically walking on air afterward. That was why I hated joining you two. I hated how happy you seemed around him."

I blinked, struggling to unpack everything in that comment. "You didn't like me being happy?"

"It's not that. It's how happy he seemed to make you. It bothered me, you know? You were never that happy with me."

I pressed my lips together. *That probably had more to do with us than him, Gina.*

"Why is this coming up now? Is there something going on between—?"

"No," I said quickly. "It came up when I was talking to my therapist the other day." Little white lie, but whatever. "So I was thinking about it."

"Oh. I see."

"Anyway, that's all I wanted to know." I drummed my fingers on my desk. "Just, um, keep me updated about the house?"

We hung up a moment later, but I didn't get back to work. That short conversation had fried something in my brain, and I needed a minute to make sense of it.

Any other time, I would have written off her answers as more gaslighting and deflection. To a degree, I was still convinced that was what all her accusations had ever been—just a mind game to keep me from noticing she was the one who was cheating, and a way for her to blame me for driving her to it. But I felt like there was a nugget of truth here. Something legitimate tucked into all the bullshit.

Or maybe I was just reading too much into it because I wanted things to make sense, and if my ex-wife had seen something in me and in Justin, then maybe that would make sense of me jerking off to the sounds of Justin getting laid the other night. Especially the part where I'd started imagining Justin going down on me, and had nearly lost my mind. *Had* she seen something I hadn't?

If she had, what did I do with that? She'd seen something. My exes over the years had seen something. The other night had happened. And...?

I exhaled hard into the silence of my office.

What the hell is happening?

"You look like you had a rough day." Justin shrugged off his jacket in the kitchen. "Everything okay?"

"Eh. I think I could use a drink. Several, actually."

"Oh yeah?"

I nodded. "Phone call with the ex-wife."

His eyebrows shot up. "Oh. Hmm, yeah, I think that's grounds for a drink or several. Why don't you go see if there's a stupid movie on, and I'll open a bottle?"

I smiled. Trust him to know exactly what I needed tonight.

And my heart skipped.

"It's how happy he seemed to make you. It bothered me, you know?"

I gulped, watching Justin peruse the well-stocked wine rack.

"You were never that happy with me."

Justin glanced up at me. "What?"

"Um." I cleared my throat. "Uh... any particular movie?"

He pursed his lips, then shrugged. "You're the one who had a shitty afternoon. You pick."

"Oh. Okay." I forced myself to break eye contact and walk into the living room instead of just staring at him while my ex-wife's words echoed in my head. What did all this mean? Or did it mean anything at all? It was entirely possible I was fixating on—

Justin came in cradling two wineglasses between his fingers and carrying the bottle in his other hand, and my thoughts scattered. He smiled at me. "Is white okay? I felt like something sweet tonight."

"Yeah. Yeah, white sounds good." I gestured at the TV. "Want to watch the *South Park* movie?"

"Oh hell yeah, I do." He dropped onto the couch beside me. "Give me crude and immature any day."

"Some things never change, right?"

"Exactly." He paused. "Food. We need some food. Should we order a pizza?"

"Pizza, cartoons, and wine?" I laughed as I picked up one of the glasses. "Sounds like the perfect evening."

Especially spending it with you.

Two movies later, Justin opened up another bottle of wine. Shit, how many had we blown through already? Eh, in the mood I was in, I was pretty sure I could kill two or three more tonight, so bring it on.

You have to work tomorrow, remember? And the class reunion is tomorrow night? Maybe don't overdo it?

All right. One more bottle between us, and then we'd be done.

He poured us each some more, took a sip, and turned to me. "Okay, so now that you're good and lubed up—"

I choked on my wine and almost spat it on him.

He laughed. "Just fucking with you. Relax." He winked. "Seriously, though—now that you've had a few gallons of wine, what's going on? What did the Wicked Witch of the East say?"

"Not much, honestly. Just an update on selling the house. We only talked for a few minutes. She thinks we have a buyer, so..." I held up my hand with my fingers crossed.

Justin didn't seem convinced. "That's it?"

"Does it need to be more than that?" I exhaled. "Just talking to her about the damn weather stresses me out."

"Hmm. Fair." He was eyeing me, though, as if he could see a card I was trying to hide.

I shifted uncomfortably. There had been more to our conversation, but was that something I wanted to talk about with Justin? Was there enough wine in this house for that?

I stared into my wineglass, wondering if I should refill it again.

"Tyler?" Justin touched my arm, and his voice was soft. "What's going on?"

"I..." I glanced at him, then drained my glass and reached for the bottle. I topped us both off, put the bottle back down, and turned to him. "We talked about whether or not she thinks I'm gay."

That seemed to sober him up in an instant. The playful smile vanished, and he looked in my eyes as he absently swirled his wine. "And what conclusion did you come to?"

"Well, she doesn't think I'm gay." I stared into my glass. "She doesn't think I'm particularly straight either."

"So, bi?"

"Maybe?" I lifted my gaze. "She just thinks there's a vibe when I'm around men. Something that isn't there between straight guys."

Justin swallowed. "Oh really?"

"Yeah. I..." I forced a laugh. "I mean, it doesn't make sense, right? I'm thirty-fucking-eight. I think I'd know by now if dudes turned my crank."

Justin laughed too, but then he shrugged. "You never know, man. I mean, have you ever tried anything with a guy?"

I almost choked again. "What?"

"What? It's a fair question."

Does masturbating while two men are having sex in the next room count?

I took a sip just to wet my mouth again. "Did you ever try anything with a girl?"

Justin snorted, waving his drink and almost dropping it. "Fuck yeah, I did."

"What? When?"

"In junior high." He rolled his eyes and sighed dramatically. "Come on, dude. What do you think us theater techs were doing backstage?"

"Uh, theater tech stuff?'

"Well yeah, that, but we were also doing the other theater techs."

I sat up. "In junior high?"

He waved his hand again, this time keeping a better grip on the glass. "Okay, we weren't fucking or anything, but I'd done enough that by ninth grade, I *definitely* knew I was gay."

"Oh." I fought the urge to fidget nervously. "So, what? I can't say I'm definitely straight until I've sucked a few dicks?"

"I did not say that." He wagged a finger at me. "Don't put words in my mouth."

"Just put a dick in your mouth?" Whoa, I was getting drunk. My filter was gone.

Justin laughed again, but he seemed almost flustered, his cheeks coloring as he dropped his gaze. "I'm always down for a dick in my mouth, hon." He took a long drink, and why the hell was it so fascinating to watch his throat work as he swallowed? Probably because I'd had a little too much wine. Or a lot too much wine.

I set the glass on the table and nudged it away.

"Look." He balanced his own glass on his knee. "I'm not saying you have to try anything. I'm just asking if *you've* ever asked yourself if you *want* to?"

I studied him, wondering if I was a tad too drunk to parse all of that.

He put his free hand on my leg, his palm hot through my jeans. "Everyone just assumes they're straight. And a lot of people are. It's okay, you know? But how many people actually think about it? Stop and ask, *am* I into dudes? *Would* I like sucking dick? It's totally okay if the answer is no. I just don't think a lot of"—he lifted his hand to make air quotes—"*straight people* have really considered it." I almost didn't catch that last part because his hand landed on my leg again.

"Huh." I swallowed, wondering if I needed some more wine after all. "I never thought of it like that."

"So, you never thought about being queer?"

"I guess not. Aside from repeatedly telling people I'm straight."

Justin shook his head. "That's not thinking about being queer. That's being defensive when someone suggests you are. And in my experience, people who've spent as much time as you have shooting down the suggestion are the people who've given it the least amount of consideration."

I furrowed my brow.

Justin sipped his wine. "If everyone would just back off and not browbeat people, or accuse them of being queer like it's some horrible thing, then no one would need to feel defensive. But they do, and then it's really easy for someone to get so defensive to everyone else that they shut *themselves* off to the possibility too." He sighed. "There's only so many times you can say 'I'm not gay' to the rest of the world before you convince yourself too."

"Unless I'm really not gay."

"You probably aren't." He shrugged. "You obviously like women. Maybe you're straight. Maybe you're bi. Who knows? But *you* won't know unless you actually think about it."

I thought about it for a moment. It was an interesting question. *Did* I find men attractive? I genuinely had never considered it. I'd asked Gina what made her think I was into men, and I'd questioned what it meant that I'd jerked off over Justin and his one night stand, but *was* I attracted to men? Was there something that my ex-wife and ex-girlfriends had seen that I'd been oblivious to?

"Huh. Maybe I should try it."

Justin's eyes widened. "Oh really?"

"Yeah, I mean..." Heat rushed into my face, and it wasn't from the wine. Was it? "You're right. I've never thought about it before. So maybe I should."

Justin set his drink on the coffee table next to mine, then sat back beside me. He seemed closer now, but I couldn't decide if that was real, the alcohol, or my imagination. "You serious?"

I gulped. "Yeah. Yeah, I am."

"So, if I offered..." He raised his eyebrows.

My pulse did things it had never done before, and I wondered if Justin's mouth had always been that interesting. "*Are* you offering?"

"Maybe." He half-shrugged. "I mean, I don't want things to be weird between us, but if we can agree it's a one-time thing to see if you like it..."

I sat up a little. "Uh, how much are you offering, exactly?"

Justin laughed and patted my leg. "Relax. I wasn't going to drop trou and offer you my ass." He winked. "Just a kiss."

"A..." I swallowed again. "Oh."

Kissing a man. Kissing Justin. The thought was oddly intriguing. Kind of thrilling. Arousing? I wasn't sure. But it was definitely doing something, and it wasn't repulsing me.

"You don't have to," he said. "But if you're curious, say the word."

I gulped, my eyes flicking to his lips. How had I never noticed how full they were? "I'm definitely curious."

Justin studied me for several long seconds before he scooted closer to me, and now his leg was against mine, touching from our hips to our knees. He was right—I'd never given a second's thought to being with a guy. Now that we were sitting this close, now that I couldn't help glancing from his eyes to his lips and back... holy shit.

"So, you want to?" He lifted his eyebrows. "Just to see what it feels like?"

I couldn't speak, so I nodded.

A little grin flickered across his gorgeous mouth. Then he put a hand on my knee, maybe to steady himself, and leaned in closer. My heart pounded as I mirrored him.

Before this moment, I'd never thought about kissing a man, but suddenly I wanted—no, *needed*—to know if his lips were as soft as they looked, and if his fingers would be warm or cool against my face, or how his stubbled chin would feel against mine, or how this was making me hard, or—

He stiffened.

I stopped.

His hand lifted off my leg, and he drew back, eyes widening with something like horror. "Oh fuck."

"What?" My pulse surged. "What's—"

"I can't. I'm sorry." He got up and grabbed his glass off the coffee table, nearly sloshing the contents onto both of us.

"Wait what?" I rose too. "Justin, what's—"

"This was a bad idea. I'm sorry I—" He shook his head. "I'm sorry."

Then he disappeared down the hall. His bedroom door closed with a quiet click, and I stood there in the living room, jaw slack and heart thumping. Into the silence, I whispered, "Justin?" I didn't even know why. I was just so stunned and confused. And hard.

What the hell just happened?

CHAPTER 16

JUSTIN

I wasn't usually the type for dramatic exits or hiding from people, but damn it, I needed to get away from him. I needed... I needed a minute. Or maybe the rest of the night. Or *something*.

Safely in my bedroom, I closed my eyes and leaned against the door. I started to bring my hands up to run them through my hair, and realized I was still holding my wineglass. At least I had the presence of mind to set it on the dresser before I dropped it on the carpet.

Restlessness kicked in, and I started pacing across the bedroom floor, arms folded across my stomach like I might be sick. Maybe I would.

God. What the fuck was I thinking?

Because it sure as hell hadn't been entirely an altruistic need to help my friend figure out if he was entirely heterosexual. Or a result of too much wine. Or because I was horny tonight. I'd wanted Tyler for years, and I'd wanted him more than I'd ever wanted any other man, but not like this. Not when it was just a wine-fueled experiment. I could take rejection, but I couldn't handle kissing the man I loved, and then having him pull back and say *"Well, that settles it. I am* definitely *straight."*

And that was exactly what would have happened tonight. I would have had my decades-old fantasy followed by the worst rejection imaginable, and it would have fucking broken me, and there would have been no one to blame but myself. I'd want to be angry at Tyler, but even in the middle of this emotional maelstrom, I knew I couldn't blame him. I'd offered, for God's sake. I'd needled him about how much consideration he'd given to being attracted to men, and then offered myself up on a silver fucking platter so he could decide if he wanted me. Wanted *men*. Not me—*men*.

Whatever helps you sleep at night.

I rubbed my eyes with the heels of my hands. Damn it. Damn it, damn it, *damn it*.

What was I supposed to do now? Go back out there, pretend everything was fine, and act like that playful little drunk experiment hadn't left me feeling like my heart had just been ripped out of my chest? I tried to tell myself I was just being a drama llama. Except I didn't think I was.

With any other man, I would've been fine. A kiss to see if he liked it? Maybe a blowjob or something? No problem. I could separate sex and love, and if a guy wanted to experiment and we both knew that was all it was, I could be totally onboard.

Not with Tyler. I'd been in way too deep over him for way too long to be so casual about touching him, especially when we both knew it would just solidify his heterosexuality. Plus we'd have to see each other every goddamned day until he moved out, and hell if I knew when that would be.

Sighing, I sank onto the foot of the bed.

And for the first time, I hoped Tyler found his own place sooner than later.

After the worst night of sleep I'd had in a long time, I gently pried my arm from under my sleeping cat's dead weight, and winced as I flexed my numb fingers to get the circulation moving again. She huffed irritably, kicked me with her hind leg, and covered her face with her front paw.

"Oh, don't be such a diva." I scratched her side, and she grudgingly started purring. "That's what I thought." Then she kicked me again, so I stopped. I got up carefully so I didn't disturb her more than I already had, and went in to take a shower.

As the hot water ran over me, my mind went back to the same place it had been for most of the night—that moment on my couch. I replayed it a few times until I'd good and tortured myself to the point of almost tears again. Then I wondered if it was bothering Tyler. He probably wondered why I'd bolted, but was that the only thing about last night that didn't sit right? Assuming he hadn't just shrugged it off and gone on with his life.

No. That wasn't like him. I had no doubt he'd noticed, and he was probably worried. He was giving me space because he knew me that well. He'd wait for me to come to him.

I hadn't gone back out to the living room last night. Tyler hadn't made any attempt to break the silence. No knock at my door. No cautious text. At some point, I'd heard him go to bed, and I'd spent most of the night wondering if he could sleep. It didn't seem fair for him to be able to sleep when I was wide awake.

Eventually, though, I'd drifted off. It wasn't anything I'd call restful, but with a little coffee, I'd get through the day. Maybe. Hopefully.

And then what? How were Tyler and I supposed to move past last night? Was it even a big deal to him?

Maybe it shouldn't have been such a big deal to me. It wasn't like Tyler had been trying to take advantage of me or use me. I'd brought up the subject. I'd offered. I didn't know if it was the wine that had lowered my inhibitions, or if I'd just wanted to grab onto the one and only opportunity I'd ever have to know what it felt like to kiss Tyler. Either way, I'd been stupid, and now I was scared shitless we'd damaged our friendship. That *I'd* damaged our friendship.

Fuck. I thumped my fist against the shower wall. After all this time, I had my friend back, and now... what if I'd fucked things up?

I was so caught up in my thoughts that I only vaguely registered the water starting to cool, and a moment later, I grunted in surprise when ice cold water hit my back. I flailed to both get out of the way and shut off the shower at the same time. Holy shit. I was awake now.

I glared up at the showerhead. Well this morning was off to a fabulous start, wasn't it?

With a sigh, I stepped out of the shower and grabbed a thick towel off the rack.

"Idiot," I muttered, and wrapped the towel around myself before I started shivering. I felt like a dumbass because I knew the lukewarm water was the brief warning before it all turned cold, but I'd been off in dramaland and...

God, I'm going to be useless at work today, aren't I?

And probably an awesome conversationalist at the reunion tonight.

I froze, meeting my own wide-eyed reflection.

That was tonight, wasn't it?

The thought of walking into that hotel ballroom made my skin crawl. My nerves came on so fast and so strong, they made me queasy. It wasn't even the prospect of facing all those classmates who'd probably forgotten who I was, though—it was the one who lived with me.

My throat tightened. Great. Just what I needed. An evening with him among all those people who thought I was really *with* him. Fuck.

But first, I had to get through this morning with him since we could never seem to avoid each other before we left for our respective jobs.

I took a deep breath. Okay. Get dressed. Get some coffee. Then maybe my head would be clear enough to look this thing in the eye and unfuck it. And if I got to the kitchen sooner than later, maybe I could get the caffeine flowing before I had to face Tyler.

Or not—he was already in the kitchen.

Coffee cup in hand, he leaned against the counter, and he avoided my eyes. "Hey."

"Hey."

And... silence. What a shock. Because how the hell were we supposed to talk about last night? I wasn't even sure I had the vocabulary for it, never mind the intestinal fortitude to get through that conversation. I knew damn well it would only fester if we tried to ignore it, but right now, this morning, on this little sleep and with this many thoughts ricocheting around in my throbbing head, I couldn't. I just couldn't.

"Listen, um..." I rocked on my heels. "I think I'm going to skip the reunion."

His eyes widened. "What?"

"I think I'm going to stay home. Get some work done on the house." I gestured at my partially gutted living room as if he might have forgotten we were living in a construction zone.

Tyler studied me. I could read the *is this about last night?* loud and clear in his eyes, but he didn't actually ask the question, and I wasn't about to answer it. I was at a loss for a lot of words this morning, and I didn't know how to tell him that I couldn't face all those people, especially not the dozen or so I'd run into over the years who'd casually asked me the same question:

"*Are you and Tyler still a thing?*"

Because everyone who'd ever known the two of us had assumed we were. Or would be. Or should be. It had bothered me then, especially whenever I'd had to smile while they'd unintentionally salted my wound, but there was no way in hell I could handle it tonight.

Tyler cleared his throat. "If you really want to go, I can skip it."

Our eyes met.

Dropping my gaze, I shook my head. "No. I... I think I'm just going to stay in tonight." I forced a smile and managed to make eye contact again for all of two seconds. "Say hi to anyone we both know."

"Justin, if you want to—"

"Don't. Okay?" I hated how bad my voice shook. "I need to sit this one out."

I thought he might argue or at least try to dig into why I was bailing. He probably knew exactly what had triggered all this even if he didn't know everything going on in my head, and knowing him, he wouldn't want to leave all this alone. He didn't like tension. I hated awkward conversations, but Tyler had always hated awkward silences, so I cringed inwardly, waiting for him to broach the subject and start pulling this thing apart even though it was killing me just thinking about it.

But he didn't.

"I'm, uh..." He cleared his throat. "I'm going to go finish getting ready for work." He dumped the rest of his coffee down the drain, put the unrinsed cup in the sink, and left without saying anything more.

As soon as he was gone, I slumped against the counter and whispered "Fuck" into the silence. I felt like an idiot for being so dramatic about last night, and I had no idea how to explain *why* I was being so dramatic about it. Why it bothered me so much. Why it hurt so much.

Down the hall, I could hear him talking to Azrael, so she must have wandered into his bedroom like she sometimes did. Usually, I would think it was cute, listening to him explaining to her why she couldn't stay on his bed while he was at work and that no, she couldn't have his shoelaces, but today it just made my heart sick.

Closing my eyes, I wiped a hand over my face. More and more, I wanted to start dropping hints about him finding his own place. I could pick up an apartment guide while I was out. Send him a link to some websites. Anything to gently nudge him in the direction of leaving.

Which made me feel like an asshole, but after last night, I couldn't shake the realization that letting him move in with me had been a mistake. I hardly would have let him wind up on the street, and I'd never kick him out, but I wasn't sure my sanity could handle this arrangement much longer. *Any* longer.

I wanted him in my life, but maybe not in my house. If last night had taught me anything, it was that where Tyler and I were concerned, there was definitely such thing as *too close*. Especially since getting closer to him wasn't an option.

So how the hell did I put some comfortable distance between us?

CHAPTER 17

TYLER

There were more people at the reunion than I'd anticipated. Our class had been huge—just over four hundred—but I was amazed at how many had actually shown up tonight. A lot of them had brought spouses and partners too, so the chain hotel ballroom was crowded as hell.

Drink in hand, I surveyed the sea of faces. I wasn't intimidated or anything. Not at all. Not me.

God, this would be so much easier with my fearless extrovert of a best friend beside me, but—

No. I was *not* going to think about that right now. Justin and I would work things out. Everything had been weird since we'd almost kissed, but it was nothing we couldn't talk over and move past. Right?

A ball of nerves had taken up residence in my stomach the moment he'd walked out of the room last night, and it seemed to triple in size right then. We *could* move past this, couldn't we?

So much for not thinking about Justin. Damn it.

I closed my eyes and took a deep breath.

Okay. When I got home, we'd talk. For now, I was here, and I wouldn't get this opportunity again for another ten years. I'd stay, catch up with people I hadn't seen in ages, and then go home to Justin.

Not that I'm putting that off or avoiding it or anything. Nooo, not me.

I took a drink and tamped those thoughts down, promising myself over and over that I *would* talk to Justin after I got home. In the meantime...

I kept to the sidelines at first, something I'd always done if I came to a big event alone. I signed the guestbook, looked at the big collage someone had made of photos of people over the years, and made small talk for a moment with someone who I thought might've sat next to me in Geometry in tenth grade, but couldn't be sure.

At the far end of the room, there was a memorial poster for our classmates who'd passed away over the last twenty years. That was a hard thing to take in. Intellectually, I'd always understood that with a class of almost four hundred people, the odds were good that at least a handful wouldn't live long enough to go to our twenty-year reunion. Still, seeing them all in one place—that was breathtaking.

I scanned the familiar names and faces. I'd gone to Katie Ratner's funeral six months after graduation. I'd heard through the grapevine about Alex Waters and Julio Ruiz, who'd been in a car wreck on their way to Stevens Pass to go skiing a few years later. Seeing Jessica Holt, Quinn Chambers, and Aaron Harvey on the board took my breath away. I'd had no idea about any of them.

I wondered if Justin knew about Kevin Pauley. They'd been good friends back then. Maybe not as close as Justin and I had been, but close.

And I couldn't ask Justin because he wasn't here now.

My gut clenched at the memory of how weird things had gotten after last night. Was that why he'd bailed on the reunion? Because of me? He'd insisted he hadn't really wanted to come, but—

Stop. Just stop.

This reunion was big enough, we could have both shown up and not crossed paths much at all, but even still, maybe spending an evening apart was good for both of us. At least until we could figure out how to make things less weird.

Desperate for more distraction, I made myself wander into the crowd in search of people I knew. I hadn't come to my ten-year reunion, so aside from Facebook, this was the first time I'd seen a lot of these people in twenty years. Turned out time had been kind to some and less so to others.

Trevor Maxwell—my lab partner in Biology and my seatmate in the trumpet section—was still the same smiling chubby dude he'd been back then, just with a few more gray hairs, an incredibly sweet wife, and slightly different glasses. We caught up for a little while before separating to keep mingling, and I was glad I came if only to chat with Trevor for a minute. He was good people—always had been —and I was happy to see that life had treated him well.

I didn't even recognize Daniel Weber until I read his nametag. He'd been a Marilyn Manson clone goth kid back in the day, but now? Jesus fuck. His light brown hair was cut neat and short, and instead of Liquid Paper white, his complexion was faintly tanned. The eye makeup was gone. He'd replaced his long black trench coat with a well-cut blazer, which he wore over a faded gray Megadeth T-shirt. Okay, so some things hadn't changed. If not for the T-shirt, I might not have believed it was actually him.

Who knew that under the attitude, the heavy makeup, and the stringy dyed black hair lurked an incredibly good-looking guy with stunning dark eyes and—

Wait.

Are you checking out Daniel Weber?

Holy fuck. *Was* I checking—?

"Tyler?" A woman's voice pulled me out of my thoughts, and I turned to see a pretty brunette coming toward me with a cocktail in her hand.

I blinked, racking my brain as I tried to place her. I glanced at her nametag—Meghan Andrews—and the piece clicked into place. She'd sat with Trevor and me in band for two years. "Meghan! Holy shit. How are you?"

She smiled. "I'm good. How about you?"

"I'm doing all right. Just moved back to the area, actually."

"Yeah? Where were you before?"

"Chicago. Went there for school and never came back." I paused for a sip of my drink. "How about you? What's been going on?"

She shrugged. "Trying to get three kids through their teenage years without killing them."

"Teenagers?" I whistled. "Wow."

"I know, right?" She made a face. "Danielle Johnson's daughter *graduated* last year."

My jaw dropped. It wasn't like I hadn't known that some of our classmates had become parents before graduation, but it would never cease to blow my mind that people who'd been teenagers with me now had teenagers of their own. I *refused* to acknowledge that there would come a time in the nearish future when my peers started becoming grandparents.

Meghan looked around. "So is Justin here with you?"

I nearly spat out my drink, but managed to calmly reply, "What? No. Why would he be here with me?"

Her eyes widened. "Oh. Oh, I thought..." Cheeks coloring, she cleared her throat. "I saw on Facebook... I mean, I... someone said you were living together, and..." She paused to clear her throat. "I thought you guys were..."

"We—" I shook myself. "No, no. I mean, I *am* living with him, but I'm just crashing in his spare room while I get on my feet after my divorce." I laughed, hoping it didn't sound as forced as it was. "We're not dating or anything."

"Oh. Wow. I..." She laughed nervously. "It's funny—I always thought you two would end up together."

I blinked, completely at a loss for what to say. Usually I'd insist I was straight, but for some reason, this time I couldn't say anything at all.

"Well. Um." She cleared her throat again. "Tell him I said hi, would you?"

"I will." *If I can figure out how to talk to him at all.*

We drifted in opposite directions, but my mind stayed cemented to that conversation. It wasn't like it was the first time someone had implied they were expecting Justin and me to announce we were a couple.

"*Fuck, dude.*" Madison had elbowed me during Justin's graduation party karaoke performance and rolled her eyes. "*Why don't you two just get a room already?*"

"*You guys seem... close.*" A girlfriend in college had mused with no small amount of sarcasm the first time she'd met him.

"*One of these days,*" my ex-wife had said through her tears, "*you're going to go to Seattle and not come back because you're going to stay with* him."

And now, even a classmate I hadn't seen in twenty years clearly remembered how convinced she was that I was—or should be—with Justin.

What the hell had they all seen that I didn't? Two guys could be close friends without it being sexual or romantic. So what if one of us was gay? Even if we were both gay, there was no reason we couldn't be just friends, but it didn't matter anyway because one of us *wasn't* gay.

"*You never know, man,*" his voice echoed in my head. "*I mean, have you ever tried anything with a guy?*"

I swallowed. Up until last night, no. But then things had gone to shit and I'd been a wreck ever since. The damn house had thrummed with the same tension that was lurking in my gut.

In my mind's eye, I could see the way he'd looked at me right before it had all gone wrong. How our eyes had locked as we'd moved in for that kiss that never happened. I didn't think anyone had ever looked at me like that before.

But then he'd broken away and walked out, and he hadn't been able to meet my eyes since. I still couldn't figure out what had made him balk. Was he just not into me enough to stomach the idea of kissing me? Or had I done something wrong?

Maybe he'd been weirded out by the way I'd been staring at him. Because goddamn, in the seconds before he'd pulled back, I'd been hypnotized by him in a way I didn't think I'd ever experienced in my life. Had that shown on my face? Bothered him somehow?

And when have I ever looked at someone like that?

My heart skipped.

Never. Not once. Not my ex-girlfriends. Not my ex-wife. Not the woman I'd almost hooked up with the night Justin and I had gone to a club.

I'd *never* looked at anyone like I'd looked at Justin last night. For a fleeting moment, there had been nothing and no one in my world except for him and the anticipation of what it might feel like to have those full lips against mine.

And right on the heels of that truth came another:

No one had ever looked at *me* with as much hurt in their eyes as he had this morning.

The sudden urge to bolt out of the room was nearly overwhelming. My heart raced like it was priming my body for a sprint from here to the car. It wasn't fight or flight—more like the realization that this was absolutely *not* where I needed to be.

Why the hell was I wasting my evening with people I hadn't bothered to stay in contact with all this time? Screw nostalgia—I needed to be with the one person who had, no matter how many times I'd fucked up at his expense, always been there for me. The one who'd always been such a normal, permanent figure in my life that I'd never once stopped to wonder if there was something else to our friendship.

And if I didn't unfuck things with him sooner than later, I might never get the chance to figure that out.

I left my half-finished drink on an empty table and, without another word to anyone, got the hell out of there.

CHAPTER 18

JUSTIN

I never thought I'd be relieved to have Tyler out of the house, but damn, I was. While he went to our class reunion and probably found some old classmate to bang for a few hours, I could stay home and be pathetic in peace.

In a pair of old jeans and a T-shirt that was way too ratty to wear in public, I flopped onto the couch with my phone in one hand and the remote in the other. I'd debated a bottle of wine or something, but I knew me—if I started self-medicating, I'd drink too much too fast. Then tomorrow would be even more miserable than tonight. No thanks. Ice cream wasn't on the menu tonight either. Eating myself sick would be about as fun as drinking myself senseless; lesson learned the hard way.

That, and ice cream made me think of sitting at Cold Stone with Tyler, and damn him, I didn't want to think about him tonight at all.

So I munched on a handful of M&Ms—hey, I could eat a *few* of my emotions—and alternated between perusing Netflix and Grindr. Nothing on either sounded appealing. I gave up on Grindr first. What was the point in trying to go out and get laid? I wouldn't have fucked me tonight. Not when I was this depressed and pissed off and pitiful. Screw it. I'd find some ass another night. All I wanted to do for now was huddle under my grandma's afghan and watch some standup comedy specials I'd seen seventy-three times apiece.

I was halfway through the third special, and starting to kind of feel better. Mostly I wasn't thinking about why I felt like shit, and that went a long way toward making me feel *less* like shit. I'd call it a win.

But then headlights arced across the ceiling—a car turning down the driveway—and I swore around an M&M.

The soft purr of an engine approached. Slowed. Stopped. The lights went out.

Nobody just showed up here, and delivery guys always left their engines running. Not that they ever came by this late unless it was Christmastime.

"Oh, fuck my life," I grumbled. I'd hoped Tyler would stay late at the reunion, but it wasn't even nine o'goddamned-clock and he was home.

Unless—shit. Was it David?

Panic shot through me as footsteps came up the porch steps, but then keys jingled, and an odd sense of relief and rising dread made me squirm on the couch. It wasn't David, which was good.

It was, however, Tyler.

And I was so not ready to be in the same building as him.

I held my breath as he unlocked the front door, shut it, and turned the deadbolt. I listened to each step he took up to the living room, and I prayed and prayed and prayed and promised my firstborn and a lifetime of celibacy to whichever god made Tyler turn right instead of left.

Don't come in here, don't come in here, don't come in—

Goddammit.

I could feel him hovering in the living room doorway, and there was no avoiding him, so I turned my head. In as neutral a voice as I could, I said, "You're home early."

"Yeah." His eyes flicked away, but only for a second. "Listen, can we talk?"

My stomach somersaulted. Hangover be damned, I needed a drink if I was going to make it to the other end of *this* conversation.

"Okay." I got up and gestured for him to follow me into the kitchen. Without a word, he did. I got as far as pulling a glass out of the cupboard before he broke the silence.

"Why didn't you kiss me last night?"

I stiffened, then slowly turned to face him. "What?"

"You backed off." He swallowed, looking me right in the eyes with so many emotions I couldn't begin to identify, and his voice shook as he asked again, "Why didn't you kiss me?"

"Did..." I tried to read him even as I was trying to pull my own emotions together. Could he at least let me get a drink in my system first? Because going at this sober hurt like a son of a bitch. "Did you really blow off the reunion to ask me that?"

Tyler shifted his weight. He started to cross his arms, then went with sliding his hands into his pockets. "It was bothering me."

"Enough for you to..." I shook my head. "I don't understand why it's—"

"Please." His voice was soft and plaintive. "Just tell me why you didn't kiss me."

A lump rose in my throat. "Did you *want* me to?" I spat out the words with more venom than I intended, and we both flinched. Breaking eye contact, I sighed. "You're straight, Tyler. If you weren't, you'd have figured it out by now, and there was no point in—" I clenched my jaw. I didn't want to spell it out to him. To tell him that even fantasizing about kissing him had been a form of self-torture, and going through with it had been more than I could handle.

He gulped. "I haven't been able to get last night out of my head. And I don't think I will until we clear the air."

Clear the air? Clear the fucking air? Did he have any idea how much this had all been eating at me? There was no clearing the air. Not in any way that didn't throw us into a whole new emotional minefield. No matter what we did or said, talking about it would just make things worse. So would ignoring it. So... well, fuck it. If we had to look this thing in the eye and make it into something even bigger and more painful than it needed to be, we might as well get it over with.

"Fine." I folded my arms tightly across my chest to keep myself from shaking. "You really want to know?"

Tyler nodded.

I set my jaw and forced—or at least tried to force—my voice to stay steady. "Because I've spent twenty-five fucking years driving myself insane wondering what it would be like to be with you. And last night, I had the chance to taste it." Okay, so much for staying steady. Fuck. "But I had to stop because I can't spend the *next* twenty-five years knowing how good something is that I can't have." I swallowed hard. "I couldn't let my biggest fantasy turn into your drunken mistake and my biggest regret."

He stared at me, eyes wide and lips apart, as if he were struggling to absorb everything I'd said.

Maybe I was scared of what he'd finally say, or maybe the dam had just broken after all this time, but I couldn't stop. "I'll do anything for you, Tyler. You know that. You've always known that. But don't fucking ask me to be your experiment. If you want to fool around with a guy and see if maybe you've got a bisexual side, be my guest. But don't ask me to do it."

He blinked. "Last night was *your* idea, Justin. You—"

"And it was also my idea to back off," I threw back. "I wanted to indulge your curiosity, but then I realized I can't do it." Jabbing a finger at him, I shakily said, "And if you came back here tonight to ask me to finish the job, then please feel free to get the fuck out."

"Justin." He put up his hands. "That's not why I'm here. I don't want to use you or experiment with you."

"Then why are you here?" My voice shook so bad it startled me, and I turned away from him so I could at least try to pull myself together. Resting one hand on the kitchen island, I squeezed my eyes shut and took some slow, deep breaths. I had just about collected my composure when Tyler broke the silence.

"You want to know why I haven't seen you in five years?"

I swallowed against the lump in my throat, but it refused to move. I didn't answer, and either he took that as a yes, or he'd intended to tell me anyway.

"After the last time I saw you, Gina and I got into it. Over you."

I shifted, but didn't turn around.

He went on. "She told me she didn't want me to see you again because every time I did, she was afraid I wouldn't come back."

"I know," I snapped without even glancing over my shoulder. "She thought you were cheating with me and every other—"

"No," he said softly. "It wasn't like that."

I forced back my emotions and faced him. Folding my arms across my chest, I silently waited for him to go on.

He moistened his lips and set his shoulders back. "Yes, Gina thought I was screwing everyone who got within ten feet of me. Man, woman—didn't matter. But it wasn't like that with you. She was convinced I was in love with you." My throat tightened and my stomach hit the floor, and goddamn but I was *not fucking prepared* when Tyler whispered, "And I think she was right."

My knees almost dropped out from under me. "What?"

Eyes locked on mine, he took a cautious step closer. "I think she was right. I've... it took until now to figure it out, but I've always felt different about you than anyone else. I just... I just..." He exhaled and threw up a hand. "I was just too fucking stupid to realize what that meant."

I stared at him, disbelieving what I was hearing. This was a hallucination, wasn't it? Was I having a stroke? Was I *dead*?

Tyler closed some more of the space between us. "I love you, Justin. I always have. I don't know what that means—if I'm bi, or if I'm..." He made another frustrated gesture. "I don't know. I am so fucking confused and lost, and I feel like an idiot for making it this far in life and not even knowing who the fuck I am, and literally *all* I know is that I love you. And that I want you."

My lips parted. "Tyler..."

"I'm sorry if I made you feel like you were an experiment, or like I was using you." His voice was shaky now, and soft. "I was curious, and I felt safe with you so I thought, what the hell? But I didn't mean to hurt you or make you feel like this."

I lowered my gaze, clenching my teeth as a fresh wave of emotions threatened to break loose. I was not going to cry, for God's sake. I was *not*. I—

Tyler touched my face, and I realized he was brushing a tear off my cheek.

Okay. Fuck. Apparently I was going to cry.

I covered my face as I released a ragged breath, and damn him and God bless him, Tyler gathered me into his arms and held me to him. All this time, my biggest never-gonna-happen fantasy had been him telling me he loved me, but I'd never imagined it playing out this way. That he'd tell me, and I'd break, and suddenly I'd be shaking to pieces in his arms because there were just too many emotions crashing through me to do anything else.

Finally, I wrapped my arms around him, and his embrace tightened until I almost couldn't breathe. I didn't care. I'd waited way too long for him to hold me like this—I wasn't going to quibble about oxygen.

Digging my fingers into his back, I whispered, "I've loved you since we were kids."

"I know." He stroked my hair and pressed a kiss to my temple. "I think I have too. I was just too stupid to realize it."

I laughed softly because I... hell, I didn't know. I was lightheaded from the flurry of emotions, creeping up on delirious as a laugh escaped my lips and another tear escaped my eye. "I swear to God, I'm not usually this..."

He chuckled, running a trembling hand through my hair. "Neither am I."

Neither... what? I drew back, and our eyes met. We were almost as close as we'd been last night. And yeah, there was a tear in his eye too.

"For the record," he whispered shakily, "I wanted to kiss you last night because I was curious." He caressed my cheek. "I want to kiss you right now because you're you."

I smiled. "Then what are you waiting for?"

He held my gaze, studying me like he thought I was going to rescind the invitation.

Not a chance, baby. But if you don't make a move in the next two seconds—

He leaned in closer. I lifted my chin. For long heartbeats, we hovered there, so close we would've felt each other's breath if either of us had been breathing at all. Never in my life had I ever had to fight so hard against the urge to kiss someone, but somehow, I stayed still. He needed to do this. He needed to cross this line.

Tyler... please...

His hand slid around behind my neck.

And then...

He kissed me.

And it was everything. All my fantasies come to life. All my prayers answered. Twenty-five years of wondering how soft his lips were and how his kiss would taste. Twenty-five years of telling myself the reality could never begin to stack up against what I'd imagined, and oh God, it was all that and more.

His arm tightened around my waist, pulling me flush against him, and his fingers twitched in my hair. As I gently probed his lips with the tip of my tongue, and as he parted them with a soft sigh to let me in, I was beyond thankful it had taken us so many years to get here. This was too perfect for teenage fumbling and second-guessing. We needed the sureness of decades behind us before we could do this moment the justice it deserved.

Moaning into my kiss, he slid his tongue alongside mine and pressed our swelling cocks together. He had to feel how aroused I was. Had to recognize that hard ridge pressing back against his own. Between that and his chin grazing mine, stubble whispering across stubble, he had to be completely and consciously aware that he had a man in his arms. Knowing he couldn't escape that reality, that he was diving in without flinching, was heady as fuck. Maybe this was his first time kissing a man, and maybe his lips and fingers hesitated here and there as he ventured into uncharted territory, but there was also certainty in his touch. He may not have known exactly what to do with me, but I could tell from his kiss and his embrace that he knew he wanted this. He wanted *me*. And I didn't think anything had ever been more exhilarating.

Tyler touched his forehead to mine, and as our lips separated, we both panted like we'd just finished a sweaty, acrobatic fuck, not a gentle kiss in the kitchen.

"Oh God," he breathed.

"Y-yeah." I licked my lips, nearly grazing his. "Was thinking the same thing."

He exhaled. His thumb traced my cheekbone, and for the first time, I realized he was trembling. Subtly, but impossible to miss when I was pressed this close to him.

"Hey." I nudged his forehead gently with mine and brushed another kiss across his lips. "You okay?"

"Yeah. I'm... it's just... I never thought..." He paused, then brought both hands up to cradle my face, and he kissed me again with more certainty this time. He pressed me back against the counter and kissed me harder and deeper. There wasn't just certainty now—there was heat. Hunger. Real undeniable *need*. His first step across this line had been confident, but tentative, and now that tentativeness was a distant memory. Whatever nerves he'd had a moment ago seemed to be engulfed entirely by pure, sweet abandon. Like he'd been fighting these urges and desires for so long, and now he wanted to fly past surrender and straight into reckless.

Bring it, baby. Give me everything you've been keeping behind those floodgates.

Tyler broke the kiss with a whispered "Fuck," and then he went for my neck. He explored every inch of my throat just like he had my mouth—tracing lines and curves with his lips, flicking his tongue, letting his teeth graze here and there.

And dear Lord, I had never felt so wanted—so *craved*—in my life. All we'd done was kiss with our clothes on, and I felt like I was water for a man who'd just come out of the desert. That it was Tyler holding me and consuming me and desiring me like this was... holy fuck.

I gripped his shoulders just to stay upright. That thing he was doing to my neck made me weak, and when he started rocking his hips in a distinctive motion against mine, rubbing his clothed hard-on against me as if we were having sex already, I was legitimately worried I might come right then and there.

"You're... God, Tyler," I panted. "You're gonna get me off if you keep doing that."

He lifted his head, grinning wickedly, and ground harder against me. "How is that a bad thing?"

"Because..." I licked my lips as I struggled to find my breath. "Don't... don't want this to be over yet."

"Over?" The grin turned into a smile. A fucking *reverent* one, especially as he caressed my cheek. "You make it sound like we're only going to do this once."

I blinked, staring into his dilated eyes. "We're..."

"It's taken us a quarter goddamned century to get here," he purred, rubbing that thick hard-on over mine again. "There's no such thing as too soon."

"Tyler..." I gripped the front of his shirt to anchor myself. My eyes tried to roll back, but I forced them open and blinked them into focus. "Let's... I want you naked."

"We'll get there. I—"

"You really want me to come in my pants? Or all over you?"

That got a moan out of him that almost made the conversation moot. In a strained voice, he said, "I don't care where you come. I just want to watch your face when you do."

"God..." My head fell back as a shudder ran through me.

He kissed along my jaw, holding me up with an arm around my waist as he rutted against me. He really was going to make me come in my pants, and with every grunt of need and pleasure he released against my skin, I cared a little less about clothes or anything besides how sexy and raunchy and primal and delicious this was.

"Christ, Justin," he murmured, teeth grazing my neck. Then he lifted his head and looked in my eyes, his burning with lust, and his voice was a low growl as he said, "How did I ever miss how fucking hot you are?"

The sound that escaped my lips didn't even sound like my own voice, and I dug my fingers into his shoulders as I came like a horny teenager.

"Oh yeah," he groaned as if he were coming too. "Holy fuck..." He kept moving his hips until I stilled him, and we both sagged against the counter, me clinging to his shirt so I didn't drop to the floor at his feet.

Panting hard, I murmured, "Shit, dude."

He laughed breathlessly. "That was one hell of a first kiss."

I laughed too, sounding drunk. "Damn. If we fuck, we'll probably burn the place down."

For the first time since he'd kissed me, a look of uneasiness crossed his face. No, that was straight up fear.

I sobered. "I didn't mean we have to fuck."

"No, I know. I..." He bit his lip.

"We don't have to do everything tonight."

"I know, but it took me way too many years just to get this far." Tyler smoothed my hair. "I'm nervous as hell, but I don't *want* to wait anymore."

I slid my hands up his chest, still disbelieving we were touching like this. Still blown away that he'd just gotten me off, and we hadn't even undressed yet. "If we move too fast, that's a good way to make things weird. It's your first time with a man, and it's our first time with each other." I smiled up at him. "If we get there tonight, fine. But let's not rush."

He watched me for a moment, then nodded. "Okay. I don't want to necessarily put on the brakes either."

"I didn't say we would." I kissed him again, lightly this time. "We just won't rush."

He glanced down. "Well, maybe we should start by getting you out of those wet clothes."

I laughed. "Yeah. Good idea. Come on."

Then I took him by the hand and led him down the hall.

CHAPTER 19

TYLER

Everything suddenly made sense.

In Justin's bedroom, as I watched him peel off his shirt, it all just... made sense. All those times when my ex-wife had thought my gaze had lingered a little too long on a man. All those accusations she'd made about not just wanting to have sex with him, but being in love with him.

It was like I'd always found men—especially this man—attractive. And maybe I had. When I'd caught myself admiring an attractive man, I'd always thought I was just appreciating his sense of style and wondering if the same look might work on me, or I'd been impressed by how fit he was. When I'd thought an actor who pulled my attention away from an actress was just that charismatic and that good of an actor.

All this time, and it had never crossed my mind that I could—and wanted to—touch a man like this.

And this man in particular.

This man who'd just led me into his bedroom and was looking at me like that and who'd already come once while we were making out and now his bed was *right there*.

My heart pounded. Oh God. We were really doing this?

And I wanted to, right?

Oh yes. Yes, I definitely wanted to.

But nervous? So nervous. So, *so* nervous.

"Hey." Justin came closer and slid his hands over my waist. "You okay?"

Gulping, I nodded. "Just nervous."

He smiled and lifted his chin to kiss me. "It's okay. There's no rush, and there's no pressure. I promise."

"It's not really rushing when it's twenty years late, you know?"

"Better late than never." He pulled me closer, his naked skin deliciously hot through my shirt. "You're calling the shots tonight, though. Anything you want to do, name it."

I wasn't sure what to say. What I wanted.

"And, um, there's nothing we have to do either." He met my gaze, looking a little shy. "To be honest, I don't even like anal all that much."

"Really? I thought that was... a thing. For dudes."

He smiled, shaking his head. "For some. It's just not my thing. I mean, if you want to try it, we can, but if you don't—"

"I don't want to do something you don't like."

"I'm not completely opposed to it, I just don't like doing it all the time."

"Oh." Weirdly, that was a relief. I'd had anal before—my ex-wife had loved it—but I'd never bottomed. And maybe tonight that would've been too much. Taking it off the table eased some of my nerves.

"We don't have to do anything," he said again. "In fact, we can start just like this, and we don't have to go any further if you don't want to." He gestured at us, probably indicating that we both still had pants on. "It's your call." He paused. "Though if we're not getting naked, I'd at least like to change into another pair of pants."

"Actually, I..." I watched my hand slide down his waist and onto his clothed hip. "I think I want to get rid of all of this."

He searched my eyes. "Are you sure? We don't have to go that far quite yet."

"Taking off our clothes?"

He nodded.

"I'm not a virgin, Justin. I've just never been with a man."

"I know, but some guys..." He chewed his lip.

"I'm not some guys either." I kissed him gently. "Just some idiot who took way too long to figure out he was bi. If you're not into it, we don't have to, but don't stop on my account."

"Oh, I'm into it," he said in a hoarse whisper. "How about if I follow your lead, and you tell me if things are going too fast?"

"Deal."

"Okay." He grinned. "So, you said something about getting our clothes off?"

"Mmhmm."

We exchanged grins, then separated and started undressing.

I made it as far as taking off my shirt before I had to stop and stare at him. Christ. No wonder the women in my life had always been prickly when I was around him—they saw, plain as day, what it had taken me twenty-five years to figure out.

Now that I saw it, though? Now that I knew what all those feelings were, and what it meant when just the sight of him made my breath catch?

I wanted more. I wanted to drown in him. I'd wasted my entire life thinking I wasn't into men, and it was even more of a travesty how long I'd gone without this man in particular.

That wasn't to say I wasn't still nervous as fuck, though. With every layer of clothing he stripped off, I wanted him more and I was also more afraid of what we were doing. Yeah, he'd gotten off in the kitchen, but I'd almost gone right over the edge with him. It hadn't been any sexual expertise on my part that had made him lose control. We'd both just been amped up and horny, and all that sexual tension breaking loose had driven us both wild.

But now we were getting naked. Could I get him off a second time?

And—

My fingers froze on my half-buckled belt.

What if he wasn't attracted to me?

He'd seen me in swim trunks and whatever when we were teenagers, but I wasn't eighteen anymore. He was ripped and sculpted, with the kind of perfect face and flawless body that turned heads everywhere he went. Five minutes on an app, and he could probably be sandwiched between a pair of twenty year-olds with six-packs.

Oblivious to my second thoughts, Justin turned down the covers of his bed and slid in. I hadn't realized how paralyzed I was by nerves and God knew what else until he patted the sheets beside him. "You coming?"

I gulped. "I... yeah." I glanced down at my clothes, which I hadn't gotten very far in removing. "Uh..."

He pushed himself up on his elbow, the playful grin shifting to a look of serious concern. "What's wrong?"

"Um." I swallowed. "Just... keep your expectations realistic, okay?"

His brow quirked. "Huh?"

I laughed self-consciously. "The last time you saw me without my shirt, I was—"

"Baby." He got up on his knees and came to the edge of the bed. With a finger hooked under my belt, he tugged me closer to him. "I want you. Full stop." He paused, smirking. "Unless you have a tattoo of my grandma's face above your dick or something."

I chuckled. "No, my appointment for that one isn't until next week."

"Good." He pulled at my belt again. "Then get these fucking clothes off and get into my bed." The command in his words—the palpable desire—shook me out of my nervous paralysis, and I did as I was told.

A moment later, I joined him in bed, and just before he pulled the covers up over us, he raked his eyes over me.

"Holy shit, Ty," he whispered. "I don't know what you were worried about." He met my gaze as the covers sank down on top of us. "I always knew you'd look good naked, but *Jesus*." He pressed himself against me, his skin hot and soft from our chests all the way down to our feet. It wasn't like it was the first time I'd been naked with someone, but this was Justin. My best friend. The guy I'd evicted from my life for way too long. It barely even registered that he was a man— only that he was the man I'd been in love with forever.

He searched my eyes, and his expression again turned serious. "I mean it—if we go too fast, just say so." His fingers drifted up my side. "I want you to enjoy this."

"I don't think that's going to be a problem." I curved my hand behind his head and pulled him into a kiss. We wrapped our arms around each other, and the kiss deepened.

Somehow I'd convinced myself that putting my hands on another man would feel alien and wrong, but sliding my palms over his body was hot and natural. Kissing his neck, shoulder, collarbone, pecs— how had I ever thought I wouldn't like this? Our bodies had always fit together so perfectly when we'd hugged, and now it was like we'd both been made for the sole purpose of having sex with each other. Whether he was on top or I was, or if we were lying on our sides and lazily kissing while we touched all over, it was... it was *perfect*.

I could have done this all night, and I was starting to think he just might let me since he obviously wasn't kidding about not being in a hurry. For ages, we just lay there under the covers, wrapped up in each other and kissing like we could make up for twenty-five years in a single night. In fact, I didn't even realize how much time had passed until I rolled him onto his back and felt his cock getting hard again. In the kitchen, I hadn't had much of an opportunity to do more than acknowledge that he'd had an erection and that had turned me on, but I couldn't see or feel much through jeans.

Now there was nothing between us. As his cock hardened beside mine, I slid a hand down and wrapped my fingers around him. He groaned, closing his eyes and arching as I stroked experimentally.

For whatever reason, I'd envisioned him being hung like a porn star. Or maybe I thought all gay men were. Had I actually *thought* about gay men's dicks?

Either way, he turned out to be as average as I was. He was slightly longer than me, I was slightly thicker than him, and stroking him didn't feel strange at all. It also didn't feel strange in the least to be turned on by his gasps and those low, throaty moans.

"You are so damn sexy," I whispered. "God, I want to do... I want to do everything with you."

"Mmm." He bit his lip and arched his back. When his eyes fluttered open, they were gleaming with lust as they looked up into mine. "Anything you want. Just say the word."

"You." The word came out without a second thought. "Just... you."

He licked his lips. Grinning up at me, he combed his fingers through my hair. "Get on your back."

My body moved before I'd fully made sense of the order. He straddled me and leaned down for a long kiss.

"I've fantasized for years about sucking you off." He paused to nip my lower lip. "Any chance I can indulge in that fantasy tonight?"

I shuddered hard under him, and breathed, "P-please do."

He grinned, kissed me again, and moved to my neck. He continued downward, kiss by kiss along my breastbone, the middle of my abs, and—

Oh, sweet Jesus. I'd imagined him going down on me the night I'd listened to him with someone else, and now it was happening for real. And holy fuck, it was hot. His lips and tongue were magic, and his little moans against my skin were amazing, and the gleam in his eyes when he glanced up at me almost sent me through the roof.

And now I wanted to know what it was like for the roles to be reversed.

"Can..." I struggled to speak while he was working so much magic with his mouth.

Justin lifted his head. "Hmm?" Now that he wasn't tonguing my dick anymore, I should've been more articulate, but the sight of him and his swollen lips just above my rock-hard cock... *fuck*.

Still, I managed, "Can I return the favor?"

His eyes widened, and he shivered as he said, "Hell yeah, you can." Beat. "If you want to, of course."

I nodded. "Yeah. I do."

We switched positions, and after a long kiss that almost made me forget what I wanted to do, I started kissing down his neck and chest. Okay, I was going to do this. I was really going to do this. Before tonight—before just now—I'd never imagined what it would be like to suck dick, so I had no idea what to expect. I wasn't put off or repulsed —in fact my mouth watered at the thought of doing to him everything he'd just done to me. I was a little intimidated, though.

I looked up from kissing my way down his abs. "Just remember I've never done this before, okay?"

Justin threaded his fingers into my hair. "If you suck dick *half* as well as you kiss..." He trailed off into another moan.

No pressure, right?

I kissed his hip bone, then lifted myself onto my arm. Hoping my nerves didn't show, I experimentally ran my tongue around the head of his cock. His skin tasted faintly of cum, and the reminder of him losing it in the kitchen gave me goose bumps. I licked him again, searching for more.

"Fuck..." Justin squirmed, though he somehow managed to keep his hips perfectly still. He let go of my hair, and I glanced up to see his fingers curling in the sheets instead. Oh, now wasn't this a view— Justin laid out in front of me like a gift, clawing at the bed while his abs tightened and his back arched. His head was thrown back, so I couldn't see much of his face, but I could make out enough to know his eyes were squeezed shut and his lips were pulled tight, and this had to be the single sexiest view I'd ever had. I'd thought it would be hot for him to glance up at me while he sucked my dick, but switch those roles? Oh my God.

I wanted him to make more of those breathless, helpless sounds, so I gave his cock more attention.

"Yeah, baby," he whispered. "Oh. Fuck."

I loved the sounds he made, and I loved how his cock felt sliding between my lips and across my tongue. I hadn't thought of this as something I would enjoy, but hey, I wasn't going to argue.

I started to take more, but Justin gently stopped me with a hand on my forehead.

"D-don't have to." He stroked my hair. "You don't have to deep throat."

True—I enjoyed more attention to the head too. It was fun to get deep-throated, but lips and tongue around the head drove me wild.

And balls. How often had I begged my ex to give my balls some attention?

So maybe Justin would be into that too.

I shifted around a little, moving down the mattress a few inches, and trailed kisses down the shaft of his cock, past the base, and onto his balls. All it took was a gentle flutter of my tongue against the soft skin, and Justin was moaning again. I swirled my tongue in the same place, and he rewarded me with a helpless whimper.

"If you keep doing that," he purred, "I'm gonna come again."

I instantly decided I liked the idea of sucking him all the way off, but... not this time. I'd never been in bed with a man, and I wasn't about to rush through this.

So, I gave his cock one last lick, then I crawled back up to him.

"I was enjoying that," he grumbled in protest.

"Me too." I moved on top and grinned down at him. "I was enjoying it a lot."

"Then keep going, you bastard," he growled, raking his hands through my hair. "I was so close."

"I know." I brushed my lips across his. "But I'm having too much fun to stop."

"Who said anything about stopping? Give me twenty minutes, and I'll be ready to fuck your face again."

I shivered hard. "You have three rounds in you tonight?"

He seemed to think about it, then shrugged. "Okay, that third one's not a promise." He teased my nipple with his thumb. "And it *is* your first time. My first time with you too, so yeah, I want it to last." He lifted his head and kissed me. "Get on your back again."

I paused for one more kiss, then did as I was told, and Justin climbed on top of me. He sat up and gazed down at me, grinning as he slid his hands up over my chest. I could barely breathe—the sight of him straddling me, and the weight of his body over mine, was seriously the most erotic thing I'd ever experienced.

I still hadn't quite gotten my head around the fact that I was in bed with a man, especially since I was too busy being blown away that I was with *this* man. My best friend. The one who'd been there for me without question even when I'd all but disappeared on him for half a decade. The person who'd always been able to make my world stop by belting out a song or smiling or just walking into a room.

Of course I love you. Of course I want you. How did I ever not know that?

"Kiss me," I whispered.

Justin leaned down, and our lips met, and it was the first time all over again. My body tingled and my brain short-circuited and my dick couldn't possibly get any harder—God, why the fuck had I waited so long to want him?

I ran my hands up his powerful thighs and onto his ass, and he groaned into my kiss. When he rocked his hips, the friction of our dicks rubbing together made me gasp.

"You like that, don't you?" he asked.

"Uh-huh. In the kitchen it... seemed like you did too."

"Oh yeah." He lifted himself onto his arms and kept sliding his dick alongside mine. "This is probably my favorite thing."

"Yeah?"

He nodded.

"Mmm, then keep doing it," I said. "'Cause it's growing on me pretty quick."

He grinned, then came down to kiss me. We made out, and he rocked his hips, and I just ran my hands all over his feverishly hot body. I still couldn't get over how well we fit together, not to mention how he seemed to know exactly how to turn me inside out. Or hell, maybe I was just so far gone that everything he did drove me wild.

He slowed to a stop, and murmured against my lips, "Spread your legs." Then he sat up, and I did as I was told. We rearranged our legs so that instead of him straddling me, I was straddling him—only I was on the bottom. It was an odd feeling, being on my back with my legs apart as he came down on top of me again, his hips settling between my hips. It was odd, but hot. Really, really hot.

Then he rocked his hips, sliding his dick back and forth against mine, and I made a sound I'd never heard myself make before. Kind of a moan, kind of a whimper, completely primal and helpless. He did it again, and slowly fell into a rhythm until he was fucking against me, the friction driving me wild.

"This okay?" he asked.

"Yeah." I licked my lips. "Feels... really good."

He thrust a little harder. "Tyler... God..." He shuddered and buried his face against my neck. His hot huffs of breath rushed across my skin in time with the rhythmic jerks of his hips, and all I could do was lie there and let pleasure crash through me. I dragged my nails up his back, and we both moaned when his rhythm faltered. He recovered, and now he was even more frantic, the bed creaking in time with his sharp movements.

"Oh God..." I arched under him. "Oh God, I'm gonna come."

"Yeah?" he panted. "Come on, baby. I've been... I've been dreaming about this for twenty-five years. Let me see you—"

I didn't hear the rest over my own helpless, throaty cry as I unloaded between our bodies. Justin kept thrusting, driving my orgasm on and on, and then he shuddered too, and I forced my eyes open because like hell was I missing this view. Above me, Justin's eyes were squeezed shut, his lips moving soundlessly, his skin flushed and sweaty, and then a tremor went through him, rolling up his spine until he threw his head back and cried out as his cum mixed with mine on my stomach.

And just like that, we both collapsed, me onto the mattress and him on top of me.

And everything was still.

Eyes closed, I wrapped my arms around him. We both panted. His heart probably pounded as hard as mine did.

As my breathing slowed and the trembling eased, I looked down at us. He was still slumped over me, both of us completely debauched and drenched in sweat. Justin's hips between my spread legs. Cum all over both of us.

And it was perfect.

Lying like this, there was no question left in my mind—I was absolutely bisexual. I was absolutely attracted to and in love with and completely lost without Justin.

Holding him tight, I stroked his damp hair and thought I might break down again as a million emotions rushed over me. It was like all the upheaval in my life over the last few months hadn't been random chaos, but a strong wind guiding me straight to this moment in this place with this man. And now that I was here, the relief was beyond profound.

It's been a long road.

But I made it.

I kissed Justin's temple and smiled to myself.

I'm finally home.

CHAPTER 20

JUSTIN

In the last hour, I'd lived out almost every fantasy I'd ever had. I'd had sex with Tyler. Tyler had told me he loved me. That he'd *always* loved me.

And now I was in the one place I'd never thought I'd actually be—tangled up with him, naked and satisfied in my bed.

Please God, don't let him change his mind.

It was irrational and I knew it. If he were actually straight, he probably would have had a change of heart—or cock—sometime before we'd gotten each other off.

Still, some part of me couldn't quite settle. Couldn't quite accept that this was real and not just a dream of mine or a fleeting phase of his. I kind of wanted to ask him if it was, but I was too afraid of the answer, so I didn't move. Nothing wrong with indulging in a few more minutes of his naked warmth.

It was Tyler who finally moved, but he didn't go far—he just rolled onto his side and rested his hand in the middle of my chest. "So. We're..." He blushed. "We really..."

"Yeah. We did." I lifted my eyebrows. "And we... are?"

He smiled shyly. "I know I want to."

"Me too. So does this mean you're bi, or... what?"

"I guess so." He trailed a fingertip along the edge of my jaw. "It's kind of hard to tell when I can't look at anyone except you."

I couldn't help laughing, and lifted my head to kiss him. "You know, I'm really liking this kind of corny but totally sweet romantic side of yours."

Tyler chuckled, stroking my cheek as I settled back on the pillow. "Yeah I guess it is kind of corny. It's true, though. I mean, at the reunion tonight, there were some insanely hot women. And they just..." He shook his head. "All I could think about was you."

Sobering a little, I mirrored him and turned on my side so we were facing each other. "And this is just out of the blue? Being into... well, me or men?"

"No." He watched his palm slide down my waist. "Like I said, Gina figured out there was something. I think I've been attracted to guys all along, but I never let myself think about it." He fell silent for a moment, eyes unfocused like he was deep in thought, so I stayed quiet until he'd finished mulling over whatever it was. Finally, he met my eyes. "Yeah, I'd say I'm bi. Just never gave myself a chance to check out men until I'd already fallen too hard for you to notice anyone else."

My heart fluttered. I could definitely get used to his corny romantic side. "I have to admit, I kind of wondered when we were younger."

"About what?"

"About if you were queer. I mean, I knew you were into girls, but I don't know a lot of straight guys who are as comfortable around gay men as you are. And sometimes, just the way you'd look at a football player or something..." I shrugged. "Yeah, I wondered."

His cheeks colored. "You never said a word, though."

"Of course I didn't," I said quickly. "You said you were straight."

"Did you think I'd get mad? You knew I wasn't a homophobe."

"No, but I didn't want to be the guy who kept needling you to consider men because then you'd think I was just trying to get in your pants."

He studied me. "Were you?"

"Well, I definitely wanted you, but only if you wanted me too." I held his gaze. "The last thing in the world I wanted to be was something you regretted. I decided a long time ago I'd rather be friends and keep things platonic than have things get weird between us."

He smiled and brushed a soft kiss across my lips. "The only thing I regret is taking so fucking long to figure this out."

"Better late than never, right?"

"Still." He kissed me again, letting it linger this time. "I can't believe you were right in front of me, and I never..."

I studied him. "And you were never into any other guy?"

"I didn't think I was, but... I don't know. Maybe? I've got a long list of exes who accused me of being into you and other guys, so maybe they saw something I didn't." He absently stroked my hair. "It's like you said before—I never thought about whether I might be attracted to men. I knew I liked women, and just never considered it beyond that. Not until now, anyway."

"So this really is new for you? All of it?"

"I'm not a virgin or anything, but yeah, being with a man is new."

I fidgeted uneasily. "Well, if you decide you want to experiment a bit, and try things with other guys, just say—"

Tyler cut me off with a tender kiss. When he broke away, he whispered, "I don't want anyone else." He searched my eyes, and must have seen the apprehension still lingering. "Yes, I'm attracted to men. And yes, I do regret never being with any until now. But I'm not interested in anyone else. I just want you."

"Still, if it ever comes up..." I moistened my lips. "I want you to be happy, Tyler. You're exploring a totally new side of yourself, and—"

"And we'll cross that bridge if we get to it," he said softly. "If it ever comes up, we'll talk about it. But right now, you're the only one I want. Period."

"Just as long as you know the option is there."

"I do. And I appreciate it. But monogamy has always been more my speed. Even before my wife cheated on me."

"Mine too, actually," I whispered. "A lot of gay couples I know aren't, but... I don't know. I just like it like this. One on one."

He smiled fondly at me. "Why am I not surprised we're on the same page?"

"Guess we're more alike than we thought."

"Guess so." He kissed me again, lightly this time.

We lay like that for a while, just holding each other with his head on my chest. Then his arm started getting tired from being pinned between us, so we switched. He rolled onto his back and wrapped an arm around my shoulders, and I draped mine over his stomach as I rested my head on his chest. For a long time, we were silent. I could hear his heartbeat, and it was in almost perfect sync with mine. Not racing. Not pounding. Just beating steadily while we lay together. His fingers ran through my hair, and I closed my eyes at the gentle touch.

"Can I confess something?" I asked after a while.

"Hmm?"

"This is the part I fantasized about more than anything."

His hand stopped. "What do you mean?"

"Just... this. What we're doing." I trailed the backs of my fingers down the middle of his chest. "I mean, I'm not going to lie—I thought about, uh, a lot of things. But this is the part I kept coming back to. Even if we never had sex, and just wound up like this..."

"Really?"

"Yeah. This is the best part, you know?"

I thought for a second he might roll his eyes and accuse me of being a cheesy romantic—okay, guilty—but I should've known he wouldn't. Instead, he whispered, "It really is." Then his arm tightened around my shoulders and he kissed the top of my head. "I just can't believe no one came along and snatched you up before I got my shit together."

I smiled. "I don't think there was anyone else out there who could've put up with me like you do."

Tyler laughed, stroking my arm with his fingertips. "You don't give yourself enough credit."

"Uh-huh. And I'm thirty-eight and single, so..."

"Was." He pressed another kiss into my hair. "I think you meant to say 'I *was* thirty-eight and single.'"

My heart fluttered and I lifted my chin to kiss under his jaw. "Well, I'm still thirty-eight for a few months, so—"

Tyler laughed. "You know what I mean, you dork."

"Yes, I do." I couldn't cuddle much closer to him, but I damn sure tried. I was still thirty-eight, but single? Nope. "Does this mean I should scramble up and change my Facebook relationship status?"

"You better not." He held me tighter and grinned. "Because that would mean getting out of bed, and I kind of like you where you are."

I shivered, squirming in his arms as our naked skin rubbed together. "Mmm, I think that status update can wait."

"Me too." He kissed me again, drawing it out for a long, lazy moment. "Why do I get the feeling I'm not going to be spending a lot of nights across the hall after this?"

I lifted my head so I could look in his eyes. "You know I won't say no to you staying in my room."

"Good." He smiled. "Because I kind of like it in here."

"Me too."

The smile faltered a little. "It... almost feels like we're moving in together already. Since we live together."

"But you still have your space." I gestured toward his bedroom. "Even if you're mostly sleeping over here, the other room is yours." I paused. "If you'd be more comfortable getting your own place once you're on your feet, it won't hurt my feelings. Whatever it takes to not screw this up."

He seemed to mull it over for a moment before he said, "Let's just keep things the way they are. Honestly, I..." He broke eye contact and gnawed his lip.

"What?"

Tyler took in a deep breath through his nose before he turned to me again. "We spent a lot of years apart because I was an idiot. The last thing I want to think about is getting away from you."

I stroked his cheek. "Then stay."

He held my gaze, and my heart fluttered. God, there was that look. For years I'd sworn I would sell my soul to have that look directed at me just *one* time for just *one* moment. Now it was, and yes, it definitely would have been worth my soul and then some. And it wasn't a fleeting glance for me to torture myself with afterward. He was holding my gaze, and he wasn't going anywhere, and Jesus Christ, was this real?

Yeah. Yeah, it was. Right? Maybe someday I'd stop wondering when I'd wake up from this dream, but I didn't see that happening any time soon.

I touched his face. "I've spent twenty years wishing you would look at me like that."

"Like what?"

"Like that."

Tyler smiled. "I think I've been looking at you like this since the dawn of time." He caressed my cheek. "Just... never managed to do it when you were looking at me."

Oh my God. Yes. I could totally get used to this corny romantic side of him. "Well, you've got my undivided attention now."

He laughed and brushed his lips across mine. "Good."

I trailed my thumb along the edge of his jaw. "I love you, Tyler." Saying that to him was never going to get old. Never.

"I love you too." He stroked my cheek. "I'm just sorry it took so long for me to figure that out."

"It's okay. This was worth the wait."

He smiled. Then he drew me in and kissed me so softly, so tenderly, I almost wanted to cry again. Worth the wait? Talk about an understatement. I'd fantasized about sex with him and about him being in love with me, but I'd never actually thought any of it would happen.

But here he was. Here we were. Tyler was in my bed, holding me to him and kissing me like there was no place in the world he'd rather be than right here with me. After all this time, my best friend was back in my life. He loved me in the one perfect way I'd never imagined he actually would.

He drew back and met my eyes. "So what do we do now?"

I shrugged as I caressed his cheek. "I guess we take it a day at a time and see where this goes."

"I meant now, like the rest of the night." He grinned. "It's still early."

"Hmm, yeah. It is. Probably too early to go to sleep."

"Well, you know what they say." His fingers drifted down my chest and stomach. "Early to bed, early to rise..."

I sucked in a breath as his hand drifted under the covers. "Fuck..."

He laughed softly, leaned in, and kissed me in the same moment his hand slid over my cock. No, I didn't see us leaving this bed any time soon. I had no idea if I had a third orgasm in me tonight or not, but I sure as hell wasn't saying no to Tyler's hands, Tyler's mouth, Tyler's body...

"You have anywhere else to be tonight?" he murmured between kisses.

"Nope."

His lips curved into a grin against mine, and neither of us said another word.

I was in my bed with my best friend. With the man I'd loved since the beginning of time.

Did I have anywhere else to be?

Not tonight. Not tomorrow. Not ever.

Because I was right where I'd always wanted to be.

THE END

IS IT OVER YET?

CHAPTER 1

RHYS

The suburban Chicago house I'd lived in for the past six years came into view, and my stomach knotted tighter. It was the same feeling I'd had on my way to a job I'd hated a lifetime ago, when pulling up to the building made me groan out loud at the prospect of another shift in that godforsaken place. Didn't seem right to feel that way coming home, but there it was, same as it had been for the past two months.

By the time I pulled into the garage beside the familiar red Corolla, my jaw ached from clenching my teeth. Probably because that's what I'd been doing every night this week at the same time. Ugh. If I didn't move out of this place soon, my dental bills were going to be astronomical. That was a good enough reason to step things up, wasn't it? So I didn't grind my teeth to dust?

As if I didn't already have a laundry list of reasons why I needed to get out of here.

With an ache in my jaw and a sour feeling in my throat, I collected my coffee cup, lunch bag, and briefcase, and got out of the car. On the way inside, I couldn't help limping a little, which added to my festering annoyance. It wasn't unusual for my leg to be sore by the end of the day, especially after I'd been coaching basketball, but it wasn't doing much for my shitty mood. I couldn't think of much that would, though. Nothing short of substances that would get me fired. Or maybe finding a note on the counter that said *I moved out.* There wasn't a plant on this earth that would get me higher than reading those three sweet little words.

But unless my soon-to-be ex-husband had won the lottery since this morning, he was just as stuck here as I was.

At the door, I paused for a deep breath to steel myself, then went inside. The kitchen and living room were empty. Derek's car was here, so it was a safe bet he was home, but he was somewhere else in the house. Good enough for me. If I was lucky, he'd stay that way long enough for me to wind down.

I went through my usual motions—cleaning out my lunch bag, rinsing the Tupperware dishes, checking the cats' food and water, perusing the mail. For years this routine had soothed me. Helped me shift from work to home so I could relax. Not so much these days.

Our long-haired calico, Lucy, hopped upon the counter and chirped at me, and I managed to crack a smile as I scratched her back the way she loved. She arched under my hand and purred. I chuckled, and I didn't even mind that she was kicking the mail everywhere as she strutted back and forth on the counter.

"Hey, sweetheart. You miss me?"

More purring.

I kept scratching and petting her for a moment, trying not to think about the future. Or the fact that Derek and I still hadn't come to a custody agreement about the cats. They were littermates, and though they could fight almost as loudly as we could, they were inseparable. There was no "you take Lucy and I'll take Chico." When this was all over and we finally went our separate ways, someone was taking both cats, and someone would be living without them.

I scooped Lucy into my arms, and I hugged her tight, which just made her purr louder and my conscience burn hotter. Guilt had been a constant friend for the past couple of months, and every time I thought about either losing my cats or taking them away from Derek, I wanted to cry. As if I hadn't done enough of that recently.

I'm so sorry, guys. I buried my face in Lucy's plush fur. *I fucked everything up.*

The click of a door at the opposite end of the house made my spine stiffen. Lucy tensed too. By the time Derek was halfway up the hall, she'd stopped purring. As he cleared the corner into the living room, she wriggled in my arms, and I sighed as I set her back down on the counter. She jumped to the floor and trotted out of the room, probably to the office where Chico was likely watching birds.

I watched her go, fresh guilt gnawing at me. Things had really gone to shit when even the cats didn't want to be in the same room with the two of us.

Without the cat to hold my attention anymore, I turned to see where Derek was headed so I could make my own escape. I still needed to change clothes anyway, not to mention take off my prosthetic and sit for a while to give my joints a rest. If he was going to hang out in the living room, then I could go into my bedroom or join the cats in the office.

But Derek wasn't heading into the living room. He was coming into the kitchen. And from the way his gaze was fixed on me, he wanted to talk about something.

I swallowed. "Hey."

"Hey." He slid his hands into the pockets of his jeans. "Do you have a few minutes?"

I struggled to hold his gaze. He didn't seem like he was looking for a fight. There was some tension in his features, but it didn't read as hostility or anger.

I shifted my weight, wincing at the vicious ache in my hip. "Yeah. Do you mind if we sit, though?"

"Sure. Yeah. Living room?"

"Okay." I followed him out of the kitchen, and we sat on opposite ends of the sofa. As soon as I was seated, I leaned down, rolled up my pant leg, and disconnected my prosthetic. Derek didn't speak while I removed it; for all our inability to coexist lately, he was still in the habit of giving me a minute to get situated, particularly when I needed to kick off the prosthetic after a long day on my feet.

I leaned the prosthetic against the end table and sat back, releasing a relieved sigh. Everything ached, especially my hips, knees, and right ankle, and taking some weight off them felt *so* good. I might've even relaxed if not for Derek waiting a cushion away to have a *conversation*. Ugh. God. What now?

Schooling my expression, I twisted toward him. I stole a second just to look at him. There would come a time in the very near future when all I had left of him was pictures, and even with the constant tension hanging between us, it hurt to imagine not seeing him anymore. Seeing him like this hurt too. The dark eyes that had tongue-tied me on day one were cold now. Beside his eyes and mouth were lines that deepened whenever he smiled or laughed, and they were barely visible now. The near-black hair I'd run my fingers through millions of times, the soft lips I'd tasted more times than I could count, that spot on his neck where a single kiss could make him shudder all over—it was all out of my reach now.

Maybe it was time to take my sister up on the offer to come stay with her. I wasn't sure how much more of this I could handle.

Forcing back my emotions, I tried to sound casual. "All right. What's up?"

He mirrored me, pulling his knee up onto the cushion and drumming his fingers on his inseam. "Um." He stared down at his hand. "So, I talked to Vanessa this morning."

My gut clenched. Instantly my mind was filled with a million worst case scenarios. I'd expected him to have something on his mind about us, not about our daughter, and panic shot through me. Had something happened? Was she hurt? Sick? "What's going on? Is everything okay?"

"Yeah. Yeah. Everything's fine." He made a *calm down* gesture. "Nothing's wrong."

"Okay. Good." I exhaled, my heartbeat coming back down. It

wasn't unusual for her to call him, but the whole "we need to talk" thing had me on edge. "So..." I raised my eyebrows. Oh God, had he told her? Did he *finally* tell her we were divorcing? He'd been dancing around that for two months.

Derek cleared his throat, and to my surprise, he smiled, though he still seemed guarded. "She's, um... She's getting married."

I blinked. "She is?"

He nodded. "Corbin proposed last night."

"Oh. Wow." I actually laughed because I was so relieved that instead of something horrible, he was breaking the news that Vanessa was engaged. "That's great!"

"Yeah. It is." He met my gaze, but then he broke eye contact, and his smile faltered.

How could a conversation be this much of a roller coaster after thirty seconds? Oh, right, because it was us and we were a disaster. A disaster our daughter still didn't know about.

Derek took a deep breath and sat up a little. "Here's the thing—they want to get married sooner than later. Corbin is going to be transferring within the next year, and he'll probably deploy at some point. So they want to get all their ducks in a row quickly."

I nodded. "Makes sense. How soon is soon?"

"They're thinking February."

I whistled. "Really not letting the grass grow, are they?"

He laughed quietly. "No. But it's still three months away. It isn't like they're eloping next week."

"True." And why was this line of conversation making me apprehensive? Like it was going somewhere I really didn't want it to go? I was thrilled for our daughter and her husband-to-be, but something about this discussion with Derek...didn't feel right. After nine years together, I knew him, I knew his tells, and I knew there was more to this than just telling me Vanessa was getting married.

Chewing his lip, Derek dropped his gaze and watched his fingers drumming on his knee again. There was definitely something on his mind. Something he needed to say, but either couldn't figure out how to or couldn't quite work up the nerve.

"Derek?" I nudged. "What am I missing here? You're happy about this, right?"

"Yeah. Of course. I'm... There's just..." He closed his eyes. Finally, he met mine again. "Vanessa still doesn't know about, um, us."

I winced. In the two months since we'd decided to split up, we'd debated more than once when and how we should tell her. The holidays were almost upon us, so that hadn't seemed like the right time, and we'd agreed to keep a lid on it until after the New Year. She couldn't make it out for Thanksgiving, and she was spending Christmas with her mom, so it wasn't as if we'd have to play happy husbands right in front of her. Just keep up the illusion on social media and on the phone. Easy. Except for the part where it meant we'd had to keep it quiet from almost everyone else so no one accidentally let it slip on Facebook. And we were still stuck living together anyway because neither of us could afford to move out yet, so the whole fucking world thought everything was quiet on the home front. The closest we'd come to letting it slip was when a friend noticed our wedding portrait wasn't on the mantle anymore. Derek had quickly said the frame had broken, and the subject had dropped. For now.

"Right," I said. "So what does that have to do with her getting—" I tensed, then inclined my head. "Derek, please tell me you're not going where I think you're going."

He looked at me plaintively. "It's her wedding, Rhys. The next couple of months are going to be stressful as hell for her, and I'd rather all that stress be about planning her wedding. Not worrying about her dads splitting up."

Closing my eyes, I pushed out a long breath through my nose. We'd been married for seven years, and even though our happier days seemed like a lifetime ago, I remembered the stressful months leading up to the wedding like it was yesterday. The thought of my parents dropping a bomb like that in the middle of all that chaos? Of trying to enjoy my damn wedding while I worried myself sick about making them be in the same room? Okay, yeah, I got what he was driving at. But...*fuck*.

Facing Derek again, I said, "I get it. I do. But then what's it going to be after that? Wait until after her birthday? Let her and Corbin get settled at their new duty station? Sooner or later, we're going to have to just say it and be done with it."

The looks we were exchanging edged toward glares. A familiar tension rose in my chest: the feeling that losing my temper wasn't far off. Neither of us was particularly volatile, but ever since things had gone down—ever since I'd fucked up and sent us down this road— we'd both been on hair triggers. A conversation about groceries could spark a fight, so something like this? Debating the prospect of keeping our divorce under wraps for *three more months*? Yeah, I could totally see this devolving into a screaming match in a hurry, and I could feel my own calm disintegrating under his acidic stare.

I broke eye contact and rubbed the back of my neck. "I don't want to ruin her wedding, okay? But I don't want us to be miserable anymore either."

He laughed bitterly. "I'm pretty sure that's going to be a thing until we get rid of this place."

I gritted my teeth, which still ached from clenching earlier. "Doesn't mean we shouldn't mitigate it where we can."

"So what do you want to do?" His voice toed a very fine line between letting his irritation show and trying to placate me so this didn't erupt into a fight. "If we tell her now, we're both still going to end up at the wedding anyway."

I swallowed, and in a weird way, I was grateful that in his mind, it was a foregone conclusion that I'd go even if we were divorcing. Vanessa wasn't my biological daughter, but I'd been in her life since she was twelve. We'd always been close, and my greatest fear was losing her right along with Derek.

"We'll both be there," I said. "But which do you think is going to be harder? Staying out of each other's way? Or pretending we're still..." God, I couldn't even say it. My throat tightened, especially when he flinched. Guilt burned hotter and shame burrowed deeper.

I can't believe I did this to us.

But I did, and there was no going back, and now we had to decide who we'd be at our daughter's wedding three months from now—blissful husbands or frosty exes.

Derek cleared his throat. "I'd much rather go separately and stay out each other's way. But this isn't about what's easier for us. This is about her."

I was the one to flinch that time. "And if we do put on the happy, married, united front at the wedding?" I looked in his eyes. "What about between now and then?"

He shrugged tightly. "We keep doing what we've been doing. Go to work. Live our lives. Stay out of each other's way."

I supposed there wasn't much else we could do. So, despite the hot lump of guilt behind my ribs—or maybe because of it—I nodded. "All right. Just, um, let me know the dates. I need to make sure I have the time off work."

"I will." Derek sat up, and he hesitated like he was going to say something more but then apparently decided not to. He rose, wincing when his knee cracked. He paused for another awkward second but again let go of whatever was on his mind, and without another word, he walked out of the living room.

As soon as I was alone, I sighed heavily. From the moment things had started unraveling, it had been one thing after another. The realization that the cats couldn't go with both of us. Sticker shock over how much this whole process was going to cost, and how strapped for cash we'd both be when it was over. The prospect of breaking the news to friends, family, and colleagues, which we still hadn't done because he didn't have the heart to tell Vanessa yet.

And now this.

I kneaded my stiff neck. The thought of continuing the charade—acting like my husband and I were still happily in it for the long haul

—made my chest hurt, but what choice did we have? There were people who put aside mountains of differences and stayed together for years for their kids despite being miserable. If they could get through that, then why couldn't I suck it up and knuckle through three more months? At least I knew there was an end in sight. The recovery from my accident had been a solid year, and I'd made it through that.

I could do this. I could make it through another three months of living with Derek and telling the world outside that everything was fine. I could get through one wedding pretending Derek and I still loved each other.

Especially since I wouldn't be the one pretending.

CHAPTER 2

DEREK

"Wait, wait, wait. Back up." Maxine, my business partner and best friend, thunked her beer bottle down on the bar so hard I was surprised it didn't break. "You guys are going to the wedding, but you're not telling her you're splitting up?"

"Pretty much, yeah." I dug at the label on my own bottle. "Just doesn't seem right, you know? Like, 'Oh hey, congrats, you're getting married. By the way, Dad and I are getting divorced.'"

She rolled her eyes and brushed a strand of auburn hair out of her face. "Uh-huh. Has anyone ever mentioned that neither of you can act your way out of a brown paper bag?"

I blinked. "What?"

"Derek." She huffed. "Come on. Do you honestly think either of you—never mind both of you—can sell this? Pretend everything is fine between you? Because you can't even hide it when someone asks about Rhys."

"That's not true. I can—"

"It is true. Your poker face is so terrible, it's obvious you're trying to have a poker face, and your husb—and Rhys's isn't any better." Her forehead creased and her voice softened. "Do you honestly think you can convince your daughter to buy it? Which is to say nothing of her mother?"

I chewed my lip. Trust Maxine to see all the flaws in my admittedly shaky plan. Our daughter wasn't stupid, and her mother could sniff out bullshit from a mile away. Damn. Maybe this whole idea was a mistake. "What choice do we have? This divorce is going to *destroy* Vanessa."

"Like it's already destroying her dads?"

I winced and drank some more beer because I was way too sober for this.

Maxine sipped her own beer. "Can I ask you something you probably don't want to think about?"

I arched an eyebrow. "Since when do you ask permission before interrogating someone?"

She laughed softly. "Come on. I'm relentless but I'm not cruel."

"Well, now I'm curious. What's on your mind?"

"Do you promise you'll hear me out? Not just shut me down?"

I shifted on my barstool, wondering if I should let this line of conversation continue. Curiosity really was getting the best of me, though, so I nodded.

She studied me for a long moment, absently working at the label on her bottle. "You've got, what, three months until your daughter's wedding?"

"Thereabouts."

"Okay. Well." She looked right in my eyes. "Have you considered using that time to see if your marriage is worth saving?" Her hand went up, silencing me even before I realized I'd opened my mouth to protest. "It's plain as day to anyone who knows you, Derek. You still love him."

I dropped my gaze, a sudden lump in my throat making it nearly impossible to swallow. "Yeah. I do still love him."

"So maybe you're—"

"Max." I shook my head and faced her again. "There's no going back."

"Isn't there?"

"No. There isn't."

She pursed her lips. "Is there no going back? Or is there a lot of pride and hurt getting in the way of seeing if there's a way back?"

Sighing, I reached for my beer. After a deep swallow that did nothing to dislodge that lump, I put the bottle down again. "He *cheated* on me."

"Yes, he did," she acknowledged with a slight nod. "And then you went and cheated on him."

I winced, shifting my attention back to my beer. The bottle was nearly empty, so I flagged down a bartender.

"I know he hurt you," Maxine pressed. "But it was a one-time mistake. It isn't like he had an affair or some ongoing thing. He fucked up. *Once.*"

"Once that I know of," I grumbled, drumming my nails and trying to telepathically urge the bartender to hurry the fuck up. "How can I trust him now?"

"The fact that he told you about it should say something."

I scowled. Hadn't I tried to tell myself the same thing in the weeks after his confession? That it must have been a one-time fuck-up, and he must have really felt terrible about it to break down and confess? It wasn't like I'd suspected anything. That confession had fallen out of the clear blue sky as far as I was concerned, blindsiding me and turning my entire world on its head. If he hadn't told me what he'd done, I never would have known, and we'd probably still be happily married now.

But he *had* told me. And the anger had boiled over. And one night I'd been so furious and hurt and betrayed that I'd gone out and done the same thing. Gone out and fucked some stranger until neither of us could take anymore, and when I'd come home, I hadn't confessed. No, I'd thrown it in his face. Made sure he knew what I'd done and why I'd done it. If he'd wondered before that morning if I might forgive him, he didn't have to wonder anymore.

"I can't be with someone I can't trust." My voice barely carried over the bar's background noise. "Rhys knew cheating was a hard line for me. He knew. And he did it anyway." I shook my head. "It's not so much that there's no going back—it's that I don't *want* to go back."

Maxine watched me, but she said nothing. A moment later, the bartender appeared with another beer, and I took a long pull from the bottle.

The truth was, I did want to go back. I wanted to go back to the way things were before the night Rhys had slept with another man. Our marriage hadn't been perfect—was anyone's?—but it had been good. I'd been content. Couldn't have asked for anyone better to share my life with. If I could go back to that, I'd do it in a heartbeat.

But I couldn't. No matter what we did or said or forgave or forgot, things were different now. We would never be the couple we'd been before he cheated any more than I would ever be the man I'd been before going to combat. To this day I didn't know the who or the why, and I didn't think I ever wanted to know. Rhys had cheated. End of story.

Maxine put her hand on my forearm, the cool contact startling me out of my thoughts. "Listen. Even if you can't trust him enough to save your marriage, there's no reason you can't put this to bed enough to be civil. Especially if you have to live with each other for the fore-seeable future."

I rubbed my eyes. "That, or I need to find a faster way to get out of that house and on my own."

She frowned. I could feel the frustration coming off her. One of the reasons we'd always gotten along so well was that neither of us sugar-coated things for each other. There was no bullshit between us. We told each other when prospective partners set off alarm bells, like when she'd dated that asshole a few years ago who'd turned out to be married. Or when her gut had told her my ex-boyfriend was a manipulative narcissist. Sometimes we were wrong—I hadn't thought she and her ex-girlfriend were even remotely compatible, but they'd had three good years together before the girlfriend's job had forced her to relocate, and the long distance thing had fizzled in a few months. They were still friends, though. I'd clearly been wrong about her.

Five years ago, she'd had second thoughts about getting into another long distance relationship. Once bitten, after all. I'd encouraged her to give him a chance because she was obviously into him and he was seriously pinging my nice guy radar. Now he was living with her and they were talking about getting married.

She'd been the one to tell me that if I really did have that much of a crush on my daughter's junior high softball coach, then maybe I should see if he wanted to get a drink. That was exactly why she'd stood beside me as my "best man" both times I'd married him—first ceremonially, then legally.

So I could only imagine how hard it was for her to hold back right now. She knew me well enough to know that this wasn't a good time to push me. There were too many raw nerves exposed. I needed time to think. To process. When I'd licked my wounds a bit more, she'd be ready and waiting to try again.

As I took another drink from the ice cold bottle, I couldn't imagine changing my mind about this. This breakup was killing me, but it was a necessary evil. Rhys and I were done. Our marriage was over. The only thing left to do was move on.

And I wasn't waiting three months to get started on that.

"What's all this?" Rhys leaned on the doorframe and gazed around the garage, which was littered with cardboard boxes and plastic crates.

I looked up from a box of framed photos. "Just, um, going through some stuff. Getting rid of a few things." Our eyes met, and I didn't have to ask if he could read between the lines.

Sorting things out so it'll be easier to move.

He broke eye contact and surveyed the mess of boxes. As he did, I thumbed through a couple more framed pictures, then stole a glance at him.

He must have just come back from a run. His sandy blond hair was dark with sweat and curling at the ends, and he had on his running prosthetic—the one with the C-shaped running blade instead of the usual foot attachment, plus his usual knee brace on the other leg. How he could go out in shorts and a tank top in November was beyond me, but cold never seemed to bother him, and I'd certainly never objected to the view. Not when it meant showcasing his broad shoulders, tattooed arms, gorgeous ass—

I tore my gaze away from him. There really was no point in ogling him unless I wanted to make myself feel worse. Which I didn't. But still...

I glanced at him again because apparently I was a closet masochist.

Rhys cleared his throat. "Do you need a hand with anything?"

"No, I'm good. Thanks." I gestured at some boxes stacked up against the wall. "That's all yours, so I haven't touched any of it."

He nodded but didn't say anything.

Awkward silence descended between us, and I hated how normal that was becoming. How I was getting so used to this twitchy, unnerving quiet with the man I'd married. Suddenly all the boxes in front of me were twice as urgent. The sooner I got things sorted into his, mine, donate, and toss, the sooner I could get the hell out of this house, this marriage, and this unending tension.

After the wedding, anyway.

"So. Um." I muffled a cough and tapped my thumb on the edge of the box in front of me. "Vanessa set the date for February sixteenth."

Rhys nodded. "Okay. I think that's mid-winter break anyway, so I won't need to get as much time off."

"Oh. Good. Good." I shifted my weight because I was suddenly wound tight with nervous energy. "The wedding's going to be in Portland."

"I figured. I'm assuming we're traveling together for this?" His voice was soft. Not confrontational or snide. Maybe a little resigned and tired. "Are we driving or flying?" His eyebrows pulled together, and I could almost hear the unspoken plea: *Tell me we're driving.*

I swallowed. The thought of a road trip together made me want to break out in hives, but Rhys was deathly afraid of flying. We'd never flown anywhere unless we'd absolutely had to. Under normal circumstances, he'd have assumed that would be the case now, but I supposed neither of us could take anything for granted these days.

"We can drive," I said quietly. "Chicago to Portland in the winter —It's probably about three or four days each way, assuming the weather doesn't get too shitty."

Rhys exhaled with visible relief. "We should probably bank on four days. It is February, after all."

"Sure. Yeah. We can do that." Tax season would be upon us by then, but Maxine had already insisted that she and our other business partner could cope if I needed a week or two for the wedding.

"*You only have one daughter,*" she'd said. "*Don't you dare stay here and work when you could be there celebrating her wedding.*"

"*I owe you one.*"

"*Oh, I know.*" And from the wink she'd given me? She'd be holding me to it. Fine by me as long as I was there for my kid's wedding.

Rhys took a deep breath. "You know, if we're there as a couple, we need to be there... as a couple. Right?"

"What do you mean?"

He fidgeted. "Might turn a few heads if we have separate hotel rooms."

Aw, Christ. I hadn't even thought that far ahead. "Hmm. Yeah. It probably will. And actually, my sister said we could stay with her."

"Mmhmm. So I guess we'll do separate rooms on the road, and when we get to the wedding..." He waved a hand like he couldn't finish the thought.

"Okay. We'll figure out logistics later, but...sounds like a good idea."

He nodded. Our customary awkward silence settled in again. Was this going to follow us all the way to Portland in February? Because three or four days each way of being cooped up in a car with him and our silence was not something I was looking forward to. I was actually tempted to suggest we drive separate cars most of the way, park someplace outside of town, and then put on the happy husband show. Huge waste of gas, but *that* was how uncomfortable it was to be in the same room—never mind the same vehicle—with Rhys.

I didn't suggest it, though, and Rhys didn't say anything. He stayed in the doorway a moment longer, then went back into the house without saying anything. When *had* we become so awkward?

Oh. Right. When he'd cheated on me.

My heart heavy, I sagged back against the wall and exhaled.

I hated him for what he'd done to our marriage.

I hated myself for angrily pouring gas on the fire.

But more than anything, I hated how much it hurt every time he walked away.

Losing you is hell, but I can't wait until this is over.

CHAPTER 3

RHYS

The bell rang after my sixth period American History class.

"See you all after break!" I called to my students as they headed for the door, but I doubted any of them heard me. They'd been collectively twitching and fidgeting as the clock neared three, ready to bolt for the buses because now they had a week off for mid-winter break. Now they were free, off to relax, maybe go snowboarding, or do whatever it was they did for fun when they had a week off in mid-February.

Hopefully their week would be more fun than mine promised to be.

Swearing under my breath, I pressed an elbow into my desk chair's armrest and rubbed my forehead. I wondered how long I could loiter around the school before going home tonight. There had to be something I could do to occupy a couple of hours. Usually I'd be here later anyway because of basketball practice, but there were no practices or games until after break. I had nothing to keep me here tonight except my lack of desire to go home.

I still had to pack, but that would take me all of half an hour. The house was clean. We'd picked up our tuxes from the rental place and our suits from the dry cleaner. Various prescriptions had been refilled. Reservations had been made. There really wasn't much that needed my attention once I got home, so I didn't need to rush out of here.

Would anyone notice if I just hung out at my desk and played on my phone for a couple of hours? I supposed I could grade homework. There was a stack in my briefcase, not to mention newly submitted papers in my inbox, and I had first, third, and fourth period World History quizzes. I'd kind of planned on saving those for the trip, though. I had three nights each way where I'd be alone in hotel rooms, and grading would keep me from imploding with boredom.

Now if I could just figure out what to do in the car to stave off the tense silence. I'd probably be driving most of the way, so it wasn't like I could grade papers, but...

I shifted my attention to my laptop. I could always put together a road trip playlist. Derek and I did generally agree on music, and it would fill in where conversation wasn't happening. Plus making a playlist would give me something to do for the next few hours. Or I could download some audiobooks. We had similar taste there too, so if I loaded up my phone with maybe a dozen of them, there had to be *one* in there that we could agree on.

Or hell, maybe he'd reject anything I offered just out of spite, and we'd spend the whole damned trip in tense, miserable silence. Could I really blame him?

Fresh guilt piled on, and I rubbed my forehead as I sighed into the stillness of my classroom. It was a damn shame I couldn't go back in time and tell myself that no matter how shitty I'd felt that fateful night, the temporary relief wouldn't be worth it. Yeah, I'd felt low as fuck, and even though Derek and I had been through rough patches before, it had seemed insurmountable in the moment. They always did, and we'd always gotten through them, and we would've gotten through that one if I hadn't decided to stop for a drink instead of going home. If I hadn't let that stranger buy me a drink. If I'd taken one of a million different opportunities that night to say no and go home to my husband.

But I hadn't, and now he was working on being my ex-husband, and I had no one to blame but myself.

My classroom door opened, and I looked up as Ryan, a friend from the English department, came in. I sat back in my chair. "Hey. What's up?"

"Just thought I'd come in and chat for a minute." He shut the door behind him and flashed me quick smile. "Since I'm not going to see you for a week."

I laughed but didn't really feel it. "You have big plans for break?"

"As little as possible." He shrugged and came across the room. Leaning against one of the desks, he loosened his tie. Today's tie was bright blue with little cartoon pigs all over it. Ryan hated the school's shirt-and-tie dress code, so he always made sure to wear the most ridiculous—but still within regulation—ties he could find. At the end of every year, his students would gift him even wilder designs. The sheer volume of ties in his closet had to be driving his husband up a wall by now.

Ryan cocked his head. "So what about you? Ready for your baby girl's big day?"

"I think so. I've, um..." I scratched the back of my neck. "Haven't really had much time to think about that part to be honest."

"You're about to go to your daughter's wedding, and you haven't had much time to think about the part about your daughter's wedding?"

I shot him a pointed look. "Come on. You know what's been on my mind."

"What's—oh. Right." He slouched a bit. "Are you telling me that in three months, you two haven't been able to come to some kind of ceasefire long enough to go to the wedding?"

"Well, we're going. But ceasefire? Not so much."

"Oh my God." He rolled his eyes. "Rhys, do you want to be miserable all week or something?"

"Of course not. But I'm going on a road trip with the man who hates me for fucking up our marriage, so being miserable doesn't really seem optional, you know?"

"Uh, yeah, it kind of is."

I eyed him, hoping the expression came across as *enlighten me, then.*

Ryan hoisted himself all the way onto the desk and rested his hands on the edge. "Look, just because you're divorcing doesn't mean things have to be miserable. I mean, my parents split up after my dad cheated on my mom, and once they'd actually filed the papers and started going through the motions, they pretty much stopped fighting."

"Really?"

"Yeah. My mom told me years later she was still pissed at him, but like, they were done. There was no reason to keep punishing him while they sorted everything out."

"Tell that to my ex," I muttered.

"It's a two-way street, hon."

I lifted an eyebrow.

He sighed. "Talk to him. Apologize—again—for what you did, and tell him you just want to get through the next week. Same as him. You're not asking him to take you back or to not have feelings about what happened. You're just saying, hey, we're going to be joined at the hip for a week. Can we just drop all this bullshit and be civil to each other until it's over?"

"I don't know if he'll go for it," I said. "It's been five months and he still can't stand to look at me." Scowling, I shook my head. "You'd think if we could magically get along, we'd have figured it out by now."

"You'd be surprised. I bet it hasn't even occurred to him to just drop it. And I'd bet even more that it's draining him as much as it's draining you. Couldn't hurt to throw it out there."

I mulled it over, and the more I thought about it... hell, maybe he was on to something. It wasn't like I had much to lose by broaching the subject. What was I going to do? Make things *more* uncomfortable between us? I didn't think that was possible at this point.

So I nodded. "Okay. I'll talk to him tonight. We'll see how it goes."

Ryan smiled sympathetically. "Good luck."

It had been four months, three weeks, and six days since I'd told Derek I'd cheated on him, which meant that for the last four months, three weeks, and six days, the mere thought of approaching him about anything made me want to hyperventilate.

It didn't matter that I wasn't dropping some kind of bomb on him this time. Ever since *"Derek, there's something I need to tell you..."* he hadn't been able to look at me without his eyes reminding me how deeply I'd hurt him. As if my conscience had let me go a day without thinking about it.

And whenever I approached him, I had the same sick feeling of dread as I'd had that day, even if I was just coming to ask if he needed me to pick something up at the grocery store or if he could take the cats in for their boosters. I never knew when he was going to give me calm, monosyllabic answers, or we'd have some stilted version of a normal conversation, or when he'd blow up at me. The blowups were fewer and farther between now—Ryan was probably right that the hostility was as exhausting for Derek as it had been for me—but the approach still wasn't something I looked forward to.

Outside his bedroom—the bedroom we'd once shared—I steeled myself. Shoulders back. Deep breath. *I can do this.*

Then I knocked gently. There was some movement on the other side, though my heartbeat drowned out most of it, and then the door opened.

I tried—really tried—not to notice that Derek was only wearing a pair of low-slung sweatpants. I hadn't come in here to drool over his lean, powerful body. I'd come in here to talk. Talk about...uh...

He lowered his chin and raised his eyebrows.

Face heating up, I cleared my throat. "Listen, do you have a minute?"

He studied me like he was seriously considering telling me he didn't, but then he stood aside, letting the door open the rest of the way, and gestured for me to come in.

It felt weird, stepping into our old bedroom. Not much had changed. My dresser was gone and the nightstand on my side was bare. Otherwise, everything was the same.

Apparently I'd caught Derek in the middle of packing. He had some folded stacks of clothes on the bed alongside a garment bag and a small open suitcase.

Chico poked his head up from inside the suitcase.

I laughed nervously. "Looks like you have help."

Derek managed a faint smile as he scratched under Chico's chin. "He's always helpful."

Chico purred loud enough I could hear him from halfway across the room. At least the cats were getting less edgy about being in the room with both of us. Shame they couldn't speak, or maybe one of them could tell me their secret.

Derek pulled his attention from the cat and turned to me. "So, what's on your mind?"

Right. Right. Something on my mind. A reason I'd come in here.

He went back to taking clothes out of his dresser, but I could tell his focus was on me.

I folded my arms loosely because I didn't know what else to do with my hands. "I wanted to talk about the trip."

"I figured." Even as he neatly stacked some shirts beside the suit-case, his guard was up. I could *feel* it. He returned to the dresser and started searching through another drawer.

"I was thinking..." I shifted my weight. "We're stuck together in the car for four days. Each way."

"Mmhmm," he said over his shoulder.

I chewed my lip as I fought back my nerves. "What would you say about putting all this, um, tension on hold until we get back?"

That got his attention. Derek turned around, dark eyebrows pulling together, and he eyed me like I'd lost my mind. "Put it on hold? How the hell would we do that?"

"Just..." I shrugged. "Go back to the way things were before it all went to shit. Not pretend we're getting back together. Just..." I wracked my brain, thinking back to everything Ryan had said in the classroom. "I know you're pissed at me for what I did. I'm sure you hate me, and I don't blame you at all. But this...where we can't even be in the same room without our hackles going up? When we can't talk without both of us obviously being on guard? I mean, it's exhausting, you know?"

"It is, yeah." His tone was cold. "Actions have consequences."

It took all I had not to snap back at him. I was here to defuse things, not ignite another battle. Injecting extra calm into my voice, I said, "I know they do. That's why we're getting a divorce. But what do either of us gain by gnashing our teeth the whole way to Portland and back?"

He pressed his lips together. "Do you actually think it's that easy?"

"No. But if we both put in the effort..." I shrugged tightly. "I mean, it's your call. We can drive the whole way in miserable silence, or we can at least drop some of this enough to maybe pass the time with conversation."

His forehead creased as he stared at me incredulously. "Conversation about what?"

"Anything. I don't care. We can listen to a book or music most of the way if it's easier, but what about if one of us wants to stop? Or if we sit down to eat somewhere?" I released a long breath. "I'm not asking you to talk to me like I'm your BFF. But just...like a stranger on a bus, you know? Shoot the shit to pass the time so we don't get stir crazy." I showed my palms. "I promise I haven't forgotten and I won't forget that I fucked up and that we're done. I'm just suggesting a truce until we get back from the wedding."

Derek held my gaze. "That sounds a lot easier said than done."

"I'm pretty sure it will be. I'll put in the effort if you will."

His features hardened for a second, and I thought he might tell me where I could stick my effort. But then, little by little, the tension in his face and posture eased. He turned his attention back to his luggage as he said, "Okay. I'm game for trying anything if it means making this trip more bearable."

Relief made my knees weak. "That's all I want."

He nodded. He paused to scoop Chico out of the suitcase and set him down on the bed. As he brushed away some cat hair, he added, "What time do you want to leave tomorrow?"

"Um." I unfolded and refolded my arms. "I don't know. Should we leave before or after rush hour?"

"Doesn't matter to me." He put a stack of shirts into his suitcase. "Should take us about seven hours to get to our first hotel, and our rooms won't be ready until four anyway, so there's no point in leaving at the crack of dawn."

"Okay. Maybe...ten?" At least then we wouldn't be stuck in the worst of Chicago's morning commute.

"Sure. Ten works."

We exchanged glances. Neither of us smiled, but there was just a *skoch* less animosity than there'd been recently. It was a step in the right direction. I'd take it.

"Sounds good. I'll see you in the morning, then."

"See you in the morning."

I hovered there for a moment, wondering if I should say something else, but decided that this was a fairly positive note to end our conversation on. We'd see how things went tomorrow when the rubber quite literally met the road.

So, I started to leave.

"Rhys."

I stopped in the doorway and turned around.

Derek was still focused on arranging things in his suitcase, and his voice was quiet as he said, "Just so you know, I don't hate you."

"You don't?"

"No." He swallowed, then turned to me, resting his hands on the sides of the suitcase. "I can't trust you. I still want us to go our separate ways. But..." He shook his head and barely whispered, "I don't hate you."

"Oh." I held his gaze, but I had no idea what to say.

Derek broke eye contact first, and the moment was over. I mumbled, "See you in the morning," and continued out of the room.

Safely in my own bedroom across the hall, I leaned against the door and closed my eyes. It should have been a relief to know he didn't actually hate me.

So why did I feel even guiltier now?

CHAPTER 4

DEREK

To say the least, I was dubious of Rhys's idea about dropping all the conflict and playing road trip buddies for a week.

As we headed out of Chicago the next morning, though, I decided he might be on to something. Neither of us had said much yet, but just letting myself not be angry with him was...surprisingly effective. I hadn't realized until now how much work it took to keep grinding my teeth and seething while I counted down to that seemingly far off day when we could finally separate for good. It was exhausting, and before last night, it hadn't occurred to me that all this energy-wasting effort might be optional. Maybe not in the beginning —the emotions had been running far too hot in the weeks following Rhys's confession—but now that a few months had gone by? Surprisingly, yes.

Of course I was still hurt, and on some level I was still pissed. But there was something to be said for consciously letting it go, if only for a week and a half. Why hadn't anyone told me I could take a deep breath, slowly release it, and will myself to simply coexist with my soon-to-be ex-husband? That I could still be hurt and angry, but dial it back to a six instead of riding along at a miserable, draining eleven?

"If you want me to take over," I said to Rhys as he drove us past the city limits, "say the word."

He glanced at me, offered a brief smile, and faced the road again. "Will do. Let me know if you need to stop."

My heart fluttered, and it was a good feeling for once. We both knew he'd keep driving all the way through unless some wreck or bad weather kept us on the road longer than he could handle. And we both knew I could happily ride until we had to stop for gas without needing to stop for a restroom or food in between. But every road trip we'd ever taken had started with that exchange—just letting each other know the options were there—and starting this trip with the same gave me hope that we could get through the next several days in one piece.

After a few interchanges and some construction zones, we were out on the open road. The freeway stretched out into the distance, only a handful of cars and the odd eighteen wheeler dotting the rain-darkened pavement. On the horizon were some ominous clouds, which weren't a surprise. The weather report predicted rain as we moved west, especially as we headed into the Rocky Mountain foothills. I had an alert set on my phone in case the forecast changed to snow or something similarly treacherous. As long as it was just rain, we'd be fine. If snow came, which it probably would once we made it into the mountains, Rhys's Santa Fe had fairly new tires, and he was a more-than-competent driver in the worst weather.

If it started to snow with any kind of enthusiasm, though, we'd stop for the night. Rhys could drive just fine no matter what the weather, and the Santa Fe handled well enough, but there was no predicting the *other* drivers on the road. No amount of skill or caution could compensate for a runaway tractor trailer or some dumbshit who thought four wheel drive meant you didn't have to slow down in bad conditions.

I gazed out at the road and the clouds and stole a few glances at Rhys from the corner of my eye. We'd always been on the same page when we'd gone out on the road together. No arguing over whether we should stop for the night or push through. No tension over how many rest stops were too many or not enough. No butting heads over music, audiobooks, or the radio. Between our agreement to bury the hatchet temporarily and sliding back into our long established road trip routine, this almost felt normal. Almost.

My mind threatened to dig into all the reasons this wasn't and couldn't be normal, but I didn't let those thoughts sink their teeth in. "Want me to find some music?"

"Sure." Rhys gestured at his phone, which was already connected to the sound system. "There are a few playlists set up. See if something sounds good."

A mixture of relief and sadness roiled in my stomach as I picked up his phone. So close to normal, and still...not.

I was into his phone and thumbing through his playlists before it even occurred to me to ask if he'd changed his passcode. Apparently he hadn't.

While I perused his playlists, Rhys rested a hand on top of the steering wheel and held his soda bottle in his lap with the other. "So what's the agenda once we get there?"

"To Portland?"

"Yeah. I mean, I assume there's the rehearsal, and obviously the wedding and reception." He glanced at me. "Anything else?"

I chuckled. "We're going to be busy, if that's what you're wondering."

"Are we?"

"Mmhmm." I selected the playlist titled *pop stuff*, set it to play unobtrusively in the background, and put the phone back on the console. "Her in-laws are having a big informal party on Thursday night for all the out-of-town family members to meet. Then Friday is the rehearsal and dinner, and Saturday's the wedding." I paused, studying Rhys as best I could from the corner of my eye. "Also Vanessa texted me last night. She and Corbin want to have breakfast with us on Sunday. With *just* us."

"They do?"

"Yeah. She was hoping we could do it before the wedding, but there's so much happening, we figured it would be better to wait until everything is settling down." I turned to him this time. "We were planning to leave Sunday morning, but we could spare an hour or two, don't you think?" *Do you think we'll be able to stand each other long enough for one meal?*

"Of course. Sounds great." He tapped his fingers on his soda bottle and stole a glance at me. "Um. I mean. If you're..." He glanced at me before focusing on the road again. "What do you think?"

"I definitely want to go. And I guess... I mean, if we can keep this going, being civil..." I swallowed. "If we can do this through the wedding and everything else, there's no reason we can't keep up the act through breakfast."

Rhys winced, albeit so subtly that I might have been imagining it. "I think we can manage that. For Vanessa's sake."

"Right. For Vanessa's sake."

Silence fell. A Miley Cyrus song played softly above the road noise but seemed ten times louder without conversation over the top. The carefully cultivated peace between us felt oddly precarious right then. As if we were on that knife's edge between diving into the topic of what used to be us and wisely letting it go in the name of keeping things smooth.

Shifting in his seat, Rhys cleared his throat. "Have you met her new in-laws yet?"

I barely kept the sigh of relief to myself. "Not yet. Vanessa put them on for a minute when we were Facetiming on New Year's, but that's it. They seem nice enough. She likes them."

Rhys laughed quietly. "Well, given her opinions of her last boyfriend's parents, if she likes them, then they must be all right."

I laughed for real this time. "To be fair, she wasn't wrong about them."

"Ugh. No. She wasn't." He shook his head. As he unscrewed the cap on his soda bottle, gaze still fixed on the road, he said, "I don't think I have ever been more relieved to see that girl break up with someone."

"I know, right?" I pressed my elbow under the window and rested my cheek against my loose fist. "Obviously the stupid doesn't fall far from the tree."

Rhys choked on his soda. He managed to stay in control of the truck even as he coughed and sputtered, but he nearly dropped the bottle, so I took it while he pulled himself together.

"What?" I chuckled. "Am I wrong?"

"No." He coughed again, wiped his eyes, and held out his hand for his drink. "It just cracks me up how unapologetically catty you can be when it comes to Vanessa's boyfriends."

"I beg your pardon? I've been perfectly nice to her boyfriends. Even the ones I don't like."

"Except that one?"

"Except that one." I wagged a finger at Rhys. "And I was nice to his face. And to his family's faces. Just...not so much once I was in the car and they couldn't hear me anymore."

Rhys snickered, then took another swig of his soda, which he didn't choke on this time. Then he tucked the bottle between his thighs and screwed the cap back on. "Let's just hope Corbin's family really is an upgrade from Kyle's."

"They are. Trust me."

We both laughed, and our earlier momentary tension was forgotten as we continued down the road. The hours passed with light conversation punctuated by long but comfortable silences while the music played. If a song came on that neither of us could resist singing along to, we cranked up the volume, sang along as off key as we always did, and laughed at how ridiculous we sounded.

Just like old times. Almost.

When we'd driven as far as the Santa Fe could go without a refill, we found a truck stop and pulled in. I topped off the tank while Rhys went inside, and once it was gassed up, I went in as well. After I'd paid for my drink and a Snickers, I joined Rhys in the truck.

He was kneading his right knee when I slid into the passenger seat. Not surprising—that leg had some extra wear and tear from almost two decades of bearing his weight whenever he wasn't wearing his prosthetic. Long periods behind the wheel always meant some stiffness, especially as he'd gotten older.

"You holding up all right?" I asked.

"Yeah. Yeah." He straightened his leg with an audible pop. "I took an ibuprofen, so once that kicks in, I'll be good."

"You want me to drive until it does?"

"Nah." As if for emphasis, he started the engine. Pulling on his seat belt, he added, "If it's not any better after fifty miles or so, we'll switch."

"Deal."

———

The solitude of my hotel room was jarring after spending the entire day with Rhys. Before we'd left, I'd imagined myself climbing the walls in the car and itching to lock myself in my room for some much needed time alone. Even after things had been chill with him all day, I'd pictured being relieved to have some walls between us for the rest of the night.

Then we'd been in the hallway, found our rooms directly across from each other, and mumbled "see you in the morning" before disappearing behind our respective numbered doors. His had clicked shut first. Then mine.

And suddenly...I'd been alone.

Wanting to be in the same room with Rhys had become an alien feeling, but there it was. I told myself I just wanted him around because it had been a nice switch, being cordial like that. Plus I was always bored and restless in hotel rooms. At least having someone to talk to could temper that a little, even if that someone was the man I was looking forward to divorcing.

I didn't want Rhys here—I was just bored. In the name of killing time, I screwed off on my iPad for a while. Channel-surfed through four hundred channels of absolutely nothing. Grabbed a shower. Somehow, all that only killed about an hour. It was too early to go to sleep—even fatigue from being on the road couldn't justify crashing this early.

Food. I could go get food. There was a bar and grill across the street that had looked promising when we'd pulled in. It would be a nice change of scenery, and it had been a few hours since I'd eaten.

So I put my shoes on, collected my wallet, phone, and room key, and left the room.

I was halfway down the hall when I stopped. Heart pounding, I turned around, and my eyes zeroed in on the door across from mine.

Things had been going really well today. Would I be pushing my luck if I suggested having dinner together? I supposed there was no harm in asking. If he didn't want to, he didn't want to. No harm. No foul.

I backtracked to his door, and for several long seconds, I stood there with my hand hovering in the air, wondering if I should do this.

Eh, nothing ventured, nothing gained.

The thought made me flinch. Those had been the words on my mind when I'd worked up the courage and asked my daughter's softball coach if he wanted to get drinks, and the memory nearly made me back off now.

But before I could stop myself, I tapped on the door.

I heard some shuffling on the other end, and waited with my heart in my throat. Rhys had undoubtedly taken off his prosthetic by now, so it would take him a moment to get to the door. A moment I could take advantage of to make my escape, but no. No, I wasn't going to be a coward. It was just an offer to have dinner. What was I so worked up about?

The deadbolt clicked. The door opened.

Across the hotel room's threshold, our eyes met, and immediately, my mind went blank. He wasn't wearing a shirt, exposing the tattoos on his upper arms and the muscles of his broad chest. His eyes were tired, but not like I'd just woken him up. More like the long day had finally caught up with him.

Shifting a little on his good leg, resting a hand on the doorframe for balance, he held my gaze and inclined his head. "What's up?"

Oh. Yeah. I'd been the one to knock. Wasn't I going to say something? No, *ask* something?

Dinner. Right.

"Hey, um." I cleared my throat and gestured down the hall. "I was going to go get some dinner. At that bar and grill across the street." I swallowed. "You want to join me?"

Rhys searched my eyes, and as my question hung in the air, I honestly couldn't decide what answer I was hoping for.

After what seemed like forever but had probably been all of ten seconds, he shook his head. "I think I'm just going to relax for the night. Ice my knee, maybe order something off GrubHub."

"Oh." Apparently I'd been hoping for a yes, if the disappointment in my gut was any indication. "Okay. Well. I'll see you in the morning."

"Right. See you in the morning."

We exchanged smiles that reminded me of how strangers looked at each other before parting ways, and then I started down the hall as Rhys closed the door.

No problem. I'd extended the offer, he'd declined, and that was fine. I'd have a nice quiet dinner by myself, and tomorrow, we'd hit the road together, and everything would be *fine*.

Hands in my pockets, I strolled out into the frosty evening and headed for the restaurant across the street. Out of sheer habit, I kept an eye out for patches of ice on the ground. Rhys was good about spotting them too, especially since he'd been navigating with the prosthetic for a decade before I'd met him. After taking some nasty falls, though—one of which had resulted in a broken wrist—he was extra cautious in the snow and ice. He sometimes used a cane if the conditions were especially bad, and he was always vigilant about ice on the ground. A few weeks into our first winter together, it had become a habit for me too.

One that I apparently hadn't broken even when Rhys wasn't with me.

Even when Rhys and I weren't together at all.

At the crosswalk, I blew out a thin cloud of breath while I waited for the light to change. I'd made the decision to divorce Rhys months ago. Why was it suddenly a hard thing to get my head around?

I shook myself. The light changed, and I started across the street. This was probably part of the grieving process or something. Maybe I should start seeing a counselor again. Someone to help me iron out all the emotions and weird surprises that came in the wake of a divorce. There were books on the subject too, weren't there? And that bookstore in town was still open, wasn't it?

Okay. Yeah. When I got home from the wedding, I'd find a counselor and a stack of books.

First—dinner.

The restaurant was one of those places with a huge section full of families and a lounge area with a big flat screen above the bar and smaller TVs mounted in the corners. Some basketball games were on right now, which didn't interest me, but it looked like there were some good beers on tap.

The lounge area was self-seat, so I found a booth beside the windows, slid in, and plucked a menu from the stand beside the condiments. Typical bar and grill food—fried cheese-slathered appetizers, burgers, salads.

A waiter who looked to be about twelve—holy shit, I was getting old—came by the table, tablet in hand. "Can I get something started for you? Maybe a cranberry lime martini or a peach margarita?"

"Just a beer. What do you have on tap?"

He rattled off some brands I'd never heard of. Probably local microbrews. He personally recommended one of the pilsners, so I took him at his word and ordered one.

While he went to get my beer, I continued browsing the menu.

Was I in the mood for a steak? Or maybe something lighter? A burger didn't sound all that appetizing tonight. Where the hell did they get "fresh caught Alaskan halibut"? Because last I checked, Alaska was... not a "fresh caught" distance from here unless someone had invented teleportation.

Someone appeared beside the table, but when I looked up, it wasn't the waiter.

"Oh." I gulped, staring at Rhys. "I thought... You said..."

"I know." He had one hand in his jacket pocket, the other on his cane, and he sheepishly held my gaze. "Is the, um, offer still open?"

My heart was pounding as I nodded. "Yeah. Sure." I gestured at the bench across from me. "Sit down."

He hesitated for a split second, then took off his parka and sat. After he'd folded his cane and slid it into his jacket pocket, he freed a menu from the stand. "So. Anything sound promising?"

"Um. Well." I looked down at the menu I'd been reading, but had totally blanked. "I was going to start with a beer and go from there, I think. That was about as far as I'd gotten."

"Beer sounds like a good start."

"The waiter should be back with mine in a second." I thumbed the frayed lamination on the corner of my menu. "What changed your mind?"

Without looking up from his, he said. "Wasn't much on GrubHub."

"Oh."

His eyes flicked up to meet mine, and he breathed a soft laugh as he lowered his gaze back to the menu. "I just... I was getting stir crazy and didn't really want to eat alone, so..."

"Fair enough. Thanks for the company."

He seemed surprised by the answer. I didn't know what to say. He didn't either, apparently. That, or he just wanted to change the subject, and I was thankful as hell when he said, "What do they have on tap?"

"Local stuff, from the sound of it. I ordered a pilsner, so we'll see how that tastes."

"Eh." He shrugged. "Works for me. What about food?"

My beer arrived a moment later, and it was pretty good, so Rhys ordered the same. Once his drink came, we also ordered some appetizers, which knowing us would end up being all we ate. Especially since the description on the nachos he ordered included *Great for sharing!* in giant yellow letters.

Rhys took a sip, and made an appreciative sound. "Oh, man. This *is* good."

"Yeah, it is. I might have to get the name and see if they carry it at home."

"That snooty-ass hippy store you shop at probably sells it." He met my eyes over the rim of his glass, and there was a sparkle in his eyes. The comment didn't have any heat behind it, either.

I chuckled. "You want me to pick up a six-pack if they have it?"

"Fuck yeah, I do. What kind of question is that?"

One that almost made me think about the fact that neither of us would be buying beer for each other for much longer, but I was enjoying my beer and this restaurant and, yes, my ex-husband's presence. I pushed those thoughts aside. No sense killing my buzz before it started.

We did the same thing we'd done in the car—kept the conversation light, and didn't struggle to fill the silence when it happened. It wasn't effortless, but it was a damn sight better than things had been recently, so I had no complaints.

"Think the cats miss us yet?" he asked.

"Are you kidding?" I put my glass down. "They were probably asleep before we'd pulled out of the garage."

"Probably. They were laying the guilt trips on hard, though. Jesus."

"That's only because Lucy knows she can manipulate you," I said with a laugh. "She knows damn well you're leaving, but if she looks at you with those big blue eyes, you'll ply her with treats until we go. She's got you trained."

Rhys chuckled, and damn if he didn't blush. "She pulls the same shit whenever Becky's cat-sitting too. And Chico is just as bad."

"Chico has Becky wrapped around his paw. Manipulative little asshole."

He laughed. "Cats? You don't say."

"I know, right?"

We kept on like that, musing about how much the cats were gong to destroy the house in our absence. Then our waiter materialized beside us, balancing a small plate and a... *not* small plate. "Okay, we have an order of potato skins." He put the little plate in front of me. "And the nachos." The platter went down in front of Rhys, and we both stared at it.

"Holy shit." Rhys gaped. He looked at me over the mountain of chips, cheese, sour cream, guac, olives, and jalapenos. "Please tell me you're sharing this with me."

"I don't know. I kind of want to see if you can handle it yourself."

Rhys groaned. "You know damn well I'll try, and I'll be miserable for the rest of the night." He pointed at the plate. "Eat."

I laughed, pulled a chip free from the huge pile, and nudged a few olives into the sour cream and cheese. "You better help me with these potato skins."

"No promises, man." Rhys was about to say something, but he glanced toward the bar and did a double take. "Aw, shit."

"What?" I followed his gaze, and as soon as I saw the big screen TV, I understood: the bartender had just changed the channel from some basketball game neither of us cared about to a hockey that was about to start.

"Is that..." The table creaked as if Rhys was leaning on it. "Oh, dude. It's the Caps versus the Kings." I couldn't help grinning. Rhys wasn't from either city, but he'd been raised in a Kings household, and he was a diehard fan.

I faced him again. "Pretty sure I don't have to ask if you want to watch."

"Please. As if you don't want to." He thumped the table with his knuckle and grinned brighter than I'd seen him grin in months. "Better order up a couple of shots. It's hockey night."

His enthusiasm was infectious. Laughing, I nodded toward the bar. "First round's on you."

We collected our drinks, jackets, and appetizers, and moved to the bar. I flagged down the bartender to order a round of shots, and as she poured them, I stole a glance at Rhys.

And I smiled.

I hadn't realized until now how much I'd missed *wanting* to be with him. So right now, even if it was only temporary—even if it was little more than an illusion—I didn't fight it.

I let myself want his company.

CHAPTER 5

RHYS

"Shoot! Shoot! Come on! *Shoot!*" I shouted at the screen. "For God's sake, what are you—yes! Yes!" The puck hit the back of the net and I jumped up from the barstool a little faster than I should have, given my current blood alcohol content. I caught myself on the edge of the bar, though, and cheered alongside some of the locals because *someone* had finally scored. The game was halfway through the third period, Derek and I were probably halfway through a bottle of rum, and the score was now tied 2-2. To the bartender, I called out, "One more!"

"Hey, easy there." Derek laughed, steadying me with a hand on my arm. "I'm not carrying your ass back to the hotel."

"Pfft." I waved him off. "You're as drunk as I am."

He chuckled and shook his head, but he didn't argue because he totally knew it was true. Hockey wasn't hockey unless we were fucked up by the end of the second period.

And since we were out of town, I didn't have to worry about one of my students' parents seeing me getting drunk and loud in a public place. Might as well take advantage.

The game had been a wild one so far, with two fights already and the puck changing hands so fast we were all going to get whiplash. Several locals had gathered around the TV too, throwing back booze and shouting at the players, the refs, and even some of the sponsors because... Look, we were drunk, and it was a hockey game.

The game went on at breakneck speed, both teams *nearly* scoring so many times it was dizzying. Then, with twenty-two seconds on the buzzer, the Caps had the puck and made a run for the goal while the Kings' defense lagged behind for a few precious seconds.

"Go! Go!" we all shouted. "Shoot it! Shoot it!"

He shot it and—

Missed.

Everyone in the bar released a collective groan of frustration.

"Well." I grinned at Derek. "That's overtime. You know what that means!"

He returned the grin and gestured at the bartender, who poured us a couple more shots. At the buzzer, we both threw back the shots, slammed them down, and cheered along with everyone else.

As it often did, overtime dragged the hell on. We'd stopped drinking after the buzzer because we'd both had more than enough. By the time the Kings fucking lost after fifty-three years of overtime, we were still drunk but sobering up. Maybe we wouldn't be passing a field sobriety test any time soon, but we could at least make it across the street to our hotel.

The biting cold was like a splash of water to the face. Holy crap, I was awake now.

And with as far as the temperature had dropped, I suspected there was more ice on the ground than there'd been earlier. Fortunately, I'd brought my cane in case the ground was slick when I'd left the hotel. It hadn't been earlier, but now that the night was this much colder and I was hockey-game shit-faced? Definitely glad I'd brought the cane. We had to walk up a gentle slope to get to the hotel, and the pavement was shiny with ice under the streetlights.

Before we left the sheltered, dry pavement in front of the restaurant's doors, I unfolded the cane. Derek offered his elbow, and I slid my other hand into it. This was one of those rare times when we didn't worry too much about people noticing us touching. A man with a cane on icy ground wasn't getting frisky by holding onto the guy next to him. Especially when one of them was drunk. Or both of them.

We slipped and slid a little, but between the two of us and my cane, we stayed upright and made it up the hotel's driveway. The entrance to the building was sheltered so people could unload their cars without getting wet, and the pavement under here was dry. No more ice.

Still holding onto Derek's elbow, I bumped his shoulder with mine and slurred, "We made it. I didn't bust my ass or anything."

He laughed as we walked in through the automatic doors. "Don't get too cocky. We still have to get to the rooms, and you're—" He stumbled, but caught himself on the door and my arm. "Drunk."

I snorted. "I'm drunk? Look who's talking."

"Fuck you." He righted himself. "It's what I get for trying to hold your ass up."

"Pfft. I'm not the one tripping on stripes in the carpet."

"Jackass."

I laughed as we continued toward our rooms. We didn't have very far to go, thank God, and we weren't going to slip on any ice in here, so we were home free. Score.

We stopped in the hallway between our rooms. I started to slide my arm free from Derek's and tried to remember which pocket my room key was in.

But then I looked at Derek. And he looked at me.

And there was this beat of still silence.

And suddenly we were against each other.

I had no idea who'd initiated it. My rum-soaked mind couldn't keep up enough to figure out who'd crossed the distance and made first contact. Or hell, maybe it could, and it had, but the instant we were kissing, my brain went blank and it didn't matter anymore who made the first move. His lips were still cold from being outside, but they quickly warmed up. So did mine. My God, I'd always loved how he kissed, and now I was pretty sure it could get me drunker than anything in a bottle ever aspired to.

As I wrapped my arm around his waist, my cane clattered to the floor at our feet, but I made no move to pick it up. There was no ice in here, and even as drunk as I was, I was steady enough to stand without the support. Even if I did waver from all the booze, I had Derek's arms around me.

And...fuck, yes. We'd hit that sweet spot where we were drunk enough to be frisky, but sober enough we could still get hard. His cock rubbed mine through our jeans every time we moved, driving soft groans and whispered curses out of me as I explored his throat like it was the first time I'd ever touched him. I found that spot on his neck, just below his ear, and he gasped and shuddered, holding me tighter. God, I was painfully hard, desperate to have him naked, but I just needed another moment or two of this.

"Rhys," he breathed. "Come up... I want..."

I lifted my head, and he grabbed the back of my neck and kissed me. I shivered, leaning into him. My touch-starved skin tingled under my clothes, but my kiss-starved mouth was too busy to stop and suggest we go into one of our rooms and get naked. We'd get there. Maybe. I didn't know. All I knew right then was that I couldn't get enough of Derek's soft lips and insistent tongue.

I pushed him back a step. Then another. He gasped when his back hit the door, and I pressed my hips against him, making sure he felt every inch of my erection. He grunted softly and arched, and I dipped my head to kiss his neck again, and... Jesus. Oh my God. All the alcohol I'd had tonight couldn't send me as high as the scent of his skin and the heat of his body as I breathed him in and kissed up and down the side of his throat.

He guided my hand down between us, and I swore against his skin as my palm slid over the rock hard ridge of his erection. I squeezed him through his pants, reveling in the thrum of his voice against my lips. Derek rutted into my hand and swore into the silence of the hallway.

"We should go in one of our rooms," he slurred, probably as much from arousal as alcohol. "Because if I take your pants off out here, we'll end up in jail."

"Mmm, I love how you think." I drew back. "Which room should—"

He touched his key to the reader beside his hip, and the LED turned green. Guess that answered that question.

We exchanged grins as he opened the door. Then I picked my cane up off the carpet, and we hurried into Derek's room.

We didn't bother with slowly undressing. As soon as the door was shut behind us, the clothes started piling up on the floor like snow-drifts. Parkas. Shirts. Shoes. Jeans. After he'd pulled back the covers, I sat on the edge of the bed, slid off my prosthetic and liner, tossed my boxers onto the rest of my clothes, and then joined Derek under the thin sheet.

For the second time, he guided my hand down to his dick, but this time, there was no more denim barrier. Just hot skin on hot skin. I closed my fingers around the shaft, and he gasped as I started stroking him.

"Like that?" I murmured between kisses.

The reply wasn't words, but it definitely sounded positive, so I kept going.

I wanted to stroke him and turn him on, but his mouth was too distracting. His lips and tongue were magic, always had been, and I couldn't make out with him and concentrate on teasing his dick, so I finally gave up doing anything with my hands. I'd get there. Right now, I just wanted to enjoy this man's amazing mouth.

I pushed him onto his back and straddled him, and as I came down to kiss him, he dragged his hands down my sides and onto my ass. I'd always loved the way this man's hands felt on me. He could be rough to the point of bruising or so gentle it bordered on ticklish or anything in between, and I loved it. I was drunk already, but his touch made my head spin even faster. His erection rubbing against mine almost drove me out of my mind.

Through the haze of need and ninety proof, I was aware this wasn't the last man I'd been with. After I'd admitted to Derek that I'd cheated on him, he'd refused to touch me, and though I hadn't blamed him, I'd ached for him. Not just to somehow assuage my guilt, but because I'd never wanted anyone like I'd wanted Derek. One stupid mistake had cut me off from the breathless, needy sex I'd taken for granted for almost a decade.

Having his skin against mine now, tasting his mouth again and feeling his thick cock rubbing mine, brought tears to my eyes. Guilt. Relief. Shame. Need. I wanted him so bad it hurt, and it hurt even more to be this aware of everything I'd destroyed.

I took in a long, deep breath of his scent through my nose, hoping it also masked a subtle sniffle. Then I kissed his collarbone again, and started working my way downward, letting my lips memorize every inch of his chest and abs. This was probably the last time I'd touch him like this—a second chance to drink him in and commit all this to memory—and I fully intended to burn it into my mind.

As my lips crested his hipbone, Derek moaned. "*Oh*, yeah." He combed his fingers through my hair. "Please, baby. Suck my—*yes*."

I swirled my tongue around the head of his cock, then slowly deep-throated him just the way he loved it. He moaned again. Except...no, that was me. That was my voice, my pleasure as I licked and stroked Derek while he arched and trembled beneath me. My head was light and my whole body felt warm all over; I had no idea where the booze ended and the arousal began, but whatever. I loved it. I never wanted it to stop.

Derek shivered. "Rhys. D-don't suck me off. Not ready to come yet."

I lifted my head. "What do you want me to do, then?"

He didn't speak, but the hunger in his eyes was unmistakable. I pushed myself onto my arms and came back up to kiss him, and... yeah, that was what he wanted. Deep, passionate kissing while our naked bodies tangled up all over again. Derek rocked his hips, rubbing his dick on my hip, and I returned the motion, adding some friction as my own cock rubbed against him.

He slid his hands down my back and squeezed my ass. "I so wish I had some lube with me."

"Mmm, yeah. But I think we can make do without." I nipped the side of his neck hard enough to make him gasp. "Plenty of things we can do."

The helpless sound he released gave me goose bumps. He was always so fun when he was this turned on. When desperation rolled off him in waves that were nearly visible to the naked eye.

We made out and groped and nipped and gasped, and every time he stroked or so much as grazed my cock, it was a wonder I didn't come. I was so turned on I couldn't see straight. Wanted him so bad I couldn't *think* straight. Somehow, we found ourselves on our sides, pumping each other's cocks while we made out. We thrust our hips too, fucking into each other's fists, and if I'd been sober, I probably would have come after two or three thrusts. The alcohol slowed me down, though, and thank God for that. Now I could enjoy this frantic neediness. His. Mine. Ours. I was drunk enough to slow down and get drunk on him. Fuck *yes*.

Derek shuddered, his hand's rhythm faltering slightly. Then he moaned. "Ungh. Don't stop. *Fuck.*"

I was panting too hard to speak, and I definitely didn't stop. I dug my teeth into my lip, pumped his cock for all I was worth, and wondered if there was anything sexier than Derek when he was this close to coming. His features were tight, his eyes squeezed shut, his fair skin flushed, and when he held his breath, I held mine too, and I mentally urged him on as I kept stroking him and thrusting into his fist.

"Fuck!" The word burst out of him in the same instant his entire body jerked, and then he gasped, and his cum landed on my hand, our stomachs, and my dick.

I was probably three strokes from coming myself, but Derek

suddenly stopped, pushed me onto my back, and—before I knew which way was up—went down on me.

"Oh God!" I groaned as his lips and tongue went to town on the head of my dick. I was so close to the edge anyway, and he licked and sucked and stroked me like he was hell bent on making me come as quickly as possible. I shuddered hard, gripping the sheets and not even trying to fight my orgasm. I let him take me there as only Derek had ever been able to, and in seconds, I cried out and came in his eager, talented mouth.

Derek sat up, cleaned his own cum off both of us, then flopped onto the bed beside me, and we lay there panting as the room spun. I didn't let myself think about how long it had been since I'd felt this good, or why it had been so long—I just basked in it and savored it.

"Oh my God," I murmured. "I needed that."

"Me too." He was quiet for a moment, then laughed softly.

I turned to him. "What?"

"Just thinking." He let his head loll toward me, and he gave me a delicious leer. "I forgot how much I loved drunk hockey sex."

I chuckled, finding his hand on the rumpled sheet. "I know, right? I mean, gotta do something with all that adrenaline."

"Uh-huh." He slid closer. "Whatever you say, baby."

We cuddled up together, my arm draped over him and his encircling my shoulders. With my head resting on his chest and the heat of his body against mine, post-sex drowsiness kicked in fast. Now that we'd both come, everything—the road trip, the alcohol, the sex—came crashing down. My eyelids were suddenly heavy.

"I'd suggest a round two, but I..." I trailed off into a yawn.

Derek breathed a warm laugh across my forehead and pressed a kiss to my hairline. "It's been a long day."

"And we're drunk. Don't forget that."

"And we're drunk," he acknowledged with a nod.

"*So* drunk."

"Pfft. We're not *that* drunk."

"Sure you're not." I patted his shoulder. "Whatever you say."

"I got it up, didn't I?"

"Uh-huh. Doesn't mean you're not drunk."

"But it means I'm not *super* drunk."

"Mmhmm."

"Fuck you," he said with a laugh.

I laughed too, and let my eyes slide closed as I enjoyed his warm embrace. I didn't let my mind linger on whether it was a good idea to fall asleep in this bed. I wasn't sure I could have lingered on the thought if I'd wanted to.

Wrapped up in Derek's warm arms, I did the only thing I could do.

I let sleep carry me away.

CHAPTER 6

DEREK

I woke up with two sensations I hadn't experienced in a long time.

One, the obnoxious throbbing of a hangover.

Two, the warmth of soft, naked skin pressed against mine.

It only took a few disoriented seconds for my brain to catch up. Last night was faintly fuzzy around the edges, but most of the details were clear enough. I knew exactly who had his arm slung over me. Whose soft breath was whispering over the nape of my neck. I remembered everything we'd done, and how much I'd loved every brush of his lips and stroke of his hands.

I found his hand and gently clasped it. As I ran my thumb along the backs of his fingers, I grazed the faint indentation where his wedding ring had been. I thumbed my own ring finger, finding the corresponding groove.

Eyes closed, I released a long breath. Last night had been fun. I wouldn't deny it, but while the hangover left a terrible taste in my mouth, it was nowhere near as sour as the regret burning in the back of my throat. Rhys and I were *over*. There was a reason we'd spent the last five months in separate bedrooms. A reason I couldn't ignore and couldn't erase.

Except, apparently, long enough to have sex.

I grimaced. Well, lesson learned. No good could come of drinking with Rhys on this trip. Oh, and also that my libido was still alive and kicking, and I was absolutely making a Grindr profile when I got home. And a Tinder profile. And...well, profiles on whichever apps people were using to get laid these days.

In the meantime?

I gently lifted his arm off me and sat up. Rhys mumbled into the pillow, then stilled. Fine. Let him sleep a little longer. I wanted him to collect his clothes and get the hell out of my room so I could get my head together, but if he slept for a minute or two, that would give me time to get dressed. Whatever conversation came after this seemed like it would be less awkward if I wasn't bare-ass naked.

I picked up our clothes off the floor and put his on the bed beside him. Then I started getting dressed. As I did, I indulged in a long look at him. That was one thing even the bitterness and resentment couldn't chase away—how gorgeous my ex-husband was. All those smooth planes and angles. How many times had my fingers traced those grooves and contours? The edges of his tattoos?

Unwelcome emotions tried to bubble to the surface, so I pulled my gaze away and swallowed hard to force them back. I didn't want to still be grieving what I'd had with Rhys. I wanted to be over him. Like, now. I sure as shit didn't need to start tearing up while we figured out how to navigate the most awkward morning after in the history of mornings after.

As I was pulling on my shirt, Rhys stirred. He scrubbed his hand over his face, grumbled a bit, and then sat up. "What time is it?"

"Um." I glanced at the clock beside the bed. "Almost eight."

He wrinkled his nose. "Fuck. Why the hell are we awake?"

I chewed my lip.

Rhys looked up at me. I could practically hear the "what?" on the tip of his tongue, but then he straightened, eyes widening slightly as if he'd remembered where he was, who he was with, and everything that had happened. He broke eye contact with what sounded like a defeated breath, then eased himself toward the edge of the bed. He glanced at the clothes I'd laid beside him, then leaned down to pick up the prosthetic and its liner. As he started to put the liner on, that all too familiar uncomfortable silence hovered between us.

My head pounded. I was way too hung over to think about this, never mind talk about it, but we couldn't just ignore it either. "Um. So. Last night. Just so we're clear, what we did doesn't mean..." I couldn't say it. Why the hell couldn't I say the words? "Things haven't changed."

Avoiding my eyes, Rhys nodded. He was still intently focused on rolling the liner into place, probably to give his hands something to do. "I know. I didn't expect them to."

"So we're—"

"Derek." He met my gaze, his expression plaintive. "We got drunk, and we got carried away. I'm not reading anything into it. I promise."

I swallowed. Then nodded. Good. Good. We were on the same page.

So why didn't it feel like the *right* page?

Neither of us spoke as he dressed. Once he was done, he gathered his jacket, phone, wallet, and cane.

I cleared my throat. "When did you want to hit the road?"

Our eyes met.

When do we have to stuff all this awkwardness into a single vehicle for the next several hours?

"I still need to grab a shower." Rhys didn't look at me. "I'll, um, text you when I'm ready to go."

"All right."

Neither of us spoke, and I didn't watch him go. It was only when the door clicked shut behind him that I released my breath.

Alone in the silent hotel room, I sank onto the edge of the bed and kneaded my throbbing temples. At this point I wasn't even sure what was making my head hurt more—the hangover or the barrage of thoughts banging around in my tender skull.

Fuck. *Fuck.* I had no idea how I felt about last night. Or how I should feel. Or how I wanted to feel. The only thing I knew for sure was that I'd gotten drunk, tumbled into bed with Rhys, and had some seriously hot sex that I hadn't realized I'd been needing. I'd broken the longest dry spell of my adult life with the man who was the reason for that dry spell, and it had been amazing, and I hated that I felt like shit now.

At least there was no question that this changed anything. That this was somehow a step toward going back to us. We'd slept together. End of story. If I was honest with myself, I hadn't started feeling bad about last night until I'd started over analyzing it. Basically until I'd convinced myself to feel bad about it.

Did it have to be like this, though? Was there anything that said I *had* to feel bad about last night? I'd been dubious of Rhys's suggestion that we could put aside our differences enough to be friendly for the duration of this trip, but he'd been right. Yesterday had been surprisingly relaxed—even kind of fun—and that was making me look at everything else with some new perspective too.

We'd had a good time at the bar last night, and then we'd come back here and screwed around. I'd been sober enough to know what I was doing, drunk enough not to overthink it, and... I shivered at the memory of Rhys's body against mine. Even while I'd been drunk and hard, I hadn't been under any illusions that we were returning to the way things had been before Rhys cheated. I hadn't had stars in my eyes or hearts fluttering above my head, thinking everything was forgiven and all was well again. I'd been turned on, and I'd felt good, and it had been that simple.

It was just the morning after when things had started to feel complicated.

But did they *have* to be complicated? Did they *have* to be weird and uncomfortable?

What if we could turn off the weird just like we'd been able to turn off all the resentment? It was only for ten days. Less than that, really. And we'd already slept together once on this trip. So which was better for keeping things civil between us—fucking or not?

Ugh. I didn't know. I had no fucking idea because there wasn't a *Road Tripping with the Cheating Ex-Husband You Still Want to Fuck* instruction manual for some goddamned reason.

What I needed was some advice from someone who had no problem telling me when to pull my head out of my ass. Fortunately, I knew for a fact she'd be awake because she'd told me yesterday she planned to come in today to get some work done, and when she had to come in on the weekend, she came in at the crack of dawn so she wouldn't kill her entire day.

"Don't tell me he left you on the side of the road," Maxine said instead of hello.

I laughed dryly. "No, we're at a hotel. We're actually getting along all right."

"Oh really? What did you do? Spike his drink?"

"No, actually... Actually, it was his idea."

"His idea, what?"

"To put everything on hold and at least pretend we can stand each other until this trip his over."

"And that's working out...how?" She sounded dubious. "I'm assuming you're not calling just to chat, so what happened?"

"Um. Well." I coughed. "We, uh..."

"Christ, Derek." She groaned. "You fucked him, didn't you?"

"I..."

Maxine sighed with palpable exasperation. "For God's sake. What were you thinking?"

That someone was touching me and I needed more because it's been too long.

I swallowed a sudden lump in my throat. "To be fair, we'd had a bit to drink."

She snorted. "Uh-huh."

"Look... I know. It wasn't the smartest thing we could have done. And yes, now things are weird again, and I..." I pressed my elbows into my knees and wiped my free hand over my face. "I can't change last night. He can't change last September. We're stuck together for the next week and a half. And that whole thing he suggested? About just putting aside being pissed at each other? It really did work. Yesterday was... Hell, it was great. So now I just don't know if... I mean, would it be crazy to think..."

"Derek." I could feel her glare over the phone. "Are you calling me because you want me to say yes, it's totally a smart thing to jump into bed with your ex-husband in the name of keeping the peace until you get home?"

"I..." I chewed my lip. "Well, when you put it like that it sounds insane, but yeah, I guess that's kind of why I called."

"I see." She fell silent for a moment. Then she sighed. "Honestly, it doesn't sound as insane as you might think."

"It doesn't?"

"No, and I hate that I can't think of a better alternative, but..." Another heavy sigh. "Damn you for making me say this, but you two might as well keep screwing until you get home. At least when you're fooling around, you're getting along, and you're *both* a lot less insufferable when you're getting laid on a regular basis."

"Gee, thanks."

"Hey, you called me for advice. And don't act like it isn't true."

I rolled my eyes, but couldn't help laughing. "So you're serious. You think I should keep sleeping with Rhys."

"I'm assuming that at least on some level, you want to sleep with him?"

I fidgeted on the edge of the bed. "Well, yeah. I can be pissed at him all I want, but I don't need beer goggles to want him naked."

"That's what I thought." She paused. "And let's face it—once you're in Oregon, you and Rhys are going to be so focused on the wedding and everything, it's going to be a moot point anyway because you'll probably be too tired for each other. If screwing around on your road trip means you're not trying to kill each other at your daughter's wedding, well, that seems like the best possible outcome to me."

I blinked. "I swear, sometimes it's frightening how much sense you make."

Maxine laughed. "What can I say? I know you. And we both know this trip is short, so anything you and Rhys do is a temporary fix. Why not do everything you can to mitigate the stress between the two of you?"

"Assuming this doesn't make that stress worse?"

"Why would it? You said yourself you got along with him all day yesterday. Sex only makes things as complicated as the people involved *want* make it. Plus if you're fucking, you're not fighting, am I right?"

"I guess." I rubbed my fingers along my unshaven jaw. "I still feel weird about it. I told myself after he cheated, that was it. I was done. I wasn't touching him."

"That's because he hurt you," she said in a gentler voice. "Nobody blames you. Including him, if I had to guess. But you also said you would never be able to look at him again without wanting to break down or read him the riot act."

"I did, yeah. So you don't think I'm back-peddling on something I promised myself?"

"When you promised yourself that you wouldn't touch him again, did you foresee being stuck with him for a week and a half like this?"

"Hmm, no."

"Exactly. You can still be mad at him for what he did to your marriage, and you can still divorce his sorry ass when you get back. If banging him during your trip keeps you from being at each other's throats at your daughter's wedding or driving yourselves insane in the car? I don't see how anyone—even you—could hold that against you."

I huffed. "You and your...logic."

Maxine laughed, though she sounded more sympathetic than anything. "You're overthinking this, honestly."

"Are you surprised?"

"Not in the least. Now go talk to him and get him back into bed."

I laughed. "All right, I will. Thanks for the advice."

"Any time. I'll see you when you get back."

"See you soon."

After I'd hung up, I sat for a moment, letting everything she'd said percolate. I tried to tell myself it sounded just as crazy coming from her as it had inside my own head, but no, it made more sense than it had any right to.

"Plus if you're fucking, you're not fighting, am I right?"

She really did have a point. In fact, throughout our relationship, Rhys and I hadn't been above shelving a fight, having sex, and then talking things through afterward. Nothing ever seemed like it was worth a screaming match once we'd blown off some steam together, and most fights were smoothed over in pretty short order.

This time, I wasn't asking myself to suck it up, screw him, and then smooth over the fact that he'd cheated. That was settled. We were done. Any sex we had now was just to keep the tension to a minimum so we could make it through the road trip and the wedding. Plus we probably would get along better if we were sleeping together. Maxine was right about Rhys and me being easier to deal with when we were getting laid. So...why the hell not?

Okay. Rhys had been right about the being civil part. My gut told me Maxine was right about the sex. We could do this, and we could get through this trip without killing each other. We might even like each other by the end of it. Enough to finish going through the motions of our divorce with minimal headache, anyway. After the last few months, I'd take what I could get.

I pushed myself to my feet and took a deep breath. First things first—shower. Then get dressed. Then pack.

And then came the really fun part—broaching the subject with Rhys.

CHAPTER 7

RHYS

I was in no hurry to hit the road, and Derek didn't seem to be either. We took our sweet time with showers, indulging in the hotel's modest continental breakfast, and packing, and by the time we finally checked out, it was almost noon. Getting coffee at the place next to the gas station took longer than it probably should have too; apparently Derek wasn't in any more of a hurry to be cooped up together than I was.

We couldn't dawdle and put this off forever, though, and finally, we were on the interstate. The weather had turned to shit, too—fat snowflakes swirled in all around us, reducing both my speed and visibility. If this kept up, we wouldn't make it to our hotel until late tonight, but...meh. We had reservations. I wasn't worried. Our rooms would still be there. We just had to get there, ideally without driving each other insane with this never-ending silence.

Because surprise, surprise—so much for keeping things relaxed on the road. As I trudged west through the wind and snow, neither of us spoke, and yesterday's cautious but easy vibe seemed like a distant memory. We were back to uncomfortable silence. Of course we were. Fuck.

Damn. I should have trusted my gut and not second-guessed my decision to join Derek at the restaurant last night. I should have kept some comfortable distance between us. Or if I'd gone to the restaurant, maybe just this *one* time I could have bowed out of the excitement of a hockey game, stuck with sodas—something besides riding that wave of alcohol and adrenaline right into my ex-husband's bed. There was no way that was going to end well, and I'd known it then as surely as I knew it now.

How could I have been so stupid?

Oh. Right. Because I'd been drunk, horny, and touching a man who was second to none in bed. I'd let myself forget all the reasons why it was the first time we'd touched in months, and now I got to deal with the fallout. New rule: no more drinking on this trip.

I kept driving, all the while fighting the urge to drum my nails or fidget in my seat. At least driving through crappy weather gave me something to concentrate on. I even wondered a time or two if that was why we weren't talking—Derek usually stayed quiet when I drove in the snow so I could focus.

I doubted that was what was happening here, though. We hadn't said two words before we'd hit the snowy road. At least the air between us wasn't hostile. I didn't feel like we were a breath away from snapping at each other and fighting. We may as well have been, though, for as wound up and nervous as I was. How the hell did we dial this back to the way things had been yesterday? Was that even possible after last night?

Fuck. Are we there yet?

The silence had gone on so long, I almost jumped out of my skin when Derek spoke.

"Listen, um." He shifted in the passenger seat. "About last night..."

I cringed. "Do we really need to—"

"Just hear me out," he said softly.

I pressed my lips together.

Derek studied me for a moment before he went on, voice still soft. "Maybe the way things went down last night was... Maybe it wasn't a bad thing."

Well shit. That was unexpected. "How do you figure?"

His nails tapped rapidly on the console between us. "To put it bluntly, when we're fooling around, we're not fighting."

"But what about afterward? We haven't even been able to look at each other since we got up this morning."

"Do you want to be able to look at me?"

I glanced at him, but only for a second since I didn't dare take my eyes off the road for long. "Of course I do. But I... I mean, we..."

"Yesterday was a lot less miserable than it could have been. I... actually kind of enjoyed it. The drive, I mean."

"Yeah?"

"Yeah. And last night? That was fun, and I don't just mean when we got back to the hotel."

I rolled some tension out of my shoulders. "It was, wasn't it?"

"Uh-huh. We've still got a couple of days before we get to Oregon, plus the drive back. I'm thinking it would be a lot more bearable if we spent it like we did yesterday and last night. Instead of, you know, like this."

Gripping the wheel tight, I stared intently at the striped asphalt through the flurry of snowflakes. "I agree. But this goes a bit above and beyond just pretending all our issues don't exist, doesn't it? I mean..." I stole another glance at him. "Do you *want* to sleep with me? After all the shit we've been through?"

After what I did to us?

Derek slid his hand over my thigh, and when he squeezed gently, he might as well have been squeezing all the air out of my lungs. Voice sultry and low, he said, "You really have to ask after last night?"

I shifted in the driver's seat. "That was... We were drunk. And it was the heat of the—" I sucked in a breath as his hand slid a fraction of an inch higher.

"Last night, I felt better than I have in a long time." Derek ran his thumb along the outer seam of my jeans. "Why not keep a good thing going if it'll get us through the next week?"

I gulped. The words had my head spinning, but the warmth of his hand on my leg left me tongue-tied. He knew what he was doing, too. This was a game we'd played millions of times while we were together. We'd never be reckless enough to try road head or anything, particularly in this kind of weather, but he knew just how much he could touch and tease me without distracting me from driving. He could turn me on just enough to make me squirm, just enough to spin me up and make my breath hitch, and keep me riding that edge for *miles*; there was a reason he'd sucked me off dozens of times in our garage.

"So, what do you think?" Derek asked.

I swallowed. "I haven't told you take your hand off my leg, have I?"

He breathed a soft laugh, and his hand relaxed a little, becoming a heavier, surer presence on my thigh.

"And you're probably right," I whispered. "It'll make the trip a lot more... more bearable."

He subtly kneaded my thigh, and my toes curled inside my boot. "Might make the drive seem longer, though."

"You're not wrong." I exhaled, fighting a losing battle against a shiver. "We, um, might need to pick up a few things. Before we stop, I mean."

"Pretty sure there are drugstores near the hotel."

Oh God. We're really talking about doing this, aren't we?

We're... really doing this, aren't we?

Neither of us spoke for a few minutes. I supposed there wasn't much to say. The air between us was still taut, but it crackled with a whole new breed of tension. One I loved, though there was a good chance it might drive me out of my head before we reached the hotel. Last night had left me even hungrier for Derek's touch than I'd been in the months leading up to this, and fuck my life, but we still had hours of driving before we reached our hotel. Especially if I had to keep puttering along at thirty-five instead of eighty-plus. There was no way I'd stay hard for the entire trip, but I was hard as hell right now, and it wasn't at all below Derek to keep teasing me until we were finally off the road.

Through the swirling clouds of snow, a sign came into view:
Rest Stop – 3 Miles.

Heart pounding, I fought the urge to stomp on the accelerator. Three miles. I could handle that. Any faster and I might wind up in a ditch. Though at least we'd be stopped and I wouldn't have to focus on the road.

I adjusted my grip on the wheel. "You're sure about this. Going through the next few days like..." I cut my eyes toward him. "Like nothing's changed?"

"Yeah." He gave my thigh another squeeze, making my skin break out in goose bumps. "Beats the alternative, doesn't it?"

"It does." God, I was out of breath. "But I don't want us fooling around just because it's easier than the alternative. I want us to actually *want* this, you know? Otherwise we're—"

His hand inched higher, his pinkie finger now dangerously close to the bulge in my jeans. "Wanting this is not a problem from my end. What about you?"

"N-no. It's not."

"Then I think we're on the same page."

"Okay. Okay, good."

The rest stop's entrance finally came into view, and I turned on my signal.

Derek's fingers twitched. "What are you doing?"

"Pulling over so you can put your money where your mouth is." The words tumbled out in a breathless rush. "I'm not driving three hundred goddamned miles with a hard-on."

He didn't object. Derek was the most cautious person I knew when it came to public same-sex affection, but he didn't say a word. I wasn't all that surprised, and not just because I suspected he was as painfully turned on as I was—there wasn't a soul in sight at the rest stop. Even if the place had been crowded, the falling snow would have given us more than enough cover.

The snow masked the lines of the parking spaces, but I supposed it didn't really matter as long as I didn't take a handicapped spot. I wasn't planning on parking that close to the rest stop's tiny cluster of buildings anyway. Instead, I continued to the far end of the lot, and as I slowed down, Derek's seat belt snapped back against the door. I was already unbuckling mine when I pulled into a parking space.

I threw the truck into park, and I'd barely turned the key before Derek lunged across the console, grabbed me, and kissed me like his life depended on it. Oh God, I loved how he kissed. Always had. And when he was this turned on? Fuck yes. Now that he didn't have to worry about distracting me from driving through the snow, he didn't hold back at all. He kissed me as passionately as he had in the hallway last night, forcing my lips apart with his tongue and exploring my mouth like he'd never tasted me before.

I wrapped my arms around him and grabbed handfuls of his sweatshirt. I wanted to pull it off and get him naked, but that probably wasn't happening. Not out here, since there was still a small chance we might get caught. Besides, the truck might start getting cold now that the heat was off.

Derek slid a hand down over my hard-on, and when I broke the kiss with a gasp, he started on my neck. I let my head fall back, murmuring curses as his lips skated across my skin and his fingers squeezed and stroked my dick through my pants.

"Jesus, Derek," I breathed. "Good thing I stopped. If... if I hadn't..."

"We'd have burned the hotel to the ground," he murmured, pausing to bite just above my collar. "Still might."

I didn't even try for words. Hopefully the low moan said it well enough.

Derek shifted and swore, probably trying to get comfortable. Life would have been a million times easier without the stupid console in the way. I was seriously tempted to suggest moving to the backseat, but then Derek started fumbling with the top button of my jeans, and I didn't want him to stop. I sure as hell wasn't stepping outside into the nasty weather with my pants undone.

The top button finally popped open, and the zipper came down easily, the restrictive tightness gone so suddenly it made me gasp. With a little more fumbling, he had my cock free, and I shivered from both the cool air and his warm hand. Holy shit, now he was stroking me and kissing my neck, and... "Fuck, baby."

Derek grinned against my neck. "Like that?"

"You know I do." I tried to reach across and return the favor, but with the console in the way, it wasn't happening.

It especially wasn't happening when Derek leaned down to take my dick between his lips. Jesus. I gave up on trying to reciprocate— I'd take care of him once he'd finished me off—and just sat back to enjoy the wet heat of his talented mouth. Gripping the wheel in one hand, resting my other in the middle of his back, pressing myself against the seat as his mouth teased every inch of my cock— God *damn*, this brought back memories. And out in the open like this? Even if the parking lot was deserted and the falling snow kept him hidden? This was *hot*.

"We... we should stop on the way to the hotel," I murmured, struggling to form words as Derek swirled his tongue around the head of my cock. "Get some lube."

He groaned low from the back of his throat, and the vibration sent a shiver through me. He started stroking, bobbing his head in time with his hand the way he always did when he was ready to send me over the edge. Not that I was far from it anyway. After months without a man's touch, and now being at the mercy of Derek's incredible hand and mouth? Oh God, I was close.

"Fuck... yeah..." I arched off the driver's seat. "I'm g-gonna come. *Fuck...*"

Derek groaned again, this time in the same moment he tightened his grip and gave a slick, mind-blowing twist, and I gasped as I came.

Just like he always did, he kept going until it was *almost* too much, and then let up. I sagged back against the seat, struggling to catch my breath, and then Derek kissed me and I stopped caring if I could breathe. His mouth tasted like cum, and we both groaned as I kissed him deeper and harder. Though I was still dizzy from my own orgasm, the need to return the favor was overwhelming. I didn't just want him kissing me—I wanted him losing his mind.

With my body weight, I pressed him back against the seat, and he whimpered as I fumbled with his fly. The zipper gave. One stroke had him trembling between me and the seat, and when I ran my thumb around the head, he shuddered hard.

"Mmm, yeah," he murmured.

I bent to kiss his neck, and explored the familiar contours of his throat with my lips as my hand found a steady rhythm, pumping him fast but not fast enough to get him off. "That good?"

"You know it is." He slid his hand up my arm and squirmed against the seat. "Oh yeah…"

"Too bad we don't have more room."

"Uh-huh," he panted. "We will tonight."

"Yeah. We will." Just the thought of all the things we could do with that much space almost made me hard again. "Tons of space, and the whole night to—"

"I want to fuck you," he blurted out. "When we get to the hotel. I want… God… Rhys…"

"Not gonna say no to that," I purred against his neck. "We're definitely gonna need some lube."

He groaned, tilting his head to offer up more of his throat. "If we had lube right now… I would so… I'd… ungh, Jesus…"

I kissed the corner of his jaw. "That'll just give us both something to look forward to for the next few hours."

The sound he made was a mix of arousal and frustration; as if the thought of everything waiting for us in the hotel turned him on beyond words, but he wasn't sure he could wait that long.

"You'll be looking forward to it, won't you?" I growled, stroking his dick a little faster. "Fucking me into the mattress?"

He whimpered. "Rhys..." I knew that helpless sound from a mile away—Derek was close. Right on the edge. *Right* there.

So of course that was the moment I went down on him, and he cried out as his hips almost came up off the seat. The console bit into my ribs, but I ignored it, and I licked and sucked Derek's cock while he moaned and swore.

"Rhys... God..." His fingers slid through my hair. He was the only man who'd ever been able to keep a hand on the back of my head while I went down on him. He never put any pressure behind it. Never made me feel like I was going to choke. That had always been a rush for me, trusting someone enough to let him be in a position where he *could* have gagged me if he wanted to, but knowing with absolute certainty that he wouldn't.

He swore again. Gasped. Jerked. "I'm...gonna come. Fuck, Rhys, I'm—" He groaned from deep in his throat, fingers twitching against my scalp, and then he shot cum onto my tongue. Like he did with me, I knew exactly how long to keep going before it would be too much, and when I lifted my head, he shuddered and sank back against the seat.

I pushed myself up, found his lips with mine, and lost myself in my favorite thing in the world—kissing Derek after we'd both gotten off. The kisses were tender now. Lazy. Not trying to get each other spun up, just enjoying the softness of affectionate lips. Savoring the afterglow and the closeness. Even with the stupid console biting into my ribs.

After a while, Derek broke the kiss and met my eyes. Caressing my cheek, he said, "We should probably get on the road. The sooner we get moving..." He let a grin finish the thought.

"Mmm, I like this plan." I went in for one last kiss, then returned to the driver's seat.

Of course with the bitter cold outside and all this heat inside, the windows had fogged up. That, and either we'd been stopped for a long time or the snow had really been coming down, because a thick drift of powder had accumulated on the windshield.

"Oops," Derek said without a hint of contrition in his voice.

I chuckled. "Right? Guess we should clear all this off so we can get moving."

"Good idea."

While the air blasted to defog the windows, we got out and used ice scrapers and hands to get most of the snow off the windshield. We brushed as much as we could off the hood too, though the idling engine was starting to melt some of it.

With the windshield mostly clear, we got back in and blew on our hands to chase off some of the cold. Snow was starting to accumulate again, so I put on my seat belt and shifted into Reverse.

As I backed out of the parking space, Derek and I exchanged grins. Oh, tonight was going to be hot. I broke out in goose bumps just thinking about him riding my ass the way we both loved.

Still grinning, I focused on the road.

And as I eased us up the ramp and back onto the interstate, I decided that yeah, maybe this trip wouldn't be so bad after all.

CHAPTER 8

DEREK

It was a damn good thing Rhys had pulled into that rest stop. Thanks to the weather, there were a number of accidents between there and our destination, and it was almost eleven when we finally arrived in the town where we'd be spending the night.

"Still want me to swing into a drugstore?" Rhys asked. "Or should we just call it a night tonight?"

"You've been driving all day. You tell me."

He shrugged, and when he glanced at me, a smile played at his lips. "I'm pretty sure I could come up with a second wind. With the right motivation, of course."

"Mmhmm." I slid my hand up his thigh. "So you're saying you can still handle getting fucked tonight?"

Rhys shivered. "Oh hey look. A Walgreens." He started to change lanes.

I chuckled.

He parked in front of the store and kept the engine idling while I unbuckled my seat belt. We had no way of knowing the political climate of this town, so the prudent thing was for one of us to go in rather than both. Two men buying personal lubricant or even walking through that aisle could raise some eyebrows and turn some heads.

So, to fly under the radar, Rhys would wait in the car while I went in.

I started to get out but hesitated. "Do we, um..." I drummed my nails on the door handle. "Do we *just* need lube?"

Rhys searched my eyes. Then, apparently reading between the lines, he nodded. "I haven't been with anyone since..." He swallowed. "Since we were both tested."

"Same." That included after I'd gone out for the revenge fuck that I'd immediately regretted.

Our eyes locked, and the moment threatened to go from awkward to excruciating before he softly added, "So, uh, just lube is probably good. Right?"

I nodded. "Yeah. I'll be right back."

The pavement was slick on the way in—I made a mental note to give Rhys a heads up before we went into the hotel—but I managed to get inside without sliding. Hands in my pockets, I scanned the signs above the aisles until I found the one I was looking for.

I slowed a little as I approached the section with the lube and condoms, though. Second thoughts? Oh yeah. Just a few.

After everything had gone down a few months ago, I'd immediately gone out and gotten tested, and I'd demanded Rhys do the same just to be absolutely sure. He had, and our results had all come back clear. At the time, it had been out of panic and anger. How many men had he been with? Had he exposed me to anything? Though he'd insisted at the time there'd only been that one transgression with that one man, I hadn't believed a word out of his mouth because why the fuck should I? He'd cheated. I couldn't trust him.

But today, when he said there hadn't been anyone since then... I believed him. I still didn't trust him—I'd never be able to trust him again—but I believed him. Maybe because there hadn't been any tells. Maybe because he'd looked me in the eyes and said it without flinching. Or, hell, maybe because I wanted and needed to believe him because I wanted and needed him. Not just a road trip's worth of peace—*him*.

At the rack marked *Family Planning*, I gave the selection of condoms a cursory look but decided to go with my gut. I pulled a bottle of lube off the shelf, left the condoms where they were, and headed for the checkout line.

Moments later, I was in the truck with Rhys, and we continued across town to our hotel.

"Whoa," he said as he pulled in the hotel's driveway. "Looks like we're not the only ones with this idea."

"No kidding." The covered unloading area was packed two cars deep, and there were three more waiting to take their places

Rhys drummed his fingers on the wheel. "Think we should wait until we get to the front? Or just park and walk in?"

"Either way. Fair warning—the parking lot at Walgreens was really slick."

He nodded. "Good to know. Thanks." He glanced at something in the backseat. "I've still got my cane handy, but let's maybe wait until we're under the cover where the concrete is drier." He grinned slyly. "No point in being sore when we get started, right?"

Grinning back, I shifted in my seat. "Sounds good to me."

Fortunately, it only took about twenty minutes for the cars ahead of us to clear out enough to let us under the overhang. As horny as I was, twenty minutes seemed like forever, but that was okay. Once we let go of all this pent-up restraint, it would be well worth the long wait.

Rhys parked and we got out. The ground was dry and here, but he took his cane anyway. Couldn't be too careful in weather like this.

Inside, the reception desk was even busier. Apparently the weather had forced a number of travelers to stop here for the night to stay here in town instead of passing through, and the hotel was out of rooms. Thank God we had a reservation. For that matter, since we were only going to be using one of our rooms, we canceled the second, which worked out great—there was a family trying to figure out what to do next since every hotel in town was full. They snagged our second room, and everyone was happy.

Now all Rhys and I needed to do was park, get our stuff, and haul ass to that room so I could finally get him naked.

Since the parking lot was mostly full and looked seriously slick, I parked the truck while Rhys waited by the door with our luggage. I fought the urge to jog back; though I wasn't quite as likely to fall on the ice as he was, it would be just my luck that I'd slip, break something, and spend the night in an emergency room instead of that hotel room. Not happening tonight. No fucking way.

Needless to say, I walked back *carefully*.

As I approached, Rhys grinned, but he said nothing. Nothing needed to be said.

I took the handle of my rolling suitcase, he took his, and we hurried through the crowded lobby to the elevators. I couldn't say for sure if the elevators really were slow, or if everything just seemed slow because I was *so close* to having Rhys where I wanted him. Quite possibly a little of both.

Finally, we made it to our floor and our room. Rhys swiped the keycard. For a split second, I had visions of the light turning red, and us having to go back downstairs to have the keycard redone, but no— it turned green, and the door clicked.

The instant we were in the room, Rhys shoved me up against the door, using my body to force it shut, and—just before he kissed me— he murmured, "God, finally."

Finally was right. I clawed at his clothes and kissed him hard because I *finally* had him right where I'd wanted him all afternoon and evening. Knowing him, the blowjob at the rest stop had only taken the slightest edge off; he wasn't going to stop squirming until he was coming again, this time with me balls deep in him where I belonged. I could definitely relate.

He snaked his hands under my jacket and ran them up my back. He closed his fingers around my shirt, and growled, "Ugh, fuck winter. Too many clothes."

I laughed drunkenly. "We can do something about them, you know."

"I know, but that..." He kissed me again. "Means letting you go, and..."

"Letting me go for a minute." I slid my hands down over his ass. "But when you get me back, I'll be naked."

Rhys shivered, rubbing his hard cock against me. "You make way too much sense for a man who's this turned on."

"Just don't ask me to figure out anything more complicated than getting you naked."

He laughed, kissed me lightly, and pried himself off me. "Then get naked."

"Yes, sir." We exchanged wicked grins, and quickly got out of jackets, boots, and all the stupid clothes that winter demanded.

Rhys pulled back the covers, then sat on the edge of the bed. While he removed his prosthetic and liner, I found the newly purchased bottle of lube and dealt with the safety seal. One less thing to hassle with when he was ready for me to fuck him.

"Much better." Rhys put the prosthetic and liner beside the bed, and he grinned as he stretched out beneath the covers.

Returning the grin, I put the lube bottle aside, then joined him in the middle of the mattress. Oh God, yeah, this was so much better than making out while we were dressed or with that stupid console between us. Now there was no fear of getting busted. No cramped space to keep us from getting close and comfortable. No clothes in the way. It was all naked skin and ragged breaths and long, deep kisses while hands explored bodies like we were two men who'd never touched before.

Rhys pushed me onto my back and straddled me. I ran my hands up his sides, his back, his arms, his thighs—anything I could reach was fair game. We stroked each other's cocks. Gripped each other's hair. Squeezed each other's asses. My heart was going a million miles an hour and I was painfully hard—had I ever been this turned on? If I had, I couldn't remember, and I couldn't think clearly enough to *try* to remember. He just felt so good, touching me with those strong, insistent hands while we made out and wound each other up.

Why has it been so long since we did this?

Oh. Right. Because—

I forced the thought back again, and kissed Rhys even harder and held him even tighter as if that might chase away everything else. I couldn't change the past. All I wanted was to enjoy tonight, and to get through the next few days without things being so icy with Rhys.

Which they wouldn't be in the first place if he hadn't—

I broke the kiss and went for his neck, and his ragged groan made all my doubts scatter. I wanted this. I wanted him. Tonight, I *had* him, and that was all I cared about.

He nudged my cheek with his chin, and when I lifted my head, our lips came together in another long, deep kiss. As we kissed and groped, our hips started moving, rocking as if we were already fucking, and the pornographic pantomime was almost as delicious as the friction between our dicks.

"Been thinking all day about you fucking me." Rhys nipped my lower lip. "Don't want to wait."

"Then get on your back," I breathed.

"Ungh, yeah." He bent to kiss me again. "And you better lube that thing up quick."

I laughed, one hand still on his thigh as I reached for the lube with the other. "Oh really?"

"Uh-huh." He grinned. "Don't you dare tease me, or I'll keep you just like this and ride you."

I arched an eyebrow. "That's...not exactly a deterrent, you know."

"Hmm, good—"

"Just get on your back."

"Fine." He started to move, and I gave his ass a light slap, which earned me another dirty, wicked grin.

Good thing I'd already gotten the safety seal out of the way—I didn't need anything between me and the lube. I quickly poured some onto my fingers, and I fingered Rhys's tight ass until he'd relaxed, and then fingered him some more just because I loved to watch him squirm and listen to him moan.

"Derek..." He closed his eyes and arched. "Fuck... c'mon."

"Just want to make sure you're ready."

He clawed at the sheets beside him. "You know damn well I'm ready."

"But I—"

"Derek." He met my eyes, his filled with desperation. "Please."

I slid my fingers free, and he whispered "oh thank God" as I reached for the lube again. When I positioned myself between his powerful thighs, he bit his lip, his brow creasing as if he were struggling to stay in control. Knowing him, he probably was.

I slicked myself up, then leaned over him as I guided my cock to him. He held his breath. So did I. As I teased his hole with the head, making little circles just to drive him wild, he groaned, squeezing his eyes shut and arching under me.

"Derek..."

He trailed off into a moan as I pressed in. No teasing now—one slide into his tight ass, and I was overcome with the need to fuck him. It had been so damn long, because—no, not thinking about that. I furrowed my brow and concentrated on easing into him, giving him a little at a time as he yielded to me.

"Oh yeah," he purred. "Yeah..."

My sentiments exactly, especially because I had the most amazing view. I'd always loved watching his face as he took my cock. The way his lips parted and his eyes squeezed shut—he was always the picture of pure ecstasy. He loved to top too, but he was the most enthusiastic bottom I'd ever been with, and this sexy view alone had nearly done me in dozens of times.

"Oh my *God*, you feel good," he moaned, running his hands up my chest.

"So do you." I closed my eyes as I pushed deeper, but then forced them open again because I didn't want to miss a second of him in this blissed out state.

Because I've already missed too much.

I swallowed back a surge of emotion.

I miss this so much.

I miss you so much.

The thoughts made me falter, and as I gazed into Rhys's eyes, my throat tightened.

Why did you do this to us?

I tried to tamp down those feelings, but the sudden intense ache in my throat was impossible to ignore.

No, damn it. Not now. Just enjoy this and—

He reached up and touched my face, and the caress of his fingertips raised both goose bumps and my hackles. I wanted him, and I *wanted* to want him, but I hated myself for it and I hated him for... for *everything.*

I abandoned my slow, easy pace, and fucked him hard. He liked it that way, and so did I, but it wasn't the need for rough sex that drove me. I thrust hard enough to knock the breath out of him. Gripped his hips tight enough to bruise. My jaw ached from clenching it, and the cable-tightness in my neck and shoulder muscles was painful, but I drove on, fucking him hard. Fucking him *angry.*

I wasn't out of control, and I wasn't trying to hurt him. Maybe convey to him what I couldn't say aloud—how much I hurt and how angry I was—through touches and thrusts, but actually *hurt* him? No. I just couldn't do slow and sensual. Not tonight. Not when my emotions were suddenly this raw and everything between us was suddenly rising to the surface at the worst possible moment.

I tried to concentrate on sensations. On sex. On getting us both off. Anything but all those feelings that weren't welcome now. They were too intense to ignore, though. Last night I'd been too drunk to think beyond getting him off, but tonight I was too sober to pretend we hadn't touched in months or that I didn't know why. I couldn't ignore all the reasons there was so much cold air between us. Why I'd slept alone all those nights leading up to now, and why it hurt as much to imagine sleeping beside him tonight as it did to imagine another night alone.

My eyes stung, and I couldn't even begin to tell myself it was from anything but tears. Tears of pain, anger, loneliness, betrayal— too many emotions that had no business sharing this bed with us.

I slowed down. So did he.

We both panted. Trembled. Stared at each other.

What are we doing?

All at once, the anger flamed out, and my arousal waned so fast it was jarring. Sighing, I pulled out before I started to go soft, and I rolled onto my back beside Rhys. He didn't try to stop me. He didn't roll over to cuddle up against. For a painfully long time, we lay in silence, a few chilly inches between us on the mattress where we'd been having sex just a minute ago.

Well, shit. Now what?

I scrubbed a hand over my face. We just had to cancel that second room, didn't we? And the hotel was full, so there was no going back down and saying, "Hey, could we grab that extra room after all?" No, we were stuck in this room together. One room with one bed. We'd be sleeping next to each other whether we liked it or not. Half an hour ago, I'd been all over that. The closer we slept together, the more times we could fool around between now and sunrise.

Now...damn.

I closed my eyes and gritted my teeth. Tomorrow would be fun. So would the weekend, since we were using my sister's guest room, which, if memory served, had a bed even smaller than this one.

Fuck. I needed a shower or something. A minute to myself to clear my head.

I sat up and swung my legs over the side of the bed, but didn't get any farther than that. Resting my hands on the edge of the mattress, I stared at the blank wall, wondering if it was even possible to make sense of all the emotions crashing around in my head.

Behind me, Rhys sat up too. "You all right?"

I almost let go of a bitter laugh. Maybe if I hadn't been this drained and exhausted right then, not to mention this close to tears, I would have laughed, but I just...couldn't.

"Not really, no." More silence, but only for a moment. Before I could stop myself, I said, "Tell me why."

Rhys tensed. I didn't see him, or even hear him, really. In ways I couldn't explain—or maybe ways I was imagining—I felt it. "Tell you why...what?"

Still staring at the wall, I fought back a surge of frustration. "Why did you do it?"

He exhaled slowly. "Derek, it's done. Does it really matter why—"

I jerked around and faced him. "Yes. *Yes*, it fucking matters."

He blinked. "Why?"

"Because it's been killing me for months, and as long as things are shitty tonight, we might as well drag it all out into the daylight."

His eyes widened, but he kept his voice level. "You know we have to spend tomorrow in the car again, right?"

"Yeah. I do. And I don't need a crystal goddamned ball to know it's going to be miserable no matter what. So let's just get it all out and over with like we should have done in September."

Rhys flinched away. He stared down at his hands, watching his fingers pluck at the sheet draped over his lap. "There's no point. There is nothing I can say that's going to make the truth go down any easier for either of us. I fucked up, and I've regretted it every minute of every day since then." He swallowed hard, and when he turned back to me, damn if his eyes hadn't welled up. "What more do you want?"

"I want to know *why*," I ground out. "We had a good thing going. Hell, we had a *great* thing going. Why the hell did you go and—"

"Maybe it didn't feel so great to me at the time," he snapped.

We both froze.

He dropped his gaze, again and his shoulders sagged too. Wiping a hand over his face, he sighed heavily. "Nothing I say is going to justify anything, okay? Not to you, and not to me. I fucked up. I know

I fucked up. If I had it to do over, I'd walk away from him in a heartbeat and never think twice about it."

"But you didn't walk away from him, so just tell me." My voice had softened to a shakier, more pleading tone. For months I'd resisted asking him why because I'd been afraid of the answer. Now that I'd asked, I needed him to tell me because I didn't see myself asking again. "Why did you sleep with him?"

Rhys winced. He kept his gaze fixed on the rumpled comforter as he slowly released a breath. "We were going through a rough patch, remember?"

I gritted my teeth. "Not rough enough to make me want to put my dick in another guy, but okay."

His jaw worked, and his eyes narrowed, though he didn't look at me. "Around that same time, I hit a bit of a rough patch of my own. I... I don't know if it was a funk, or some depression or what. I just..." He sighed and shook his head. "I didn't feel like me, and I didn't know what to do about it, and I got it into my head that I couldn't come to you about it because things were iffy between us. So I got into this... this weird spiral, where I felt like shit, and then I felt worse because I didn't think I could come to you, and then I resented you over it, and..." He swallowed, pushed his shoulders back, and finally turned to me. "I'm not blaming you or excusing what I did. It was entirely my fault, and I own that. But that's where my head was."

So there it was. The truth. The reason my husband had spent a night in another man's bed and sent our marriage into a tailspin it couldn't get out of. Knowing that truth didn't make me feel any better. I wasn't sure I'd expected it to. Or what I'd expected to gain from knowing.

"Look, I know it doesn't change a damn thing," Rhys said in a shaky whisper, "but I mean it—if I had the chance to do it over, I never would have touched him."

I held his gaze for a long moment, not sure what it was I was searching for in his eyes. Whatever it was, I decided it wasn't worth continuing this staring contest with the man it hurt to look at, so I broke eye contact and rose. "I'm going to take a shower." I didn't wait for a response, and Rhys didn't offer one. He probably needed some space from me as badly as I needed it from him.

In the hotel room's cramped shower, I pressed my hands against the walls and closed my eyes as hot water cascaded over my crawling skin.

Rhys had been right—knowing didn't help at all. I'd convinced myself I couldn't possibly feel any worse about how things had gone down, but I'd been wrong. Somehow, knowing that he didn't think he could come to me when he was hurting cut deeper than finding out he'd been in another man's bed. He'd felt like we were too far apart, and he'd resented me for it, and he'd found comfort somewhere else.

Yes, we'd been in a less than perfect place when this had all happened, but it hadn't been that bad. Had it? Life was peaks and valleys, and that had felt like just another valley to me. Not even a very deep one. We hadn't been at each other's throats. If anything, we'd just been...on different wavelengths. On other planets, sometimes. There hadn't been much talking, and our sex life had taken a nosedive, but I hadn't been worried. It wasn't the first time we'd gone through that, and I'd assumed it wouldn't be the last.

Even when he'd texted me to say he'd had a couple of drinks and was crashing at a friend's house, I hadn't worried. I'd had no idea that we were hours away from the conversation that would spell the end of our marriage. That as I'd goofed off on my phone and watched some TV and eventually made my way to bed, Rhys had been—at that very moment—having sex with a man whose name and face I still didn't know.

That while I'd thought we'd ride things out, Rhys had felt so far away from me that...

I exhaled, then turned away from the spray and wiped the water out of my eyes.

Maybe Rhys had done us a favor. If we were that far gone, was there any coming back?

Yes.

Yes, there was.

Or at least there had been right up until the moment when Rhys had made the decision to cheat on me.

A fresh wave of anger replaced this sick, sad feeling.

All he'd had to do was come talk to me. It didn't matter how hard that was, or how afraid he was to approach me. If he'd cared about me, our marriage, or the life we'd built together over the last nine years, he'd have sucked it up and talked to me. Or at least done something to try to bridge that gap.

But he hadn't. He'd blown up what was left of the bridge, and now here we were on opposite sides of a chasm that I not only couldn't cross, I didn't want to. We were done. *I* was done.

I shut off the shower, pulled open the curtain, and yanked one of the gritty white towels off the shelf. Tonight would be miserable, sleeping in the same room as Rhys, but I'd get through it. I'd get through everything, because it was just a few more days. We'd survive tonight, get to Portland, plaster on smiles, make it through the wedding, and then come home, divorce, and get the hell out of each other's lives.

Mental note—look up rental car prices for the return trip.

CHAPTER 9

RHYS

I was physically and emotionally drained, but sleep? Not a chance. My mind was whirring too fast, and after a solid three hours, I finally stopped fighting it. Lying on my back, hands laced behind my head, I stared at the ceiling of the hotel room I was sharing with Derek.

Entirely too close to me, he was asleep. I envied him that much, but I knew it wasn't because his mind was at ease. He'd been in the Army for eight years, and he'd done three combat tours. That was more than enough for a soldier to develop that superhuman ability to sleep any time, anywhere because there was no telling when the opportunity would arise again. There'd been a time when I could do it too, but my own military career had ended prematurely, well before that ability could stick.

At least one of us could sleep. If I didn't drop off in the next hour or so, I might have to let Derek drive tomorrow. For now, I was too busy reliving tonight and a few other glaring red dots on my life's timeline.

On that day last September, the moment I'd realized what had happened—the moment I'd truly grasped the magnitude of what I'd done—had felt similar in a way to how I'd felt when I'd woken up from my accident almost twenty years ago. Physically, I'd felt different of course, but mentally, there'd been the same horrifying awareness that my entire world had changed and that there was no going back. I'd been overwhelmed with panic, trying to mentally do damage control and find some angle that would make everything normal again, and at the same time, felt a cold, heavy blanket of calm resignation around my shoulders. My world had changed. There was no going back. Might as well get used to it.

Back in Airborne School, I'd known as soon as I'd hit the ground that my career was over. Not just as a paratrooper, but most likely in the Army. There'd been too much pain for this to be anything less than a catastrophic injury. Too many bones bending where there were no joints. In the blink of an eye, everything from mid-shin down on my left leg was changed forever. I wouldn't say I'd made peace with it, but within a matter of seconds of that fateful impact—before my instructors and the medics had even realized anything was wrong —I'd known nothing would ever be the same.

A few drug-fogged days later, when the base docs had told me amputation was the best course of action, I'd had the same sense of my whole world being irreversibly changed. A weird feeling of wanting to freak out from sheer panic and at the same time thinking I should probably start getting used to the idea.

And years later, as I'd dropped onto the bed beside a man I never should have touched, I'd had that exact same feeling. There was no taking anything back. I could no more pretend that I hadn't fucked him than I could pretend my ankle and lower leg hadn't shattered.

Except I'd recovered from my injuries. I'd learned to walk again. I'd learned to run. Prosthetics were still a pain in the ass, and life would be easier without missing half my lower leg, but I'd adapted to my new reality and moved on.

Tonight, in this too-small hotel room, I stared at Derek's silhouette in the milky glow of the streetlights. The similarities between my accident and what I'd done to our marriage ended with that sense of irreversible change. The accident had been just that—an accident. I'd come in hot, misjudged the terrain, and landed too hard on loose ground.

Cheating on Derek... Well, there was definitely blame there. And Derek wasn't something that could be replaced with plastic and carbon fiber. I could eventually move on to someone new, but I didn't *want* someone new. I wanted him. I'd been in love with him since our second date, and that hadn't changed. Every time he looked at me with all that hurt and anger in his eyes, I wanted to break down sobbing because I hated myself for what I'd done to him and to us. I had never been more profoundly aware of how much I loved him than I'd been the morning after I'd torpedoed everything.

Apparently it's true what they say—you don't know what you've got until it's gone.

Gazing at him now, I swallowed to force back the threat of tears. Yeah, it was definitely true, and Derek was definitely gone.

With a heavy sigh, I closed my eyes and ran a hand through my hair. Sometimes I wondered if I should have told Derek at all, but that thought was always fleeting. The only thing worse than having him hate me was having him go on loving me without knowing I'd betrayed him. He'd deserved the truth so he could decide whether to stay with me or go, and I'd known even before I'd opened my mouth what his choice would be.

But I couldn't lie to him. Not directly, and not by omission. If he left me, which I'd known he would, then I deserved it for cheating on him. I didn't deserve to have him unknowingly continuing to love me as if nothing had changed. Because it had. As surely as if bones had shattered, there was no walking this off. No going back and pretending things hadn't happened.

How do I move on from doing this to us?

Beside me, Derek jerked. Then again. He sucked in a breath, and it came out as a faint whimper—a sound I'd long ago learned to recognize as the beginning of a nightmare.

Years of habit had me moving before I could think twice.

"Derek." I put a hand on his arm, as much to let him know I was there as to keep him from taking a startled swing at me. "Hey." I shook him gently. "You're okay. Derek?"

He tensed. Then stilled. Slowly, he exhaled, and the tension melted away. Sometimes he'd wake up fully after I'd shaken him out of a nightmare. Other times, he'd drift back to sleep as if nothing had happened. That was what he did this time—sighed into the pillow, and fell back into that familiar steady rhythm that meant he was asleep.

My heart was racing as I eased back onto my own side. That was pretty normal after he'd come out of a nightmare, mostly because I knew how quickly and violently he could surge out of a dream before he woke up and realized where he was. I was hardly afraid of him—though I was mindful of flailing hands and elbows—but it was always unsettling to watch the man I loved going through that.

And how many times had he had those nightmares since we'd broken up? They were always worse when he was stressed, and God knew he'd been stressed all to hell for the last few months.

Guilt made me cringe inwardly. As if I didn't already feel like shit for making him so miserable. Now his combat nightmares were probably stepping up too. Because of *me*.

Gazing at his silhouette, I fought the urge to touch him again.

I wish I could show you how sorry I am.

I wish you knew how much I still love you.

But even if I could, it didn't matter.

Because although he was lying here beside me in this quiet hotel room, Derek was gone, and he wasn't coming back.

Another silent morning. Hooray. Without exchanging more than the absolute minimum of monosyllabic words, we showered, dressed, packed, checked out, and loaded our things into the truck. More than once, I'd considered speaking up just to ask if he was doing all right. He'd had several nightmares throughout the night, and judging by the circles under his bloodshot eyes and the lack of color in his face, they'd taken their toll. They usually did.

But I didn't say anything. I had a feeling he was miserable enough without being expected to talk to me, and maybe this just needed some time. Did we need to cool down? Catch our breath? Fuck if I knew. All I knew was I was worried about him, worried about myself, and worried about how we were going to get through the next several days.

Now if I could just figure out what to do about that.

Just like yesterday, it was Derek who finally broke the standoff, this time before I'd even started the engine.

"Wait. Before we go."

I let go of the key and turned to him. "Hmm?"

Derek wasn't looking at me. Instead, he stared down at the coffee cup in his lap. "We still have to get through the wedding."

"Yeah. I know."

He chewed his lip. "So how do we do this?"

"I..." I pressed back against the driver's seat and stared out the windshield. I had no idea what to say. I still wasn't quite sure what happened last night. What exactly had flipped the switch in him and turned some much-needed sex into...that. Not that it mattered. "You tell me. Where do we go from here?"

Derek stared out the windshield for a long, quiet moment. Finally, he took a deep breath and faced me. "Let's just...take a break today. I'm still getting my head around everything from last night, and I just..."

"It isn't like we can get away from each other."

"No, but I've got headphones. Can we just call it a ceasefire, do our own thing until we get to the next hotel, and maybe regroup in the morning? Figure things out from there?"

That sounded like several hours of quiet, awkward hell, but I really didn't have any better ideas. If he was half as raw as I was this morning—and I suspected he was, especially after so many nightmares—then we were asking for an even worse flavor of hell if we kept the communication channels open right now.

"Okay." I cleared my throat. "Okay. Yeah. I guess... I guess that works."

There was nothing left to say, so neither of us said anything else. Derek slipped on a pair of noise-canceling headphones. I found an upbeat playlist on my phone that wouldn't put me to sleep and set it to play on the truck's speakers. Loud enough I could hear it, not so loud it would bug Derek through his headphones.

And I was right.

It was several hours of quiet, awkward hell.

CHAPTER 10

DEREK

Weather and traffic made the drive stretch out for an extra two hours, but not a moment too soon, we made it to the next hotel. Without exchanging more words than absolutely necessary, Rhys and I unloaded our handful of luggage, checked in, and got into the elevator, which crept up to the third floor.

Our boots and the wheels of our suitcases were the only sounds as we followed the hallway to our respective rooms. The rooms turn out to be next to each other this time instead of across the hall, but whatever. As long as we didn't have to spend tonight and tomorrow morning getting in each other's way.

We stopped beside the first door, which was his. Rhys turned his keycard over in his hand. "So, um." He didn't look at me. "Text me in the morning, I guess? When you're ready to get moving?"

"Okay. Will do."

He disappeared into his room. I continued to mine, keyed myself in, shut the door behind me, and dropped onto the bed.

And now... Now I was alone. I had the breathing room I'd desperately needed since last night. As I stared at the wall dividing his room from mine, though, it felt like too big of a barrier. Too much distance.

At the same time, it didn't seem like enough. Would the hotel let me swap rooms with the people next door? Put an entire room between me and Rhys? Hell, maybe give me a room on another floor at the other end of the building? And would that make me feel better or worse?

It didn't matter; I was being ridiculous. Releasing a long breath, I sat on the edge of the bed. Then I lay back across the mattress, laced my fingers behind my head, and stared up at the dusty brass light fixture.

Taking a break of sorts from interacting had been a good idea, and I was glad we'd done it, but I couldn't say I felt better. Not worse, though, so that had to be a win.

Throughout the long, silent hours on the road, my emotions had run the gamut between sad, angry, hurt, and guilty. For a while, I was just numb. Then I wished I was.

Now I was tired. Tired of being in the truck. Tired of not being home with my cats and my own bed and anything familiar besides Rhys. Tired of being a million miles away from Rhys, and that being both too far and not far enough.

Closing my eyes, I sighed. I was utterly exhausted. Rhys and I really, really needed to go our separate ways sooner than later because this? What we were doing? It didn't matter if we were in the same bed or on opposite ends of the building—it was going to drive me insane. Something needed to give, and it needed to give *soon*. As for the next few days? Well, either we went back to pretending we were friendly—maybe even fucking because it was more fun than fighting—or we stopped pretending we were anything but over.

I wondered what Rhys was doing right now. What he was feeling. We'd agreed to give everything a rest today and tonight, and we'd talk it through tomorrow. But what about now? Was he okay? And did I really care?

Of course I cared. Divorcing or not, he was still the man I'd loved for most of a decade. I could be angry about things he'd done and still give a shit if he was okay. I didn't really *want* to give a shit at the moment, but I did.

In the car, he'd been listening to an audiobook for the last couple of hours. I'd only caught brief snippets when I was between songs, but I'd caught the narrator's voice and a familiar character name, and I was pretty sure the book was another installment in the suspense series we'd both been hooked on for a while. Realizing that had made my heart heavy. Ever since those books had first started coming out in audio, he'd talked about them like a kid who'd just discovered Harry Potter. He'd gotten me hooked, and before long, we were both devouring chapters during our commutes. Sometimes when he came home from work, he'd linger in the garage for a few minutes to finish a chapter, and after he came in, we'd both go on and on about the latest twists and turns and our theories about what would happen next. He'd always been so good at figuring out who the killer was, I'd teased him about reading ahead, but no—he was just that in tune to the stories.

I was tempted now to download the latest book so I could listen to it, but I didn't. I couldn't. As much as I loved the series and had been itching for a new installment, I couldn't bring myself to listen. Not now. Everything about those books was tied to Rhys. Yeah, I loved the plots, and the narrator, and the characters, and everything about them, but the real joy of the series was in fanboying over it with my husband.

Damn. Who knew this would be the hardest part about breaking up? Not just the hurt and betrayal, not just the upheaval of our peaceful life, but realizing that small things were gone. All those evenings spent making dinner while we rambled about the books. Hanging out on the couch watching TV or movies. Talking in bed after we'd turned off the lights but hadn't gone to sleep yet. It was all those quiet, mundane moments that hadn't seemed like much at the time. Turned out there was more to them than I'd thought.

The moment I'd known we were in for the long haul probably sounded silly to anyone but me. We'd been cuddled up on my couch to watch TV, and Rhys had dozed off on my shoulder. The show ended, and there was another one after that I didn't care to watch, but I couldn't reach the remote to change the channel or turn it off. I'd had to either wake him up to get the remote, or sit through the show until he did. The choice had been a no-brainer.

And the moments that followed had been a game changer. Something about sitting there with Rhys and whatever show it was playing in the background while I ran my fingers through his hair, I'd simply known. There was no dramatic epiphany. No skies opening up or angels singing. Just that quiet realization that I was home. That I not only didn't want to disturb him in the name of getting the remote, I didn't want him to move at all. Ever.

In the silence of my hotel room, I wiped my eyes and sighed. I missed feeling that way about him, and damn it, I missed having him next to me right now. Wasn't it supposed to be simple when someone cheated? Weren't you supposed to be angry and hate them and be done with it? I wasn't supposed to have fond memories cascading through my mind and making me want to go next door, knock, and ask if he wanted to watch a movie together.

Fuck. I'd expected divorce to be hard. I just hadn't realized how hard and in what ways.

I turned my head and glared at the wall dividing me from Rhys.

I hated him for what he'd done to us.

And I hated myself for wanting him here beside me.

***

Breakfast?

How could a one-word text trigger so many emotions? As I stared at Rhys's message, I gnawed my lip and debated how to answer. Last night had been enough of an emotional roller coaster, and I'd only just started to decompress and pull myself together. Would sitting at a breakfast table with him make me feel better or worse?

Well, I was going to be cooped up in a car with him in fairly short order, so maybe it wouldn't hurt to test the water by sitting together at breakfast. At least then we could get up and walk away under the pretense of acquiring more coffee and without jumping from a moving vehicle.

Christ. This felt like a dry run for a combat mission, not stuffing our faces before a road trip.

Hoping a text couldn't convey all the weirdness bouncing around in my head, I wrote back, *I'll meet you there in 15.*

Fifteen minutes would be enough time, right? It was enough time to shower and shave, and that would wake me up even though I hadn't slept for shit.

I groaned, rubbing my gritty eyes. The therapist I used to see had warned me that stress would make the combat PTSD worse, and she'd been right—fucking nightmares every damn night. Maybe I should start seeing her again. I was so threadbare from lack of sleep, I decided I could use all the help I could get.

For now...shower. Shave.

Then breakfast. With Rhys. Great.

After I'd gotten dressed, I gathered my phone, wallet, and keycard, and headed out. I had just closed my door when Rhys's opened. My stomach fluttered with nerves as we made sleepy eye contact.

"Hey." He pulled his door shut.

"Hey."

We exchanged an uneasy look, and then he nodded toward the elevators. Without speaking, we started walking.

It only took a couple of steps for me to notice that Rhys's gait was stiff and he was favoring his right leg. His knee must have been acting up after a few long days of driving.

I glanced at him. "You want me to drive today?"

"Nah, I've got it."

"You sure? Your knee seems sore."

Rhys shrugged. "I'll just wear the brace for a couple of hours and take a few ibuprofen. It'll be fine."

I pressed my lips together. On a normal day, I'd argue with him, remind him that there was already a knee replacement sometime in his future, and that giving the joint a rest for a day was probably the best thing.

This wasn't a normal day, though. I wasn't the concerned husband anymore. Pushing him to take it easy had too much potential to be incendiary, so I let it go. If he was in enough pain, he'd suggest letting me drive. I hoped.

As we rode the elevator down, I stole another glance at him, trying to gauge how much pain he was in from his posture. He seemed all right when he was standing still, which usually meant he could put weight on it. Maybe it was just stiff from driving, so it was tender when he walked.

He knew his limits, I reminded myself. I had always followed his lead when it came to his pain and mobility. Sometimes, though, I worried he was pushing himself harder than he should and he'd pay for it later. As it was, his orthopedist figured he had another five, maybe ten years before his right knee had to be replaced. That was a hell of a recovery anyway, but it would be extra complicated for an amputee. One of the reasons his knee was in such bad shape was years of wear and tear because of the amputation. Things like standing on his right leg in the shower since he had to take off his prosthetic. Hopping took its toll, and even though he'd long ago let a physical therapist talk him into using a shower chair, the joint was still damaged.

A newly replaced knee on the right and a prosthetic on the left? That was going to be complicated until things had healed. We'd always assumed I'd just work from home during that period so I could help him recover.

Now part of me kind of wanted to tell him to go easy on that knee because I wouldn't be around to help when it finally needed to be replaced.

Oh. Yeah. That wouldn't be incendiary at all.

The elevator let us out into a thinly crowded lobby. A few people were checking out and heading into the blustery weather outside. Others were leisurely eating breakfast and either checking their phones or watching the news.

It was a typical continental breakfast—a small buffet of basic breakfast items and decent coffee. The sausage was a bit questionable, but there was plenty of ham and bacon that looked fine. With some meat and enough hashbrowns that my trainer would have given me some serious side-eye, I joined Rhys at a table that was somewhat separated from everyone else, giving us some semblance of privacy.

We ate in silence for a moment, though my appetite was mostly MIA.

Rhys idly tapped the end of his fork beside his plate. "So, I guess this is where we have another uncomfortable talk and try to figure out how to play the next few days."

"I guess so, yeah." I picked at the hashbrowns that had seemed so appetizing a few minutes ago. "We're going to be rooming together when we get there." *Oh God. There's only one bed in that room.* "We might as well iron things out as best we can now."

Rhys nodded, avoiding my eyes. "Exactly. So, um..." He hesitated, then chanced a look at me. "Any ideas?"

Damn. I'd been hoping he'd already thought of something.

"Um. Not really." I put my fork down because I really didn't feel like eating now. "Obviously sleeping together is off the table."

With a quiet grunt of agreement, Rhys nodded again.

That was weirdly disappointing. I knew it was for the best, and I didn't want us to continue sleeping together, because it would just complicate things. But somehow it was hard to accept that yet another chapter of our life together was over.

Rhys broke a piece of bacon off the strip and popped it in his mouth. "Maybe we should take today the way we did yesterday. Headphones and all that."

"You think so?"

"I don't know." He sounded equal parts tired and resigned. "But I don't know how else to make sure we're not ready to kill each other by the time we get there. We're going to need our game faces all weekend, and the weekend is going to be nonstop stress even with-out..." He gestured at both of us. "So let's stick with how we played it yesterday, and save our energy for the weekend."

It hurt to imagine that pretending we liked each other required that much energy. Six months ago, it wouldn't have required a second thought.

"Okay. We'll do that, then." I picked up my coffee, which had cooled during the long silences between us. "I'm going to get a refill." Without waiting for a response, I got up and headed for the buffet again. Might as well enjoy that freedom while I still had it. Once we were on the road, well...

I sighed and poured some fresh coffee.

It seemed like a couple of adults should be able to come to enough of a truce for the car ride to be bearable without blocking each other out with headphones. The first day hadn't been so bad, after all.

Things were just too raw now. Too many emotions had come to the surface the other night, and I got the impression he couldn't ignore them any more than I could. Digging into it and unpacking it all—I was exhausted just thinking about it.

Maybe Rhys was right, though. If we were going to get through the chaos of a wedding weekend, then maybe disappearing into our own little worlds for a while—me with my headphones, him with whatever he put on the car's speakers—was our best bet. We'd have to pretend soon enough that we were happily married. If we were going to have the energy to put on a convincing show, then another day of quiet distance was probably what we needed.

Something told me that tomorrow, I'd be begging for that distance again.

CHAPTER 11

RHYS

Things were bearable after we'd talked, but it was still another six long, uncomfortable hours before we pulled into Derek's sister's driveway.

"Okay." I shut off the engine. "We're here."

"Finally." Derek tucked his headphones into their case. "I think I'm about ready to call it a night."

"Me too." It wasn't even that late, but the road was tiring, and the ongoing silence between us had been draining in its own way too.

I unbuckled my seat belt, but before I could open my door, Derek said, "Wait."

I turned to him, suddenly nervous. What now?

Derek swallowed. "Before we go in, we should put our rings back on."

"Oh." I looked at my left hand, which was on the door handle. "Yeah. Good idea." And good thing I'd remembered to pack it. I'd stopped wearing it a long time ago, and I'd been so stressed before this trip, it had nearly slipped my mind to bring it. "Uh, mine's in my shaving kit." I motioned toward the back. "Let me get it."

He nodded.

It was dark out, and the night was cold enough that ice was a possibility, so I pulled my cane out from under the seat. Moving carefully, I went around to the back of the truck, opened the hatch, and pulled my shaving kit out of my suitcase. The ring was in a small box, and I took it out and put it on.

Wow. This was... weird. I opened and closed my hand, eyeing the ring in the dim floodlights in front of Amy's house. The tan line hadn't even faded yet, but the smooth, cool band already felt alien on my finger. As if it had been off longer than it had been on, even though I'd worn the thing for seven years.

Kind of like my relationship with Derek, I guess. Great for years, and then so shitty it's hard to remember all the good years that came before.

I shoved my shaving kit back into my suitcase and zipped the lid. In silence—the oh so familiar damned silence—we gathered our things and headed up the walk to the front door.

Before Derek had cleared the top step, the door swung open.

"Hey!" Amy grinned and spread her arms wide. "Gimme hugs, boys!"

Derek and I both laughed, and in turn, we hugged her on the porch.

She took us inside and we greeted her husband, Nate, and their teenagers, Jackie, Robbie, and Kelly. I was seriously ready to take everything into the guest room and flop facedown on the bed for the night, but then she uttered those magic words that gave me reason to stay out here: "Do either of you want some coffee?"

Yes. Yes, we did.

While her husband and son took our things into the guest room, we sat on her huge, comfy sofa, and a moment later, she brought in a couple of steaming cups of coffee.

Unfortunately, after the last few hours—the last few days, really —the coffee didn't do much. Within half an hour, I was flagging, and Derek was starting to get that spacey look in his eyes that meant he was running on fumes. I really hoped it was because we were tired from being on the road and not solely from the monumental effort of pretending everything was peachy between us. If we couldn't handle an hour of that, we were fucked for the weekend.

Whatever the case, we both tried to stay engaged as Amy and her family caught us up on everything they'd been doing lately, but it just wasn't happening. The minds were willing but the bodies were weak.

We glanced at each other, and I suspected Derek recognized my expression as easily as I recognized his—we were both just *done*.

"Well," he said to his sister. "I think we're going to call it a night. It's been a long day."

Amy grimaced. "I bet. And you're going to be running yourselves ragged this weekend."

"Don't remind me," he muttered.

I tried not to take that personally. He meant we'd be running ourselves ragged with all the wedding festivities, not our secret charade. That was all.

We said good night to everyone, then shuffled to the guest room. Derek shut the door behind us, and just like that we were alone in this familiar guest room with its familiar bed.

Knowing we'd be sharing a bed tonight, I'd expected a certain amount of tension and maybe even some sniping once we were in here, but neither of us said much of anything. We got ready for bed, got into bed, and shut off the light, and that was the end of it. Maybe that was good. Maybe it wasn't. Maybe it meant we could do this. Maybe it meant we were both too tired and resigned to fight.

At least things were calm for the time being. I'd take that for as long as it lasted.

The first night in Amy's house was, unsurprisingly, miserable. The bed was slightly smaller than a queen, so I didn't dare move for fear of brushing up against Derek. I spent most of the night clinging to the edge, keeping my back to him and trying like hell to fall asleep.

Though we'd yet again come to something like a truce, the damage was done. Maybe we could pretend to be happily married in front of everyone at all the wedding festivities, but when it was just the two of us? Forget it. We both knew the truth, so there was no point in pretending we believed the lie. So now the air was cool between us, and I couldn't sleep.

It didn't help that my right knee throbbed mercilessly for most of the night. Four days of driving had definitely taken their toll, and now I regretted not taking Derek up on his offer to drive for a while. And of course whenever I was out of the car, I was favoring it, which meant putting extra weight on my prosthetic, which meant my left knee and hip were sore too.

By the time the sun rose and I gave up, I was running on maybe two hours of sleep. Fortunately, my brief stint in the Army and over a decade as a teacher had left me with a seriously valuable superpower: the ability to function at ninety percent or better even when I was running on fumes. I might feel like shit, and I'd crash hard once there was nothing left standing between me and a bed, but in the meantime? I'd be fine.

A brisk jog in the biting cold helped wake me up too. A short one, though—both knees and my left hip were sore, so I went easy. Just a half mile or so around Amy's neighborhood at a low speed. Enough to work some stiffness out of my joints and muscles without overly taxing anything. As a bonus, while it was cold as hell, the roads were clear. No ice to slide and bust my ass. Perfect.

When I came back in from my run, everyone else was starting to come out for breakfast.

"Did you have a nice run?" Amy asked cheerfully.

"Yeah." I smiled. "I'm just going to grab a shower, and then I'll join you."

I was halfway out of the kitchen, when Robbie said in a disgusted voice, "Ugh, how can you run in that?"

Derek, who was sitting at the kitchen table, tensed.

I glanced down at my running blade, then back at Robbie. "Uh, why not?"

He gestured out the window. "It's cold as balls out there."

"Robbie," his mom scolded.

"What?" He shrugged. "It is."

I chuckled, relieved he'd meant the weather. Derek relaxed too. We should've known better—Amy's kids were all well aware of my disability and they'd seen both my everyday prosthetic and the running blade before.

"It's not that bad," I said. "Not once you get moving."

The kid shuddered and clung to his coffee cup. "No, thank you."

"Wimp."

"Hey!"

I shrugged. "What? It's not *that* cold."

He just shook his head, and the rest of his family laughed.

While they continued with coffee and making breakfast, I returned to the guest room for a shower. We'd stayed with Amy enough times that I didn't even have to ask for a shower chair anymore—she'd left it propped against the wall before we'd arrived. Or maybe Derek had reminded her. Either way, I appreciated it.

By the time I'd finished my shower and come back into the room, Derek had returned as well. He went into the bathroom to shave while I got dressed, and that silence from last night lingered while we went about our morning routines.

I was just sliding my wedding ring back on—weird—when Derek broke the silence.

"So, um, we're still on for the party tonight, right?"

Party? Tonight?

Oh. That one. Fuck. It was supposed to be an informal gathering so the families could actually meet before the wedding. Derek and I had met Corbin a few times, but neither of us had met his extended family. Well, aside from Derek briefly Facetiming with the kid's parents.

So, I'd have the opportunity to meet Vanessa's new extended

family, and Derek and I could have a dressed rehearsal of pretending to still be happily married loving husbands. Yay?

I glanced down at the ring I didn't feel right wearing. "Yeah. Yeah, we're still on."

"Okay. Good." He paused. "And, um, as far as anyone but us knows, everything is fine between us." His tone was flat, tinged with more fatigue than anger or bitterness. "I guess tonight will give us a chance to see if we can pull that off."

"I think we can." My voice didn't sound much better. "It's just for tonight and the next couple of days. We can do this."

Derek met my gaze, and to my surprise, he cracked a small smile. "Yeah, we can do this."

I managed to smile back just as faintly. "Um, what time do we need to leave for the party?"

"Probably around four."

"All right. I'll be ready."

I was so not ready for this.

I mean, I was dressed and dutifully wearing my wedding ring, and we were in the truck with time to spare to get to the party on time. Ready? Eh, not so much.

We'd spent most of the day just relaxing. Catching up with Amy and the family now that we were awake. Running a few errands to pick up things Vanessa's mom had texted saying she frantically needed. Helping Amy wrap her wedding gift because no one in Derek's family had gift-wrapping game like I did.

Before I'd known it, it was almost four. Time to go be around people. A lot of people. *So many people.*

The party was being held in the VFW hall not far from the reception hall. I parked in the mostly full lot outside, and we headed in.

At the door, we stopped, and we both took deep breaths, straightened our jackets, and set our shoulders back. Then Derek offered his elbow.

It was easier than it should have been to slide my hand into the crook of his arm. Habit, probably. We'd been good at this longer than we'd been cold toward each other, so I let chalked it up to muscle memory.

When we stepped into the crowded VFW hall, two things were immediately apparent—Corbin's family was huge (oh God so many people), and he was not the first to join the military. Though everyone was in civvies, the haircuts on the younger generation were hard to miss. He had a number of older relatives who stood with that conspicuously stiff posture that came with wearing a uniform for most of their lives.

I glanced at Derek. Hopefully he was in a steady state of mind tonight and could handle people comparing war stories. Most of the time he was fine. If he was a bit brittle or his PTSD was acting up, he'd quickly bow out of those conversations. Easier said than done in a room full of military.

"You going to be okay?" I asked.

Derek nodded. "Yeah. I'll be fine." He glanced at me, and though he didn't look particularly happy to be looking at me, nothing in his expression said *get me the fuck out of here.* Good enough.

It didn't take long for us to find Vanessa. She was talking to some people I didn't recognize, dressed in a blue cocktail dress with her blond hair tumbling over her shoulders and a couple of her tattoos showing.

She turned, and the instant she saw us, her eyes lit up. "Hey!" She threw her arms around Derek. "I'm so glad you guys made it!"

"Like we'd miss this." Derek hugged her tight. "Congratulations, kiddo."

"Thanks." She let him go, turned to me, and pulled me into a hug too. "How was the trip?"

"Long," we both said, injecting enough good humor into it to avoid her suspecting just *how* long the trip had been or why.

"You'll have to fill me in on—" She glanced past Derek, and her lips pursed. "Damn it. Corbin's mom needs me for something. I'll be back."

"Don't worry about it," Derek said. "We'll be here."

She released a long-suffering sigh, then hurried off to see what her new mother-in-law needed.

The party was, as these things often were, a whirlwind of faces and introductions. We'd met most of Vanessa's mom's family before, and of course we'd met the groom, but we hadn't met his family before. And there were a lot of them. At one point, while catching up with Corbin, an older gentleman leaning heavily on a cane came up to offer his congratulations.

"So, this is my Great Uncle Bill." Corbin gestured at us. "Uncle Bill, this is Derek and Rhys. Vanessa's dad and—" His eyes darted toward me as if he'd suddenly drawn a blank.

"Stepdad," I said.

"Stepdad?" Bill looked around. "When in the world did Sara get remarried? Did I miss that?"

"No. No." Corbin waved a hand at us again. "They're married to each other."

"*Oh.*" Bill glanced back and forth between us. "Well, I got no problem with two men being married, you know."

I could feel Derek bristling beside me, though he had a damn good poker face.

"That's great," he said with a convincing smile. "We're pretty okay with straight people being married too."

"Eh." I made a so-so gesture. "Long as they don't throw it in our faces, though. That's obnoxious."

Bill looked puzzled.

I put up a hand. "And as long as they're not asking for more special rights."

"Ugh." Derek made a dramatic gesture of rolling his eyes. "Always with the special rights."

Bill was definitely confused now, and I struggled not to snicker.

But then he cleared his throat. "Well, one of the boys at my office married a man the day they legalized gay marriage." He laughed dryly, shaking his head. "Not even a year later, the dumb kids got divorced. Can you imagine? Making such a big stink over wanting to get married, saying they should be able to do the same as the rest of us, and they can't even make it work."

Derek and I exchanged uncomfortable glances. Even his poker face had slipped.

"Bill, really?" Corbin touched his great uncle's shoulders and gently steered the man toward the bar. "Looks like you could use a refill."

Bill looked at the mostly empty drink in his hand, grunted in agreement, and headed toward the bar, muttering something about men marrying men when there's so many perfectly good women out there.

Corbin sighed and turned to us. "I'm sorry about him. He means well—I think—but he has no filter at all."

"You don't say," Derek said into his glass, but he sounded amused.

"How's everything else going?" I asked. "Wedding prep in between"—I nodded toward the great uncle in question—"relative wrangling?"

"Crazy," Corbin said. "Vanessa's mom says that's normal, though."

"It is," Derek and I said in unison.

Corbin chuckled. "Great. I'm probably going to spend half the honeymoon just catching up on sleep."

"Good plan," I said with a laugh. "I think I collapsed for almost eighteen hours after our wedding."

"Me too." Derek's laugh was halfhearted. "I thought it was over the top to leave the reception in a limo because we could just drive ourselves. Good thing we did, though—I was asleep before it pulled out of the parking lot."

Now I was the one struggling not to sound halfhearted. That had been one of my favorite memories from our wedding—that quiet ride in the limo with Derek dozing against me.

"Aw, crap," Corbin muttered, snapping me out of my thoughts. "Will you guys excuse me for a second? Bill is stirring shit up again."

"Go get him," Derek said with some more genuine amusement.

Corbin hurried off to corral his great uncle, and a second later, Vanessa's mom, Sara, came out of the crowd, arms outstretched. "Oh there you guys are! Sorry, I've been running around putting out fires."

"It's a wedding," Derek said with a laugh as he hugged her. "Wouldn't be right if there wasn't nonstop chaos."

She let him go and shot him a pointed look. "Says the man who hasn't been neck deep in the chaos this whole time. Ugh, why do weddings always seem like such disasters?"

Derek and I chuckled but didn't look at each other.

"Well, I'm glad you two made it." Her eyebrow flicked ever so slightly upward as her eyes darted back and forth between us. "In one piece, too."

I glanced at Derek, not sure what to make of the comment.

He shifted a little, clearing his throat and avoiding her eyes and mine. "Yeah. Yeah. Made it one piece." When he finally met her gaze, his smile was the least convincing one I thought I'd ever seen on him. "Wasn't so bad after all."

Sara nodded, shifting her eyes toward me. Her expression was still more or less pleasant, but steely too. A distinct *"you better be glad there are people around."*

I gulped. Great. I was now on the shit list of the stressed out mother-of-the-bride who was also really protective of her daughter's father. That boded well for the rest of the weekend.

After Sara left to put out some fire or another—something about the caterer, I thought—I cut my eyes toward Derek. "She knows, doesn't she?"

"Yeah." Derek slid his hands into his pockets. "She's, uh, known for a while. Pretty much since the beginning."

Oh. Awesome. So she'd gotten the story when Derek had still

been spitting nails over what I'd done. That explained the warning in her eyes. God help me if she got me alone this weekend.

"Thanks for the heads up," I muttered into my drink.

"I needed to talk to someone about it," he snapped. I glared at him, and he returned it, but in the same moment I remembered where we were, he seemed to do the same. Expression and voice softening, he said, "She's not going to say anything. I told her we're keeping things on the DL until after the wedding. We're good."

"Uh-huh."

He leveled a glare at me. "Rhys. Just—"

"Don't." I lowered my drink and returned the glare. "You just could've mentioned that she knew, okay? That's all. Nobody wants any surprises this weekend, and that includes me."

His lips pulled tight. I could hear the *this could have been avoided entirely if you hadn't...* coming from a mile away, but he didn't say it out loud. Something told me he would before the end of the weekend.

Pretending everything was fine, we continued mingling at the party. By the time we caught up with Vanessa again, we'd schooled all traces of our marital bullshit out of our voices and expressions.

"So do you and Corbin have any idea where you'll be transferring?" Derek asked. "Or when?"

"Don't know exactly when yet," she said. "But he's probably getting orders sooner than we thought. He's thinking somewhere on the East Coast, but we don't know for sure yet."

Derek furrowed his brow. "How's that going to work with you going to school?" I could practically hear him crunching the numbers on in-state versus out-of-state tuition, and I was doing the same. Along with her mom, we all contributed as much as we could so Vanessa wouldn't have to cover it all with student loans, but out-of-state could get hairy.

Vanessa waved a hand. "Oh, I'm probably going to continue the program I'm in. They have online courses in the same field, and Corbin is looking into waivers for out-of-state tuition because I'm a military dependent. If we can't swing that, there are some schools that have locations on bases that don't charge out-of-state rates."

"Oh. Good." Derek visibly relaxed. "Just let me know if you need help with anything."

"Thanks, Dad." Vanessa glanced past us and straightened. "Oh! Corbin's grandparents just got here. I need to go say hi. I'll catch up with you guys!"

She hurried off, and Derek chuckled. "She's going to be exhausted by the end of the weekend."

"No kidding." I turned to him. "By the way, keep me in the loop if her tuition does go up. Money's going to be tight for a while, but I'll help as much as I can."

"I will. Thanks." We exchanged uneasy smiles. At least we'd managed to keep the façade going in front of Corbin, his weird great uncle, Sara, and Vanessa, even if we flagged a little when no one else was looking.

Vanessa was going to be tired at the end of this weekend? *We* were going to be *wiped*.

And as much as I knew Derek was ready to break off contact with me, I hoped he took me up on my offer to continue helping with our daughter's tuition. How I'd do that... well, I'd figure it out one way or another. I still wasn't entirely sure how I was going to live on my own on a teacher's salary. Even with my disability pay from the military, money was and probably always would be tight.

Guess I'd add *find a roommate* to my list of things to do after this trip was over.

CHAPTER 12

DEREK

Parties wore me down. Too many people and too much noise. Back in my early military days, I'd gone out partying, but that was before I'd spent any time in combat. Now, I got nervous in crowds, though the PTSD was more or less under control now. It had been relatively mild to begin with—I wasn't as badly triggered as some of the people I'd served with—but large groups in small places did make my neck prickle and my stomach knot in unpleasant ways.

As I was getting another drink, my daughter's mom appeared beside me. "Hey. You doing okay?"

"Yeah." I rubbed the back of my neck and pretended not to notice how much I was sweating. "Just...crowds. You know how it is."

Sara nodded, and I thought she might have shuddered. "You want to go out and get some air?"

"I would love to."

We grabbed our jackets and slipped out the back. I wasn't worried about anyone thinking it was weird; anyone who knew us was well aware that my daughter's mother and I were close.

Calling her my ex would be generous. We'd never married. Hadn't really dated. We'd just fooled around a few times during our early years in the Army, back when we'd been stupid kids and I'd still been in the closet. The sex was fun, we were careless, and the next thing we knew, we were expecting Vanessa. In the years since, we'd done the best we could to co-parent our daughter. There'd never been much of a breakup because there'd never been much of a relationship. No divorce. No custody battles.

It had gotten complicated when Sara was posted to Germany for a couple of years, and we'd had to fight our respective commands a few times to keep our deployments from overlapping. Once I'd been discharged, that part got easier. Now Sara was retired, and though our daughter was an adult, we still emailed and even Skyped pretty regularly just because we wanted to. She was good people, and I was grateful we'd stayed friends despite some bumps in the road.

Standing outside in the cold, Sara lit a cigarette and hugged herself as she took a drag. After she'd blown out a cloud of smoke, she turned to me. "So how are you holding up?" Her eyebrows pulled together. "With..." She pointed her cigarette toward the room we'd just left.

"Like I said." I shrugged tightly. "Crowds."

Sara pursed her lips. "I didn't mean the party. I meant your plus one."

My teeth snapped together and I stared at the ground. "Oh." Well damn. That was a complicated question. "I'm doing okay, I guess. Things are, um..."

"Tense?"

"Tense." I nodded emphatically. "Yes. Yes, that is the word you could use. Tense." Somehow it didn't seem to encompass all the emotions and discomfort of the last few days, but I was at a loss for a word that would.

Sara took a drag off her cigarette, then turned her head away so she could blow out the smoke. "Did you two really drive all the way here together? With all that tension?"

"What else could we do?" I sighed, leaning hard against the cold railing. "Rhys is terrified of flying, and it would have raised eyebrows if he'd driven and I'd flown. Vanessa definitely would have noticed."

Her lips quirked. "Okay, I suppose that's true. But how in the world did you two make it through—what, three days on the road?"

"Four." I sighed. "And it was... rough. I'm thinking I should just rent a car on the way home. It's a waste of money and makes the environmentalist in me cringe, but I just don't think we can handle another four days cooped up in a car."

"I hope you got separate rooms at the hotels."

I shifted my gaze away, gnawing the inside of my cheek.

"Derek..."

"We..." I rubbed the back of my neck and sighed. "We started out that way, yes. And then there was one night where everything seemed really good, and we thought, hey, why not enjoy this since it's better than fighting?"

"Didn't last?"

"Didn't last." My shoulders sagged. Hell, my whole body felt like it was sagging. I needed a break from everything, especially from my ex-husband, and I wouldn't get one for a solid week. "We tried to shelve everything for this trip and at least act like everything is fine, but it's not working as well as I'd hoped."

"Could be because everything *isn't* fine?"

"You think?" I rubbed my eyes. "But there isn't much I can really do, you know? No one here except you knows what's happening, and I'm sure as shit not announcing it at our daughter's wedding."

"No, I would hope not." She scowled. "I don't understand why you haven't told people. And kicked him out already, for that matter. Even before you found out Vanessa was engaged."

"You make it sound like I could afford a mortgage on my own *and* a lawyer." I took a long pull from my beer. "Trust me, we're not still living together because it's fun."

"But you could have at least said something. And I still think you should have told Vanessa before this weekend." She inclined her head. "She's not stupid, Derek. She's going to notice something isn't right between you two."

"We'll be okay." Why didn't I sound convincing? Or convinced? "We've done just fine so far."

Sara arched an eyebrow. "Have you?"

"We..." I gulped. "Why? Have people noticed?"

"Not that I know of, but you two looked about as comfortable as two actors who hate each other trying to film a love scene."

I looked away, stomach roiling. "Great."

We stood in silence for a while. Sara finished her cigarette and crushed it in an ashtray sitting on the railing. "I still can't believe he did that to you. Why in the world would he cheat on you?"

I didn't tell her he'd explained things (sort of). What difference would it have made? All that knowledge had done was make me feel worse. "Does it matter? It's done."

She didn't respond.

I shifted my weight. Then, resting my forearms on the railing, I leaned over them and gazed out into the night. "You know what the worst part is?"

"Hmm?"

I took a deep breath of the icy cold air. "After all this shit, I still love him." My own words were like a swift kick in the balls. Eyes stinging, I gritted my teeth and whispered, "And I fucking hate him for that."

With a heavy sigh, Sara stepped closer and hugged me. "I'm sorry he did that to you. I always thought he was such a good guy."

"Yeah. Me too."

As she let me go, she said, "I can kick his ass if you want me to."

I laughed, swiping at my eyes. "No, that's okay."

"I mean it. Wouldn't be any trouble at all."

"Yeah, yeah, I know. But...it's fine. I just want to get through this weekend, get home, and start getting on with my life."

Sara frowned. "You're not going to get very far with that until you and your ex start being, you know, exes."

I nodded.

"Step one—stop living together." She glanced back at the party we'd abandoned, then met my eyes, brow furrowed and expression totally serious. "Get that man out of your house before seeing him every day drives you insane."

"Have to wonder if that ship has already sailed," I muttered.

Sara scowled but said nothing.

Deep down, I knew she was right. I needed to tell Vanessa the truth, and I needed to tell Rhys to hit the road. If I had to bring in a roommate or take out a loan or get a second job—maybe all three—to get by, I would. But he had to go.

Which shouldn't have hurt like this, except on some level, I still thought—*knew*—that Rhys was a good guy. He was a great guy.

And knowing that made what he'd done cut even deeper.

You're good to everyone.

Why not me?

Fortunately, the second full day in town meant tons of preparation and running around. The instant someone realized Rhys had an SUV, he was conscripted into helping with last-second errands like picking up some extra chairs and some desserts for the rehearsal dinner. Meanwhile I went between the church and reception venue, helping set things up. There was just enough stress and distraction to keep us out of each other's hair without anyone noticing.

At some point, after we'd finished unloading some tables at the reception hall, Sara and I were pulled in to help put flower center-pieces together with Vanessa and Beth, Corbin's mother. In an effort to save money, they'd foregone a professional florist, bought boatloads of silk flowers, colored marbles, and dollar-store mini fishbowls. Vanessa had assembled one centerpiece already, and it actually looked quite nice.

While we tried to make ours resemble hers as closely as possible

—or at least not look like Pinterest rejects—Beth worked on making matching boutonnieres for the wedding party and ushers.

"You should save some of these flowers," Beth said as she hot-glued a purple rose to another boutonniere. "They might come in handy decorating for a baby shower."

Sara and I exchanged looks, both pressing our lips together.

"Nope." Vanessa poured some marbles into another vase. "No baby showers in my future."

Beth laughed. "Every Army wife is pregnant by her first anniversary. I'm pretty sure there's something in the water in base housing."

Vanessa laughed, shaking her head. "Well, looks like I'm drinking Coke until he retires, then. Or staying out of base housing. *No* babies."

"Well." Beth gave her a knowing smile. "You're still young. You have plenty of time."

"I don't need time," Vanessa said matter-of-factly. "We're not having kids. Period."

Beth scowled. "Corbin would be such an excellent father, though."

"He'd probably be a great lion tamer too, but it's not in the cards."

Her mother-in-law's scowl deepened. "Think about your parents, though." She nodded toward me. "You're their only child. How else are they going to have grandkids?"

"If they wanted grandkids, they should have had more kids so their odds would be better."

I snorted. So did Sara.

Beth glared at us.

"What?" Sara shrugged. "One kid with him was more than enough, thank you."

"You're one to talk," I muttered with exaggerated exasperation. When I realized Beth was decidedly not amused, I said, "Look, grandkids would be great, but she and Corbin are the ones who'd have to do all the work raising them. If they don't want them?" I shrugged. "They're not going to catch any hell from me."

"Same," Sara said. "And you're an Army wife. That means you're guaranteed to be a single mom for months or even years at a stretch sometimes."

Vanessa wrinkled her nose. "Ugh. No thank you."

Beth huffed. "I always thought deployments went faster when I had kids to keep me busy. What else are you going to do during that time?"

"Study?" Vanessa said. "Get a Chia Pet? I don't know. I don't need toddlers to fill my time, though, and I'm not having them just so I have something to do while Corbin's deployed."

Her mother-in-law glared at her, then tsked and shook her head. "I just don't understand your generation. Not wanting kids? At all? I don't get it."

"That's okay." Vanessa smiled brightly. "We do."

Sara and I exchanged glances again, and we both smothered smiles. If Beth thought she could wear down her new daughter-in-law's stubbornness, she was in for a shock. Vanessa probably didn't need the pressure, and God knew there'd be more once she was in the military spouse community, but she was no one's doormat. If she didn't want kids, she wouldn't have them, and she wouldn't have married someone without being on the same page with him. No way in hell was someone badgering her into something she didn't want to do, least of all something like motherhood. We'd always suspected she'd go that route anyway. She'd never had much interest in things like babysitting except as a means of earning money, and kids had just never been her thing. She would coo and fawn all over a puppy or a cat, but babies? Not so much.

Rhys wandered in a moment later and looked at the craft supplies laid out in front of us. "Can I help with anything?"

"We need all the help we can get." Vanessa gestured at an empty chair.

He shrugged and sat down. "So what are we doing?"

"Turning those"—she pointed to rows of empty vases beside bags of marbles and piles of flowers—"into that." She nodded toward the growing ranks of finished centerpieces.

"Okay." He pulled an empty vase toward him. "Looks simple enough."

"Should be." She smirked. "Dad's handling it okay."

"Hey!" I threw a stalk of silk baby's breath at her. "That's enough out of you."

"Children," Sara warned with a grin. We all laughed.

Except Beth of course. She started on another boutonniere, and looked pointedly at Rhys. "So what about you?" She gestured at Vanessa. "Did you know she doesn't want children?"

He froze, his hand hovering above the silk flowers. "Um. What?"

"Beth is trying to convince me that Corbin and I should have kids." Vanessa shook her head and emphatically jabbed some flowers into the marbles in her vase. "Not happening."

"Oh." Shrugging again, Rhys picked up the flowers he'd been reaching for and started separating them into smaller piles. "Yeah, I've known that for a long time." He glanced at Beth. "You didn't know?"

"Well, I knew," she said with palpable annoyance. "I just figured they'd change their minds eventually."

Sara, Rhys, and I all laughed.

"Yeah, no," Vanessa said. "I mean, if I *was* going to have kids, I'd have done it the way Rhys did."

We all paused, and Rhys and I glanced uncertainly at each other.

"Um." He cleared his throat. "What do you mean?"

"You know." Vanessa didn't seem to notice the ripple of tension between us. "Find some dude whose kid is already past all the diapers and annoying stuff."

Rhys barked a laugh. "Oh yeah. Because the preteen stage is so past all the annoying stuff."

Vanessa laughed and threw a marble at him.

Chuckling, he ducked, caught it, and tossed it back. "What? I'm just saying."

"Jerk," she said, but there was no venom behind it.

"Brat," he retorted in a similar tone.

"Just be glad you missed me during my toddler years."

"Ugh," Sara groaned. "We should've gotten medals for getting through those years."

"So true." I bumped fists with her.

Beth scowled. "Well, I can see why she isn't keen on having small children."

"Nope," Vanessa said with an unrepentant smile. "I'd rather start when they're older, so blame Corbin. If he'd come into this with like a twelve or thirteen year-old—"

"He's twenty-four!" Beth scoffed.

"Pfft." Vanessa shook her head disapprovingly. "And he didn't plan for his future at all, did he?"

Rhys, Sara, and I were struggling not to laugh too hard, since Beth clearly wasn't as amused by this as we were.

Fortunately, Sara stepped in, changed the subject to something wedding-related, and steered us away from Beth and Vanessa butting heads over grandkids. That kept things a bit less painful until Beth had to leave to pick up the champagne she'd ordered for the reception.

Vanessa watched Beth go. As soon as her mother-in-law was out of earshot, Vanessa said, "I don't think she likes me."

"Oh, I'm sure she likes you," Sara said. "You're just crushing all her dreams of having loads of grandbabies."

Vanessa shuddered. "She's got two other sons. If she wants grandkids, she should be talking to them instead of barking up this child-free tree."

"No kidding," the three of us said in unison.

She eyed us.

"What?" I showed my palms. "It isn't like any of us are surprised."

"At all," Sara supplied.

"Eh." Vanessa shrugged again. "Fair." Her humor faded a bit. "I really wish she'd give it a rest, though. I'm already tearing my hair out over the wedding—can we stop with the grandkid guilt trips for, like, two days?"

I swallowed. When I glanced at Rhys, his eyes reflected my own unspoken thoughts—we definitely had to keep our bullshit under wraps. Vanessa was handling everything as well as could be expected, but she had her limits, and she was probably getting closer to those limits than she was letting on.

Rhys cleared his throat and turned to Vanessa again. "You can use all the stress to your advantage, you know."

"Yeah? How?"

"If she starts badgering you," he said, "just bow out and say you have something you need to take care of."

"Good idea." She paused, glancing at each of us in turn. "And for real—you guys don't mind if you're not getting grandkids?"

"No," we all said.

"Honey." Sara shook her head. "Grandkids are great, but it's your life. The three of us all know how hard it is to be a parent, so we're not going to push that on you just so we can show off our grandkids a couple of times a year."

"It was totally worth it for us," I said. "But yeah, it's hard. It's not something you should do for someone else."

Vanessa's gaze slid toward Rhys. "How was it for you?"

Rhys straightened. "What do you mean?"

"I mean, did you want kids? Like, of your own?"

"I hadn't really decided, to be honest." He tucked another flower into the vase and slid it across the table to join the others. "I was still kind of on the fence, and then I met your dad, and...instant family. You and your dad were all I needed."

My throat tightened. Rhys's eyes darted toward me but only for a second. Sara shifted uncomfortably between us.

Fortunately, Vanessa was mostly focused on hot gluing a ribbon around one of the vases. "See? So people can be perfectly happy without biological kids. If Corbin and I ever change our minds, we'll just adopt."

"Good plan." Sara picked up her phone and huffed. "All right, kiddo. We've still got errands to run, and we need to go now before places start closing."

Vanessa got to her feet but paused to glance at us. "You guys don't mind?"

"Of course not," I said. "Go."

She and Sara left, and just like that, I was alone with Rhys and a bunch of flowers in dollar-store vases. Somehow the conversation with Beth about our daughter's choice not to have children had been less awkward than the silence joining us at the table now.

Rhys cleared his throat as he pushed a completed vase toward the others. "Corbin thinks they might need some more chairs for the reception. So, um, he might be dragging me off to pick them up."

"Okay. Sure. Just, uh, keep me posted. If you're out when everyone heads to dinner, I can probably get a lift with Amy or Vanessa."

"Dinner. Right." He swallowed, and we exchanged another one of those *oh God what did we get ourselves into* looks. "I'll text and check in. We'll figure it out from there." Right then, his phone buzzed. "That's Corbin." He pushed his chair back and stood. "I'll, um, see you at dinner?"

"Yeah. See you at dinner."

He headed out, and I surreptitiously watched him go. We'd done a pretty damn good job of playing the happyish couple so far. Vanessa didn't seem to suspect a thing.

But that conversation had been more heartbreaking than she—and probably he—could possibly know.

Vanessa and I were all you ever needed.

When did that change?

And why?

CHAPTER 13

RHYS

If there was one thing I'd learned at my sister's wedding and at my own, it was this: the rehearsal was where stress came to a head. My sister and her fiancé had gotten hammered at theirs, which led to a screaming match in the parking lot. My dad and I had been circling each other like sharks over some unresolved issues that had nothing to do with me marrying Derek, and those issues had exploded into us shouting at each other for twenty minutes before dinner. I'd heard plenty of horror stories from other weddings too. It seemed like if there was any trouble brewing, it either came out at the rehearsal and everything was fine the next day, or it simmered until the wedding and blew up at the worst possible moment.

By the time everyone had sat down to dinner at my rehearsal, Dad and I had run out of steam, and we talked things through later in the evening, and everything was great the next day. My sister and her fiancé had done the same. The arguments weren't even that serious—they were just the result of weeks and months of stress snowballing into the eleventh hour before the wedding. Marinate all that in alcohol, and... Well, the results weren't exactly a surprise.

So at Vanessa and Corbin's rehearsal, I steered clear of any booze. I noticed Derek was doing the same, and I was grateful for it.

Sara, however, was not steering clear of it, and every time she cut her eyes toward me, I got nervous. Especially after her third or fourth pre-dinner drink.

We'd always gotten along, and though she'd been understandably cautious about a new man shacking up with her daughter's father, she'd never been hostile. We'd met early in my relationship with Derek. He'd been open with her from day one that he was dating me and let her know when things were turning serious enough that living together was on the table. Hell, she'd come to our commitment ceremony and our legal wedding, and not just because our daughter was there.

But all through tonight's rehearsal, and as we'd all pitched in to make dinner in the reception hall's giant kitchen, and throughout dinner, and as Vanessa's soon-to-be in-laws insisted that everyone drink the gallons of booze they'd brought, the air between Sara and me grew steadily colder.

In the name of keeping the peace, I surreptitiously avoided her as much as I could. That wasn't much, though. Derek and I were supposed to walk up the aisle with her and sit beside her. At dinner, Derek and I couldn't really avoid sitting together, and Sara ended up sitting across from us.

No one did or said anything. Dinner was as uneventful as anyone could ask for. But just being there, occasionally catching each other's eye as the air between us grew frostier and frostier, was miserable.

And could I blame her? I'd brought this on us. I was the reason Derek was probably wearing himself down by putting on that almost believable happy face. I was the reason Sara was livid and drinking herself into a rage. I was the reason for the divorce that could ruin Vanessa's wedding.

So no, I didn't blame her. I just hated the constant scrutiny. I wanted to glare at her and tell her I hated myself enough. Could she not see how much this was eating me alive? It had been for months, but today? With the hours ticking down to the wedding that was stressing Derek out more than it should have?

I don't need you, lady. I'm flagellating myself just fine on my own.

Finally, dinner was over, and I had the chance to escape and catch my breath. While Sara and Vanessa were checking to make sure all the tables were ready for tomorrow, I helped Corbin's mom wash dishes in the big kitchen.

At least washing dishes didn't require much thought. Beth was annoyed at someone else about God knew what, so she wasn't chatty. And me... fuck. I was elbow deep in soapy water and up to my neck in regret. I felt like a kid being punished—I knew I'd fucked up, and I was going to be reminded of it at every turn until someone else decided I'd been miserable long enough. Derek had kept his polite, civil game face all day, but I knew he wished I wasn't here. Sometimes we'd catch each other's eye when no one else was looking, and the hurt would show in his, and all my regret would start throbbing with renewed vigor. As if it had stopped this entire time; the whole trip and this whole damn day, it had been there like a relentless toothache—impossible to ignore and not a dentist in sight.

By the time I'd found myself in this kitchen with dishes to keep me occupied, I felt like I had while recovering from some of my surgeries. Not in pain, per se, but when my emotional threads started to fray because I was worn ragged, sleep-deprived, and frustrated that the simplest things were suddenly complicated. With a road trip, my looming divorce, and my battered conscience, I was pretty sure I was down to my last thread, and it wasn't going to hold much longer.

I just need some downtime. Some time to myself.

God, yes. That's what I need. Will it be too cold to go for a run when I get back to the house?

That might be a bad idea. There'd been some frosty patches in the shade when I'd gone out yesterday morning, and the ground had been wet today. With the sun down, there was a good chance of ice forming, and an even better chance of me not seeing it before I stepped on it. Apparently a run would have to wait until tomorrow.

Though I was seriously tempted to hunt down a twenty-four hour gym in the area. After all I did have a car, and I doubted Derek would mind if I left for a while.

Yes. As soon as I was done washing dishes, I'd look up gyms in the area, and after all the rehearsal shit was over, I'd blow off some steam on a treadmill. Hopefully that would help.

Now if I could just hold myself together until then, I'd be golden.

At the other sink, Beth peered at the drying rack, which was full of plates. "I think we're missing a few. I'll go check."

"Okay. Sure." I flashed her a quick smile, then continued scrubbing burnt cheese off the side of a lasagna pan while she went back into the reception hall. Admittedly, I was glad to have a moment alone. We hadn't exactly been chatting, but I'd take what I could get.

Not thirty seconds later, though, footsteps behind me raised the hairs on my neck. I hoped it was just Beth coming back in with more plates, but somehow I knew it wasn't. And when I turned... Oh shit.

Sara gave me some unmistakable side-eye as she plunked a handful of glasses down on the counter next to the sink. "Need any help?" The chilly offer came through gritted teeth.

"Uh. No. I'm... I'm good." I chanced a quick look at her before fixing my attention on the pan I was still working on. "I've got it. Thanks."

"All right." But she didn't move. She just...stood there. Right outside my peripheral vision, eyes burning holes in my shoulder at the same time her glare brought the temperature in the kitchen down twenty degrees. Finally, though, she turned to go, but before I could sigh with relief, she halted. "You know what? I can't keep my mouth shut."

I gulped, and when I turned to her again, she was glaring at me hard. "Uh. Okay." I put down the sponge and pan, mostly so I didn't drop the glass pan and break it. Then I picked up a dishtowel to occupy my hands. "What's up?"

"I think you know what's up."

I returned the glare. "No, I don't. I know that if looks could kill, you'd have dropped me before dinner, but beyond that—"

"Oh, cut the crap." She set her jaw. "Don't play stupid."

My teeth snapped shut. Well, that answered that.

"Why, Rhys?" Sara folded her arms and held my gaze, shooting daggers from her eyes. "Why the fuck did you do it?"

"Is anything I say going to change any—"

"Don't answer my question with a question." She came closer, the glare hardening. "Tell me why. Tell me what in God's name was going through your mind when you made the decision to do that to him when he has been *nothing* but good to you. Oh, and while you're at it? Tell me why the fuck you did something that you *know* is going to break my little girl's heart."

The last fraying thread of my composure was dangerously thin now. Sara had me dead to rights, and I didn't have an answer for her. Not one that would excuse anything. Nothing could excuse that fuck-up that had thrown my family's entire world into chaos. And the reminder that this was going to hurt Vanessa pretty much knocked my legs out from under me.

I leaned against the counter and clenched my jaw so hard it hurt. It didn't matter how raw I was after the last few days with Derek. There was no way in hell I was breaking down here. Not where Derek or—God forbid—Vanessa could walk in and see me.

C'mon, Rhys. Pull it together.

Except...I couldn't. I'd been trying like hell to hold it together for months, and especially for the last few days. I'd even put on the face of a happily married husband for the last twenty-four hours, refusing to let it show that I was dying inside.

Sara may as well have been putting a mirror in my face and forcing me to look at who I was and what I'd done, and the guilt was too much.

"I fucked up," I whispered shakily. "I know I did. There is nothing I could possibly say that'll justify it to you, because there's nothing that'll justify it to me either." Before I could stop myself, I sniffed, and with an unsteady hand, swiped at my eyes. "There's nothing you can say that's going to make me feel worse than I already do." My voice shook and threatened to break as I whispered, "I hurt Derek. I fucked up our marriage. It's going to devastate Vanessa once she finds out. I messed up so bad, and... I mean, I don't even know how to live with that. I don't... I..."

Sara's expression softened, and that didn't help me pull it together at all.

I covered my eyes as I tried like hell to pull it together anyway. I failed. Miserably.

She touched my shoulder. "Rhys, slow down. Just take a breath and—"

"Hey, Mom? Did you find the—"

I dropped my hand and turned just as Vanessa appeared in the doorway, and her gaze went straight to me. Horror and concern took over her expression. "Dad? What's going on?"

I cleared my throat and once again tried to compose myself, but the damage was done. There was no hiding the fact that she'd walked in while I was fighting a losing battle against tears. Didn't stop me from making a valiant effort, though.

Sara stepped between us and started to herd Vanessa toward the door. "Why don't we go back out and—"

"What? No." Vanessa side-stepped her mom and stepped closer to me. "Dad? What's wrong?"

"Nothing, sweetheart." I sniffed and forced a smile. "It's—"

"Like hell it's nothing." She stared at me with wide eyes. "I've seen you cry twice, and it was never over nothing."

Fuck. How was I supposed to explain my way out of this one?

And of course Derek picked that moment to join the party in the kitchen. As soon as he saw us, he halted abruptly, eyes darting to each of us in turn. "Um. What's going on?"

All eyes were on me again.

Beth stepped in behind Derek, a stack of plates in her hands, but instantly seemed to realize there was a tense moment in progress.

She set the plates down and quickly left, and the standoff continued.

"What's wrong?" Vanessa repeated.

So many things that I can't even begin to explain to you.

Sara tried to nudge them both out of the room. "You know what? Why don't we all give Rhys a minute? This isn't the time for—"

Vanessa planted her feet. "Would someone please tell me what's going on?" she asked through gritted teeth. "Because there's no way it's nothing, and now I'm going to worry myself sick until someone tells me."

Derek and I locked eyes. Then he exhaled and turned to her. "Look, we're not trying to hide anything from you. We didn't want..." He shook his head. "We wanted you to enjoy your day and—"

"What aren't you telling me?" Vanessa snapped. "Is someone sick? Are you guys splitting up or something?"

The simultaneous flinches from Derek, Sara, and me could not have been more conspicuous.

Vanessa's jaw went slack and her eyes were huge. "You are, aren't you?" Beat. "What the hell? Are you serious?"

Derek swallowed. "Like I said, we didn't want to tell you until—"

"Screw that. I know now. What... What *happened*?"

Derek and I exchanged another look. We hadn't planned to tell her yet, so we hadn't worked out how much we would tell her.

I took a deep breath. "Listen, we were going to tell you, but then when you told us you were getting married, we wanted to hold off until after—"

"What? I told you guys that months ago! Has... Has this been going on since... *November*? For God's sake, why the hell wouldn't you tell me? I've been tearing my hair out over this wedding, and now you're going to drop this bomb on me the night before? What the hell?"

"We weren't going to drop it on you the night before." Derek made a placating gesture. "We didn't want to tell you until after—"

"Yeah, and how'd that work out for you?" she threw back.

I winced. Vanessa was about as even-keeled as they came. She rarely raised her voice to anyone, never mind one of her parents, but I knew all too well how stressful weddings were. They wore everyone down to their last fraying threads, and even someone as level-headed as Vanessa was bound to snap. Especially if she found out at T-minus eighteen hours pre-wedding that her dads were divorcing.

As the silence in the kitchen wore on, Vanessa's anger evaporated in favor of pure, bone-deep hurt. "I can't believe this." She wiped her eyes with a shaking hand. "You guys should've told me." Before either of us could reply, she walked out.

"Vanessa," Derek called after her, but as he started to follow her, Sara stopped him with a hand on his elbow.

"Let me talk to her," she said. "She might need a minute."

Derek opened his mouth like he was about to protest, but then he deflated and motioned for her to go.

A second later, she was gone.

And we were alone.

A couple of silent seconds ticked by before Derek spun on me and growled, "What the fuck?"

"Hey, don't look at me," I gritted out. "Your ex brought it up. Not me."

"What do you mean?"

"I was in here washing goddamned dishes, and she came at me sideways and started giving me the third degree, and I—" My own anger and defensiveness dropped out from under me like a bone snapping beneath my weight. Shifting my gaze from my angry ex-husband to the doorway our daughter had fled through, I said, "I just couldn't... I can't justify what I did. I'd never try to. And I just..." I had to grit my teeth hard as my emotions threatened to get the best of me again. Damn him and Sara for stomping on that nerve. For picking tonight of all nights to do it. Anger tried to surge forward again, and I grabbed onto it as I faced Derek again. "We shouldn't have kept this from her, and you fucking know it."

"And you shouldn't have fucked him, but that didn't stop you, did it?"

We stared at each other, jaws set and eyes narrow.

Then he shook his head, muttered something I didn't catch, and stormed out of the kitchen.

The instant I was alone, I slumped against the counter. I rubbed my forehead and swore into the empty kitchen. Later, I'd get angry at Derek taking that cheap shot. Later, I'd get pissed at Sara for coming at me like that.

Right now, I was too busy feeling guilty and ashamed, not to mention worrying about Vanessa. We'd known this would devastate her. That was exactly why we hadn't told her before this weekend.

But she knew. There was no putting this cat back into the bag, and with just hours to go before her wedding, she knew.

And I hated myself more than I had in recent memory.

Which said a *lot*.

CHAPTER 14

DEREK

From the slack-jawed, wide-eyed looks I got from the other guests, they'd seen Vanessa leave the kitchen and knew something was wrong. Question was, where did she go? I didn't see her or Sara anywhere.

I did find Beth, though. "Hey, do you know where Vanessa went?"

"I think she and Sara went into the ladies room." She pointed down the hall. "What's going on? She seems so upset."

"Just some family drama. I need to go talk to her. Thanks." I hurried past her and down the hall. At the ladies room door, I hesitated, then knocked.

The door opened a crack, and when Sara saw me, she opened it farther and stepped out into the hall to join me. It didn't shut quite fast enough to mask the sound of my daughter sobbing on the other side, and my heart fucking hurt.

Baby, I am so sorry.

"She's really upset," Sara said. "She had no idea."

"No kidding," I snapped. "We were trying to keep it that way until after this weekend."

She scowled.

"Next time I tell you to keep something between us? Keep it between us." I didn't give her a chance to respond, stepped past her, and pushed the door open. At the sinks with her fiancé, Vanessa was facing away from me, leaning against the counter. In the mirror, there were muddy smears of makeup below her eyes as she cried. I schooled the anger out of my expression, took a deep breath, and approached. "Vanessa?"

She didn't turn, but she sniffed and started wiping her eyes. Corbin shot me a dirty look as he ran his hand up and down her back. He didn't have to say a word—his contempt was palpable.

"Can I have a minute with her?" I asked in a soft voice.

His jaw tightened. He turned to Vanessa. "Babe?"

Without looking at either of us, she nodded.

"Okay." He put an arm around her shoulders, kissed her cheek, and whispered, "I'll be right outside."

Another nod.

He let her go, shot me a murderous glare, and left.

As the door shut quietly behind Corbin, I inched closer to Vanessa, forcing back how much it hurt to see her like this. Especially knowing it was because of me. "Hey, kiddo."

She turned around and looked at me with red eyes, then covered her mouth as she felt apart again.

"God, I am so sorry." I crossed the small bathroom and pulled her into my arms, and I just held her for a moment while she cried on my shoulder. Vanessa was usually tough to a fault—giving the impression she had it together even when she was about to lose it. It was part of why her mom and I had sent her to a therapist in her teens. Not only to adjust to having a stepfather, but so she could learn to express and vent her emotions before she hit her breaking point. She was better about it these days, but she would just never be the kind of person who cried at the drop of a hat. Too much like her mom, I guessed. And even, I thought sadly, her stepdad. Rhys and Vanessa had gently teased me over the years for tearing up during sad movies while they'd effortlessly stayed dry-eyed.

So whenever she did let go and get emotional, it was hard to see because I knew it meant something had well and truly hurt her. And I'd known she'd be devastated by our split. Having that news crash down on her in the middle of all the wedding stress? We'd pushed her beyond her breaking point. Here it was, the night before her wedding, and she was shaking and sobbing in my arms, and it was my fault. Rhys's too, but... I should have told her long before tonight.

After a while, she pulled back, wiped her eyes, and leaned against the counter. Hugging herself, she met my gaze. "What happened?"

I released my breath and rolled my shoulders. A part of me that would die angry at Rhys wanted me to tell her the truth, but I couldn't do that to her. Honestly, I couldn't even do it to Rhys. Maybe he'd ruined what we had, but I wouldn't touch the bond he had with Vanessa.

"Things have been rough for a while. We just..." My voice wavered. Why did telling Vanessa make me feel as brittle and raw as the morning I'd heard Rhys's confession? "We tried to make it work. I guess we just reached a point where we realized we'll be happier apart than together."

She was shaking her head before I'd even finished. "That doesn't make any sense. You can't just work it out? I mean, don't you still love each other?"

Fuck. She might as well have just hit me in the chest. There was no simple answer to that question. Did I still love the man I'd been married to up until the day he'd come home and said he'd cheated? Yes. God, yes. There was nothing I wouldn't do for that man.

But that man was gone. He hadn't existed at all. One night, one confession, and the man living in my house was a stranger to me now. A walking, talking reminder of someone I'd thought was real. Someone I felt stupid for trusting and whom I hated for betraying that trust.

"Dad?"

I exhaled. "It's complicated, I guess. All I know right now is we're not happy being together. So, we're moving on."

"Are you guys at least going to stay friends?"

Another punch to the chest. "We'll see how things play out after we actually separate."

"You...haven't separated?"

"Not yet. We're still figuring out finances and..." *Living together so no one lets it slip to our daughter before her wedding.* I cleared my throat. "It doesn't all happen overnight. Once that part's done, we'll catch our breath and see how the rest shakes out."

She stared at me in disbelief, her eyes closer to dry now, but muddy streaks still marking where tears had slid down her face. "And you've known all this time. Why didn't you tell me?"

I rubbed the back of my neck and sighed. "We knew you were going to be dealing with finals, the holidays, and planning the wedding. We just... we didn't want to pile more on you." I scowled, cutting my eyes toward the door. "This wasn't exactly how we thought things would go. In fact we were trying to avoid it."

Vanessa pursed her lips. "It's out now."

"It is. I'm sorry." I studied her. "Are you going to be okay?"

She took a deep breath, then let it out slowly. With a shaky hand, she tucked a blonde curl behind her ear. "I think so. I'm just... It came out of nowhere, you know?" Her blue eyes started to well up again. "I always thought you and Rhys were happy."

"I know." *I always thought we were too.* "Neither of us is going anywhere, though. We're both still here for you, and we want you to enjoy your day."

Vanessa dropped her gaze and nodded. "I will. And I'm sure you guys know what you're doing. It was just a shock."

I couldn't think of a damn thing to say. No, we didn't know what we were doing. Yeah, it was a shock. I couldn't explain to her how and why it had been a shock to me too, and why it still didn't seem real sometimes. But unless I wanted to tell her—now, the night before her wedding—the real reason Rhys and I were splitting up, I couldn't let it show how badly this was tearing me apart. How lost and betrayed I felt. How I couldn't begin to decide if it hurt more to see Rhys walk into a room or watch him walk out of it.

So I settled on comforting her without words. Silently, I drew her into another hug, and she wrapped her arms around my waist and leaned against me as I rested my chin on top of her head. For the longest time, we just stood there in silence.

I wondered if she felt Rhys's absence as acutely as I did. Something about this moment felt like those years when it had just been her and me, and at the same time, it didn't. As if Rhys had left an indelible mark on both of us. During the years before he'd come along, I'd dated a little, but had been more or less content just doing my job and raising my daughter. She had me and her mother, even if we didn't live together. It didn't seem like anyone was missing.

And then Rhys had been there, and from that point on, it had been impossible to imagine that there'd ever been two of us instead of three.

He was probably still in this building right now. For all I knew, he was just outside the ladies' room door.

But more than he had since the moment he'd told me the truth, Rhys felt like he was on the other side of the world. Like he was, in every way imaginable, gone, and nothing would ever be the same.

Why did you have to go?

I stayed with Vanessa for another twenty minutes or so. We mostly talked about where things would go from here with me and Rhys, but I managed to steer the conversation to the wedding. By the time we left the ladies room, she was smiling again, though she still had some tears in her eyes.

Corbin was waiting outside as he'd promised, and he gathered her into a hug. "You okay?"

"Yeah. I think so."

He looked at me over her shoulder. Some of the venom had left his expression, but he was still obviously not happy with me. Couldn't say I blamed him.

While he stayed with Vanessa, I returned to the banquet hall where tonight's rehearsal dinner had been and tomorrow's reception would be. Some people had left, but most were milling around with obvious questions in their eyes. Two steps into the room, I had everyone's attention.

I kept my head down even as I searched for Rhys and Sara. He was nowhere in sight. She was having a quiet conversation with Beth near the kitchen. I didn't really want to talk toeither of them, but I needed to, so I headed her way.

My sister stopped me, though. "Hey. Is it true? You and Rhys are splitting up?"

I had a feeling I was going to be answering that question a lot this weekend. Well, I deserved it. With a sigh, I nodded. "Yeah. It's true."

"Oh my God. I had no idea." She touched my shoulder. "How are you doing?"

"I've been better, to be honest. I'll be okay, though. I just wish Vanessa hadn't found out like this."

"I believe it." She straightened, a hint of panic in her expression. "Oh, you and Rhys are staying together at the house!"

I barely kept myself from groaning. "Yeah, we are."

"Uh, do you want... Would it be easier...?" Her eyebrows rose.

It was so tempting to suggest tossing him out and making him find a hotel for the night, but things were fraught enough between him and me. The name of the game now was damage control and keeping the tension from getting worse.

"Let him keep the guest room. I can sleep on the couch or something."

"Are you sure?"

"Yeah. His back and couches..." I shook my head. "It'll be fine."

"Okay. I'll text one of the kids and have them put out some sheets and a blanket for you."

"Perfect. Thanks." I paused. "Is there, um, any chance I could ride back with you, too?"

"Of course." Her brow furrowed. "How bad *are* things? Everything seemed fine when you got to the house."

I grimaced. "We've been trying really hard to look like it's all fine because we didn't want anything getting out quite yet. But yeah, things are, um... They're not great."

"Jesus. I would never have guessed."

"That was the idea." I glanced around. "Have you seen him, by any chance?"

She pursed her lips. "I think he was helping Corbin's dad take out some trash, but I haven't seen him for a little while."

"Thanks. I'll see if I can find him."

As I walked away to track Rhys down, I paused to steal a look at Sara. She'd been drinking pretty heavily earlier, but as she spoke with Beth, it was clear she'd sobered up. She'd actually seemed pretty sober by the time I'd walked into the kitchen after she'd confronted Rhys. Now she was even steadier on her feet, though she winced at the light, as if she were already getting hung over.

Normally, we got along well, but I was feeling less than charitable toward her tonight, and I decided the visibly unpleasant headache served her right.

Which...made me think that maybe now wasn't the time to talk to her *or* Rhys. I could catch her tomorrow before the wedding. I could wait to talk to him until we were back at my sister's house. At least then if things blew up, Vanessa wouldn't hear any of it. She'd been through enough for tonight.

So instead of my daughter's mother or my ex-husband, I went looking to see if I could help with any cleanup from tonight or prep for tomorrow.

The uncomfortable conversations could wait.

It was almost ten when Amy and I made it to the house. Rhys's truck was parked on the curb, so I didn't have to ask if he'd already come back. Great. I supposed it was too much to ask for him to be in the shower when I slipped into the guest room to collect my things? Probably, yeah. And my shaving kit was in the bathroom. Damn it.

On the other hand, we still needed to talk before tomorrow. Whether we liked it or not, our *"pretend we can stand each other"* act was about to be more crucial than ever. The truth was out that we were divorcing, but we had to put on a united front for the wedding. We *had* to.

So, after I'd said good night to my sister, I dragged myself down the hall to the guest room. I gave it a light knock so I didn't startle him, then stepped into the room.

Rhys was reclining on the bed with his phone propped against his thigh. As I closed the door, he sat up. "Um. Hey."

"Hey." I swallowed. "Amy is going to let me crash on the couch. So we, uh, can have a little space."

"Okay. Good." He put his phone aside. "What about Vanessa? How is she?"

I winced. "She's not happy, but I think she'll be okay. I hope she will."

"Yeah, I hope so too."

We exchanged glances. I wondered if mine was as unreadable to him as his was to me.

I broke eye contact and cleared my throat. "Anyway. I should just get my stuff and go downstairs. We probably both need to sleep."

"Yeah." He paused. "And, um, I'm sorry it came out this way. Sara caught me off guard, and I didn't think Vanessa would come in, and..." He exhaled, shoulders drooping. "I didn't mean for it to come out this way."

"I know. I don't think anybody did. Not much we can do about it now." The words came out with a bit more venom than I'd intended, and it only took a glance to confirm that he'd caught it.

His features tightened. "We should have just told her from the start and not tried to—"

"Or *you* could have kept your dick in your pants," I snapped. "Then we wouldn't have to deal *any* of this."

Rhys blinked. He stared at me with a mix of surprise and hurt, but that quickly dissolved into anger. "You really want to fight that fight tonight, don't you?"

"Why the fuck not? I've been biting my tongue all—"

"You know what?" he ground out. "You can blame me for what's happening to our marriage. I won't deny that's my fault. But what happened tonight?" He stabbed a finger at me. "That's on you. You wanted to hide this from Vanessa, and you vented all my sins to your ex, so tonight? *You* get to own that. Not me."

It was my turn for a blink of surprise, but Rhys wasn't done.

"What did you think was going to happen, huh?" He narrowed his eyes at me. "Vanessa isn't stupid. Did you really think we could fly under her radar? And what if we did? Were you going to wait until she came back from her honeymoon, then drop it on her? What's the—"

"What difference does it make now?" I snarled. "She knows. She's pissed. We might've just ruined her fucking wedding. You happy?"

"Of course I'm not happy. Do you actually think I'd be *happy* about something like this? I don't want to be right if it means wrecking our daughter's wedding. I've—" His voice hitched, then suddenly softened. "I've wrecked enough for one lifetime, thanks."

"Yeah," I said through my teeth. "Maybe it'll make you think twice in the future."

Rhys flinched, but he didn't get defensive this time. He avoided my gaze, and he said nothing. Maybe there was nothing left to say.

If there was, it could wait until some other time. Tonight, I needed to at least try to get some sleep so I wasn't a zombie at the wedding.

So much for unfucking everything—or anything—before tomorrow.

I gathered my shaving kit and suitcase, and without speaking to Rhys, I left the guest room for the living room.

There was a downstairs bathroom, thank God, so I used that to get ready for bed. One of Amy's kids had made up the couch, and I sighed with relief as I settled onto the cushions and pulled up the covers. Time to sleep. Recharge as much as I could before tomorrow.

The house was still now. In a weird way, it reminded me of the calm after a firefight. After the bullets had stopped flying, wounds had stopped bleeding, and damage had been assessed. When everything was just...quiet.

It wasn't peace. Maybe the immediate conflict and danger had passed, but the war wasn't over. Sometimes during my combat tours, I'd wondered if those periods were worse than the actual fighting. At least when we were taking enemy fire, we could react. We could determine where it was coming from, how to get out of its way, how to neutralize it.

When this quiet fell, there was no telling when or how it would be broken.

Of course this bullshit with Rhys wasn't the same dangerous, traumatic insanity that had gone on during my combat tours, but there was definitely some déjà vu in the quiet between the storms. We weren't done fighting. That much I knew. It was just a matter of what would set us off and when.

I closed my eyes and exhaled.

Nothing to do now except wait for the next firefight or the orders to go home. Whichever came first.

The next morning, I dressed, borrowed one of my sister's cars, and headed over to Sara's house, where Vanessa was staying before the wedding. I'd texted Sara to let her know, and she met me at the door with a sheepish look.

"Hey," she said as she let me in.

"Hey. How's Vanessa?"

"Oh, she's still upset. I think she'll be okay today, but..."

I nodded as I shrugged off my jacket. "She's a tough kid. This is one of those times I just wish she didn't have to be."

"Yeah, I agree." She cleared her throat. "Listen, um. While we have a minute, I wanted to say I'm sorry. About blindsiding Rhys last night. It really wasn't my place, and I knew that. I just..." Sighing, she shook her head. "Seeing you hurting like that, I guess I lost it."

I chewed my lip. I desperately wanted to be pissed at her for it, but she'd always been protective of people she loved. Asking her to put on a happy face and pretend she didn't know what was going on between Rhys and me would be like asking me to pretend I didn't know some horrible truth about my new son-in-law.

Also, whether I was pissed or not, I had to coexist with Sara today as much as I did Rhys. If nothing else, for our daughter's sake, I didn't want this blowing up. I still needed to contain the fire with Rhys.

"Don't worry about it," I said. "Everyone's stressed. Shit happens."

"It does. But I shouldn't have put Rhys in that position. Especially since you asked me not to. So, I'm sorry."

"It's okay." I touched her arm and managed a slight smile. "I mean it."

She studied me uncertainly. Then she broke eye contact and gestured down the hall. "Vanessa just got up a little while ago. I'll go get her for you."

"Thanks."

Sara disappeared down the hall. A moment later, Vanessa emerged, dressed in jeans and a button-up blouse.

"Hey." I smiled. "I just came by to see how you're doing."

She shrugged tightly. "I'm okay, I guess. I just can't get over everything with you and Rhys."

My smile fell. "Yeah, it must have been a shock." *Sure as hell was for me.* "But you know we're all still here for you, right? And we're all thrilled to be watching you get married today."

She chewed her lip. "Is it weird that I'm scared Rhys won't be around after this?"

"Of course he will be."

Her eyebrows rose.

I took her hand. "You don't even remember Mom and me being together, but we've both been there for you from day one. Right?"

She nodded. "But you're my *parents*. Rhys is..." Her brow pinched.

"He loves you, kiddo. That hasn't changed." I gave her hand a gentle squeeze. "This thing, it's between Rhys and me. It has nothing to do with you. If you still want him to be part of your life after this, that's up to the two of you."

She studied me. "So, if I want to stay in touch with him...you won't be upset?"

"Of course not."

"Oh thank God."

"Did you really think I'd tell you to cut things off with him?"

"I..." Vanessa shook her head. "I have no idea. I'm just glad you're not."

"Never in a million years."

"Good. I need to talk to him, though. Before today gets going." She tapped a nail on her phone's screen. "Do you know if he's awake? I don't want to text him and wake him up."

"I'm not sure, but he'll probably be on his way to the church in a little while. I can let him know you want to talk to him."

"You...don't mind?" Her brow pinched. "It looked like things were heated between you guys last night."

I forced myself not to visibly react to the reminder of how volatile I'd left things with Rhys. "They were. Which is why I need to talk to him myself." I gave her another gentle squeeze. "I promise, things will be better today. We'll talk some things through, and then I'll have him come talk to you. We'll all be fine, okay?"

She nodded. "Okay. Thanks." She checked her phone and took a deep breath. "I guess Mom and I should get going."

"All right. I'll catch up."

She smiled, though it still looked a little sad. "I'll see you there." We shared a quick hug, and I started to go but hesitated.

"Vanessa?"

She met my eyes, eyebrows up.

I swallowed. "I mean it—I'm sorry I didn't tell you before this weekend. I should have..." I shook my head. "I'm sorry."

A small, sad smile appeared on her lips, and she came back over and hugged me again, tighter this time. "It's okay. It just caught me by surprise."

"I know." I squeezed my eyes shut and stroked her hair. "And like I said, I'll tell him as soon as I see him that you're looking for him."

"Thanks."

We let each other go and exchanged smiles. Then we joined Sara outside and headed for the church.

As I followed Sara's car, my stomach was in knots at the prospect of talking to Rhys. It was something we needed to do, but I definitely wasn't looking forward to it.

My conversation with Vanessa replayed through my head. I wasn't sure why I was choked up at the thought of them staying in contact after the divorce. It wasn't jealousy. I didn't want her to cut him off. In fact, I was relieved she still wanted him in her life. They'd been close for a long time, and continuing that relationship would be good for both of them.

Rhys's transition from softball coach to Dad's boyfriend to stepdad hadn't been entirely smooth. Vanessa was twelve when Rhys came into the picture, fourteen when he'd become her stepfather, and he and I had both known there would be bumps. There had been, and we'd all taken them as they came.

What we hadn't expected was... Well, shit. Almost everything.

Rhys hadn't elbowed his way in and taken over some role that had previously been mine or Sara's. My role and Sara's hadn't changed when he'd entered the picture. His relationship with Vanessa, their stepfather-stepdaughter dynamic, had been their own from the start, complete with head-butting, pushback, and plenty of frustration from both sides. There was no reason for that to change now, and despite my bitterness toward Rhys, I genuinely hoped it didn't. I wanted them to stay close. No one ever had or ever would be what Rhys had been for her. I prayed like hell he still wanted that too, but that praying seemed kind of pointless. I could say a lot about Rhys. That he'd disappear from Vanessa's life just because we were done? Not a chance.

Way back then, when it had become clear that Rhys was going to be a fixture in both our lives, Vanessa had asked what she could call him. I hadn't had any preference. Rhys hadn't either. We'd both been more than a little blown away when she'd settled on "Dad." She still called him by his first name when she needed to differentiate between him and me, but the rest of the time, he was Dad.

And no matter how much my heart ached at the thought of him, I knew he would always be Dad to her, just like I would be.

Talking to him this morning wouldn't be easy. But if it was to let him know his daughter needed to see him so he could reassure her that she could still call him Dad?

Hell yeah, I'd talk to him.

CHAPTER 15

RHYS

As I tied my bowtie, I avoided my own gaze in the closet door's mirror. Dressed head to toe in black, I felt like I was getting ready for a funeral, not my daughter's wedding. Hopefully today's mood was more wedding than funeral. At least better than last night. That wasn't too much to ask for, was it?

Derek had already left, apparently riding in to the church with his sister, so thank God for that. I drove in my own truck and just prayed—repeatedly—that today was peaceful and focused on the kids getting married, not the two jackasses getting divorced.

I'd barely stepped out of the truck, though, when Derek appeared beside me. I bristled but tried not to let it show.

He cleared his throat. "Hey. Vanessa's asking for you."

"Oh." I looked around. "Where is she?"

He motioned toward the church. "Go inside, go left, and it's the third door on your right."

"Okay. Sure." I paused. "How is...uh...everything?"

Derek avoided my gaze. "I think it'll be better after you talk with her, but everyone's calmer than last night."

"I guess that's something." I glanced at the church steps. The morning was bitterly cold, and there'd been ice on the road on my way in. Just to be on the safe side, I pulled my folded cane out from under the driver's seat.

As we started up the steps, Derek paused. "Do you, um..." He tentatively offered his elbow.

Pride and a whole lot of other things made me want to insist I could make it on my own. Past experience—not to mention some shiny spots on the steps, especially closer to the metal railing—made me think twice.

Without a word, I took his elbow, and we carefully and silently made our way to the top. The steps weren't as slick as they could have been, but better safe than sorry. Vanessa had dealt with enough bullshit without one of her soon-to-be-divorced dads winding up in the ER on her wedding day.

As soon as we'd cleared the top step, I let go of Derek's arm, but he stayed close until we were through the door.

"Thanks," I murmured, folding my cane as we stepped inside.

"Don't mention it."

We exchanged uncomfortable glances. Then he gestured down the hall. "She's, um..."

"Right. Yeah. Thanks."

I followed his directions to a Sunday school classroom that had apparently been designated for the bride and bridesmaids to get ready. Inside, Vanessa's dress hung in a garment bag beside the door, a pair of white pumps arranged on the floor beside them. She was in jeans and a button-up shirt, her hair and makeup already done, but the tears she was valiantly trying to hold back were smudging the hell out of her mascara. The second she saw me, the dam broke, and so did my heart.

Without speaking, I set my cane on the table by the door, crossed the room, and hugged her, and she held me tighter than I thought she ever had.

"I am so sorry," I said, stroking her hair. "We really, really didn't mean to drop this on you today of all days."

"I know. But I mean...even after I talked to Dad, I just can't get my head around it." She sniffed. "You're really leaving?"

My heart broke all over again at the childlike softness of her voice. Christ. She was supposed to be focusing on getting married today, not grieving my marriage to her dad.

All I could say was, "I'm sorry, kiddo."

"Have you guys at least *tried* to fix it?"

I squeezed my eyes shut. What was broken here wasn't getting fixed. "We've tried."

She sighed, and she was quiet for a moment, as if she was absorbing everything. "Will it be weird if I stay in touch with you?"

"Weird?" I pulled back and stared at her. "What? No. Of course not." I clasped her hand between both of mine. "Your dad and I are splitting up, but it's not like I'm going out for cigarettes and just not coming back. All our problems—they're between me and him. Nothing has to change here."

That seemed to ease some of the tightness in her features and her shoulders. "Okay. I..." She laughed bitterly and kneaded her forehead. "I still can't believe this."

"God, I'm so sorry. We should have told you so you didn't find out like you did." Sighing, I squeezed my eyes shut. *And I'm so sorry your dad and I are getting divorced at all.* Then I looked in her eyes and gently took her shoulders in my hands. "I know you're upset. I don't blame you at all. But this is still your wedding, and the one thing your dad and I want more than anything is for you to be happy. We want you to enjoy your day, not worry about us."

Her shoulders sank beneath my hands. "I guess it's just a shock."

"It is, and it's not one you should have to deal with today of all days. But I promise it's bigger than it sounds. We're still here this weekend for *you*, no matter what."

Vanessa sniffed. "But if it sounds than bigger it is, why were you crying when I walked in last night?"

I winced. "It hurts. I won't pretend it doesn't."

"If it hurts that much, then why are you guys still splitting up?"

Because I hurt your dad too much for him to stay with me.

"It's not quite that simple." I sounded resigned even to myself. "There's a lot of emotions to sort through. I guess last night, it got the best of me at the worst possible time." *Probably because your drunk mother came at me at the worst possible time, but you don't need to know that.* "It's a wedding. There's a lot of stress and a lot of emotions. I'm just sorry this one came out."

She nodded slowly.

"And yes, we'll absolutely stay in touch. I promise." I gently took her hand between mine. "Remember when your dad and I got married, and we had you come up to the altar with us? Because we wanted to have some vows that included all three of us?"

A tear rolled down her cheek, and she sniffed sharply as she nodded.

"Do you remember what I said?"

She pressed her lips together, then whispered, "You said you weren't just marrying my dad. And after that day, we'd be a family."

"Exactly." I brushed the tear away. "And even though things didn't work out with your dad, I'm not going to just ride off into the sunset and disappear. I made a promise that day to be there for you and love you like you were my own daughter. Because as far as I'm concerned, you were, and you still are. Nothing is changing there."

She searched my eyes as hers welled up again. To my surprise, she laughed as she wiped her eyes. "I kind of feel stupid now for asking. I didn't really think you'd...you know, disappear."

"It's okay." I squeezed her shoulder. "You can ask whatever you need to ask to get through this. Even if you think it's stupid or it'll hurt our feelings. Capisce?"

Vanessa smiled. "Capisce."

I smiled back.

She took a deep breath and, as she released it, rolled her shoulders. "Ugh, I need to pull myself together." She wiped her eyes and cheeks, then glared down at her hands. "My makeup is going to be all fucked up if I'm puffy, and... ugh."

"You've got time. Don't worry."

"I'm a bride. I'm going to worry."

"You're also your father's daughter."

"True." She hugged me tight. "Thanks, Dad. I'm sorry I—"

"You don't have to apologize. I'm the one who's sorry." *For reasons I can't begin to tell you.* "We came together and kept things on the down low because we want today to be about you. That hasn't changed. So, whatever you need from us to make sure today is still perfect, say the word."

She pulled back and met my gaze, and there was a flicker of *"don't split up,"* but she didn't say it out loud. She was far too pragmatic for that. Upset, yes, but realistic. Which was probably why she was so upset—she was all too aware of the reality of the situation and what little she or anyone else could do to change it.

"I'm going to duck out so you can get ready." I glanced at my phone. "I think the photographer's going to be here soon."

Vanessa nodded.

I hugged her one more time, and murmured, "Love you, kiddo."

"Love you too, Dad."

I smiled, then left her to get ready. The wedding wasn't for a few hours yet, so she'd have plenty of time to get the redness out of her eyes and cheeks.

As soon as I was out the door and out of earshot, I stopped to release a heavy breath. This was not a conversation I'd ever thought I'd have to have with my daughter on her wedding day. It was not an exaggeration to say I was having some serious regrets right now about things I'd done in my relatively recent past.

There wasn't much I could do about any of that, though, so I focused on whatever it took to keep today from going to shit for Vanessa. Step one, while she got ready, I needed to have a talk with Derek, so I went looking for him.

I found him outside the sanctuary, sipping from a Styrofoam cup of coffee. "Hey." I steeled myself. "Can we talk?"

He glanced at me, features tightening. Then he drained his

coffee, tossed the cup in a trash can by the door, and slid his hands into his pockets. "Yeah. Sure. How's Vanessa?"

"Better. I think she'll be okay. She just needed some reassurance that we're okay. Each of us, I mean. Not...um..."

"I know what you meant."

"Right. So yeah, she's upset, but she'll be all right. I, um..." I thought for a moment. "Listen, that agreement we made before we left on this trip? I know it's easier said than done now, and it kind of blew up in our faces, but I think we *need* to go back to that. Put it all aside and don't make today about us or our problems." I swallowed hard. "Today has got to be about Vanessa."

"I know it does. There's just been..." He exhaled, rubbing his neck with both hands. "The last few days... Especially last night..."

"I know. It's been rougher than I think either of us bargained for. But for her sake..."

He nodded slowly. "Yeah. I agree. I'm just worried... I mean, we've been trying all kinds of truces and..." He waved a hand. "Look where we are."

"I know. But it's not just us now. And I mean, you were still willing to give me your arm on the way up the stairs this morning. Which—thank you again, by the way. But the point is, there's no reason we can't do the rest of the day the same way, you know? Think of it like keeping each other upright so a fall doesn't ruin everything."

Derek's lips quirked as if he were mulling it over. "Yeah, I can work with that, I think." He still seemed skeptical. Not that I blamed him.

"We already know we're over and we're not going back. Everything that needs to be said has been said." I struggled to hold his gaze and forced a cautious laugh. "If you can act like you like me for the next twenty-four hours, at least enough to not let me fall down the stairs and break my neck, I promise I won't read anything into it."

He actually chuckled too, avoiding my eyes for a second. "All right. I, um...yeah. I think we can do that."

"So...truce?"

Derek hesitated, but nodded. "Okay. Truce."

I released my breath and managed to smile. "Okay. Good. Good." I looked around, clearing my throat. "So, do they need us anywhere?"

He shook his head. "Not really. The photographer's going to want some portraits before and after the ceremony, though, so kind of hover around the sanctuary, I guess."

"I can do that."

He gestured at the cane in my hand. "You, um, want me to stash that in your truck so you don't have to carry it around? And so it doesn't disappear?"

I glanced down at it. "You don't mind?"

"Nah. I'll grab it before we need to leave for the reception. Doesn't sound like the weather's going to get any warmer, so it might get icy."

"Okay. Yeah." I handed it to him, then fished my car keys out of my pocket. "Thanks."

He met my gaze, and we both managed subtle but genuine smiles.

Then he left the sanctuary with my cane and keys, and once I was alone, I exhaled just like I had after I'd talked to Vanessa. None of this meant our shit was resolved, but if we could get through today and tomorrow without any more blowups or breakdowns, if we could focus on our daughter's happiness and nothing else, then I'd call it a win.

Please God, let us hold it together this time.

CHAPTER 16

DEREK

I was relieved that Rhys had suggested a truce. I'd been thinking along the same lines, but I'd been second-guessing myself all morning. That seemed stupid now—there was a lot I could say about Rhys, but I should have known he'd prioritize Vanessa as much as I did today. The last few days had left me questioning whether we really could put our differences aside in the name of functioning together, but of course we could do that today of all days. We were adults. Today was about our daughter. We could do this.

As the ceremony started, Rhys and I stood at the beginning of the aisle with Sara. We all exchanged nervous glances, followed by reassuring nods and nervous but still somehow reassuring smiles. The air was taut between the three of us. A lot of things had been said that shouldn't have, and a lot of things still *needed* to be said, but there wasn't much we could do now. Sara, Rhys, and I could sort last night out later. Today...Vanessa.

When it was our turn to start down the aisle, I offered Sara my elbow. She took it, and with her other hand, took Rhys's, and the three of us walked down the aisle to our seats in the front row. I was tempted for a second to have Sara sit between us as well, but that would be too conspicuous. So, I sat with Sara and Rhys on either side of me while Corbin's family took their seats on the opposite front row.

The bridesmaids and groomsmen made their entrances as well. The best man was Corbin's older brother, who wore his Navy dress blues, and the second groomsman was their youngest brother, who was Army like Corbin. The rest were in tuxes.

Corbin joined his groomsmen, also in his dress uniform. He took a deep breath and stared up the aisle with a huge smile on his face.

Then the music changed, and everyone stood and turned.

Being her father, I was probably biased as hell, but as Vanessa started walking down the aisle, she looked amazing. Two seconds in, I was getting choked up because holy shit, my daughter was coming down the aisle in a white dress with a rose bouquet, gaze fixed on her soon-to-be husband and a big, bright smile on her face. She was getting married. My little girl was getting married.

Standing to my left, Sara made a subtle gesture of wiping her eyes. To my right, Rhys did the same. Someone sniffed. Well, at least it wasn't just me.

As she passed our row, Vanessa turned to the three of us. Her smile faltered for just a second but then brightened again. There were wheels turning that she'd discovered at the worst possible moment, but right now, we were focused on her, and I think she saw that in all our eyes. Whatever else was going on in the world, nothing could change how happy the three of us were to see her marrying Corbin today.

We all sat down, and sitting between my two exes, I just beamed up at our daughter. I was so proud of the young woman we'd raised. She was smart, kind, strong, ambitious. I'd admittedly questioned her taste in guys a few times, but I liked Corbin. Though they were young, they both had their heads screwed on straight. Their future together would be a good one, I was sure of it.

And to think, her mother and I had worried ourselves sick before Vanessa was born that we wouldn't know what we were doing. To be fair, we hadn't, but we'd done the best we could, and our daughter had turned out just fine.

It wasn't only me and Sara, either. Rhys had come into the picture late in the game, but it would be disingenuous to say he hadn't had a profound impact on Vanessa. In fact, he'd already started having one before we'd started dating. As her softball coach, he'd given her just the right amount of encouragement and criticism, balancing the need for motivation with the information to improve her technique. When she was in high school and didn't make varsity softball, he was the one who'd stayed outside in the backyard, tirelessly helping her with her form. Every morning, rain or shine, they'd jog together. By the time tryouts rolled around the following year, she'd been a shoo-in for varsity and had led the team to back-to-back state championships.

That was to say nothing of how much he helped with her schoolwork. Academia had never been my strong point, but Rhys was a teacher, and when she'd struggled with a subject, he'd been the one hunched over textbooks at the kitchen table, walking her through the material until she understood it. Her mother or I could have helped her through it, but not like he did. He was one of those teachers who could explain things clearly without talking down. Vanessa had struggled with her schoolwork in elementary school, and she was touchy about anyone who made her feel stupid, and Rhys never did. Not once. Even now, while she was in college, they Skyped or instant messaged when she needed help studying.

My throat tightened around my breath. There was no denying that Vanessa wouldn't be the woman she was today without the man sitting beside me. As I watched her saying her vows to my new son-in-law, I had to wonder if that alone should give Rhys some amnesty. Yeah, he'd fucked up. But look at the woman he, Sara, and I had raised. Look at the life we'd made together—a home, careers, friends.

For the past few months, thinking about that made me want to lash out at him and demand to know why he was willing to throw it all away over one night of sex with a stranger.

Today I couldn't help but ask myself the same thing.

And for the life of me, I couldn't come up with an answer.

The reception kicked off with dinner, and I sat between Sara and Rhys. While it wasn't the *most* comfortable arrangement, we all stuck to our truce. As long as we kept conversation light, things stayed peaceful, and nobody made any attempts to steer it away from those light topics. No snide comments. No backhanded remarks. No subtle digs. Man, if Rhys and I could keep this up, maybe I wouldn't need a rental car or a plane ticket for the return trip after all.

As with all receptions, there were toasts. Rhys and I each read ours after the best man, the maid of honor, and Corbin's father, and we even managed to laugh a few times during the other's brief speech. I nearly choked on my drink at Beth's disapproving scowl when Rhys made a comment about Vanessa probably being too mouthy to hang out with the Army wives, and he snorted audibly when I made our daughter groan with embarrassment over a story about her junior prom. If I squinted hard enough, I could almost believe that everything was fine between us. Almost.

After dinner, the deejay called Vanessa and Corbin out onto the floor for their first dance.

My heart fluttered from the joy of seeing my daughter so happy with her new husband, and also from the relief that everything from last night hadn't been enough to kill that joy. Her wedding would probably be a bittersweet memory, something I would regret until the end of time, but there'd been a lot more tears of happiness than anything else today. I could live with that.

Their song had barely begun to fade when the deejay said, "Now it's time for Vanessa's father-daughter dance. Derek? Where are you, Derek?"

"Oh." I put my drink down. "I guess I should get up there."

"Yes you should." Sara nudged my shoulder. "Go!"

I laughed and joined the couple in the middle of the dancefloor, shook hands with Corbin, and then he stepped aside while I took Vanessa's hand.

And...wow. Jesus. My daughter. A bride. All grown up and married. Didn't she just start kindergarten last week?

"You're not going to get all choked up again, are you?" Her voice was a little thick.

"What do you—" I cleared my throat. "What do you mean, *again?*"

"Oh come on." She rolled her eyes. "Don't act like you didn't."

"Okay. Maybe a bit."

"Uh-huh."

"What can I say? It's kind of mind-blowing watching your kid get married." I smirked. "You'll understand once you're watching your own kids getting—"

"Oh shut up." She laughed, and so did I.

"Seriously, though," I said. "I'm so happy for both of you."

Vanessa smiled up at me. "Thanks. His family's a little nuts, but I like him."

I chuckled. "Well, I would hope you like him. You're kind of stuck with him now."

She laughed too, but then our humor faded as what I'd said really sank in.

"You know what I mean," I said softly.

"I know. I know. And I..." She shook her head. "I just wish you guys had told me. But as long as you and Rhys are happy..."

Happy? I'm the farthest I've ever been from happy.

"Don't worry about us. He'll be okay. I'll be okay." *When?* "It's not the end of the world."

She sighed.

"We'll all be all right," I said. "He's still your dad even if we're not together. I just wish we could have done this without putting a damper on your wedding. We thought—"

"Dad. Don't. Yes, it's a tough thing to get my head around, and yes, I wish you guys had told me sooner, but we can't change it. As long as you and Rhys are going to be okay after you split up, I'll live with it."

I put on my best *Dad's okay even though he's dying inside* smile. "We will be."

"That's all I can ask for."

We continued our dance until the song started to fade, and then the deejay came over the microphone again. "Rhys? Where's Rhys? Your daughter would like a dance with you too."

Vanessa and I stopped, and I gave her a tight hug before I let her go. Rhys and I met each other's eyes as he came onto the dancefloor, and... Damn. We really were getting good at hiding this, weren't we? Nothing in his expression—or hopefully mine—betrayed everything beneath the surface.

As I stepped back, he took my place. We exchanged smiles, somehow hiding all traces of awkwardness, and then his attention was on Vanessa.

I slipped back into the crowd and watched them.

As they danced, sharing a conversation only they could hear, all the emotions I'd had during the wedding came crashing back in. All the memories of what a fixture Rhys had been in Vanessa's world. Of how we'd been a small, perfect, complete family.

I'd been itching for the moment when he and I could finally separate, but as I watched him sharing a dance with our newly married daughter, the thought of him exiting stage left after this suddenly took my breath away.

For months I'd told myself that I'd done the right thing by breaking things off. What kind of self-respect did I have if I took back someone who'd cheated?

After that, we'd forced ourselves to stay together (sort of) in the name of economics and, more recently, flying below Vanessa's radar, and now I wondered if that forced proximity had been a blessing in disguise. Instead of separating and moving on, we'd had no choice but to stay close enough that I could see the effect this had on him every single day. I couldn't delude myself into thinking he felt nothing about what he'd done. That he was cold and spiteful.

Because the fact was, Rhys had been nothing but contrite. He'd never denied what he did. He'd come clean about it almost immediately, and he'd worn his conscience on his sleeve ever since. In all the months that had gone by, he'd never once tried to downplay it as just one night, or tell me that at least he hadn't done more than have sex with someone. From the get go, he'd been devastated and repentant, and whenever it had come up—especially when I'd angrily thrown it in his face—another crack would show. As if he were crumbling under the weight of his own guilt, and he was one verbal slap in the face away from collapsing.

Maybe that was what he'd done last night. Sara had confronted him, and he'd broken. The weight of his own guilt had toppled him, and did I have any right to be surprised? It wasn't like I could pretend he hadn't been hurting all this time, and it wasn't just when people were looking, either. There'd been dozens of times where I'd come into a room and found him with tears in his eyes or that distinct blotchiness of someone who'd been crying recently. He'd usually try to hide it, too. Maybe he was embarrassed that he was so emotional. Maybe he was afraid I'd notice and accuse him of trying to make me feel guilty.

Maybe...maybe he was right.

I cringed, swallowing hard as I watched him and our daughter dancing. I'd *wanted* him to feel that bad about what he'd done. I'd *wanted* him to wallow in his own mistake and not go a day without knowing how badly he'd fucked up.

But now...

"*I mean, don't you still love each other?*"

Getting a lump in my throat at the sight of Rhys wasn't an unusual thing these days, but this felt different. It wasn't that feeling like I wanted to break down because he'd hurt me and I couldn't stand the sight of him.

It was because...

Oh, fuck me.

Sitting quietly a lifetime ago on the couch with him sleeping on my shoulder, I'd realized I was in love with him.

Standing here now at the edge of a dancefloor while he danced with the daughter he'd treated like his own child from day one, I realized I was *still* in love with him.

I had to swallow hard to get that lump to move. As I gazed at him and Vanessa, I couldn't deny the truth—I still loved him. Not in that *"I'll always love him even if we're not together anymore"* kind of way. No, I loved him. Deeply. Fiercely. As profoundly as I had the day we'd been the ones saying "I do."

The song ended, and he and Vanessa shared a long hug. Then her new husband politely cut in, and Rhys watched them with a fond smile for a moment before he bowed out and walked off the dancefloor.

Our eyes met. Only for a second, but long enough for a million unreadable emotions to register in his expression and God knew how many to ping pong through my guilt-addled mind. He quickly dropped his gaze as his smile evaporated.

Christ. He'd been the picture of pride and joy while he'd danced with Vanessa. One look at me, and he once again had his conscience on his sleeve.

My mouth dry and my heart sick, I watched him walk away.

He'd fucked up. *Once.* I had no reason to believe it had happened before that night. I'd told myself for months that I could never trust him again, but now I wondered if, with as mercilessly as he'd been beating himself up over it, the opposite was true. If Rhys had become the last man on earth who'd cheat because his conscience couldn't take it.

Or maybe that was all wishful thinking because, for the first time, I wanted to believe we could come back from this.

Oblivious to me watching him, and definitely oblivious to everything going on in my head, Rhys went to the bar for another drink. Once he had the glass in hand, though, he didn't return to the table.

Instead, he stepped outside through a door the staff had propped open to let some air into the stuffy room.

I didn't follow. I wanted to—more than I had in a long time, I wanted to be where Rhys was—but I held back because this wasn't the time or place to hash out our problems. I needed to think things over, too. Right?

My mind just kept circling back to the thought I'd had during the ceremony. That I'd hated Rhys for killing our marriage with that one night in a stranger's bed, but now I had to wonder—was I, on some level, doing the same thing? No, I hadn't been the one to break my vows and cheat, but I'd let that one night end everything we had.

Rhys had fucked up by going to bed with that guy.

Was I also fucking up by letting that one mistake end our marriage?

Cheating *was* a deal-breaker. There *was* no going back. It *was* a red line. Our fate *had* been sealed the moment he'd decided to sleep with someone else.

So why did I want to run after him and try to unfuck our marriage?

As I stared at the door Rhys had stepped out of, it was hard to conjure up the certainty I'd had the morning after he'd cheated. On the heels of that kind of betrayal, it had been easy to hate him and be done with him. After watching him dance with our daughter at her wedding, after thinking back to everything he'd been for her and for me for the last nine years, after realizing the lump in my throat was grief and not anger... *Was* I really sure about where things went from here? Or could I—and did I want to—course correct?

Someone stepped up beside me, and I almost expected it to be Rhys. To my surprise—kind of—I was disappointed it wasn't.

"There you are." Sara offered a tight, uneasy smile. "I've been looking for you."

"Oh." I swallowed and managed a halfhearted laugh. "Well, you found me."

The smile warmed a little, though she still seemed uncomfortable. "I, um, just wanted to tell you again that I'm sorry about last night. I shouldn't have confronted Rhys like that."

I nodded but wasn't sure what to say. Though I'd been angry with her last night, I'd steered most of that anger back where it belonged—to myself. "I never should have kept the divorce from Vanessa."

"Maybe not, but last night wasn't my place." Sara took a deep breath. "I just... I saw how much you were hurting, and I was so angry at him, but...it wasn't my place, and if I hadn't done that, then we all could have saved Vanessa some heartache today. So, I know I told you this already, but I mean it—I'm sorry."

"I know. And with all the stress of the wedding and everything, I shouldn't have unloaded it all on you and—"

"No, you always know you can vent to me." She sighed, shaking her head. "Apparently I just shouldn't drink while stressed *and* in the same room as the person you're venting about. I should have known that wouldn't end well."

I laughed softly, though I didn't really feel it. We stood in silence for a moment, watching our daughter dancing with her new husband in the middle of a crowd of their friends and family. My mind kept going back to when Vanessa had been dancing with Rhys, and my heart kept sinking lower and lower. He still hadn't come back in from outside. Maybe that was good. Maybe a little space was what we needed tonight. Or what I needed.

Because I'm a coward who can't face my own feelings, never mind talk to him about them.

Before I could stop myself, I blurted to Sara, "Do you think cheating is a deal-breaker?"

She seemed to mull it over, then shrugged. "Depends on the situation, I guess."

"What do you mean?"

"I mean if someone had an affair, yeah. Deal-breaker. I'm not going to forgive a man who gets emotionally invested in someone else." She looked past me, as if watching Rhys through the windows.

"A one-time fuck-up, though? I guess it would depend on how sorry he was." Her eyes shifted back to me. "If I really believed that *he* believed he fucked up."

"Like if he came and told you about it?"

"Oh God, yeah." She said it without hesitation. "If he lied about it and tried to cover it up, he can eat shit and die. But if he came clean on his own? I might be able to forgive him." She cocked her head. "Why? Are you, um, reconsidering?"

I pressed my lips together. Yeah, I was, but for some reason I couldn't bring myself to say it out loud.

"For what it's worth," Sara said softly, "if there's one thing I took away from last night before everything blew up, it's that Rhys absolutely regrets what he did. He's not sorry he got caught. He's sorry he did it."

"He didn't get caught," I said quietly. "He confessed. I never would have known if he hadn't said something."

She was nodding as I spoke. "And I could tell last night that he really does regret it. I mean, I went in there guns blazing, ready to read him the riot act and then..." Her shoulders drooped. "Then I just wanted to give him a big hug because here I'd been thinking he was an asshole, and it turned out he was hurting so bad. Even if it was because of something he did, he was still hurting, you know?"

My throat tightened. "I think he still is."

"I'd bet money he will be for a long time."

Releasing a long breath, I let my shoulders sink.

"Why don't you go talk to him?"

"Now?"

"Well, yeah." She looked at me like it was the most ridiculous thing she'd ever been asked. "Why not?"

"Because..." I made a sweeping gesture at the reception going on around us.

"But you're both miserable. Maybe if you guys can talk some of this through, you can actually enjoy the rest of..." She mimicked my gesture.

Okay, she had a point. I shifted my weight. "Except I don't want to leave the wedding and—"

"Go talk to him." She nudged me toward the door Rhys had gone through. "Vanessa will understand."

I hesitated, but finally nodded. "Okay. I will."

She gave my arm a squeeze. "Good luck."

"Thanks."

And without another second thought, I went outside to find Rhys.

CHAPTER 17

RHYS

I barely felt the bitter cold. An Oregon February was less brutal than a Chicago one, and my tux fended off the wind while the burn of my drink made me forget how chilly my face and fingers were. Mostly I was numb, so I didn't feel much of anything. Just...empty. I'd thought everything in my world had come crashing down five months ago, but apparently there was more collapsing and crumbling left to do. Couldn't wait to see how the next few weeks went.

I took a deep swallow from my glass. Not that it helped.

I'd come out here for some air because not only was my soon-to-be ex-husband in there, but the venue had started getting hot and stuffy. The staff had propped open the door and cracked some windows to let in some air, but it hadn't been enough, and the biting February cold actually felt pretty good.

Thanks to the open door and windows, noise and music from inside spilled out here. There was some pop song playing right now. Probably a newer band, since I didn't recognize them. Just another sign that I was getting old, Vanessa would helpfully point out if I ever mentioned it.

I chuckled halfheartedly as I brought my drink to my lips. Vanessa, Derek, and I all shared a love of what her mother called "pop drivel," but admittedly, even being around teenagers all day didn't keep me up to speed on the latest bands. Maybe she was right. Maybe I was getting old.

My humor lasted about as long as the thin cloud of breath hung in the air. The vapor dissipated, as did my quiet laughter, and I stared out into the night.

It hadn't been a bad day. Quite the opposite. Despite everything last night, Vanessa had still enjoyed her wedding, which was the most important thing. There'd been a few moments here and there when I could tell she was thinking about the divorce, but she'd still seemed happy during the ceremony and throughout the reception. Under the circumstances, that was about the best I could ask for, and I hoped she forgave us for last night, not to mention everything that was still coming. At least she wasn't living with us anymore. I couldn't imagine having her there in the middle of the crossfire or the arduous process of dividing up everything we owned. She didn't need to go through—

Sharp footsteps came out onto the patio. Probably someone looking for a smoke.

I glanced over my shoulder.

And froze.

No, it wasn't someone coming out for a smoke. Not unless Derek had picked up the habit again over the last twenty-four hours.

He didn't seem at all surprised to see me. In fact, he was looking right at me. And walking right toward me.

I gulped. There was something on his mind. The creases in his forehead and the intensity in his eyes told me that much, but right now I couldn't read him to save my life. Did he want to talk? Fight? Let me know they'd be cutting the cake? No idea.

I couldn't hold eye contact with him anymore, though, so I shifted my gaze away and stared out at the darkness again. The hair on my neck prickled as he came closer. The cold didn't register at all anymore over Derek's unavoidable presence.

"Rhys?" His voice was softer than I'd expected. And...tentative? Was he nervous?

I turned to him again, and it wasn't the smile that surprised me. It was the outstretched hand, palm up. Not an offer of a handshake—an unspoken invitation for a dance.

So many questions. *So* many. Why this? Why now? If I took him up on it, what happened when it was over?

Of course I knew what would happen when it was over—we'd be right back to where we'd been all this time. We'd still be divorcing. He'd still resent me. Everything we'd been would still be gone.

But right now, if only for one song, he was asking me to dance with him one more time. Though I knew it would hurt like hell to let go after the music stopped, I couldn't say no.

With my heart in my throat, I hesitantly reached for his hand. Then I took his, the warmth of his skin making my breath stutter. As he laced our fingers together, he stepped closer and slid his other arm around my waist. I rested mine on his shoulder.

He started to move in even closer, and I thought for a fleeting moment that he might kiss me, but instead, he touched his cheek to mine as our feet started moving with the soft, distant music. Neither of us made a sound.

Muscle memory kept me dancing, but my mind was fixed on how it felt to be this close to him. The cold around us made me extra aware of the warmth everywhere we touched. He wore a faintly spicy cologne that had become synonymous with him. Any time I caught a whiff of it, even walking through a department store or catching it on someone else, my mind went to Derek. Just a few weeks ago, a student's father had come in for a parent teacher conference, and the hint of that same cologne had nearly broken me down in tears right there in my classroom. I inhaled it deeply now, committing it to memory. I didn't care if smelling it in the future hurt; I always wanted it to make me think of this.

The familiar weight of his arm around my waist was heartbreakingly familiar—something I'd always taken for granted. I'd never realized until now how much I loved the way it felt. It was one more thing I'd miss once we were done for good, along with the way his eyes sparkled when he laughed, and how nice it was to lean against him on the couch while we watched TV, and the simple pleasure of domestic things like cooking or shopping together.

Pulse pounding, I squeezed my stinging eyes shut. There was so much I wanted to say right then, but this moment felt so delicate. Like anything could break the spell and send us back to an arm's length apart.

We'll be there soon enough; just let me have this.

It was Derek who finally spoke. His cheek was still pressed to mine, our bodies still swaying gently to the music, and the single syllable came out as little more than a ragged breath: "Rhys?"

My stomach somersaulted. "Hmm?"

He ran his thumb over the top of mine, and his voice was unsteady as he whispered, "I miss you."

My heart... God. What *was* it doing? Pounding? Breaking? Skipping? Melting?

Voice wavering as badly as his, I said, "I miss you too."

Our feet weren't moving anymore. When we'd stopped, I wasn't sure. All I knew was that we were standing now, just holding on to each other.

Cheek still pressed to mine, he said, "I have no idea how to come back from this. Up until this weekend I didn't think it was possible, but now..." He finally drew back and looked in my eyes. "I don't know how to come back. I just know I don't want you to leave."

I stared at him in mute disbelief for a long moment before I found my voice. "You'd... You'd really take me back?"

Derek nodded. "I never should have let you go."

"But...after I..."

"I don't care." He shook his head, and his eyes welled up as he looked in mine. "You fucked up once. I was hurt and I was angry, and yeah I still am, but... I don't know. Today, watching our daughter getting married and watching you dancing with her, I just... it drove home how big a presence you've been in her life and mine." A tear slipped free, and he quickly brushed it away. "I thought you were throwing all that away, but isn't that what I'm doing, too?"

I swallowed, unable to process everything he'd said, never mind respond.

"You've never given me any reason to believe you'd cheat again," he whispered shakily. "When you tell me you're sorry... I believe you. Because I know you."

"But how do we do this if we can't trust each other?" I moistened my lips. "If you can't trust me?"

"We find a way to bring that trust back."

"Do you think it's that simple?"

"Simple? Yes. Easy? No." He pulled me a little closer, and his voice was soft and unsteady as he said, "It took me until tonight to realize that whatever it takes will be worth it."

I was speechless. Completely and totally speechless. And even if I'd been able to find words, I didn't trust myself to articulate them without breaking down from both relief and guilt.

So I did the next best thing—I wrapped my arms around him and hugged him tighter than I had in ages.

Derek hugged me back just as fiercely, burying his face in my neck and exhaling a warm breath across my skin. I squeezed my eyes shut and held on as I released my own breath. It was like I hadn't been able to find enough air for the last few months, and now, wrapped up in Derek's embrace where I belonged, I could breathe again.

And finally, I found my voice: "I love you, Derek." I stroked his hair. "I know I've said it a million times, but I am so sorry."

"I know." He pulled back to meet my gaze, and for the first time in ages, he smiled at me like he used to. That warm smile, the softness in his eyes—I hadn't realized until now just how much I'd missed that look. Caressing my cheek, he said, "And I love you too."

Oh my God, my heart. I forced back my emotions and whispered, "Do you really think we can do this?"

His smile broadened as his hand slid up into my hair. "We're off to a pretty good start, aren't we?"

"I guess we are. I just... I mean, you're serious? About fixing this?"

Derek didn't answer.

He just lifted his chin and pressed his cool lips to mine, and the whole world came to a gentle halt beneath our feet.

This wasn't like that messy, demanding kiss in the hallway of our hotel the other night. Instead, it reminded me of the last time we'd put on tuxes and danced at a wedding—our own wedding. It felt just like when we'd sealed our vows with a long, tender kiss, when everyone else in the room had disappeared for one perfect moment, and everything had been right in the world.

Tonight, with a long way to go before we were back to that kind of solid ground, this soft, sweet kiss was like a taste of what would be waiting for us once we'd done the work to rebuild everything we'd been.

I broke the kiss and touched my forehead to his. "I didn't think we'd ever..." I ran out of breath and words.

"I didn't either." Derek ran this thumb along my cheekbone. "But I'll work for it if you will."

"You better believe I will. Whatever it takes."

He smiled, then kissed me again, and he deepened it this time, gripping the back of my neck as he gently prodded my lips apart. The undercurrent of desire made me briefly entertain the idea of dragging him off to find a coat closet or something, but we were supposed to be at our daughter's wedding. We could be forgiven for taking a few minutes to put our marriage back on the rails. The rest could wait.

Derek broke the kiss this time. "At the risk of ruining the

moment," he said with a wry grin, "should we take this inside so we don't freeze our balls off?"

I laughed, and so did he. God, it felt good to laugh with him after all that tension and bitterness. And now that he mentioned it, it really was cold as hell out here.

"All right." I slipped my hand into his. "Let's go inside."

CHAPTER 18

DEREK

As Rhys and I walked hand in hand back into the warm reception hall, Vanessa turned. Her eyes darted right to our hands, and her face lit up. Lifting her skirt so she wouldn't trip, she hurried toward us from where she'd been chatting with some guests.

"Are you guys...?" Her forehead creased and she stared at us with a hopeful smile on her lips.

Rhys and I glanced at each other, both smiling. He raised his eyebrows, a look I recognized as *I'll follow your lead.*

I turned to Vanessa. "We're going to give it a try. It's not going to be fixed overnight, but we're—"

"Oh my God, that's awesome!" She threw her arms around me, nearly bowling me over, and I laughed as I hugged her back. She embraced Rhys too, and when he glanced at me over her shoulder, his eyes damn near melted me all over again.

I almost lost you.

We almost lost this.

Suddenly I was almost overwhelmed with the need to hug him—hell, hug both of them. So I stepped in, wrapped one arm around her and one around him, and tried my damnedest not to cry because my little family felt whole again. It would take a lot to fix everything that was broken between us, but nothing in the world motivated me more to put in the effort than this moment right here. Whatever it took to get us on the rails and keep us there, I was all in.

The three of us separated, and Vanessa glanced back and forth between us. "So you guys are really okay?"

"We're getting there," I said.

Her forehead creased. "Getting there?"

"Hey, it doesn't happen overnight." I kissed Rhys's fingers and smiled at him. "We're off to a good start, though."

She still didn't seem entirely convinced.

"Hey." Rhys put his free hand on her shoulder. "Don't worry about us, okay? Today's about you."

"Yeah, yeah." She waved him off. "That's like telling me not to be nervous about the wedding."

He laughed. "Fair. But there's nothing to worry about here. We're..." He turned to me, a soft smile forming on his lips. "I think we're back on track."

I wrapped my arm around his waist. "Yeah. Me too."

"Thank God." Vanessa hugged us each again. "Jesus, I am so relieved."

"So am I, believe me," I said. "Now come on. You're supposed to be enjoying your wedding."

She grinned broadly. "I'm enjoying it a lot more now."

I smiled through the guilt that still prodded at me. It would take a while for my conscience to stop feeling quite so raw thanks to my near-divorce casting a shadow over our daughter's wedding. "I think your man's waiting for you on the dancefloor." I nodded past her. She turned, and Corbin flashed her an *are you coming?* smile as he kept dancing with some friends near the edge of the crowd.

Vanessa turned back to us. "You guys better get out there too."

"We're right behind you, sweetheart," Rhys said. As Vanessa headed for the dancefloor, he faced me. "You want to dance again?"

I grinned. "Thought you'd never ask."

He took my hand and led me out into the crowd. Eyes locked, we pulled each other close again.

There were a handful of people in the room who obviously didn't care for two men showing affection—including Corbin's great uncle—but quite frankly, they could all go fuck themselves. After teetering on a precipice for so long, and finally stepping back into the safety of each other's arms, we weren't letting go. I needed to hold him while the dust settled all around us. Touch him while I caught my breath. Tell myself again and again that we'd put on the brakes before we'd passed a point of no return.

Whatever came next, I had a feeling we'd benefit from some outside help. So, as I continued dancing with the man I'd almost divorced, I promised myself that as soon as I had a few minutes alone, I'd start scouring the internet for a queer-friendly marriage counselor.

After a few songs, we both needed a break from the thickening crowd on the dancefloor, so we stepped away to get something to drink. While we were standing in line at the bar, my arm loosely wrapped around Rhys's waist, Sara appeared in beside us. "And here I thought Vanessa'd just had too much to drink and started imagining things. But..." She gestured at us. " I guess not."

"Nope," I said. "She wasn't imagining things."

"Good. I'm glad." She smiled, but then sobered as she looked at Rhys. "Listen, I wanted to apologize for last night."

"It's okay." Rhys smiled, tightening his arm around my waist. "I think it knocked over a few dominoes that got us here, so..."

"Still. I'm sorry."

Rhys let go of me and hugged her. "It's all good. I promise."

Sara closed her eyes and sighed. "Thank you, Rhys." She let him go. "And I'm really glad to see you two back together."

"Yeah." I wrapped my arm around him. "Me too."

Not surprisingly, it was late when we let ourselves into my sister's house. Amy and her husband had left the wedding a couple of hours earlier, but we'd stayed to help with some of the clean-up. Now, everything was done, and we were finally back at the house.

In the living room, Rhys's eyes flicked toward the sofa where I'd slept last night. A blanket was spread across the cushions, and a couple of pillows were propped on the armrest.

"You're, um..." He shot me a mischievous look as he pointed at the makeshift bed. "You're not planning on sleeping in here again, are you?"

I tugged my bowtie loose. "Keep looking at me like that, and neither of us will be sleeping any time soon."

Rhys hooked a finger under my belt and pulled me closer to him. "I'm absolutely wiped, but I'm pretty sure I can find a second wind."

"Yeah?"

We both grinned. Then we headed upstairs to the guest room. I was mentally, emotionally, and physically exhausted, but I needed Rhys tonight. If I collapsed under the weight of my own fatigue, I'd spend the whole night dreaming that things had played out differently. That we hadn't shared that dance out in the cold wind, and we hadn't agreed to do whatever it took to make us work. No, I fully intended to fall asleep still aching from him so my mind and body knew damn well that everything was the way it needed to be again.

He closed the bedroom door behind us, and we got as far as taking off our jackets before we sank onto the bed together. I couldn't remember the last time we'd kissed like this, and promised myself this wouldn't be the last time. We needed to fool around like this more often. Kissing hard and deep. Clawing at each other's clothes in an effort to get to the hot skin underneath. Making each other gasp and curse.

"We should really take all this crap off before we tear something," he murmured between kisses.

"Mmm, I was thinking we should take it all off so I can put my hands on you, but not tearing something works too."

Rhys laughed, a light, carefree sound that was so, so good to hear.

His hands slid down over my ass, and we both groaned as he pulled me against him so there was no missing either of our hard-ons between us. "Derek..."

"Get out of those clothes," I breathed. "I want you naked."

We were both unbuttoning our shirts before we'd even fully separated. Rhys sat on the edge of the bed to take off his prosthetic and liner, and then we slipped back into bed beneath the covers. We came together in the middle, naked and hard and hungry for each other, and for ages, we lay like that—on our sides, kissing lazily and stroking each other's cocks as if we had all night just to touch and tease.

A shiver pushed me closer to him, and I thrust my cock into his fist. He groaned, so I did it again, and then he was doing the same. We picked up speed, but then the bed creaked and we both froze.

"Damn," he murmured. "Stupid bed's going to give us away."

"Mmhmm. But there's... God, Rhys..." I shuddered. "There's stuff we can do. Quieter stuff."

"Yeah?" He grinned against my lips. "Like what?"

"Well..." I tightened my grip on his cock, and it was his turn to shiver and moan. "If you promise to be good and quiet, I can fuck you."

Holy hell—that helpless whimper had to be *the* sexiest thing I had ever heard. "Yes, *please.*"

I laughed softly, stroking him harder. "That what you want?"

"God, yeah." He pushed his dick into my fist. "So want it."

"Promise you'll stay quiet?"

"I can if you can."

"That a challenge?"

"Maybe."

I slid my thumb over the head of his cock, making him gasp. "Sure you can—"

"Just fuck me, damn it," he whispered.

I chuckled. "You still have that lube?"

"Uh-huh." He licked his lips. "Should we get it?"

"Well unless you want me to fuck you dry or something."

He shuddered, and I chuckled.

"Where is it?" I asked, sitting up.

He nodded toward the bathroom. "My shaving kit."

It only took a second to find it, and I swore just getting my hand on that little bottle of clear liquid made my cock even harder. The anticipation was driving me out of my mind. I slid into bed beside him, and from the way he pulled me into his arms and kissed me, he was definitely on the same page. We made out breathlessly while we groped and ground, the bottle tumbling onto the bed somewhere between us.

"Derek," he pleaded. "C'mon."

I felt around and found the bottle again. It took a few tries, but I got the top open. Breaking the kiss took a few more tries, but I managed to do that too, if only because I needed to see what I was doing so lube didn't end up everywhere except where it needed to be.

Rhys bit his lip as I poured lube on my fingers, and he parted his thighs. I capped the bottle again, dropped it somewhere I could easily find it again, and ran my palm up his inner thigh. I'd barely started teasing his hole with my fingertips before we were kissing again. He'd always loved kissing, and so had I, and tonight, there was a sense of urgency that had never been there before. Like we both needed to make sure we really had come back to this, and we also desperately needed to make up for so much lost time. Whatever was driving it, I didn't complain.

Rhys exhaled sharply through his nose as my fingers slid into him. He gripped my shoulder and kissed me harder, squirming beside me as I worked them deeper. It didn't take long to get him ready— never did—but I fingered him for ages just because I could. Because I knew he loved being fingered, and also because it was fun to tease him, knowing he loved taking cock even more than he loved this.

When his nails started to dig in and his breath was coming in short, sharp gasps, I knew he couldn't wait much more. And I couldn't wait either.

Sliding my fingers free, I murmured, "Turn over."

"On my knees or my stomach?"

I grinned. "You know how I like fucking you."

He visibly shuddered as he returned the grin, and then he turned onto his stomach. I positioned myself over him, heart thumping as I guided myself to his well-prepped hole. I started to ease my cock into him, and we both sighed, which turned into low groans as I slid past the tight muscle. I molded myself to him as I pushed deeper. There was more resistance than I was used to with him, though; he was probably still tense because of everything that had gone down.

"Hey," I murmured into his hair. "Relax."

"I'm..." He exhaled, letting his head fall forward. "Trying. I just... There's been so much..."

"Shh." I kissed beneath his hairline. "Only thing that matters right now is us. We'll work everything out." I withdrew slowly, then eased back in. "Right now, I just want you to feel good."

"I do. Always... Always do when..."

"Then just breathe. Relax. Don't worry about anything except enjoying this."

"I am. God, Derek..."

"Breathe," I whispered. "Everything's good tonight."

He closed his eyes and exhaled, and he started to yield to me. Carefully, I continued my slow, easy strokes, and little by little, he relaxed. He took me deeper, moaning every time I bottomed out, and I slid fluidly in and out of him.

"Fuck, baby," I whispered. "I love...love the way you feel."

He responded with a wordless sound that I knew meant he agreed. He stretched his arm out and gripped the edge of the mattress, muscles rippling under his tattoos. "Derek..."

I bit his shoulder. "Like that?"

He moaned, a sound I'd long ago learned to recognize as *don't you dare stop*.

No, I definitely wasn't stopping. I gave myself over to this with a degree of surrender I didn't think I'd ever experienced before. Letting myself move in him and with him and over him, getting lost in the sheer ecstasy of being with him.

I couldn't believe we'd made it back to this. It didn't even matter that there was still a lot of work to be done—just the fact that what we had was salvageable at all gave me a profound sense of relief. I'd walk through fire for Rhys. How I'd ever thought that had changed, I couldn't begin to imagine now. We still needed to find some forgiveness and close some wounds, but nothing that had happened seemed worth letting go of this. Letting go of *him*.

My eyes stung, and I buried my face against his neck. This was the second time in a matter of days that sex with Rhys had overwhelmed me to the point of tears, but this was nothing like the last time. I wasn't fighting anything back anymore. I wasn't trying to pretend I wasn't angry or hurt, or that this was just a Band-Aid over something we couldn't fix.

It was all just so real and perfect, and I was so overwhelmed with emotions and disbelief. The invisible weight of the world rolled off my shoulders. Tension I hadn't even noticed before melted away.

I rocked my hips and held him as close as I could. I was pressed up against him, buried inside him, breathing in his scent and body heat, and I still couldn't get close enough. I couldn't say if it was because we'd been so far apart for so long, or if I just needed to feel as much of him as possible to make sure we weren't that far apart anymore.

"God, Derek," he breathed, arching under me. "Baby..."

I exhaled against his neck as I slid an arm under him and hooked it over his shoulder, and we both groaned as I used the leverage to thrust deep inside him. It felt so damn good to give myself over completely. There was no holding back anymore, and that total surrender was the most liberating thing I'd ever experienced.

Beneath me, Rhys shivered. "Fuck..."

"Mmm, baby..." I let my teeth scrape the side of his neck. "I'm... I want to come in you, and then..." I thrust hard. "Then I'm going to blow you."

Rhys moaned. "Yeah. Yes. *That.*" He rocked his hips in time with mine. "You feel so good..."

I buried my face against his neck again to keep myself quiet, and I held on tight and fucked him for all I was worth as my orgasm closed in. The need to hold back and draw this out was nonexistent—the sooner I came, the sooner I'd get to have him like this all over again.

He released a ragged whimper, and that was all I needed. A shudder forced me all the way inside him, and I pressed my teeth into his shoulder to force back my own cry as Rhys kept rocking his hips to keep me coming. He kept going until I stopped him with a hand on his hip, and after I'd paused long enough to let the spinning room slow down, I carefully pulled out.

"Turn over," I said, and kissed the side of his neck before I got out of his way.

Rhys didn't hesitate. As soon as he was on his back, I pushed his thighs apart and eagerly went down on him.

"Mmm, yeah," he whispered. "Fuck..."

As I took him deeper into my mouth, I pushed two fingers into his ass, and he gasped. Again when I crooked them inside him. His back arched, and his fingers kneaded my scalp, raising goose bumps all the way down my neck and back, and he moaned my name as I licked and sucked his rock-hard dick.

"God, you're so good at that," he slurred just loud enough for me and no one else to hear. I hummed around his cock because I knew he loved that, and he rewarded me with a soft moan. Once we were home and didn't have to stay quiet, his voice would be echoing off the walls while I blew him, but tonight, his restrained and barely audible sounds of pleasure were more than enough.

It didn't take long to get him to the edge. Never did if I'd been fucking him before I went down on him, especially since I knew all the ways he loved to be licked and stroked and fingered. He held his breath, every muscle in his body tensing as he hurtled closer to the edge, and then all at once, he released his breath and the tension gave and hot cum shot into my mouth. Like he'd done for me, I teased him to keep his orgasm going, and when he'd had enough, I stopped.

I pushed myself up on my arms and came back to up to him, and as soon as I was within reach, Rhys wrapped his arms around me and drew me down on top of him. We kissed breathlessly, still tangled up and trembling. Fatigue was closing in even faster now, and my body wanted to flop onto the mattress and go to sleep, but...not yet. I needed a few more minutes of holding him like this.

After a while, I broke the kiss, and our eyes met. He smiled. Then I did. And then we both laughed. I wasn't even sure why. Nothing was funny—it just felt good to let go and be happy with him again. Like we were returning to a place I thought had been burned to the ground, and we were both giddy with the relief of coming home.

I can't believe we made it back to his.

But all I said was, "I love you, Rhys."

He pressed a kiss to my temple. "I love you too."

CHAPTER 19

RHYS

Everything was right in my world again, and it was surreal. I'd accepted on some level that things had changed and could never go back, just like they'd changed after my accident. And to some extent, maybe they wouldn't. My relationship with Derek would never be the same as it was before I'd fucked everything up.

But maybe there was a chance it could be...better? Like now that we were this aware of how much we had to lose, we wouldn't take anything for granted. *I* wouldn't take anything for granted.

Derek cuddled closer and rested his head on my shoulder, our hands loosely clasped in the middle of my chest. "I really thought I'd lost you."

"Tell me about it." I kissed the top of his head. "Still doesn't seem quite real, you know? Having this back?"

"No, it doesn't." He turned and lifted himself onto his elbow. "It isn't going to be perfect overnight, though. You know that, right?"

"Yeah, I know." I stroked his hair. "Maybe we should get some help from someone who knows how to handle all this."

"That's what I was thinking."

"Fair warning—I'm probably going to be apologizing for the rest of my life."

"You don't have to."

"I know." I let the backs of my fingers drift down his stubbled cheek. "But that's not going to stop me."

He came down, kissed me softly, and whispered, "I love you."

"I love you too." I caressed his face. "Whatever it takes to make this work, I'll do it."

"So will I. But we don't have to do all of that tonight." He covered my hand with his and kissed my palm. "Let's just enjoy us."

"We will. We are. But when we get home, whatever we need to do. I don't want to lose you again."

"You won't." He leaned in for a kiss. It started out light, like he'd only meant for a brief brush, but then he came back for more, and I wasn't about to stop him. The kiss went on, and after a while, Derek tilted his head and teased my lips apart with his tongue. I held him tighter as he deepened the kiss. My cock was starting to get hard again, and as our hips brushed, I felt his doing the same.

His lips left mine enough to let him murmur, "How much lube do we have left?"

"Enough for the moment." I nibbled his lower lip. "Might need to get some more before we hit the road, though."

"Mmm, pretty sure that can be arranged." And then he kissed me full-on, and neither of us said anything more.

I wrapped my arms around him as we indulged in this long kiss that was both lazy and suggestive. As if we were both signaling loud and clear that we wanted to go another round, but no one was in any hurry.

I sure as hell wasn't. I was much too busy savoring his touch and this closeness.

For the rest of my life, I would regret cheating on Derek, but in a small way, I was glad we'd gone through this. I wished I could go back and bring us to this point without hurting Derek, but at least by some miracle, we'd made it to this. Maybe it was the cleansing fire we hadn't realized our marriage needed. Maybe we'd just gotten damn lucky.

Whatever the case, I had him back, and I planned to spend the rest of the night making sure he knew how relieved I was.

As we'd promised before we'd even left for this trip, we met Vanessa and Corbin for breakfast—more like brunch—the day after the wedding.

The restaurant was one of Vanessa's favorites. It was a locally owned place that she always took us to when we were in town, and they had an amazing breakfast menu. Fortunately for us, they also served breakfast all day.

Derek and I got there first and found a booth. Maybe fifteen minutes later, as we were sipping our second cups of coffee, our daughter and new son-in-law arrived. Both had on sunglasses and looked like they hadn't slept in weeks.

"Did we party a little hard last night?" I teased as I got up to hug her.

"Ugh." Vanessa groaned. "I probably should have stopped after that third glass of champagne."

"Aww, come on." Derek patted her arm. "It's your wedding. You're supposed to wake up hung over."

"He didn't." She pointed an accusing finger at her new husband, though she was grinning.

"I'm a soldier, sweetheart." Corbin tenderly tucked a strand of hair behind her ear. "If I drank enough last night to be hung over, things would have gotten out of hand."

"Showoff," she grumbled.

Derek and I exchanged glances and laughed as we all took our seats.

"I remember those days," I said. "My liver is probably grateful I didn't serve my full enlistment."

Derek snorted. "Mine says 'lucky you'."

"Hey, it isn't like anyone poured it down your throat." I bumped his shoulder with mine. "You could have stopped any time."

"Well, yeah." He bumped me back. "But I didn't want to. So there."

"Then you have no one to blame but yourself if you fucked up your liver."

"Shut up," he laughed.

I chuckled, and realized Vanessa was staring at us incredulously. "What?"

She shrugged, shaking her head. "It's just... After everything that happened, it's so weird to see you guys, you know, being *you guys* again."

We glanced at each other, and instead of that tight, uneasy feeling that I'd gotten every time I'd looked at him recently, it was a flutter in my chest. I smiled as I put my hand over his. "It's kind of a novelty for us too."

"Yeah, I bet." She gestured at each of us. "So, what happens next?"

"Well," Derek said. "First things first, we're going to start seeing a counselor as soon as we can. Then we'll go from there. It'll take some time, but..." He brought my hand up and kissed the backs of my fingers. "I think we'll be all right."

I barely suppressed a shiver. I wondered how long this would go on, feeling so profoundly relieved every time Derek reminded me that we had a shot at being all right. I kind of hoped it didn't stop any time soon.

It was funny how on our road trip, I'd been dreading this post-wedding breakfast. After days on end of pretending we were okay, a quiet meal with Vanessa and Corbin sounded like torture because we'd have to keep the charade going. There'd be nothing to distract her from us, and we'd have to be extra *"look how great everything is"* in order to fly under her radar.

Never in a million years did I imagine we wouldn't have to pretend.

And all too soon, the breakfast I'd been dreading came to an end. We'd all finished eating and had been chatting over coffee for a while when Vanessa sighed, turning to her husband. "We should get to the airport."

Derek glanced at his phone. "We should probably get on the road too."

"Yeah, we should." I couldn't help being disappointed. After all the chaos recently, was it really too much to ask for us to take some time to bask in everything being okay?

They had a plane to catch, though, and Derek and I needed to get going so it wasn't super late when we made it to our hotel in Boise tonight.

So we paid the bill, and the four of us trooped outside into the bitterly cold but sunny early afternoon. Beside her car, Vanessa turned to us. "Thanks for breakfast. And I'm glad you guys worked things out."

"Me too." I kissed her cheek. "Now go enjoy your honeymoon. And don't forget the sunscreen this time."

Vanessa rolled her eyes. "Yeah, yeah, yeah. I know."

"Hey, if you want another second-degree sunburn..." I showed my palms.

She shivered, chafing her arms. "Ugh. No thanks."

"Well then," Derek said. "Sunscreen."

Corbin laughed, wrapping his arm around her shoulders. "We'll get sunscreen. Don't worry."

There were more hugs and goodbyes, and then our daughter and her new husband got in the car to head to the airport for their honeymoon.

As I watched them drive out of the parking lot, I said, "Think they'll actually remember the sunscreen?"

Derek barked a laugh. "I give it three days until there's a sunburned selfie on Instagram."

I chuckled. "Yeah. Me too." Then I turned to him and grinned. "I guess we better hit the road too. We've got a ton of lube to go through tonight."

He shivered as he snaked an arm around my waist. "Think we'll have to stop and get more before we make it home?"

"That sounds like a challenge to me."

"Mmm, does it?" He pulled me closer. "Are you accepting that challenge?"

"You better believe it."

"Then yeah—we better hit the road."

I kissed his cheek, and we headed for my truck, smiling the whole way like a couple of dorks.

I had no illusions that our future would be easy or that there was no work left to be done to bring our marriage back to life. It was going to take time, counseling, and *so* much patience.

But we really were off to a damn good start.

EPILOGUE

Derek

About a year later.

"Ducking out early?" Maxine smirked at me from my office doorway.

"Early?" I glanced at the clock on the wall before I resumed tucking some files into my briefcase. "It's six o'clock."

"I know. But it's still kind of a novelty, you not finding every possible excuse to stay here as late as possible."

"I haven't done that in a long time."

She smiled. "No. Still. It's good to see you actually wanting to go home."

At that, I smiled too. "It's a nice change, isn't it?"

"Yes, it is." She tilted her head. "How are things with Rhys these days, anyway?"

"They're good." I pulled on my jacket. "We still have our moments, but I don't think that'll ever change."

She snorted. "I'd be worried if it did."

"Hey!"

"What? I know the two of you. Couple of stubborn assholes."

I chuckled. She had me dead to rights and we both knew it.

After I'd said goodbye to Maxine, I left the office. Rhys wasn't coaching any sports right now, so he was probably already home. Admittedly, it was still kind of novel to be looking forward to seeing him.

Going to a marriage counselor had probably been the single best decision we ever made. He didn't sit us down and walk us through a step by step plan to put our marriage on the rails. Instead, he'd listen to us, and he'd ask questions that always seemed to magically lead us to the answers we needed.

Not surprisingly, the first few months had been rough. Although we'd both been committed ever since Vanessa's reception, putting everything back together had been easier said than done. There'd been some fights that had—in the heat of the moment—made me wonder if we were going to make it after all. Once we'd calmed down, though, those thoughts scattered in no time.

Even during the roughest of the rough times, things had been promising. We'd agreed to keep separate bedrooms for a little while, but more often than not, we ended up in the bed we'd shared since we'd bought the house. In fact, something about the near miss—about coming so close to losing each other—had *seriously* reignited our sex life. I didn't know if it was this need to make up for lost time or to make up for the time we'd almost lost, but we'd been screwing like newlyweds since we'd gotten back together. We'd even picked up some books on ways to spice things up, which had resulted in a few blowjobs in my office and a few marks he'd had to awkwardly explain to his physical therapist.

Keeping our sex life active and hot made everything else easier to work through, too. Whenever we saw our marriage counselor, we came home and tumbled in to bed together. Didn't matter how the session had gone. Could've been smooth, could've been rough—didn't matter. Spending some hot, sweaty time between the sheets afterward always landed us back on the same page.

Twice, we'd been in the middle of an argument that threatened to turn into a fight, when one of us had stopped and—like we'd done during the earlier years of our marriage—suggested we call time out, blow off some steam in the bedroom, and then sort things out. And like it had during the earlier years, it worked like a charm.

I wasn't going to lie—sex and counseling weren't magic fixes. I'd expected that bringing back trust would be hard, but holy shit. It was *hard*. Though I believed Rhys when he apologized and swore he'd never cheat again, there were moments when doubt crept in. If Rhys didn't answer his phone or respond to a text. If he stayed late at work. If he was home while I was at work. Whenever he'd gone out of town with the softball team he was coaching.

I told him as much whenever he came home, too. Our counselor had encouraged us to be open and honest about it, so we had been, even though it was hard. I didn't accuse him or demand he justify where he'd been and what he'd been doing—just calmly explained what I'd been feeling. I could tell it hurt Rhys whenever I admitted I'd been worried. But it was all part of the process, and it was paying off as time went on. He texted me more often. His *oh my God look at this pile of exams I have to grade* selfies made me laugh now. So did the lazy selfies with both cats parked on his chest. It became less about him making sure I knew he wasn't doing something deceitful and more about him just sending me silly pictures or random texts. I did the same just because. The result? We were communicating more, even when it was just to say hello.

More and more, I didn't worry. Not about him cheating, and not about us falling apart. Life wasn't perfect, but it was better. Even though there was still a long road ahead of us, it was good to be on that road with him. It was good to have little things back that I'd thought were dead and gone. Texting throughout the day. Entertaining ourselves with the cats and a laser pointer. Watching movies no one but us seemed to appreciate.

There were the not-so-little things too. Not being constantly worried about how I was going to make it on my own. Having someone to talk to. Waking up from a combat nightmare to strong arms around me and a soft voice in my ear. I shivered just thinking about the nights I'd woken up alone while we'd been separated. Rhys would never cure my PTSD or make the nightmares go away, but there was something to be said for waking up from one of those horrific dreams with him there to calm me down.

In the driver's seat of my car, I shivered. It had only been a few nights since the last bad one. Thank God for Rhys.

I turned down our street, then into our driveway. As the garage door rose, a familiar pang of suspicious worry hit me. Rhys's truck wasn't there. He hadn't said anything about working late. The suspicion died away pretty fast; it was more of an old knee-jerk habit now than anything.

And five minutes later, I felt ridiculous about even entertaining that worry—I'd just started finished unpacking my lunch bag when the garage door opened again. The familiar sound of the Santa Fe's engine purred, then cut off, and as the garage door rumbled shut, a car door opened and closed.

Then Rhys came into the kitchen, a couple of plastic shopping bags hanging off his arm and a bag of cat food on his shoulder. "Oh hey. Did you just get home?"

"Yeah. A few minutes ago."

He put the grocery bags on the counter and the cat food bag beside their dishes. As he opened the cat food, he said, "I'd have texted you, but I thought I'd get home before you did." He gestured at the cats, who'd come trotting in at the sound of their food. "The overlords were running on empty."

Okay, I definitely felt ridiculous now. And I really hadn't had any actual suspicions about where he'd gone or why. I didn't need to keep tabs on him every minute of the day. More than I'd ever believed I would, I trusted him. There was just that nagging voice in the back of my mind that hadn't forgotten what had happened, and I supposed it would just take time for it to shut up.

"Get out of the way," he said to the cats as he started pouring food into their hopper. "If you get your head in—really, Chico? Really?"

Chico stepped back, shaking himself and sending kibbles flying everywhere. He looked pretty pleased with himself.

Lucy was about to shove her head into the falling food, so I scooped her up into my arms until Rhys had finished. Once he'd closed the hopper and put the bag of food away where they couldn't get into it, I set her down again.

We caught up while I cleaned my lunch dishes and the cats crunched happily. The day had been uneventful for both of us. That was fine by me. I'd had enough excitement a year ago and was more than okay with dull and mundane.

As I was putting my last container on the drying rack, though, Rhys wrapped his arms around my waist and kissed the side of my neck. "Hey. What's up?"

"I..." Shit, had he noticed my mini freak out? I exhaled, leaning back against him. "Nothing. I'm good."

His lips brushed beneath my ear. "You were worried again because I wasn't home when you got home." It wasn't a question.

Closing my eyes, I let my shoulders sink. There was no point in hiding it. The only thing worse than feeling stupid about it was realizing he'd caught on and knowing it hurt whenever he did.

"Hey." He nudged my hip so I'd turn around, and when I met his gaze, he said, "I should've texted you. I'm sorry."

I sighed and smoothed his hair. "And I should be cutting you more slack by now instead of—"

"Derek." He shook his head. "We're in a better place than we were a year ago or even a few months ago. If you have a minute or two here and there of wondering why I'm not home when I'm supposed to be..." He half-shrugged. "It's not like you're grilling me or trying to chase me down, right?"

"Well, no."

"Because we both know I'm not going to fuck up like that again, but there's a part of you that still worries I will." He raised his eyebrows as if to ask, *right?*

And he *was* right. Our counselor had walked us through this a million times. I was long past any desire to hammer at Rhys's conscience or make him prove himself. This wasn't about making him feel guilty or punishing him for something he'd repented for in every way imaginable. My reaction to the empty bay in the garage had been driven by caution, not resentment or anger. It was about walking out onto the ice with him, trusting that it would hold, but still jumping whenever it creaked.

"I do trust you," I whispered.

"I know." Rhys lifted his chin and pressed a soft kiss to my lips. "We're getting better. It'll just take time."

I nodded and wrapped my arms around him for another kiss, one we let linger for a long moment. Still holding onto him, I said, "You don't have to text me every time you leave the house, though. Just so we're clear."

He smiled and brushed his lips across mine. "But you can always text me if you don't know where I am."

I said nothing and went in for one more long kiss before we let each other go.

"So." He cleared his throat. "Want me to order something horribly unhealthy while you find us something to watch?"

"That sounds perfect. Comedy or action?"

He pursed his lips, then shrugged. "Either or."

Admittedly, I still felt kind of guilty for my momentary doubts, but he was right—things were getting better. Those moments were getting fewer and farther between. I really did trust Rhys, and I was grateful every day we'd put in the work to get back to where we were now. The rest would go away over time.

Once our food had arrived, we took our usual places in the middle of the couch with Rhys leaning against me and my arm around his shoulders. Chico curled in Rhys's lap while Lucy perched on the armrest. Rhys idly scratched behind Chico's ear, and I queued up *The A-Team*, which we'd seen hundreds of times. Tonight was looking like another perfectly boring evening of hanging out with our cats, watching TV, and eating dinner.

And I couldn't think of a single thing I'd rather be doing.

THE END

For more books by L.A. Witt, please visit

http://www.gallagherwitt.com

Romance * Suspense

Contemporary * Historical * Sports * Military

ABOUT THE AUTHOR

L.A. Witt is a romance and suspense author who has at last given up the exciting nomadic lifestyle of the military spouse (read: her husband finally retired). She now resides in Pittsburgh, where the potholes are determined to eat her car and her cats are endlessly taunted by a disrespectful squirrel named Moose. In her spare time, she can be found painting in her art room or destroying her voice at a Pittsburgh Penguins game.

Website: www.gallagherwitt.com
    Email: gallagherwitt@gmail.com
    Twitter: @GallagherWitt

www.ingramcontent.com/pod-product-compliance
Lightning Source LLC
Chambersburg PA
CBHW030538020726
47494CB00005B/1423